THE MISTS OF MORNE

AN OWENS ODYSSEY

BOOK I

Justin B. Hodder
2021

Copyright ©2020 Justin B. Hodder

ISBN 978-1-7774393-0-9

Printed in Canada.

Front cover image credit is given to https://unsplash.com/@timholmes

Back cover image credit is given to www.czgemstones.com

Cover art & design by Christopher Holmes @chrisholmes.ca

Layout & typesetting by Christopher Holmes @chrisholmes.ca

Facebook: https://www.facebook.com/justin.b.hodder/

Instagram: justin.b.hodder

Any reader who may wish to reach out to provide feedback or criticism, or if they wish to ask questions, request further copies or to show their support for the project through social media, please feel free to contact the author at the above email address, or by using either of the social media channels above.

For Uncle Geoff
How's this for a world tour?

THE MISTS OF
MORNE

AN OWENS ODYSSEY

BOOK I

PROLOGUE

"*History* is a fickle concept," the professor said nonchalantly, scuffing his loafers along the floor; it was the year's closing lesson. "For example, if history has taught me anything, it's that as soon as that bell rings, all of you will bolt from this classroom like animals freed from their leashes.

"However, I'm referring to the bigger picture. By nature, we believe what we read in books, see in documentaries, or are taught, here, in our classrooms. Statistically, no one lives much longer than one-hundred years, so to understand history and what it has to offer, humanity relies on the discovery of tangibility; photographs, scriptures, artifacts, DNA—all sufficient, leaving no room for refute."

His lecture fell on the disinterested ears of Berkeley's graduating class of 2018, whose final papers, by now, sat in some administrative filing cabinet. The class was a mere formality, the end of the semester and the last of the students' degrees.

"However," the professor continued, "what about theorized history? Stories that have been passed down through generations that eventually become something that we have no choice but to believe because it's what we've been told our entire lives. After all, history is exactly that—a story. One that, without evidence, by all accounts, can be considered fictional."

He took a moment to scan the room, observing the students texting and yawning. His shoulders sunk as his index finger pulled at the loosening knot of his tie, shaking his head.

"Who knows what really happened in those undocumented times? Without the ability to logically disprove history, it becomes reality. That is, of course, until someone else finds new indication, new proof that what we know and understand is incorrect. Sometimes it works in society's favor, a revelation to the world and life within it. For others, the discovery is minuscule, a footnote in the next printing of a university textbo—"

The bell rang while he was mid-sentence.

He hung his withered face and cringed, listening to his students grab their belongings and rush for the classroom door. Not so much as a thank you or a goodbye, just as he had predicted. Tidying the last few sheets of paper at the corner of his desk, he took a last lonely look around his empty classroom, only to find that one young woman still remained.

"Miss Owens, why am I not surprised?"

Once the door slammed behind her peers, she turned back to the forefront, unamused by their less-than-enthusiastic tendencies. Her education had always been the focus.

"You shouldn't be," she laughed. "Please, finish."

The professor side-stepped around his desk, smiling, climbing the stairs to where she sat. He eased forward, planting his palms firmly onto her desk, recognizing that ever-present glint of interest in her eyes.

"Never forget, one thing is invariable. No matter how much information on the past we have, no matter how much we think we know, history is *always* subject to change."

CHAPTER ONE

Achieving satisfaction from perforating cardboard targets had taken her a little longer than anticipated, though the last two clips of ammunition were well worth the relief of frustration.

Removing her earmuffs, she released her long, dark locks from the clutches of a hair clip, scrunching it to return the tousled waves she had worked so hard to achieve just hours before. She grabbed her dress at the thighs, hiking it just enough so that she could make a jogging exit from the shooting range.

Emily was late.

Stuck in an Uber, the driver, whose cigarette smoke billowed out the window through the park air, didn't seem bothered in the least that her ride hadn't moved in over ten minutes. She would've just gotten out and walked the rest of the way from W 96th Street to the MET and said fuck the $24.00 if it wasn't for the damn heels.

"Any sign of movement?" she asked, stretching her seat belt to lean forward and peer out the front window while clipping in her shiny hoop earrings. No response, except the stagnant glare she received from the driver in the rearview mirror.

She sat back and took another glance at the invitation she was squeezing in her hand.

Come join us to discover the Lost City of Irisagrig!
The Metropolitan Museum of Art
Private unveiling to take place on September 28th, 2019
Doors open at 7:00 pm
Cocktail hour begins at 7:30 pm

Her eyes rolled to her wrist; 8:02. *Maybe I'll be able to sneak in unnoticed.*

This was a sociable event for the rich, the classy, and the desperate, which, these days, she considered herself to be a little bit of all three.

Emily was trust-fund wealthy, having deep-pocketed parents who had always kept her comfortable through the years, especially with her desired move to the Upper West Side last year, mere weeks after her graduation from university. Even when the price tag on her dream condo had that extra zero at the end, her father whipped out his checkbook to take care of it without hesitation.

Now, however, she leaned more toward the desperate side. She'd been in what most would describe as a downturn; no leads, no fun, no adventure. The excitement of getting her archaeology degree was to discover what the past had to offer; she aspired to see the world. New York was as far as she'd gotten.

Tonight's gala proposed a great chance to mingle with some of the field's best. With a little luck, she would get a whisper of an upcoming project or expedition. In her mind, treasure hunting was a very cut-throat industry. Only one person can be the first to find something, and if it isn't you, you're just a guest at *their* unveiling.

The sound of a car horn snapped her from her moment of self-reflection. Traffic was beginning to move.

Approaching the museum, she could see the spotlights crossing in the clouds over Central Park. As much as she longed for her own adventures, she had still crossed off the days on her calendar leading up to this night, waiting to see the hundreds of newly unearthed tablets from the Irisagrig site.

Once the driver made the last turn onto 5th Ave, she could see a small crowd gathered up ahead.

"This is close enough," she insisted, already reaching for the door handle. She grabbed her clutch and slid from the car.

Ascending the steps of the MET, Emily found that she wasn't the only latecomer as guests were still filtering in the main entrance. Coming through the doors, she was halted at the security checkpoint and instructed to place her purse to the side as one of the male guards wove his metal detector over and around her body.

Her head swiveled, taking notice of the security presence, which had been stepped up quite a lot for the evening's event compared to their normal business hours. *Turns out leaving my garter knife at home was a smart idea.*

"All clear," the next guard said, flicking his fingers, signaling for her to step farther inside. "Ticket and I.D. please, ma'am."

"Ma'am?" Emily said, raising one softly-arched eyebrow, pressing her pearly white teeth into her lower lip. "I'm too young to be called 'ma'am,' you know."

The guard gave her a stone-faced glare in front of everyone.

She lowered her head, flushing, and popped the clasp of her clutch and started to rummage.

"Here you go, *sir*," she smirked at her attempt to quip him. *Nothing? Again?*

"Welcome, Miss Owens," he said as he passed her I.D. back along with the detached ticket stub, raising his arm in the direction of the coat check. She threw the card back in her wallet and continued past.

Emily removed her jacket to reveal a royal blue bandage dress with a plunging neckline, exposing the shapely curves of her bust and the sternum tattoo underneath. Handing over her coat, she turned and made her way into the Great Hall, continuing toward the Charles Engelhard Court where the exhibit and banquet were being held.

Entering the dining area, the air thickened with the hum of multiple conversations, each one overpowering the next. She moved deeper into the crowd, blending in so that she didn't feel as if all eyes were on her—not that that was likely to begin with.

"Drink? Drink?" A server's voice came within earshot.

She flagged him down with a raised hand and a nod.

"Um, yes, can I get a double vodka and water, please? Light ice, with two slices of lemon."

"At once." He turned away, shifting sideways through the guests.

Waiting, she busied herself by looking at some of the tablets that were enclosed in viewing cases nearby, plastered with the classic signage: *Private Exhibit: Do not touch. No video. No photography.*

Floating through the exhibit, she became engrossed in the depictions of battle on the artifacts. She leaned forward, holding her purse against the small of her back, reading the text below the showcase.

The Lost City of Irisagrig
Pieces from the walls of a religious temple.
Archaeologists hypothesize that the pictorial display tells of a great army that swept through the mountainous regions of the Middle East and South Asia.

Her stomach fluttered from the inside-out as the tiny hairs of her neck began to rise with each word. She rubbed her palm along her skin to settle the tiny bumps that had formed along her forearms. It was the kind of discovery that would make anyone's years of university feel worth it.

The sound of ice cubes clinking in a glass from behind pulled her to stand up straight.

"Here you are, madam. Enjoy the evening." The server handed her the drink then disappeared once more.

Emily moved farther through the exhibit, weaving carefully amongst the crowd so as not to spill any of her alcohol. There were so many pieces to see, not only the tablets but other items that had been found during the same exhibition in Iraq.

She took another glance at her watch; *9:00 pm.*

As if on cue, the sharp feedback of a microphone shrieked through the room. She turned her gaze to the podium to see a stocky, balding man, fiddling clumsily with the throat of the microphone. Covering her mouth, she laughed, pleasantly surprised to find a familiar face in attendance.

Dr. Alsafar was an old family friend, one who she had always looked up to, acting as a sponge anytime he spoke. Whether it was providing life lessons, teaching her the Arabic dialect, or giving words of wisdom on her favorite subject: archaeology. He was the top in their field after all, and had always been there when she needed that extra push or reassurance that her passion was all that mattered. He was born in Iraq, the place where he conducted the majority of his research now, but he'd worked all over the world, something she one day hoped to do.

Emily began inching her way through the guests to get closer to the podium, just as the doctor was beginning his address.

"Thank you, everyone, for gathering here this evening. It was an honor to be asked to speak a few words at an event for a discovery such as this.

"In my forty years of field research, I can say with confidence that we are closer than ever before to discovering the secrets of our ancestors. To fully understand how the world was shaped is a goal I have always aspired to achieve. And now, with this new batch of artifacts, we can really begin to look into what has been unknown for so long.

"I am glad to announce that my team and I have been selected to transport the tablets back to Iraq after the exhibit finishes in the coming weeks. We will then begin our studies, and we expect to unveil our findings to you all immediately thereafter.

"A toast! To the research, to the findings, and to the past!"

A unison clap began to build as he raised his glass high above his head, waving to the crowd.

Emily shuffled her way through the dispersing guests, hurrying to catch Dr. Alsafar as he descended from the stage. But just as she broke into the front of the crowd, he was instead caught by the handshake of another man.

The man was unknown to Emily. Tall in stature, his face looked like that of a model, as if he had stepped straight off the box of a men's hair-care product. His beard was dark and full yet sprinkled with a casual grey. His hair, dark as well, was neck length.

"Dr. Alsafar! So great to finally attend one of your showcases. It's been too long indeed." The man's voice ran formal and deep.

In an attempt not to be rude, Emily veered away, although she remained intrigued by this mystery man.

Instead, she turned toward the nearest display case, pretending to admire its contents while sipping her cocktail. She listened with intent, periodically spying over her shoulder.

"Well, if it isn't Dr. Taylor," Dr. Alsafar said. "What brings you from your work in Tuscany?"

Emily saw that the man's expression dimmed. "Let's just say it was a dead end, shall we? For now."

Dr. Alsafar chuckled, placing his hand on the man's shoulder. "It happens to the best of us, my friend."

At that moment, Emily's eyes met with Dr. Alsafar's as he glimpsed her in the background. She turned back toward the tablets, emptying what remained in her glass. *Don't say it …*

"Emily Owens?" he called out. "Is that you, darling?" *Shit.*

"Dr. Alsafar!" She spun around and stepped toward him, bending slightly to embrace him with a hug. "I had no idea you would be here tonight!"

"Last-minute summons, I'm afraid. You look lovely this evening. Gosh, it feels like years since I saw you last."

"You're too kind, Doctor. Always the charmer," she said, trying to maintain some professionalism in front of the stranger. "And you last saw me at my graduation, to be exact."

"Right, right. Have you had the pleasure of meeting Dr. Taylor before? He is one of the top archaeological principal investigators of our time." Dr. Alsafar motioned a wink in Emily's direction, nudging her with his elbow. "Very accomplished for someone just under thirty."

"No, I don't think she has." The man interjected, offering Emily his hand. "Dr. Everett Taylor. A pleasure to meet you, but please, call me Everett. I'm sorry, but I believe I missed your name earlier."

She blanked, taking a second to look him up and down, searching for a flaw.

His suit was tailored, form-fitting to accentuate his broad, athletic shoulders. His hands looked worn, which was expected after years of working in the archaeological world, but clean and capable of manhandling her if need be. Her inner thighs squirmed against each other with her thoughts, the kind that brought self-awareness to the fact that she hadn't worn any panties.

Dr. Alsafar cleared his throat, a motion for Emily to respond.

"Sorry, what was that?" she said, teetering.

"Your name?" Everett said, his hand still outstretched.

She grabbed his palm and tried to gather herself.

"Em," she blurted, his solid grip keeping her dazed. His eyes, a piercing blue, maintained firm contact with hers.

"Like the letter?" Everett said, smirking slightly as he turned to Dr. Alsafar for passive confirmation.

"I mean Emily! Emily Owens," she corrected herself quickly. "My friends call me Em."

She blushed.

Everett looked confused but unsurprised about what was happening. She knew this couldn't have been the first time he had a woman fumble in front of him.

"Well, I should get moving along, my friend," Everett said, shaking the doctor's hand one last time before panning his eyes back to Emily, scanning her from head to toe himself. "I've been admiring other things at this gala for far too long; I'm missing the exhibit. Perhaps I'll see you around, *Em*." He winked as he carried onward.

She blushed deeper, looking on as he became lost in the crowd.

The interaction had left a sought-after opening. Soon, others flooded to Dr. Alsafar, drawing his attention away, leaving Emily to stand awkwardly off to the side.

Time for another drink. She scanned the room until the server caught her eye as she rubber-necked above the crowd. She raised her glass, tapping it.

Minutes later, while watching the server saunter through the crowd with her drink, Emily's attention once again became fixated on Everett Taylor. Now that she had been introduced to him, he stood out from the other guests. She barely even acknowledged the server this time, simply taking the glass from him while keeping her focus on this new attraction of hers.

With the new vodka and water in hand, she began to move closer to the young archaeologist, hiding behind the bodies of the others who were admiring the displayed collection. Even though he couldn't see her, the more she watched, the more uneasy he appeared to become. He was fiddling with something, nervously flicking his eyes back and forth over the crowd, trying his best to make sure nobody was watching him. *What are you up to, Dr. Taylor?*

As he lifted his hands once again, she could now see that he was taking pictures of the tablets with his cell phone. *Tsk, tsk.* This behavior was clearly warned against, but here he was, as bold as he was handsome.

Continuing along the showroom floor, he would stop discreetly at each tablet to take a single picture. As he moved, she followed. Eventually having enough of their little game of cat and mouse, as he reached the final tablet, she approached him from behind and tapped him on the shoulder.

"Can't you read?" she said lightheartedly, sliding herself between him and the display case, tapping the sign with her index finger.

"Em … Emily," he stuttered, casually tucking the phone into his breast pocket. "I hadn't noticed, my apologies."

Liar.

"Come on now, Dr. Taylor." She pressed the rim of the glass into her supple bottom lip, taking a sip. "I know a man with your experience in this line of work knows the rules, or are you just privy to breaking them?"

"Must have slipped my mind." His Adam's apple bobbed as he took a deep swallow. "And as I said, 'Everett' is fine."

What are you up to?

"It's okay, *Everett*," she slurred in a whisper, hoping he'd drop his guard for a naïve, drunk woman. "I won't tell anyone. I promise." She laid her hand on his forearm, smoothing it at first then gripping it forcefully, knowing any man's ego was easily stroked.

"I think I need a drink myself. Care to join me?"

Got him.

Hours ticked by on the clock as they sat at the bar, drinks flowing freely, filled with Dr. Taylor's stories of discovery and disappointment. Emily paced herself, merely sipping her cocktails to keep her buzz under control. She needed to stay vigilant. Everett was none the wiser, too busy drinking his scotch and being distracted by his colleagues.

Shortly after midnight, the bartender announced last call, and security began making their rounds, advising the guests that the event was ending for the evening. Emily was running out of time to ask about the photos again.

"Everett," she giggled, still keeping up the drunken façade. "Really now, what do you intend to do with those photos?" She placed one hand on each of his thighs, coaxing the information from him.

"You are quite persistent, aren't you?" By now, his eyes were well glossed from the evening's drinks. "Just adding them to my collection. I'm sure you have your secrets, too, don't you, Miss Owens?"

She peered over his shoulder, seeing security moving closer by the second.

"And this, *collection*." She inched her hands farther up his thighs, so far that her thumbs were practically flanking his manhood. "When can I see it?"

"It's in my hotel room." He studied her face for a reaction.

"Perfect." Emily leaned in and kissed him deeply. "Maybe you could show me later tonight?"

"How about now?" Everett stood without hesitation and turned toward the bartender, settling their tab before placing his hand on Emily's lower back to escort her to the coat check.

As they walked outside and down the steps, a stretch limousine awaited them at the bottom. Everett cupped her hand in his while opening the door with his other, allowing her to sit and swing her legs inside the vehicle. Lowering the window just a sliver, she overheard him instructing the driver to take them to the Mandarin Oriental. *Classy.*

The limo began to make its way through the maze that is Manhattan's streets. Inside its tinted domain, darkness enhanced their sexual tension.

They had traveled only a few blocks when he draped her over his lap, rubbing her silky legs, courting her mouth with his tongue. Her hands caressed his jawline, clawing to draw him in, kissing him stronger, faster. His lips felt like the pieces of a puzzle joining to hers, locking perfectly together in sync.

Suddenly, she felt a vibration.

Under normal circumstances, it would be a mood killer if a guy she was trying to hook up with reached for his phone, but in this case, she hoped that he would.

She slowed her kissing to gently clasp her lips against his neck.

The vibration hit her again. *Damnit, just answer it!*

Everett, distinctly feeling the full intoxication of his single malts, flung his head forward and reached for his phone in his breast pocket. Placing his finger over the scanner, the limo illuminated with the light from the phone's screen.

Emily continued to kiss below his jawline, all the while peering at the text.

"Send me the photos as soon as you can."

She knew it. There was more to him than he was letting on.

He hit the lock button, and the limo went dark once again. She shifted his face, back to embracing his lips. Lifting her dress, she placed his hand between her legs. For a moment, he seemed taken aback, shocked that she wasn't wearing anything underneath.

He slipped his middle finger inside of her, smirking.

She bit his lip, moaning at how effortlessly it happened.

"We have arrived, Dr. Taylor." The driver's voice interrupted them over the speakers, just as the limo rolled to a stop.

Emily and Everett groaned, hurrying to collect themselves before the driver opened the door, like teenagers with no desire to be caught by their parents. As soon as the driver held the door for them, they scurried in through the hotel's lobby and onto the elevators.

Everett reached for the controls, repeatedly thumbing the button for the penthouse suite even though it had brightened with the first press.

The elevator climbed, stopping once they had reached the Oriental Suite.

Upon entering the room, Everett had now gained a stumble, and his head had begun to bobble. He removed his cell phone from his coat pocket, then slung his jacket over the back of the sofa.

Emily, on the other hand, waltzed into the room as sober as a judge, surveying her surroundings. Blueprints were scattered over the dining room table, and large black cases littered the rest of the suite. *Life of a principal investigator.*

"Wait here," he said explicitly, hiccupping while loosening his collar. "I need to take care of something first." Everett moved into the study, pulling the doors behind him.

She never was keen on taking directions.

The doors remained ajar, just enough so she could peek inside. She found him sitting at a desk, snaking a data cable between his phone and laptop. From the reflection in the window behind him, she could see that he was uploading the photos, just as she had hoped.

He pushed the chair back, its feet squealing against the marble floor.

Emily did a double hop backward, trying to act casual over by the sofa before his return.

"Now, where were we?" Everett emerged with a drunken grin.

"*You* were going to the bedroom." She placed a single finger on his puckered lips. "And *I* was going to freshen up."

Reaching to undo a few more buttons of his shirt, she pulled him in close, kissing him one more time before playfully pushing him away toward the bedroom. She lingered long enough to see him stagger from wall to wall, not quite swinging the bedroom door to a complete close behind him.

Here's my chance.

Emily darted into the half bath attached to the living room, immediately fumbling through the small compartments of her clutch, knowing it was in there somewhere.

Her fingers grazed the hard casing of a USB drive, concealed as a lipstick. *Here it is!*

Quietly, she opened the door, peeking down the hallway to confirm Everett was still in the bedroom. She let out a long exhale, then slipped back into the living room, creeping through the study and over to the laptop.

A large window on his computer screen had confirmed the files had been transferred to a folder named "The Duke of Tuscany." *Strange place to be sending files that have to do with relics from Iraq, Dr. Taylor.* Regardless, she jabbed the lipstick USB drive into the slot and began to transfer the folder.

"Twenty minutes!" she hissed softly as the screen flashed the download time. *Hiding more than just the photos, I see.*

Everett called to her from the end of the hall.

She lowered the screen of the computer to dim the light, then scrambled to the doors of the study. Sliding them back into place, she whipped around to him coming toward her, all of his clothing removed except for his boxer briefs.

She froze, unsure of exactly how much he had seen.

"What are you doing?" he asked, puzzled, standing with one hand against the corner of the wall.

"Sorry, I must have had more to drink than I thought. Isn't the bedroom this way?"

She could sense that he was starting to lose his interest and his patience.

Time for a distraction.

Reaching back, she unzipped her dress, the blue material parting like waves against her tanned skin. The straps, releasing with a slight buckle, trickled over the edge of her shoulders. Without resistance, the dress fell completely to the floor, pooling at her feet.

The look on Everett's face changed from annoyance to fascination. At first, he held eye contact like a gentleman, but eventually succumbed to his male instinct. *Just like they all do.* His gaze descended to admire her breasts, firm and full; her left, pierced with a barbell.

As he moved toward her, Emily's eyes shifted lower as well. She also had great admiration for the male form, and his was no exception.

His chest was shaved, curving at the base of his pecks. He also had abs that had been hidden under his two-piece suit. Her eyes kept sinking farther along his abdominal V until they became fixed on the bulge he was carrying so confidently.

That's when her eyes snapped back to his face, concerned that he may see into the study if he came any closer.

She took a step forward, grabbing him by the hand to lead him back into the hallway.

"So, is the bedroom this way?" She smiled, already knowing the answer.

I know how I can kill twenty minutes.

Emily felt the energy leave his body shortly after they finished. As they collapsed beside each other, she watched as his eyes fought to stay open. *Typical.* Nevertheless, in this situation, it was exactly what she needed.

She slid from the bed and made her way into the ensuite, glancing at her watch.

Twenty-three minutes. Not bad.

She waited a few more minutes before returning to the bedroom, and there he was, spread across the bed, passed out. She snickered at the sight of him snoring, with the condom still dangling from his flaccid penis.

Tiptoeing, she headed back out to the hall and to the study, grabbing her crumpled dress off the floor and slipping it on along the way.

She rushed to the computer. The popup on the screen read "Transfer complete."

Emily removed the USB drive from the laptop and stuffed it back into her clutch, taking one last look toward the bedroom on the way out. Everett hadn't moved. She grabbed her heels by the straps and hoisted them, grinning triumphantly as she left, quietly closing the hotel room door behind her.

CHAPTER TWO

Emily sat in the back seat of the cab twisting the USB drive in her fingers, wondering exactly what it was she would uncover in the files within. Her conscience, however, had already started to ravage her mind, telling her that maybe she shouldn't have followed through with what she had done. Not the sex, of course—that was well worth it—but to stoop so low as to steal another person's research.

Am I really this desperate?

The city's street lights dashed across her face as she laid her head against the edge of the headrest, nodding against the window in a losing fight to stay awake. She shimmied upright and pressed the button on the armrest of the car door, welcoming the influx of crisp, cool air striking her face.

As the cab turned onto W 101st Street, her condo building appeared up ahead.

Once the car had stopped at the main entrance, she handed the driver two bills and exited the car, hobbling the rest of the way to the front door. The concrete sidewalk reminded her that she was still barefoot, but wearing her heels again hadn't been an option since they came off at the hotel.

Swiping the powdered rocks away from her soles, she was greeted by Geoffrey, the building's concierge. He was posted in his usual spot, wearing his grey buttoned-up suit, his arms loosely crossed against his rounded belly.

He had been working in the building long before Emily ever moved in. He was the smiling type, one of those people who life could never bring down, constantly ready with a joke or story to brighten someone's day; somewhat of a local celebrity with the residents.

"Good morning, Miss Owens," Geoffrey said, grinning as she stumbled over the threshold. "Late night, I see."

"Good morning, G."

"Are you aware that shoes go on your feet, Miss Owens?"

"You try wearing them for six hours and see how you wind up at the end of the night."

"Nooo thank you." His face sunk into his double chin as he bellowed. "Have a good sleep, Miss Owens."

She turned and waved, continuing her walk of shame into the elevator. Leaning back against the railing, she fumbled through her purse in search of her keys, watching the numbers climb until the doors parted in front of her at the fifteenth floor.

She walked the length of the hallway to her door, unlocked the deadbolt, and slithered inside.

Emily threw her belongings on the coffee table and walked into the dining room. Her laptop awaited on the table, practically calling to her to check the stolen information. Coming around the table, she lifted the laptop's screen halfway, but pressed it closed again just as fast.

She dropped the lipstick USB drive beside it and took a step back.

Not tonight.

She left the dining area and turned in the hallway toward her master bedroom.

Removing her dress, she kicked it away across the floor of her room, at the same time removing her jewelry.

Entering the ensuite, she was greeted by a less-than-flattering reflection. The soft pastel of her ample lips had been smeared from pleasuring Everett, and her normally alluring green eyes had become two puffy, bloodshot beads, not to mention their corners, blobbed with mascara.

She reached for the nearest cloth and started to wipe.

It was shortly after noon when Emily awoke to the sound of bells emanating from the tower of St. Michael's church. She rose from the bed to draw the curtains, letting the sunlight in to provide a refreshing warmth against her skin. She stood for a moment, lingering on the brightened colors of the city, ones that contrasted the sullen thoughts of regret still plaguing her mind since before she'd opened her eyes.

She strolled down the hall and past the dining room to the kitchen, side-eyeing the laptop as she walked by. After making herself a cup of coffee, she returned to stand in the adjoining doorway, looking at her laptop, while tapping her fingernails against the mug.

The USB drive lay in wait, but Emily was conflicted about what she should do.

From the corner of her eye, the lit screen of her cell phone caught her attention before it dimmed once again: a missed call. She took one last glance at the USB drive before heading to the living room, curling up on the sofa and hitting the button on her phone to access her voicemail.

"You have two unheard messages. First message."

"Hey, Toots! It's Emmet and Willow, you know, your parents. Haven't heard from you in a while. Your mother and I just wanted to make sure you're doing okay. I wanted to let you know that I'm heading to Thailand for a couple of days for work; I have a run to do. Your mother will be home, though, in case you feel like driving up to visit her. We know you're busy chasing that ever-elusive big adventure, so if you can't make it, we understand. Anyway, call us back. We love you."

Her father had been calling her "Toots" ever since she was a baby. Emily had a strong relationship with her father, although he wasn't around as much as she would have liked when she was growing up. He was a pilot for hire, frequently getting contracted to fly people all over the world. She never did ask too many questions about where he went or who his customers were; the particularities of his job were always just kind of swept under the rug. But when he *was* around, he was the best father ever, always taking the family on vacations with endless supplies of her favorite ice cream.

He had his moments—like all fathers—but for the most part, she only remembered the good.

Oddly, her father had seemed to become more protective as Emily grew older. Not in a hard-ass kind of way, more like a making-her-take-self-defense-classes kind of way. He was the one who introduced her to the shooting range in the first place. *What kind of fifteen-year-old needs to know how to handle a gun?* It wasn't like she didn't enjoy those times, because she did, but she was always suspicious of his underlying motives.

As for her mother, she was a sweetheart. Like in most families, she was the rock that made everyone stable. Her name was actually Willene, but Emily's father had called her "Willow" since the day they'd met—a combination of Willene and Owens. He said he always knew they would be married someday, so he gave her that pet name for assurance. *Romantic, apparently.*

Her mother was also an archaeologist, which is what had led Emily to pursue a career in the field in the first place. Emily's mother would often take her on work trips, even hiding things so Emily would find them, so she would feel as if she was a part of the excitement. Emily guessed it was her mother that had set the expectations so high for her, ones that, lately, had felt out of reach.

Emily's parents had moved to Vermont once she left for university, in pursuit of a quieter lifestyle now that their kids were grown and moved out on their own. She wasn't avoiding them, by any means, but was merely trying to make her own way, and she felt fortunate that they understood that.

As Emily sipped her coffee, her eyes shifted to the glass cabinet standing against the wall. Her diploma stood framed, a constant reminder of how hard she had worked to follow her dreams. Below, the shelves were filled with awards of her success. First place ribbon: gymnastics competition; Dallas, Texas. First place trophy: free climbing summit; Arco, Italy. Gold medal: open water swim; Budapest, Hungary.

These achievements seemed to inspire her thirst for success even more. Growing up, being told she could be whatever she wanted to be in life really hit home. Her yearning for recognition, whether it was physical or verbal, had become one of her less admirable traits.

Emily jabbed the pound sign on the screen.

"*Message erased. Next message.*"

"Hey, bitch, it's Peyton! I'm still alive in case you were wondering. Where have you been? Anyway, Mom and Dad told me to check in on you. By the way, I am getting huge! You should see this baby belly. It's crazy! Don't be a stranger, or I'll come over there and kick your ass while I still can! Just kidding. Love ya."

Peyton, Emily's older sister, had always been the wild child of the family. She was much rougher around the edges than Emily ever was.

Emily always looked up to Peyton, though. Peyton was so strong and independent. That woman was her best friend, and Emily was beginning to neglect even her. With Peyton having one kid already and another on the way, it wasn't fair to anyone that Emily hadn't visited lately.

"*Message erased.*"

Emily got up and shifted to a seat at the dining room table, blankly staring at the apple-shaped insignia on the top of the laptop before her. Her fingers lifted the screen as her eyes remained fixated on the USB drive.

She removed the cap and plugged the USB drive into the port, biting her nails, waiting for it to load. Upon its completion, she hovered over the file folder named "The Duke of Tuscany."

In a wave of frustration, she closed the screen again, this time rattling the table. She batted the mug of coffee across the room, shattering it on the hardwood. *Goddamnit! I can't do this.* She had always worked hard for her achievements and couldn't understand why she had felt it necessary to take the coward's route.

Crunching over the broken ceramic and wasted brew, she hauled her gym bag from the closet and slammed the door as she left her condo.

Sitting alone in the change room of the gym, Emily was preparing to rid herself of self-disappointment and the pent-up rage it embodied. Heavy metal continued to play over her AirPods as she ripped them from the sides of her head, standing to drive a fist into the lockers on her way out to the ring.

Kickboxing had been a much-needed past time, and better yet, she was a natural. There was no better outlet to blow off some steam than to go a few rounds. With her gloves tightly strapped, she sucked at her mouth guard as she jogged in place, awaiting her opponent.

Finally, one of the gym's personal trainers climbed through the ropes, geared and ready to go. She and Emily had sparred together countless times in the past, but as Emily looked across the ring at her today, she saw only a version of herself—one she loathed.

At the sound of the bell, both women squared up, shuffling in a circle, waiting for the other to make the first move.

Emily felt the cold sting of her opponent's glove across her chin. She stumbled back, shaking her head, shifting her jaw back and forth to assess the damage.

"Wow, Em, that's the first time I've ever gotten one up on you. You good?"

Emily responded with a hard right of her own; blocked. The trainer landed a hard kick to her leg. *Focus, Emily, c'mon.*

They swayed, reading each other.

Her opponent went for a quick roundhouse, which Emily ducked before performing a leg sweep that sent the trainer to the mat, fully knowing it was an illegal move when sparring.

"Hey! What the hell was that?" the trainer shouted.

Emily paused, clenching her jaw.

The woman lifted herself back to her feet, stepping forward and rocking Emily with an elbow strike that sent her mouth guard flying to the outside of the ring. She followed with a stiff jab to Emily's midsection, knocking the wind from her.

Emily buckled to one knee, coughing, looking up at the condescension on the trainer's face.

"What's wrong, Em? You can hit dirty, but you can't play dirty?"

Emily snapped. Spearing the instructor to the mat, she began throwing a flurry of punches, each one landing harder than the last. The woman covered her head with both arms, but Emily didn't let up.

"Help! Emily! Stop!" The trainer's screams resonated from below Emily's punches.

Within seconds, a set of arms wrapped around Emily's torso from behind, ripping her away from the trainer and tossing her face down on the mat. She felt a knee driving into her spine.

"You know we don't do that here!" It was the owner, Gabrielle.

The tension she had applied to Emily's now-buckled arm was like a vice-grip—not enough to hurt, but enough that she knew she wasn't going anywhere.

Tears began to trickle from Emily's eyes, staining the canvas mat.

"Come on, girl, let's go to my office," Gabrielle whispered, pulling Emily to her feet as the other employees slid into the ring to tend to their co-worker.

"Sorry, Gabby. I'm not even sure what just happened out there," Emily said in a muffled voice as she tore at the Velcro straps of her gloves with her teeth.

"I know, Em, but I can't have you up in here wailing on people," Gabrielle barked back. "Especially the ones on my payroll. You know better than that. Don't you realize your actions have consequences? Haven't I taught you anything? Shit, what's gotten into you?"

Emily turned her head toward the lean, five-foot-ten woman who was standing with her back pressed against the brick wall opposite her. Gabrielle's dark cocoa skin blended in with the dim light of the underground room, while the unsympathetic whites of her eyes searched Emily for a response.

She and Gabrielle had been friends for a long time, so it wasn't hard for either of them to tell if something was wrong with the other. She also knew that Gabrielle still had a reputable business to run and that her misdemeanor was unacceptable, whether they were friends or not.

Gabrielle's line of work was one that saw this type of behavior constantly, and from what she had told Emily in the past, most times it would only get worse before it got any better.

Emily put her head back down, focused on the concrete floor as a mix of tears and sweat accumulated to drip from the tip of her nose. Unable to hold it in any longer, she proceeded to explain the events of the night before to Gabrielle.

When reaching the part about her feelings of regret for stealing the information, Gabrielle stopped her immediately, pushing herself off from the wall and waving her hands to cut Emily off.

"Listen, listen, listen. There is one thing that I have learned in life as a black woman opening my own gym in Manhattan, okay?" Her eyes leveled sternly with Emily's. "You do what you have to do to succeed, honey. I found out the hard way that sometimes you have to step on a few toes to get to the top. That's the name of the game.

"I'm not saying what you did was right, but what's done is done. *You* just have to believe it was worth it."

Emily pulled her in and squeezed her with a formidable hug.

"Now get out of here. Enough of this sappy shit." Gabrielle pulled away to open her office door. "And the next time you want to get that aggression out in my gym, take it out on the squat rack, all right girl?" She chuckled, slapping Emily on the backside to move her along.

Emily dropped her gym bag and was met by the smashed mug and sticky, coffee-laden floor. Grabbing a broom and dustpan from the linen closet, she started to clean, all the while glancing over her shoulder at her laptop on the table. She dumped the shards into the trash and sat down in front of her laptop, lifting the screen to reveal the previously highlighted folder.

She double-clicked.

The folder contained a multitude of information—documents, pictures, emails, profiles, testimonies. Her pupils widened as she leaned in with attempt to absorb everything she was seeing, a little overwhelmed at first.

Once the folder had finished loading, front and center was the most recent item: the pictures of the Irisagrig tablets she had watched Everett take the night before.

I'm going to need another coffee.

The rest of Emily's afternoon was consumed with sifting through the files. She was able to decipher almost all of the information that the folder contained, finding the most intriguing aspect to be that each document was either addressed to, or submitted by, someone known as "the Boar." According to receipts and bank transfer data, it looked as though Everett had been hired by this person to photograph the tablets at the gala.

After reviewing the pictures again, Emily realized that Everett had only taken pictures of the tablets that depicted the story of the great army, the one that Emily had read about on the display cases.

Why is this "Boar" only interested in these tablets in particular?

She zoomed in on every photo, examining them for clues as to why that might be.

The carvings on the tablets depicted many warriors, both infantry and cavalry. Some showed images of the warriors running across a plain or desert, with dust clouds forming around them, while others showed the warriors driving their spears and arrows into the hearts of their enemies. This was nothing out of the ordinary, as most ancient relics documented acts of war.

She swiped through a few more photos before something else caught her eye.

Magnifying one of the photos to get a better look at the edge of one specific tablet, she noticed that it appeared to have been broken off. All that remained on the tablet's jagged edge was what appeared to be an outreached arm holding some sort of item, outlined by a deteriorated yellow color.

She surveyed every single photo of the tablets again. None showed the missing half of the shattered tablet.

Peculiar. It seems as if a piece is missing from the collection.

She added this to her notes, biting the tip of her pen while contemplating its significance.

Trying not to over-think every minute detail, she moved on from the tablets, finding herself immersed in files containing what would be a historical timeline of some sort, obtained over multiple excursions.

First, she read what she understood to be an excerpt from a journal.

It is not a myth! By my own ears I have heard the tales of its existence.

Tonight, we make for Tuscany, the last known whereabouts of the Duke. My team and I feel we are on the cusp of greatness with this one. Should we not make it, I pray this book reaches you, my love.

Do not follow, for if death has taken me, I fear the stories are real.

– Frederick S.
May 11th, 1758

Emily wondered what the "it" the excerpt referred to was, as well as which Duke they were seeking. Tuscany had had many Dukes throughout the years, Emily knew for a fact. She leaned in closer, then scrolled to another document, this one a letter.

The Austro-Hungarian Empire is beautiful, brother. I wish you could have come with me.

I have discovered paintings on a church roof in Vienna that foretell of the god's relic for which I seek. I know that I must be close. I leave for the Hofburg in the morning.

There are whispers that the war will reach us soon, though I trust I will escape before it does. I will update you as soon as I can. Take care of Mother.

– Robert
Nov 1st, 1918

God's relic? With her knowledge of world history, she was well aware that the Austro-Hungarian Empire fell shortly after the date on this entry. *How has this page even survived? Better yet, how did the person who owned this folder even have access to such records?*

Emily opened the next document.

Father, I have retrieved what is rightfully ours. I took the god's relic while they slept. What fools to welcome me into their home ... such idiocy.

I am leaving Switzerland in three days' time to return home, using the money I made from the Habsburgs. I have found favor with a ship's captain who is set to cross the Atlantic.

I trust you still have shelter for me, home in Ollantaytambo. Our people will rejoice once again. Inti will be pleased.

I will see you soon.

– Luis Gomes
January 23rd, 1924

The pattern was apparent. Each story vaguely described people who appeared to be pursuing the same goal, although leaving no indication of what exactly it was they were pursuing.

Emily sat back in her chair and hung her head back to stare at the ceiling, processing.

That's when it resonated. The yellow depiction on the tablets.

It has to be. That *must be the connection.* That *must be the* "god's relic"!

The documents still left an abundance of unanswered questions. For starters, what exactly were all of these people searching for and why? Either way, she knew that if she could figure it out and find this "god's relic" herself, then it would ignite the recognition that she so strongly desired.

It was time for an expert's opinion, and lucky for her, the best one she knew just happened to be in the city. *Dr. Alsafar!*

She saved her notes, pushed her chair back from the table, and scooped up her laptop to head downstairs.

Geoffrey was waiting by the front desk, immediately trying to trap her with small talk. But Emily was on a mission. She plowed through the lobby with her head down, unwavering, toward the main entrance.

"Sorry, G. Big break! Gotta go!" She turned to blow him a friendly kiss before jogging through the exit.

Heading straight back to the MET, Emily crossed her fingers over the steering wheel as she drove, willing every red light to change to green, while turning her explanation for the doctor over and over in her head.

"Sorry, Mr. Boar," she said aloud, zipping through Central Park with a grin from ear to ear. She whipped the car into the parking garage, almost forgetting to lock it as she started to rush toward the museum.

This was it. The big break that her career needed.

Once she showed Dr. Alsafar the documents, she knew they could figure this out together. All she had to do was show him the yellow etch mark on the tablet, paired with the entries, and she knew he would believe her.

She ran through the Great Hall and down the corridor as she made the turn into the Charles Engelhard Court, practically bursting with excitement.

Emily halted, stopping in her tracks just inside the archway of the Court.

Her mouth hung open. The rosy flush of her cheeks seeped to a pale hue. Tightening her grip around the laptop, her arms fell to her side.

There was nothing. No tablets, no exhibit, no doctor. *Impossible.*

She had been here less than twenty-four hours ago. Dr. Alsafar had announced it himself; the exhibit would continue into the next month.

How could someone remove all of those displays so fast?

She dug her hand into her coat pocket to fetch her cell phone, dialing the doctor's number and pressing it to her ear.

"Pick up, pick up, pick up!" Her voice rose in volume with each repetition as the phone rang.

Other visitors began to stare at her, some even ushering their kids away from Emily while shaking their heads.

"*You have reached...*" The voicemail started in.

Emily collapsed onto the nearest bench, timidly looking around at the few strangers milling about. She laid her phone face down beside her, her lip quivering as if she was an abandoned little girl.

Where could he be?

CHAPTER THREE

The drive home felt like a much longer one. Emily tightly gripped the steering wheel as her thoughts drifted elsewhere. Instead of being annoyed by the stop of a red light, she now found herself pausing at the green ones until the incessant honking from behind her snapped her from her disillusion.

Moping her way back to her condo building, her somber attitude lingered like a shadow. Geoffrey's shift had ended somewhere during her escapade to the museum, so even he wasn't there to cheer her up when she arrived. She was starting to feel as if she would never make her name as an archaeologist. She began to think that maybe she *should* go to see her mother, if only just to get away.

Standing in the elevator, Emily glared at her zombie-like reflection in the golden door of the lift, then dragged her feet as she made her way down the hall to her condo. She placed the laptop on the table and flopped onto the sofa, burying her face into the pillows.

Hours later, a deep thumping echoed through Emily's condo, startling her awake and causing her to roll off the sofa.

What's going on? What time is it?

The condo had transitioned to a pitch black while she had slept. Another bang rattled the door.

Brushing the hair from her face, she gathered herself to her knees.

Her heart began to race as she swatted the cushions searching for her phone, but unable to find it. Her mind automatically went to Everett. *What if he somehow found out I stole a copy of his documents? What if he's here to reclaim them?*

"No, he was passed out," Emily whispered, reassuring herself while crouching on all fours between the coffee table and sofa. "He didn't see me take anything." *Right?*

Now she was second-guessing whether he *had* seen her after all. If it *was* him at her door, he was going to be pissed off. She barely knew the man—what if he was secretly a serial killer?

Her mind began spinning with unrealistic scenarios.

She crawled across the hardwood floor on her hands and knees, sliding herself underneath the dining room table. Raising a hand above her head, she felt along the table's underside for the knife she kept hidden there—another aspect of her life that her father was responsible for.

Once more the knocking sounded, more furiously than before.

As soon as her fingers grazed along the handle of the knife, she removed it from its sheath and slid from underneath the table. She pressed her back against the nearest wall and used it to slide upward onto her feet. She side-stepped her way along the wall to the door, white-knuckled from clenching the blade's resin grip.

Instinct was telling her to check the peephole, but her gut churned at the thought of Everett kicking the door in before she had the chance.

She had no choice.

Wrapping her hand around the doorknob, she leaned over to the peephole. Taking a deep swallow, her doll-like lashes fluttered against the glass as she investigated the corridor.

With a heavy breath of relief, she swung open the door.

"I told you I'd come over here and kick your ass," Peyton stated, arms crossed over her pregnant belly.

"What the fuck, Peyton?" Emily huffed, squinting her eyes as they adjusted to the light in the hallway. "What time is it?" She discreetly placed the knife in the drawer of her entrance cabinet, trying not to alert her sister to her newly developed paranoia.

"It's only 10:30, Em. Are you drunk or something? Jesus." Her sister brushed past her into the condo, flicking switches as she went. "Why are all of your lights off?"

"Come on in," Emily muttered underneath her breath, yet loud enough for Peyton to catch the underlying sarcasm.

By the time she had locked the door and turned around, her sister had already helped herself to some coconut cream pie that had been left over in the fridge. She was sprawled across the sofa with a mound of pillows placed behind her back.

Emily had witnessed this behavior before. Peyton was in full pregnancy mode.

Her usual up-kept, ash-blond hair had clearly been neglected, looking as if it hadn't been washed in days, and the roots were showing at least an inch. Her suave sense of fashion had also been reduced to grey sweatpants and her husband's hoodie, with her modelesque body now resembling that of a slender toad.

"Did you call Mom and Dad yet? You know I'll get blamed if you don't," Peyton badgered with her mouth full of whipped cream. "What? I'm pregnant—give me a break."

"I've been busy, Peyton. I'm working on a new project."

"I don't believe you."

Her brooding grey eyes could still scold Emily in the way that only an older sister's could.

"But you know ..." she continued, chewing with her mouth open, "Mom and Dad always did love to hear about *your* success stories. Maybe you can start the conversation there. You're named after Dad, for Christ's sake."

Emily could hear the hint of resentment in her voice.

"Don't you think that they would rather hear from their daughter who's about to give them their next grandchild?"

She was attempting to deflect the conversation. It was no secret that Peyton often felt that Emily was favored by their parents. She wanted to help her see that it wasn't true.

"Oh, they hear from me plenty. Ask Mom about last week, when she stayed on the phone while I hurled for twenty minutes."

They laughed together, the first time in months.

Somehow, the conversation got easier from there, both managing to keep things civil and positive for the next hour. Emily needed to get her mind off of things too, even if in the back of her mind she was constantly preparing for reality to kick back in as soon as her sister left.

As midnight drew, Peyton pushed herself up from the sofa and waddled her way over to the door. Emily followed, laying a hand on her sister's belly as she was putting on her jacket.

"Listen, Em, I know life gets tough at times. Trust me, I've been there. Even though you're too stubborn to see it, you're vulnerable just like the rest of us. Just know that your family is here if you need any of us, okay? You can ask for help sometimes, you know."

Emily stayed mute, simply giving her sister a hug before reaching to open the door.

Peyton took three steps into the hall, then spun around.

"By the way, you could use a vacation. You look like shit. Love you. Byyyye."

A grin spread across Emily's face as she closed the door, shaking her head at the mess her sister had left behind as she walked around her condo.

Circling back to the dining room, she stopped to hover over the notes she had taken earlier. Her heart wouldn't allow her to give up on this. She may not have had the help from Dr. Alsafar she felt she needed, but she was determined to see this through, no matter what. Propping herself in front of the laptop once again, she retraced her steps and reviewed all that she had learned thus far.

From what she could tell, the artifact had been traced back as far as Tuscany in 1758. It appeared as if "the Boar" had been collecting info for several years, tracking the artifact to the last reported destination, South America.

Still, she was unable to place where exactly the tablets came into play. Something wasn't adding up.

If this "Boar" has a record of the artifact from as recently as 1924, why would they need photos foretelling of it passing through Iraq in the 15th century?

She skimmed through the documents again and again, starting from the beginning each time.

That's when she noticed that almost every page had a recurring symbol that she had somehow missed before. The symbol seemed to represent the sun. Inside, there was an upside-down cross, with what appeared to be three nails shooting upward.

Clicking on the symbol brought her to maps that were full of red markings, mostly appearing to depict dig sites, all of them corresponding to the locations of the journal entries.

The comment she had overheard from Everett when Dr. Alsafar questioned him about Tuscany replayed in her head:

"Let's just say it was a dead end."

She could only assume that Everett had been contracted to go to Tuscany in search of this mysterious relic, meaning that whoever had hired him still hadn't found it.

Emily caught herself smiling at the screen.

She delved further, finding a folder labeled "Itinerary." Opening it, she leaned in to see that it was filled with a list of travel documents and itineraries for flights that were due to leave LaGuardia

Airport, heading to Alejandro Velasco Astete Airport in Cusco, Peru on October 3rd, in four days' time. The tickets had been redacted with black markings to conceal the names of the people they had been purchased for. She was willing to bet her degree that these people were headed to Peru in search of the aforementioned "god's relic."

She discovered that Ollantaytambo—the location mentioned in the most recent document—was only a few hours north-west of Cusco. *No doubt that's where they're headed.*

Emily stopped. She knew better than to get ahead of herself. *What if these people are dangerous?*

More research was needed on the strange symbol before she could make a sound decision.

A quick internet browse gave her multiple hits on symbols that were similar in design, but nothing exact. However, similar symbols were continuously referred to as "Christograms," which were a combination of pictures and text relating to religion. After cross-referencing the symbol with other Christograms, she found a match.

It wasn't a perfect resemblance, but the markings were unmistakable: the same cross and nails, surrounded by a sun, although this time, they were pointed downward. In turn, this led her to a plethora of links and articles discussing a group of people referred to as the Jesuits, some sort of society that had been established in the 1540s.

She had heard the name "Jesuit" before in history class, maybe in high school, but to her recollection, they were simply people of God, not treasure hunters, and certainly not dangerous.

She kept going.

"The Society of Jesuits believed that the Lord would bless his children with gifts from the heavens so they may share it with the impure of the world. As soldiers of God, they were to defend and propagate faith, and progress the souls of Christianity."

Scouring over the information into the early hours of the morning, she fought to retain every detail, which she knew would be required if she was going to try and spearhead some sort of expedition.

Based on her research, the Jesuits didn't seem to pose an immediate threat, which in turn made Emily feel more confident than ever that this treasure was fair game. Still, she would need to act fast if she was going to get a jump on the discovery. Even though these Jesuits had failed before, she had a feeling that this next location would be the big one.

Fortunately, there were still seats available on a flight leaving for Cusco from New York on the evening of October 1st. The bad news was that it was full of layovers. She had hoped for a direct flight, but there was no such luck on such short notice. One stop in Bogota, another in Lima, then onward to Cusco. Even so, this gave her at least a twenty-four-hour head start.

It has to be enough.

Without hesitation, she booked the flight.

She spent the next two days scouring the internet for information about the artifact called the "god's relic" and the mysterious "Boar"—with very little luck.

As the departure time of her flight quickly approached, she found herself scrambling to get ready.

Pushing her chair back from her dining room table where she had been lost in her research, she headed into the bedroom. Rifling through her closet, she grabbed her suitcase and flung it open on the bed, filling it with clothes and travel accessories.

She retrieved a tactical knife and thigh-holster from the closet, unsheathing it halfway to run her thumb along its sharpened edge.

Her father had always taught her to know her way around a weapon, to expect the unexpected. He showed her how to defend herself, how to prepare, how to be aware of her surroundings. He always said that keeping these things in mind was an occupational hazard of his, often telling her that humans are predictable beings and if you have something they want, they *will* try to take it from you.

Emily was now starting to realize she had become that person. *She* was the one who wanted to take something belonging to someone else.

A cut-throat industry, right, Em? She tossed the knife into the suitcase with the rest of her things. *Just in case.*

She removed the USB drive from her laptop and threw it into a satchel along with her passport, iPad, and wallet. Grabbing her cell phone from the countertop, she looked down at it with reservation before thumbing the contact for "Home."

"Hey, Mom, it's Em. I'm sorry I haven't called you back. I've just been … busy. But good news! I'm onto something I think will be really big. I'm trying not to get too excited, in case it doesn't work out. But if it does, I think you and Dad will be proud. I'll be in South America for a few days. Not sure how the service will be there, but don't worry, my team and I will be fine. I love you."

Lying to her parents was not something she had ever done, not even as a teenager. But in this case, she deemed it necessary, knowing they would never approve of her going on an expedition alone. This was *her* adventure. She needed to do this for herself. To be taken seriously and to make a legitimate name in her field of work; she knew this discovery was what it would take.

Guess I'll take that vacation after all, Sis. Emily smirked, zipping up her suitcase.

Geoffrey was just starting his shift when Emily exited the elevators, suitcase in tow.

"Bags in hand, cab outside … Off to the airport I presume? Anything to do with that big break from this weekend?"

"Sure is, G! I'm going to be out of town for a few days. Keep an eye on the place for me, will you?"

"Will do, Miss Owens. Please, allow me to see you out."

Geoffrey helped load her suitcase into the trunk of the cab. Emily waved back at him through the rear windshield as the car pulled away.

Opening her bag, she removed the iPad and powered it on. The half-hour drive to the terminal gave her a little extra time to get her accommodations in order.

First, she combed the internet for hotels and transport once she reached Peru.

Luckily for her, the local resorts still had rooms available, and it looked as though she could take a shuttle from Cusco to a town called Urubamba, then another half-hour shuttle from there to Ollantaytambo.

Next, she laid out everything she knew so far.

If the Society of Jesuits were indeed after this artifact, it must have some religious connection, hence the name "God's relic." But, why were they only heading to Peru now? Her only logical conclusion was that they were finding clues at the prior sites that lead them in this direction, discovering the last journal entry at some point in their search through Austria.

According to the itineraries, eight flights were booked to Cusco, meaning there were at least eight people she had to keep an eye out for; confrontation was not at the top of her priority list. The plan was to get in, find what she could about this mysterious relic, then get out. *Simple.* Even if these people weren't dangerous themselves, she didn't want to be tangled up with the local authorities should anything happen.

The cab came to a halt at the Departures section of the airport.

Emily grabbed her things and began working her way through the crowd to get inside. She approached the check-in desk, checked her suitcase, then proceeded to security, where everyone was herded like cattle through the screening area.

She had forty minutes before boarding, which any normal person would use to rest, but she still had work to do. She had copied all the stolen data over to each of her devices for the sake of ease. Using her iPad once again, she compiled most of her findings into an email and sent it to Dr. Alsafar with a message for him to review the information and report any feedback.

"Flight 1554 is now asking passengers seated in Zone 1 to please come forward and board the aircraft," the electronic voice wailed over the waiting area.

Emily looked down at her ticket: first class. *That's me.*

Her nerves felt like bugs crawling in her stomach as she walked through the gangway to board the plane. Once aboard, she swooped into her seat and watched the rest of the passengers filter on board. She tilted her head back, closed her eyes, and took a deep breath through her nose. Something about the smell of planes always reminded her of her father.

She withdrew her phone from her carry-on just as the last few people were boarding. While the flight attendants demonstrated their emergency protocols to the passengers, Emily distracted herself with her phone.

She sent a text to Peyton, a selfie with a message that read, "*Thanks for the push. #vacayfordays.*" She wanted her sister to think that she was just taking a short trip, in case she got worried. Then she texted Gabrielle, apologizing again for her behavior at the gym on the weekend.

After hitting send, she received a tap on the shoulder by one of the flight attendants.

She ripped the AirPods from her ears, her heart thumping.

"Excuse me, sorry to startle you, but we are about to take off. We ask that you turn off all transmitting and receiving functions on your device. Thank you."

Emily blushed and nodded, standing to place her phone in the overhead compartment before sitting back down to buckle herself in.

As the plane pushed forward and lifted from the runway, she finally relaxed, listening to the landing gear grinding its way back inside the plane. Reaching a few hundred feet in the air, she balled up her jacket against the window and laid her head down, shutting her eyes.

As the plane ascended, her phone illuminated, buzzing in the hollow of her bag above.

"Incoming call – Dr. Alsafar"

CHAPTER FOUR

It wasn't until the wheels of the plane bumped onto the tarmac that Emily stirred in her seat, rubbing her knuckles into the sockets of her eyes. She slid into an upright position, squinting around as if, for a moment, she had forgotten where she was.

"Attention passengers, we have arrived in Bogota, Columbia. If you are connecting to another flight, please see the board inside the gate for more information."

Emily grabbed her satchel from the overhead compartment and shuffled with the crowd off the plane.

Once inside the gate, her stomach burbled and grumbled. Her mouth began to salivate at the sight of a burger and fries on a poster in the airport's food court. Ordering something was imminent.

Propping her bag onto a table in the waiting area for her food, she removed her phone and immediately saw that she had missed a call from Dr. Alsafar. *He must have received my email!*

Unfortunately, as soon as she thumbed the screen, it faded to black.

Maybe charge the damn thing next time before you set off across two continents.

She plugged the phone into the nearest outlet; returning the call would have to wait.

In an attempt to kill time, Emily started to people-watch, settling on a thin redhead who was clumsily carrying two laptop bags. With a strap slung over each shoulder, she was trying to wiggle her way to one of the food stands, constantly bumping into other people who were just trying to order their meals.

"Order 142!" a cashier shouted from behind the counter in Spanish.

Emily stopped gawking and jerked her head around. She realized it was for her. *Seems like completing that Spanish Studies Program at UCB will come in handy after all.*

Retrieving the tray of food, she walked back to her seat and devoured the meal within minutes. Following a less-than-attractive belch, she wiped the grease from her mouth and checked her phone again: still charging.

She took another look around. No sign of the redhead anymore. *There goes my entertainment.*

Her boarding broadcast sounded overhead.

Emily removed herself from the table and unplugged her phone, then headed back toward the gate. Fortunately, the next leg was less than three hours.

She boarded the plane and sat, patiently awaiting the announcement for departure. A hefty man flopped down in the seat to her right. His strong body odor smelled like cigarettes and deep fryer oil. Emily plugged her phone in again while reaching for the drink menu.

As the plane filled with people making their way to their assigned seats, the seat to her left remained unoccupied. The flight attendants had already closed all the luggage compartments and were about to start their cross-checks. Emily hoped that with a little luck, it would stay empty, allowing her to breathe air that was somewhat fresh.

"Hold the plane! Hold the plane!" a shrill voice shouted, barreling down the loading ramp.

A unified sigh released from the passengers, pure disdain for the person who was holding up the plane.

Emily was too far back to see who the voice belonged to, but she soon heard a loud thud followed by an eruption of laughter from the passengers and crew alike.

Emily slowly raised herself out of the seat to get a glimpse of the commotion.

It was the redhead from the food court.

The young woman, who looked to be no older than twenty, collected herself from the floor. She pushed her glasses back onto her face, then placed an inhaler to her mouth and pumped it as the flight attendant dusted her off.

"I'm so sorry! Please forgive me!" The young woman began stumbling over her apology. "You see, I misplaced my ticket, then I found it, then I went to the wrong gate–"

"Please take your seat, ma'am," the flight attendant said, cutting her off.

Lowering her head, the young woman moved swiftly down the aisle, laptop cases still hanging at her sides, smacking every passenger in an aisle seat along the way.

Emily slunk back into her seat, tightly closing her eyes.

Please don't sit here. Please don't sit here.

Placing one laptop in the overhead bin, the young woman crashed into the seat next to Emily, tucking the second laptop beneath the seat in front of her.

"Hi! I'm Maggie. Nice to meet you!" The young woman jutted her palm forward.

Her smile was bright and innocent, one that pushed her glasses up to rest on her cheekbones when she grinned. Her nose and cheeks were covered with a light sprinkle of freckles. Her hair, a natural orange, was propped into a messy bun.

"Hello. My name's Emily," Emily said as she reached for the stranger's hand. "Nice to meet you as well."

"Is that your husband over there?" Maggie asked, pointing to the obese man to Emily's right.

"Him? God no."

"Oh, sorry. Someone should really tell him he needs to reapply his deodorant."

The comment caught Emily off guard, causing her to snort with laughter.

"I'm sorry, was that rude of me?"

"No, no, it's quite fine." Her chuckle dragged on. "But I think you're right."

Once the plane climbed high enough that the seat belt sign had turned off, Maggie reached down to retrieve her computer, placing it on the lunch tray table folded down in front of her as Emily watched conspicuously from the corner of her eye.

Maggie could really type.

Her fingers danced across the keyboard rapidly and with great accuracy. Before Emily knew it, schematics were popping up all over the screen, followed by intricate CAD drawings and location markers.

Emily would periodically turn away nonchalantly, but eventually Maggie caught her looking at the screen.

"Do you wanna see?" Maggie chirped with excitement.

"Sure! What is all this stuff?"

"This is my passion! I graduated from MIT when I was eighteen, with a master's degree in explosives and mining engineering, then started my own company. I'm on my way to Chile right now, finishing up a contract utilizing explosive mining. So far so good!

"The mine has since run dry, so I'm on my way to tie up the loose ends and dispose of the dormant devices. Then I just wait for the next job to come along!"

"So, what's the name of your company?"

Maggie bent over and reached into her laptop case, withdrew a business card, and handed it to Emily.

Maggie Riggs
Explosive engineering & disposal
I build 'em, I Rigg 'em, I blow 'em
1-701-555-8745

"You can keep it," Maggie blurted. "I've got new ones on the way. The last line of my slogan wasn't very well thought out on my part. Let's just say, I've gotten a lot more calls for 'business' than I ever expected I would."

Emily couldn't help but laugh. Maggie may have been a bit ditzy, but it made for some great entertainment.

"So, what's the other laptop for?" Emily asked as she tucked the business card into her pocket.

"Oh, that's for my other business! I'm a bit of a computer geek, a grey hat, you could say. I've been a hacker for most of my life, so I decided why not get paid for it? Haven't landed anything major yet, mostly just catching a few unfaithful spouses sending some very revealing pictures. I'm capable of doing so much more, but hey, it pays the bills, right?"

"Sounds like you live an interesting lifestyle. I'm a little jealous."

The girls conversed for the entirety of the flight, although Emily decided to keep her reason for travel a little closer to her chest. Instead, listening to Maggie tell her eccentric tales seemed to shorten the time it took to reach Lima. Emily was required to remain on the plane as it was carrying onward to Cusco, but Maggie had to disembark to catch yet another connector.

"It was nice meeting you, Emily! Not many people can stand listening to me natter on for three hours straight," she giggled at herself.

"It was a pleasure, Maggie. Take care."

Emily shook her head, smiling, watching as her new acquaintance, once again, hit both seats and their passengers with her laptop cases on her way off the plane.

Looking out the window, Emily could see the ground below as the plane began its final descent into Cusco. There were mountain ranges as far as her eyes could see, a mixture of greens and reds protruding from the earth. Once the aircraft breached below the clouds, a city revealed itself, nestled amongst the hills.

Rolling to the gate, everyone was shuttled from the plane and on to the baggage claim. Emily grabbed her suitcase, then promptly made her way outside, taking a welcomed breath of fresh air as she scoped out her surroundings.

It was 8:00 am, and already the sun was beating down. She dropped her bags at her feet, standing on the blistering sidewalk with a hand waving above her head. Most taxis seemed to favor groups or families, leaving her standing alone, sweating until, finally, one driver acknowledged her. He helped her load her things into the trunk and she gave him the name of the hotel she was staying at.

The route first took her past the Oval Pachacutec, a giant bronze statue in Cusco's main town square. Emily lowered her window, resting her head on her arm as it hung at the side of the car. What looked like a *pueblos jóvenes* could be seen off in the distance, a mix of shanty houses staggering into the hills.

Driving through Plaza de Armas, the Catedral Basílica de la Virgen de la Asunción came into focus. It was a magnificent structure that every archaeologist had heard of before, housing many artifacts and relics, and accented with artwork and religious symbolism. The aura of Cusco city, with its breathtaking landscapes and architecture intermingling with one another, created a sight to behold.

Emily withdrew her cell phone to take some photos, when once again, the missed call from Dr. Alsafar came to her attention. Conflicted, she didn't want to overlook the passing wonders, but she also very much needed to talk to him.

She dismissed the notification.

The taxi began to swerve through narrow streets encompassed by small shops and venues where people were selling whatever they could to make a living. The taxi broke out into a small plaza surrounded by white buildings before stopping in the middle of the street.

The driver turned slightly, sputtering furiously in Spanish while motioning for Emily to get out. He was speaking a little faster than she was capable of understanding. The only word she could make out was *"caminas." You walk?*

Looking through the front window she could see various tapered pathways tangled amongst the buildings, realizing he could drive her no farther. She realized he was telling her that she had to get out and walk.

The moment her bags were taken from the trunk, he sped off back the way they had come.

Emily pulled up the GPS app on her phone. With her face to the screen, she followed the little red pin that showed that her hotel was only a short distance away. The cobblestone road pressed hard against her feet as she winded between the rows of houses, with nothing but the sound of the wheels from her suitcase rattling over the bumpy thoroughfare for company.

Upon entering the hotel, Emily was greeted by a withered, elderly woman who was stationed behind the front desk. Propping her satchel on the counter, she pulled out her passport and credit card, voicing her reservation. The woman presented a key, then ushered her in the direction of a small staircase that led to her suite.

The door opened to reveal an open-concept room, housing a large, king-sized bed at its center. As Emily walked in, she flung her things on top of it and continued toward the balcony that overlooked the large garden at the heart of the hotel. Orbs of light and fountains were scattered throughout the garden. Turning, she glanced into her bathroom, which contained a full-sized, walk-in hot tub, and immediately envisioned herself floating in a pool of bubbles.

Her phone vibrated in her palm; 5% battery life remaining. *Again?*

Moving to plug her cell phone in by the nightstand, she knew a bath would have to be put on hold. The streets were calling her to head back outside with her hopes of asking the townspeople if they knew the history of the elusive artifact.

With her iPad gripped at her hip, she visited a variety of establishments, swiping through the pictures to show people, in hopes of finding someone who recognized the images depicted on the tablets. Emily got the feeling that no one had time to help an American. Mostly, the locals firmly shook their heads to dismiss her, or they casually avoided her altogether. There were some, however, that, when asked, became uneasy and shuffled away from her, as if they knew something but didn't want to say anything.

In time, she found her way to an old, worn-down church, that had been condemned, according to the signage outside. Its architecture was full of spiraling archways and carved opal detailing. In its old age, the walls had become tattered and rotting wood accented the altar area. The floors creaked with her every step. Her nose also detected the faint scent of urine, presumably feline, based on the number of cats she'd seen wandering the streets.

Farther inside, she shuffled through the thin layer of dirt and grime that had accumulated over the years of neglect. At the church's center, glass crunched beneath her feet she walked. She knelt, carefully wiping the floor to reveal a shattered, circular mirror. Within its reflective shards, she noticed a painted mural on the domed ceiling above. She stood, craning her neck to admire it. Although it had faded over time, it had somehow remained far less deteriorated than the rest of the structure.

Emily lingered, attempting to appreciate the display, though it was too dark inside the church to view it properly. She moved to the nearest window, tugging at its ruffled curtain until it fell to the ground in a crumpled heap.

A cloud of dust whirled through the air causing her to cough into her fist as sunlight poured into the room. Before she had a chance to calm herself, an unnatural yellow hue filled the entire hall of the church.

Wondering where the bright light was coming from, she turned to find the sunlight hitting the shattered mirror on the floor, sending scattered beams of light bouncing around the room, including toward the ceiling's mural. Inching her way back into view of the mural, she noticed that the sunbeam was striking an outreached hand that was clutching what appeared to be a yellow fragment.

Emily's eyes widened at the sight, consumed by a rush of familiarity.

She quickly withdrew her iPad and began flipping through her photos, eventually landing on one that Everett had taken back at the MET. She held it above her head, positioning the ceiling in its background.

There it was. The same depiction of an outstretched hand holding the same yellow object! Both depictions showed what appeared to be an army being led by the person holding the artifact, both shrouded in clouds of dust. The figure holding the object in this particular mural, though, was depicted in the same color as the object itself; their skin a distinct yellow.

The resemblance was uncanny, leaving no doubt that it had to be one and the same.

But how are the two connected?

She switched to the camera screen and started to take photos, uploading them to her cloud storage. She shuffled closer to the mirror on the floor, trying to zoom in to ensure she was capturing everything in the mural. Propping herself onto her tiptoes, she stretched her arms as far as she could while trying to maintain her balance.

Just as she was focusing a shot, the floor gave way beneath her.

Emily yelped, reaching forward to catch herself on the rotten floorboards as she dropped. Her armpits hugged flush with the wood, holding on as tightly as she could. Dust from the floor made it hard to keep a steady grip as her legs dangled in the darkness of the hole.

"Help!" Emily yelled, coughing once again, choking on the puff of particles created by the crash. "Somebody! Please help me!"

Kicking the air with her feet, she grazed a solid wooden beam. Planting her toes, she began hoisting herself, her body rising from the hole, inch by inch, until her chest and stomach emerged. With half of her body now free, she kicked off from the beam, thrusting with her arms to push herself out of the hole.

The floor broke away again.

Her chin smacked the wooden edge of the hole on the way down, sending her senseless body falling to the hard basement floor.

Emily's back arched, accompanied by a thunderous cough as she regained consciousness. Her face and body were covered in dirt, her lungs apparently full of it as well. Her body had been laid across one of the church's pews, far from the abyss that had just swallowed her whole.

"Calm down, miss! You're safe!" a man's voice came from beside her.

Emily flinched, seeing someone crouched just a few feet away, staring.

He reached for her, but she timidly drew away.

"Who ... who are you?" she asked.

"My name is Diego. I heard you scream, then a loud crash. You really shouldn't be in here."

Finally, someone who speaks English.

Remembering what had happened, she frantically looked around, her bottom lip protruding when she saw her smashed iPad lying on the floor beside her.

"I am sorry about your device. I found it like this on the ground next to you."

"Thank you. Thank you for helping me," she mumbled, still coughing from the inhalation of dust.

She raised her index finger, pointing to the yellow-colored object in the mural on the ceiling.

"Can you tell me what that is?"

Diego spun around, glancing in the direction she was pointing.

"You mean the sunstone?"

"Is that what it's called?"

"The tale of our sunstone is a long one, but if you have time, I will be happy to share it with you. You seem to be a determined woman, coming here alone."

"Yes, please. Tell me everything."

Diego stood and walked toward the newly formed hole in the center of the church, his eyes fixated on the mural above, drawing a long breath through his nostrils.

"It is said that long ago, when the world was succumbing to sin and darkness, the Inca cried out to our god, Inti. They prayed for a better world, a light to repel the evil.

"One day, a piece of the sun fell from the sky, a gift from the almighty Inti. Hence the name, sunstone."

Could this be "God's relic"? Is it possible that the relic isn't referring to the Christian God at all, and is instead the "god's relic"?

"The person in the mural above, the one holding the stone, is known as the keeper, the person elected by the people as the one most trustworthy enough to wield it. The keeper, if pure of heart, would become one with the stone, a leader draped in holy garb, resonating a golden aura.

"The gift was infused with a great army, warriors who were at the full disposal of its possessor. The story tells that the sunstone was used by the people to bring prosperity back to the land, ridding the world of the dark-hearted and hateful."

Emily sat still and wide-eyed, immersed in the story.

"What are those clouds surrounding them?" she asked.

"You mean the mist?"

Diego smiled, seemingly already giddy about what he was going to say next.

"When called upon by the keeper, a dense mist would pour from the stone, bringing forth the aforementioned army it contained.

"Sadly, it is said that, over time, some people became selfish, wanting to control the warriors for themselves. One day, while the keeper rested, the stone was stolen and whisked away to another part of the world, intended to be used for self-gain. Or so it is said."

It was then that Emily connected his story to the tablets of Irisagrig.

Surely this is all some sort of myth. Pieces of the sun? A stone that releases mist and contains an army of warriors? It has to be a tall tale passed down through generations. Doesn't it?

She hobbled to her feet, bracing herself with the backrest of the pew.

"So what happened to the stone after that?" Emily asked.

"My ancestors retrieved the stone almost one hundred years ago and returned it to our Sacred Valley. Although, instead of using its power, they sealed it away. Nobody knows where, but we have seen much prosperity since its return. Our crops are always full, and poverty in the region has declined significantly."

Emily's skepticism remained. Regardless, she had to see this stone for herself.

"So where is this sunstone now?" she asked sarcastically. "Are you saying no one knows where it is?"

"No one that is living, no. That's the thing; it was hidden so that the clutches of an impure heart may never possess it again. Few have come to seek it, but all have failed."

Emily reached down to pick up her cracked device, staring at it with despair. She was technically no further ahead in her quest, and now, knowing that others had come for this sunstone without success dissuaded her. Would she be able to find the relic when others could not?

"Are you all right now? I am afraid I must return home to my family. Mrs. Gomes gets very angry with me when I am late for dinner."

"Yes, I'll be fine. Thank you, again, for helping me and for the story."

Diego wandered out of the church with Emily following close behind. As he disappeared between the houses, she sat on the steps of the church, tossing her useless iPad into her satchel and placing her elbows on her knees while holding her head in her hands. Her back ached, her neck was stiffening, and dried blood had trailed its way down her chin to her collar.

Wait … Gomes?

She jumped to her feet, the feeling of defeat dissipating as Diego's final words resonated in her head.

Emily burst through her hotel room door, grasping for her phone on the nightstand. Slouching into a nearby chair, she seated herself at the table and pulled up the folder to thumb her way through the diary entries.

Just as she had thought: "*Luis Gomes, January 23rd, 1924.*"

If this journal entry is legitimate, then maybe there was *a sunstone.*

She still found it hard to believe all of Diego's story, but some aspects did correlate perfectly.

Biting at her thumbnail, she sat wondering if she should continue on or just let it go, unsure if she was onto something big or simply chasing a pipe dream. Still, she couldn't shake the feeling that if she could somehow find this god's relic, it would cement the Owens name in history.

Over and over, she flipped through the photos that she had taken at the church, until eventually, her eyes veered to the ensuite to rest on the jacuzzi.

I could use that bath right about now.

Shuffling into the bathroom, she struggled to remove her t-shirt and shorts, which had become stuck to her body, leaving a trail of blood-stained clothes wherever they landed as she walked.

Reaching for the faucet, she laid her phone on the edge of the tub, letting the hot water pour over her hands as she closed her eyes to the comfort of the steam. She opened the shutters of the window, letting the breeze of the cool night air filter in.

Striking a match, she lit a few of the scented candles surrounding the bath and watched it fill. Removing her bra and panties, she placed them on a chair, then released the knotted ponytail from her hair with a grunting tug.

She dipped her toes into the bath first before wading in, coming to rest against the back wall of the tub. The water stung at her scratches like the licks of a flame. She winced at first until the pain subsided. With her arms now spread across the rim of the tub, she laid her head back onto a rolled towel, staring at the ceiling before closing her eyes for a moment of peace.

A vibration suddenly shook the ceramic.

Emily opened her eyes and hesitated, slightly annoyed. She reached to lift the phone. *"Incoming call – Dr. Alsafar"*

"Shit!" she said aloud before answering, realizing that she had totally forgotten to return his call earlier that day.

"Dr. Alsafar, I'm so, so, sorry I forgot to call you back but–"

"Emily! Listen! Where are you?!" His voice sounded frantic.

"Whoa, Dr. Alsafar, calm down. It's okay, I'm okay. What's the matter?"

"I have received your files. You need to delete everything you have immediately. Those are dangerous people, Emily!"

"Wait, what? Who's dangerous? What people?"

"The symbol you sent me, it's the sign of the Recreant Order! They are a group of defectors, people not to get in the way of. Please tell me you have not yet pursued your findings."

Emily slid forward, her face taking on a concerned expression as Dr. Alsafar continued his rambling plea.

"If what I am seeing is correct, they will be heading to Peru as soon as possible. Whatever you do, do not follow them! They will kill you just for knowing what their agenda is. They shut down the whole Irisagrig exhibit once they knew it was related to the artifact that they were seeking. I was escorted onto a plane and sent back to Iraq the next morning.

"You have to trust me, Emily, I beg you!"

She had never heard him speak so frantically before.

The Recreant Order?

What the fuck have I gotten myself into? Deep shit, apparently!

"Emily? Emily?" the doctor's voice rang over the phone's speaker.

"Yes, sorry. I'm here. I hear you loud and clear, Doctor. I'll drop this right away. I promise."

"I will be in New York again in a few months. We can talk more privately then. Take care of yourself."

Emily slowly lowered the phone as the call disconnected, her mouth hanging slightly open.

She tossed the cell phone onto the armchair with the rest of her things, then floated back to her resting place, becoming dazed by the flickering of the candle flames.

Little by little, her body started to sink beneath the waterline. Her breasts, then shoulders, then mouth, which curled into a smug grin as she disappeared beneath the water's surface.

CHAPTER FIVE

Emily leaned against the wall of the plaza, patiently waiting for her shuttle to arrive. Checkout was at 11:00 am, and it was now 11:47 am; still no sign of the bus.

Her feet cradled her bags while her eyes and thumb moved over the screen of her phone.

The Recreant Order

The first known records of this group started to appear in approximately 1710. A rebel branch of the Society of Jesuits, their intention was to undertake humanity and shape it in the eyes of God.

"Recreant" is/was derived from the notion that they were unfaithful to the Jesuits' beliefs, and "Order" from their authoritative direction in terms of what they considered to be holy. Due to their apostate ambitions and acts of dishonor, the Recreant Order was shunned.

As an extremist group, they sought to use any means necessary to "cleanse the world of sin." The Society of Jesuits, however, were immediate to disassociate themselves from the Recreant Order, claiming the Society was there to guide the sinful, unlike the Recreant Order who were motioning to destroy them.

The Recreant Order was believed to have disbanded by 1792, disappearing from the public eye. This remained the case until acts of unexplained violence began to occur in the mid-1800s, surrounding the rise of treasure hunters.

By the late 1800s, it was believed that the Order had amassed many followers who kept their identities secret, known only to one another. How they would signal their allegiance is still unknown, though some suspect that it was a secret phrase or gesture.

By the mid-1900s, the Recreant Order had established themselves as major players in the world of recovering religious artifacts and scriptures. Using their financial leverage and intimidation tactics, they chose to pursue anything they felt was rightfully God's. It wasn't until the late 1900s that their influence once again subsided, which is believed to be attributed to the increased awareness of their existence by any figures of authority.

The Recreant Order's agenda seemed to change at every turn of the century, but one thing remained constant: They would stop at nothing to bring their illusion of peace to the world.

It has been recorded that over eight hundred arrests of the Recreant Order's members have been made since 1710. As of this publication, there have been no reports or sightings of the Recreant Order since 1989. Most believe that they have demobilized entirely, but we may never know for sure.

Dane Kowalchyk – The Renegade Reports
November 1st, 2017

So the Society of Jesuits isn't trying to find the god's relic after all …
The sharp sound of a drawn-out honk snapped her from her reading.

She waved to signal her acknowledgment of the driver's arrival, picked up her bags, and jogged over to climb aboard the bus.

"Urubamba, sí? Tambo del Inka?"

The driver smiled a toothless grin, nodding profusely.

Confident her Spanish was adequate, Emily still had little confidence that this bus was going anywhere near Urubamba, but she had no other choice but to climb aboard. She shuffled her way to an empty seat near the back, slouching down next to a Swedish fellow who apparently thought it was fashionable to wear a tracksuit depicting his country's flag as an outfit.

The old, rundown shuttle was probably the bumpiest ride she had ever been on, but she tried her hardest not to let it distract her from the sights along the way. Cliffs on the horizon and the fields full of pink cantutas in their foreground contributed to the natural beauty of Peru. Emily wished she had more time to appreciate it, to really soak it in.

With each stop, the shuttle became lighter and less compacted, eventually leaving Emily as the lone passenger. Her hand gripped the malleable leather of the seat ahead of her, raising herself with a sigh of relief when she saw the hotel signage as they veered through the stone walls into its parking lot.

Tambo del Inka
A Luxury Collection Resort & Spa

Once the bus came to a stop at the front door of the hotel, Emily wasn't able to exit fast enough. From outside, the hotel looked very quaint, encased by snow-capped highlands and the dramatic Urubamba River, which made for a majestic combination.

Pausing from her moment of clarity, Emily hadn't even realized that she had been left in the middle of an angled parking space with her suitcase tipped on its side. Luckily, the staff were friendly, ushering her from the lot into the main lobby of the hotel to begin her check-in. The bellhop promptly followed, assisting her and her belongings to her suite, a welcomed service, as she was still sore from the day before.

The room was sunlit, with direct access to the terrace garden behind the hotel. She opened the sliding glass door and stepped barefoot across the grass. The fresh air mixed with the sounds of rushing water from the river was a combination that would make anyone forget their worries.

She pulled out her cell phone, searching for the next available means of transport to Ollantaytambo. There was a bus leaving at 3:00 that afternoon. *Maybe a little luck is coming my way after all.*

She hurried to purchase the e-ticket.

Sitting immersed in her phone, she pondered what she might uncover if she continued her journey. The more she thought about the story Diego Gomes had told her, the more it made sense that this place was called the "Sacred Valley."

She needed to do more research to determine if there was any validity in his tale—if such information even existed. She turned to the internet.

The Inca were an ancient tribe that arose sometime in the 13th century, inhabiting the Sacred Valley and surrounding areas. They were also known to worship Inti, the sun god and deity of the holy city of Cusco.

Emily began pulling up old records and portraits of the Inca, most of which contained some reference to the sun.

What if the person depicted in the mural—the first keeper of the sunstone—was an Inca?

Her phone screen switched to notify her of an incoming call, vibrating in her hand.

"Hello, Emily speaking."

"Hello, Miss Owens. This is Rosa from the shuttle service provider. I am very sorry, but we must advise you that our shuttle has been canceled for this afternoon. We have been made aware of a rockslide that has temporarily closed the roadways leading into Ollantaytambo."

Of course.

"When will the next shuttle be?"

"Road crews are working diligently. They expect it to be re-opened first thing in the morning. We will reschedule your booking for 10:00 am sharp. We sincerely apologize for any inconvenience this may have caused."

Emily slammed the phone down beside her on the sofa. *There goes my whole day, wasted. So much for being one step ahead.* But on a positive note, she knew about the sunstone, which was more than she could say for the Recreant Order—or at least she hoped.

She left her room and went down to the hotel lobby, wondering what to do with the rest of her evening before flagging down one of the employees who was walking by.

"Excuse me, what do people do for fun here in Urubamba? Any recommendations?"

"Oh, you are looking for fun? To party, perhaps? There's a nightclub about a ten-minute walk from here. You should go; it will be busy tonight!"

"Great," Emily said sarcastically.

Hours later, Emily was standing in front of the bathroom mirror applying her makeup. A vodka water sat half-finished on the vanity, coated with beads of sweat from the humidity.

She dragged ruby red gloss across her lips, smacking them together as she finished. She reached back, drawing on her ponytail to ensure its tightness. She was wearing a black one-piece jumpsuit with a sheer lace bodice and a straight-leg pant. Something about going out always made her feel like she had to look her best, hoping that maybe Urubamba had some untapped resource of hot men.

Might as well make the best of a bad situation.

She slid her phone into her pocket along with her hotel room key card and credit card, then downed what remained in her glass before heading downstairs.

The evening sky was scattered full of stars as Emily walked through the labyrinth of stone walls that led into a bustling part of the town. The hum of chatter and sputtering of motorbikes echoed in the streets. As she rounded a corner, the thump of music pulsated from a small, two-story building—nothing like the larger New York clubs she was accustomed to.

The nightclub was packed inside. She scooted her way to the bar area where it surprisingly wasn't as crowded, the dancefloor seeming to hold most of the people.

Kudos to that hotel employee.

Perched atop a stool at the end of the bar, she swirled her drink, soon realizing that a place like this would be a lot more fun if she had some friends around. Loud music and laser lights just weren't the same without someone to let loose with.

By the time she had finished her second drink, boredom had started to set in. There was only so much people-watching she could do, and it seemed that everyone was having a great time except for her.

Maybe the hotel has a good movie selection?

She settled her tab, waved to thank the bartender, then turned toward the exit.

Seemingly out of nowhere, a hand appeared on her arm. She instinctively grabbed its wrist, looking up to find the owner wearing a shocked expression.

"You may want to let that hand go if you're going to let it buy you a drink, sweetheart," a man said with an English accent as he grinned confidently.

"My apologies, but a girl can never be too careful in a place like this." Emily eased her grip, smiling through her embarrassment.

"Apologies as well. My friends and I just arrived, and right away I could see you were the prettiest girl in this place. Although, if I may say so, you don't look like you're having very much fun. The drinking not helping?"

He was cocky, but Emily found it somewhat attractive. His attitude, mixed with his cleanly shaven face and taper fade, were all complimented by his hooded hazel eyes.

Emily didn't mind giving him her time. It wasn't like she had anywhere else to be.

"How about we give that drinking thing another try?" She batted her eyelashes, looking back toward the bar.

The man escorted her through the crowd, leading her to a table near the rear of the upper level of the club. Something a little more private Emily noted.

"Allow me to get us those drinks," the man said, leaving her behind as he headed to the bar.

He hadn't even asked what she wanted, leaving her half expecting him to bring her back a fruity cocktail or something—definitely not her style.

"Here you go, sweetheart. A couple of pisco sours for us this evening."

"Ahh, the national drink of Peru. Very clever, Mr. ... ?"

"The name's Dominik," he raised his glass to cheers hers. "And yours?"

"Emily." She picked up her drink, clanking her glass against his.

"So, what brings you to Urubamba?"

"Oh, you know, just trying to get some sun," she said flippantly as she took a big swig of her drink, using the glass to conceal her smile at the inside joke.

"That skin already looks sun-kissed, if you don't mind me saying."

There he was, being brazen again.

"Does the lady dance?" Dominik said, sliding his arm across the table while gesturing for her hand.

She placed her palm in his, allowing him to lead her down to the dancefloor.

Along the way, he waved in the direction of a small group of people, who all raised their glasses in acknowledgment, yet rolled their eyes when he stopped looking.

Must be those friends he came with.

"I'm not keeping you from a night out with your friends, am I?" Emily shouted.

The music had made it difficult for them to hear one another.

"No, no. They're just jealous that I'm having a better time than they are, that's all. Fuck 'em!" He laughed, tipping his glass back.

Dominik was having no trouble busting moves, even in his tailored suit. He spun and dipped Emily around the dancefloor, neither one caring about the people they bumped into while doing so. But once a slower rhythm began to play, she took control, turning around to push her body against his. The smell of his Jean Paul Gaultier cologne was becoming intoxicating as she slid her hand upward to caress his head, grinding against him sensually.

His hand made its way across her stomach, holding her close.

Turning her head to the side, she stared up at him, rubbing harder against his body. He leaned down and kissed her. She spun back around, throwing her arms around his neck, biting his bottom lip as they locked together.

"You want to get out of here?" Dominik asked, gazing into her eyes.

"You know I do."

They left the dancefloor in a hurry and headed back up to the table to gather their things.

Dominik motioned for Emily to stay put while he went to let his friends know that he was leaving, but while he made his way down the stairs, her curiosity drew her to the edge of the railing to look down below.

His friends looked angry, seemingly giving him some sort of lecture before he dismissed them with a middle finger and stormed away.

Watching him stomp back up to the second floor, Emily slunk back toward their table.

"Are you ready, sweetheart?" he called.

"Is everything okay?"

"Yeah, yeah, my friends are just a bunch of assholes."

Just as they were about to leave, a server walked by with a full tray of drinks.

"One last shot for the road?" Dominik said. "What do you say?"

"Sure, why not."

As he stretched his arm above the crowd, trying to signal to the server, the cuff of his jacket shortened, revealing an unmistakable tattoo on his wrist.

A sun, an inverted cross, and three nails pointing skyward.

Emily's stomach became queasy. Her eyes narrowed and her throat shriveled.

The Recreant Order—they're ... here?

She backed away, her eyes watering. Not with fear, but with disgust. She reached behind herself, grasping for a chair, a table, anything to keep her from falling.

Dominik turned around with the shot glasses, handing one to Emily while pinching the other, unaware that she was in a state of shock.

"All right, sweetheart, bottoms up!"

Flinging his head back to take the shot, Emily did the same, except she tossed the drink over her shoulder instead. He squeezed her by the hand to lead her through the club, but she became immobile.

"What's wrong? Change your mind?" Dominik said in an agitated tone.

Emily's mouth parted, but no words came out. Instead, she pulled him in tightly, planting another drawn-out kiss on his lips to provide him with false reassurance while casually sliding her arms down his back until they reached just above his waistband. Her hand grazed cold steel.

A gun.

Emily sprang backward, doing her best not to allude to her discomfort.

Was this his plan all along? To lure me back to a private location so that the Order can take me out? Surely his "friends" are Recreants as well.

Walking out the front door wasn't an option, and there was no apparent exit from the second level.

"Are we doing this or not?" Dominik was demanding now moreso than asking.

She grabbed him by the hand and pushed through the crowd, leading him away from the stairs. She flung open the door to the men's bathroom, hauled him inside by his collar, then sat him on the lid of the toilet. Maintaining her composure, she stared at him seductively while closing the door and locking it behind her.

"Is this what you wanted?" she whispered. "To get me all alone?"

He was already licking his lips, tugging furiously at his belt buckle.

She walked toward him and leaned in to nibble his earlobe, playfully drifting her hands around his torso. His eyes closed with satisfaction.

That's when Emily jolted back, kicking him in the chest to pin him against the toilet tank.

Dominik's eyes popped open, staring down the barrel of his own Glock.

"Who are you?" Emily screamed, twisting the butt of her heel into his ribs. Her hands were shaking, clammy on the grip of the gun. "What do you want with me?"

"Whoa, sweetheart! What do you think you're doing? I just wanted that sweet ass."

She fired one round into the tiles on the wall beside him. "Bullshit!"

He threw his hands up above his head. The music was thumping too loudly for anyone to hear the shot, and he was well aware of it.

"That tattoo on your wrist." She could see it now in plain sight, making her certain. "You're one of them, right? A Recreant?"

"You don't know who you're messing with, girly," he sneered.

Three thunderous knocks rattled the door, startling Emily as she turned her head toward the entrance at the untimely distraction.

Dominik knocked the gun from her hands, lunging forward to squeeze his hand around her throat as he forced her back against the door.

"I don't know who you are, sweetheart, but it looks as though your vacation is going to end a little early."

He tightened his grip.

Emily gasped for air, all the while eyeing the gun lying on the floor.

Her body began to rise as he lifted her from the ground by the throat, her legs flailing in midair.

He had left his face wide open. *Perfect.* It was a shame she had to ruin it.

She lifted her right arm above her head then dropped it just as rapidly. Her downward elbow connected with his face and she could hear the cartilage of his nose fracture.

Dominik stumbled backward, releasing her to the floor while she coughed for relief.

She was thankful Gabrielle had shown her that move.

"You broke my nose, you bitch!"

He shouted through his hands, cupping his face as blood filled his palms.

Emily kicked off her heels, which were not much good to her now.

She positioned herself in a street-fighting stance, commonly used for defensive maneuvers. She noticed him squinting through the tears building up in his eyes from the blow. Being a man of his size, she knew he had no choice but to rush her.

As predicted, he lunged forward again, swinging his arms to try and grab her.

She avoided him, causing him to crash onto the ceramic floor. With the opportunity presenting itself, she leaned in and hit him with two strong punches to the mouth.

Dominik spat a mouthful of blood onto the floor, looking up at her with a shit-eating grin, his teeth covered in red.

Emily noticed the gun lying on the floor beside him at the same time he did.

They both slid for it across the grimy floor, their hands and arms intertwined, trying to stop each other's attempt. He punched her in the ribs first, causing her to flinch, then rolled over and climbed on top of her while pinning her arms to the ground beside her head.

"Now you've just gone and pissed me off," he sputtered, blood still spewing from his gums.

He released his grip on her arms and placed a hand around her throat again, leaving Emily clawing helplessly at his forearms. Tearing at his skin with her nails, she glimpsed the urinal hanging on the wall to their left. With both hands placed around her throat now, Dominik was squeezing tighter with every breath she took.

But once again, he had left himself exposed.

With a swift thrust, she kneed him firmly, crushing his balls against her leg.

He howled as he collapsed backward onto his knees, which allowed her to slide out from underneath him.

She used a wet floor sign as a crutch to help push herself up.

Standing tall, Emily folded the sign and smacked him across his face with it. In a last-ditch effort, she dug her fingers into his hair and smashed his head against the rim of the porcelain urinal. The blow was so hard that the bottom lip broke off as his face connected with it.

Dominik's body fell lifeless onto the floor as the urinal water began to leak onto him, the gash above his eye turning the water red as it began to flood the floor of the room.

Emily leaned against the nearest wall, rubbing her throat, taking deep breaths.

There was no time to rest.

Opening the window above the toilet, she gauged the two-story drop before turning back around to grab Dominik's gun. Seeing a small dumpster below, she dropped her shoes and the gun first, then gripped the window ledge to let herself fall into the pile of garbage.

Scrambling her way out onto the ground, she put her heels back on and tucked the gun into her pocket.

She jogged to the edge of the building, then looked around.

Clear.

Darting across the alley, she hurried in the direction of her hotel.

Emily hadn't noticed the older man standing in the shadows farther down the alley behind the club, the side of his face illuminated by the screen of his phone.

"She's here ..."

CHAPTER SIX

Daylight had broken some hours ago, brightening the hotel room with an orange hue through the sheer curtains. The local news flickered on the television that hung from the wall, muted, while Dominik's gun lay dormant next to Emily's phone at the foot of her bed.

She was curled into a ball next to the window. Her eyes, dark and dry, twitched each time her mind wandered back to the events of the night before. She couldn't shake the fact that she may have killed a man. With every sound of an animal or the rustling of leaves, she peeked out from behind the curtains, expecting *them* at any moment.

Emily reached for the remote, periodically activating the volume on the television. There had been zero mention of any incident at the disco. Urubamba was not a large town, which led her to believe that a homicide would surely get the top story.

She muted it again.

Finding the courage to stand, she headed into the bathroom, her legs numb from being confined to the chair since her return. Staring at herself in the mirror above the vanity, she could see the faint bruises left on her neck from Dominik's hands. She delicately traced them with her fingers, remembering how it felt to have her arteries throb inside his squeezing palms.

She turned on the tap to run hot water over her knuckles, the dried blood dissipating into a swirling pink spiral down the drain. Cupping her hands, she leaned over the sink and splashed her face twice before reaching for a towel to pat herself dry.

The landline on the nightstand rang abruptly, causing her to jump. She dropped the hand towel to the floor then inched her way toward the phone.

Who would even be trying to reach me this early?

"Hell … hello?" Emily said, holding her breath.

"Good morning, Miss Owens. This is María from the front desk. Just calling for your scheduled 8:00 am wake-up call."

Shit, I totally forgot. I guess killing a man would do that to you.

"Oh, yes, thank you. I'm awake."

"Have a good day, Miss Ow–"

Emily ended the call and laid the phone back down.

The buzz of the air conditioning created white noise in the background of her thoughts. With two hours left until the shuttle arrived, she knew that she couldn't sit around idly any longer.

I need to see it for myself. I have to go back to the club.

Emily removed the clothes she had been wearing from the night before and changed into something more appropriate for the day ahead: shorts and a tank top. Proceeding to remove her knife from her suitcase, she strapped it around her thigh before grabbing the Glock and stuffing it into one of her packed shoes.

Once outside the confines of the hotel, Emily hugged the walls of the alleyways, performing a double take around every corner. As the nightclub drew closer, she half expected to see flashing red and blue lights or trails of yellow tape.

Instead, it was silent. No movement, no sirens, nothing.

This left her scratching the base of her neck, lingering just a few steps from the club's entrance.

Suddenly, a man barged out through the front door. He glared over his shoulder while locking the deadbolt before turning to face her.

"Can I help you?" he asked in Spanish, scowling.

She had no idea what to say. It wasn't like she could just ask, "Hey, just wondering if there is a dead man on your bathroom floor?"

Then it hit her. A little move Peyton had shown her once while she was chasing a bartender's number after last call.

"Yes, hello sir, I am so sorry to bother you this early." Her Spanish was rusty, but she was trying to make herself sound extra sympathetic. "I was at the bar last night and I think I left my purse behind."

"We're closed. You will have to come back later tonight. I cannot help you."

The frustration in his voice was building. Her case was lacking desperation.

Moving closer to him, she pouted her lips, and as if on command, her eyes began to well.

"Please, sir, my passport and wallet are in there. I'm leaving Peru today and I need it."

He stared at her for what felt like ages, then finally, with a roll of his eyes, he reached back to unlock the deadbolt. "You have five minutes. No funny business."

"*Gracias! Gracias!*" Emily slid past him timidly, while his eyes remained fixated on her with disdain.

She was in.

The club looked much more dated now that all the lights were on. She pretended to look around the bar at first, trying to make her act more believable. Shuffling stools and rooting through the trash, all a part of her ploy.

The man's cell phone rang.

He pulled it from his breast pocket and looked down at the screen, then looked back at Emily. Seeming reluctant to answer it, he finally stepped outside the front door to take the call, immediately yelling at someone on the other end.

As soon as he left, Emily swung herself around the railing and up the staircase, rushing over to the men's bathroom and pushing open the door.

Stepping inside, she was baffled more than ever.

There was no blood on the floor, nor any signs of a struggle. She turned to look at the urinal; it was completely fixed. Even the bullet hole she'd put in the tiled wall had been grouted over.

This is crazy! How could this even be possible?

The true power of the Recreant Order was becoming apparent.

"What are you doing in here?!" the man barked from behind her.

Emily spun around, keeping her distance from him.

"Ahh ... *baño?*" she said, gesturing toward the bathroom.

"Your five minutes are up. Get out!"

He grabbed her by the arm and tugged her downstairs. The front door banged behind her as he shoved her back outside into the street.

She flipped him her middle finger as if the door was transparent, then trotted her way back to the hotel. *What do you have yourself tangled up in, Em?*

Emily kicked her suitcase under the bed and grabbed for her satchel, which was more compact and much easier to travel with. Inside, she placed a bottle of water, a notepad and pen, her passport, and her cell phone. Staring down at her shoes on the floor, she reached inside and removed the gun, this time tucking it into a hidden pocket within her bag.

Back down in the lobby, she blended herself into a small crowd that had gathered in the parking lot, the air brakes of the tour bus hissing as the bus came to a stop. She and the tourists packed themselves inside, eager and ready for the next leg of the journey.

The route to Ollantaytambo took them along the Urubamba River; she was able to see its might as she peered out her window, mountain ranges accenting it as far as her eyes could see. Crossing over the town's limits, the roadways had become very narrow, with barely enough room for one vehicle to pass. Winding into the heart of the city, the shuttle stopped at the Plaza Ollantaytambo, a square at the town's center.

One by one, the passengers exited the bus, instructed by the driver to meet back at 8:00 pm as he handed everyone a tourist brochure. There was more than enough time for Emily to look for information on the sunstone, hoping the locals here would be more helpful than in Cusco.

A half-hour into her visit to the Sacred Valley, Emily was already dripping with sweat. Crowds of tourists continued to arrive, making the shuffle around in the heat difficult for even a solo traveler like her.

Shading her brow with her hand, she could see the great terraces in the distance surrounding the town, her eyes drawn toward the skyline as she admired the great Inka Watana, also known as the "Temple of the Sun."

Her eyes lowered to the brochure.

The Temple of the Sun was a large defensive structure built by the Inca for protection in the 15th century. Created using extensive layers of rock from the nearest quarry, the structure was also used as a place of prayer and worship to the sun god, Inti.

The stone staircases leading to the top of the valley were seemingly endless, weaving their way around the ancient fortress. At the halfway point, the clouds surrounding the mountaintops caused Emily to halt, eerily, yet optimistically drawing her in with their hovering crescents around the peaks. Taking several sips of her water, she recalled what Diego Gomes had told her about the mist, and for a moment, she believed his story.

As she climbed farther, the city beneath her receded, shrinking by the minute until she finally reached the top. From there, she passed through an arched gateway that led into what was considered the sacred area, one that provided a view for miles of the farmland stretching across the valley.

How did the Incas ever drag so many boulders up here to create this vast structure?

She bent over to catch her breath, resting her hands on her knees as she looked up ahead.

Before her, on the structure's highest point, was what the brochure referred to as the "Intihuatana", a ritual stone. This one in particular looked like a large, free-standing wall, accented by four identical, rectangular indentations.

She moved ahead, observing the unique piece of Incan history.

It was said that the Inca would stand in the rectangular indentations of the Intihuatana and look toward the sun as a sacrifice to Inti. As they grew older, those same Incas would be able to hold their gaze into the sun for longer periods of time, eventually never having to look away.

Emily stepped onto the platform and entered the first rectangular indentation. She placed her back flat against the stone, then looked into the sky, directly at the sun. Within seconds, her eyes began to water and sting, forcing her to look away.

Wiping her eyes, she looked forward to the sun once more, blinking through her discomfort.

"Excuse me, *señorita*, you can't be up there!" a tour guide shouted in a disappointed tone. "That's a sacred monument."

Behind him, four or five tourists snickered at her being scolded.

"My apologies, I didn't realize," Emily lied. "I just wanted to try staring into the sun."

While trying to explain herself, Emily proceeded to point into the sky, immediately noticing writing carved into the roof of the cavity she was standing in.

Intrigued, she traced the markings with her fingers.

"Excuse me, *señor*, can you tell me what this is?" Emily shouted to the tour guide, pointing to the carvings.

"That is the prayer of the Inca, performed in the shadow of the sun during rituals," replied the tour guide, his tone becoming increasingly irritated.

She stepped out of the cavity and walked along the wall. Studying the roof of the other three indentations, she discovered more writing etched into each.

"But what does this prayer say exactly?"

The tour guide, realizing the quickest way to get Emily down would be to answer her questions, resigned himself to respond.

"Loosely translated, we believe it says, 'As close to the gods as one can get, atop the morne I lay in wait. If one should need to hold the sun, rise up to open the gate.' Now, I won't ask you again; please, get down from there!"

Emily took some quick photos before jumping down and joining the group of sightseers. She asked the tour guide to repeat the translation so she could record it with her phone.

"One last thing," Emily continued. "What is a 'morne'?"

"No one is quite sure of the origins of the word, but in the context of the prayer, we understand it to mean 'summit' or 'one who stands alone,'" the tour guide said in a cool, clipped tone.

Realizing that she was no longer welcome in the tour group, Emily decided it was time to make her descent.

While making her way back down the hill, Emily kept replaying the recording, listening for some sort of clue. Something about the prayer didn't make sense to her.

First, the climb she had made was hardly worthy to be called a "summit." Second, there were many other mountains around that were higher than the one on which the Inka Watana had been built—definitely closer to the gods in respect to the sky.

Deep in concentration, she was so engrossed in her thoughts that she almost didn't see the crowd of people walking toward her. Stepping aside to let them pass, her eyes lifted from her phone, scanning the tourists scaling the hillside.

Mixed in the swarm of people headed in her direction were Dominik's friends from the night club.

Five men, one woman.

Emily scrambled to put her phone away, trying to blend into a different group of people that were heading back to the base of the hill. She buried her hand into her bag, gripping the pistol within its pocket. Keeping her face low, she peered at the group over the shoulders of the other sightseers. None of them seemed concerned with the sights, but were instead strictly focused on making their way to the top of the structure. Dominik, however, was nowhere to be seen, further reassuring Emily that he hadn't made it out of the club alive.

Yet, something still wasn't sitting right.

There had been eight flight itineraries on the USB drive, but only seven Recreants had been accounted for in Peru thus far.

Where is the last one?

Continuing downward, she darted to one side just as the group of tourists reached the bottom of the hill. One last look over her shoulder confirmed that she hadn't been spotted, so she finally released her hand from the gun in her bag. She had kept one step ahead of the Order so far and was not planning on losing that advantage now.

After turning down a small side street, Emily stopped at a small café situated next to the Urubamba River. She ordered a cup of iced coffee and sat on the shaded deck that overlooked the rapids. It was a secluded spot where she could be alone to regroup, to process.

She laid her phone in front of her on the table.

"As close to the gods as one can get, atop the morne I lay in wait. If one should need to hold the sun, rise up to open the gate."

The recording continued to play. Retrieving the notepad and pen from her bag, she made notes as the recording of the prayer repeated.

Maybe this is nothing, Emily. Maybe it is just a prayer.

However, the fact that one of the journal entries specifically referenced Ollantaytambo was too much to ignore. She had to keep an open mind while trying to determine what was real and what was simply legend.

Let's assume that "holding the sun" is, in fact, a direct reference to the sunstone itself. According to Diego Gomes' story, the sunstone was meant to repel evil when needed—maybe that's why a clue was left

THE MISTS OF MORNE

behind. Now, for "as close to the gods as one can get" and "morne" mean-ing "summit" ... That's probably referring to a mountaintop, isn't it?

She began to bite the end of her pen, crushing its cap with her back teeth.

The sharp ringing of bells at the opposite end of the street broke her from her concentration. She leaned her chair onto its back legs to look through the trees, her eyes landing on a small train station with a colorful banner next to it.

Inca Rail
Come with us to Machu Picchu!
Explore one of the 7 wonders of the world!

Goddamnit! How could I have overlooked it? Machu Picchu stands at eight thousand feet—now that's a summit!

Emily knew that Machu Picchu was often referred to as the "Lost City of the Inca," but was now a world-renowned natural landmark. She had studied it countless times during her schooling.

If Diego Gomes' story is true, maybe Machu Picchu is where the Inca were first gifted the sunstone from the sun god, Inti. Is it possible that the sunstone was returned to its place of origin?

She abruptly removed herself from the table and dashed down the street to the train station.

"I need one ticket!" she exclaimed, slamming her credit card down onto the counter in front of the wicket. "And I need it now."

Emily boarded the train forty minutes later. Seeing that only the first two of the five cars had occupants, she moved toward the back of the train and sat alone in the fourth car. While waiting for the train to depart, she unfolded a pamphlet that had been pro-vided with her ticket, outlining the history of the Machu Picchu citadel, which was built amongst the mountain's highest ridge.

Originally built sometime in the early 15th century, Machu Picchu was constructed for the Inca emperor Pachacuti. It remained inhabited for approximately a hundred years until the Spanish conquest finally expanded into Peru, ultimately causing the depletion of the Inca by the mid-1500s.

Some say it was conflict that destroyed the Incan civilization, while others say it was unfamiliar disease introduced by the Europeans.

She refolded the pamphlet.

Okay, let's assume this emperor Pachacuti was one of the stone's original keepers. According to Diego Gomes' story, the stone was robbed from a keeper. Perhaps word traveled abroad that the Inca no longer had an invincible army at their disposal and were defenseless. The Spanish moved in to conquer, and so fell the Inca Empire.

Of course Luis Gomes would want to return the sunstone to its rightful place, his home in Peru, centuries later!

It was a bit of a reach, but everything seemed to coincide. With her interest piqued more than ever, Emily knew she had to start by placing her faith somewhere.

Suddenly, a unison scream of terror wailed from the front-most train cars.

Emily propped herself up in her seat, looking through the windowed doors between the cars for the source of the commotion.

A loud series of gunshots rang through the air, followed by another wave of screams.

Was that an assault rifle? The sound was unmistakable.

"Everyone off this fucking train now!" A gravelly voice barked the command from outside on the platform.

Men, women, and children leaped from the cars onto the railway platform, grabbing their loved ones to head for shelter among the shops and houses.

Another barrage of shots echoed from the front of the train, followed by more screaming.

Emily ducked, inching her way between the cars to get a better look through the glass. With the train now completely emptied, she gained a clear sight.

An older man dressed in black tactical gear was placing one hand on each of the handrails as he hauled himself aboard the train. Emily presumed he was in his late fifties by the way his cement-grey widow's peak had thinned, fading into the ghost-white stubble that encased his square jawline. He stood still, his hands firmly gripping the collar of his bulletproof vest, surveying the car before his scolding eyes landed on the retreating conductor.

Emily could faintly hear them arguing. It seemed the conductor was unwilling to leave the train.

The older man's voice was instantly detestable, and raspy, like he had prematurely yanked a breathing tube from his throat. It soon became apparent that their conversation was going nowhere, which was when the older man waved his hand to someone outside of the train.

Within seconds, five other men and a single woman boarded with duffle bags. It was the same group of people from the night-club and the trail, but now they had all shed their civilian clothes and were wearing tactical outfits. *The Recreant Order.*

Two of the men moved like clockwork to the outside of the train and back again, loading boxes into the first car while another two forced the conductor to his knees. The older man then walked among the others respectably, as if he was assessing them, acting as a mentor.

Could this be the Boar?

He approached the conductor and grabbed him by the scruff of his neck.

Emily could see the conductor's lips moving in what she assumed was prayer as the Recreant leader dragged him to the doorway then placed the barrel of his handgun to the back of the conductor's head. There was little recoil when he pulled the trigger, sending the defenseless body crashing onto the platform below.

"Now that wasn't so hard, was it?" the leader said, turning back to his comrades.

The woman rolled her eyes, a small diversion from the resting bitch face she had been carrying since the night before at the nightclub. Her ink-black, side-swept hair and shaven undercut only added to her aggressive demeanor, accentuated by a nasty scar along her hairline near her temple. She carried herself like a woman who owed the world nothing and took no shit from anyone in the process.

She bypassed the man calling the shots and entered the conductor's cabin. Moments later, the train began to move.

Five of the men stood in the first car and clung to the straps above their heads, staying vertical as the train picked up speed. The older man, however, sat cross-legged at a table, his pistol laid in front of him as smoke wisped from its chamber. He grabbed a pear from one of the original passenger's bags and took a bite, slurping on it like he hadn't just ended a man's life.

"Rico, go sit up front with Alex," he commanded. "Make sure we don't run into any surprises."

Without hesitation, the most robust of the men released his grip from the overhead strap and joined the woman in the control car of the train, closing the door behind him. He was undoubtedly the enforcer of the group: low body fat, high muscle mass. He was solid. His arms and neck were covered in what looked to be Samoan tribal tattoos; the Recreant Order symbol was placed discreetly within them.

"Jason, Drew, prep the gear in the second car. Anthony, I want you on comms. See if you can get that antenna set up on the roof. No doubt some asshole in that crowd of people will have squealed to the authorities by now. We're going to need that chopper ready."

"What about me, Cardinal Valerius?" the last man spoke up, taking a step forward. Another brawny henchman, though significantly less hulking than the first.

"Caleb, I want you to sweep the train. Make sure there are no stragglers, and if you find any—kill them."

At his words, Emily ducked down below the window. Her heart began to beat like a drum inside her chest as she gently banged the apex of her skull against the paneling.

Springing forward onto all fours, she crawled along the metal floor to make her way back through the adjoining doors between the cars until reaching the fifth and furthest train car. Once there, she reached above her to draw the curtains.

The train was now moving full speed ahead, making it impossible for her to jump from the back. She had reached a dead end.

The sound of sliding metal rang through the cars; the door between cars one and two had been opened.

Emily rose to a stand and parted the curtain just enough to peek toward the front of the train. Two men had started carrying in the boxes, spacing them around the second car.

The man called Drew looked to be merely a teenager. The state of his facial hair made it seem as if his puberty had halted halfway through its growth. He was tall, but clumsy—an obvious novice. His beady eyes kept flicking to everyone else to see how they were operating.

The other man, Jason, was sturdier and more seasoned. He irritably stroked his gingered beard every time Drew made a mistake. And yet, across both of their hips hung what looked to be automatic Remington R4s, making them equally threatening.

From behind them, the man called Caleb entered the car, also with a gun at his hip.

He brushed past Jason and Drew, heading straight for the third car while methodically looking from side to side, moving any bags or blankets that were strewn about. He even checked the overhead compartments; he was thorough.

Emily surveyed her train car, unable to find a single place to stow away. She then remembered her bag that she had idiotically left in the fourth car, which contained the Glock—her only hope of making it off the train alive.

"Be conscious of your surroundings, for in clarity, you hold your greatest weapon: your mind."

Her father's teachings were embedded in her for a reason.

She hastily grabbed some pillows from overhead and bunched them underneath a wool blanket, something she and Peyton used to do when sneaking out to parties in high school. She needed Caleb to believe that someone was asleep in the seat, to grab his attention.

Now for the hard part.

She pulled her knife from its sheath, staring at herself in its gleaming reflection.

Grabbing a hair elastic from around her wrist, she tied it tightly halfway down the length of her hair before placing the blade against the bunched strands.

Hesitating, Emily heard the sound of the door between the third and fourth cars slide open. She peeked over her seat to see that Caleb was closing in.

Time to get over yourself, Em. It's now or never.

She closed her eyes, and with one swift motion, sliced the blade across her ponytail to sever it from her head. For a second, she stared down at her fistful of hair, mourning as if she had lost a limb of her body. Then, she draped the disembodied ponytail over the backrest of the chair to make it seem as if it were originating from underneath the blanket.

She reached over and opened a window, causing the hair to lightly flutter as the wind rushed in. Satisfied, she dived across the aisle and crouched on the floor between the seats opposite her setup.

The door between the fourth and fifth cars opened.

The sound of her heavy breathing was drowned by the knock of Caleb's thick rubber soles walking in her direction.

"Heavy sleeper, are we?" he mumbled, just as his eyes lighted on the lumpy mound of blanket.

He raised his gun over the top of the seats, turning to his left to focus on the staged body, exactly as she had wanted.

Overconfident, his left hand deviated from the handguard of his rifle as he reached for her illusion.

CHAPTER SEVEN

The rattle of the train's wheels passing over the tracks resonated through the car.

Emily had retreated, breathing cathartically while crouching back into her hiding place between the seats. Loose strands of hair were stuck to the sweat that was beading down her nape. Her arms were wrapped around her shins as she rocked herself back and forth. Tears seeped from the corners of her eyes, all the while remaining fixated on the back of Caleb's head.

He turned around slowly and dropped the blanket from his clenched fist, his face masked with a look of surprise and pain. As their pupils locked, Caleb lifted his arm and began pawing at his neck, bringing his hand to the ribbed shaft of the knife that Emily had just shoved into his jugular.

A hiss of static fluttered from the radio in his holster, followed by the Cardinal's voice.

"Status report. We're two hours out."

Fading, Caleb dropped his gun, allowing it to swing to the side of his hip. He reached for the radio, one last attempt to alert the others of Emily's presence.

She stilled, her eyes unblinking, unwavering.

"Anthony here. I'm almost finished setting up the antenna. All clear."

She watched Caleb lift the radio, thumbing unsuccessfully at its button while attempting to form words. Trying to catch a breath, his Adam's apple was bobbing against the blade in his throat, preventing him from swallowing as curdles of blood burbled over his bottom lip.

"Cardinal, Drew and I almost have the cargo assembled and repackaged. All clear."

More static.

"Caleb, report. Everything okay back there?"

Hearing the Cardinal say Caleb's name caused Emily to stir. She snapped to the realization that even a grunt over the radio would alert the others that something was wrong.

Using the base of the seats to lift herself, she reached ahead and snatched the radio away from Caleb, clipping it onto her belt behind her back. She gripped the handle sticking from his throat, and in swift succession, kicked his sternum and withdrew the knife as he fell away.

She hadn't thought of what would happen next. Someone would undoubtably come looking for him if he didn't respond at all.

The remnant trickle of Caleb's blood trailed from the sharp edge of the blade and onto her knuckles. She grabbed the blanket from the floor and swiped the knife to clean it, before sheathing it again and looking down at Caleb. Every time his heart would beat, a squirt of blood would launch from the hole in his neck.

Seconds later, the squirting stopped.

"Can someone please go find Caleb? I don't need another idiot pulling stunts on this mission," the Cardinal's raspy voice ordered from the radio.

Emily bent over and grabbed Caleb's body by the shoulder straps of his vest, using them to drag him to the back of the train car. With every tug, her feet slipped against the blood-laden floor, making the disposal of his limp body slower than she would've liked. Her eyes bounced from the back door of the train car to the gangways, watching for the approach of the other Order members.

As her shoulder butted against the steel doorway, she slid it open, and from a crouch, rolled Caleb's body from the train, watching as it slumped onto the tracks and quickly disappeared from sight.

Once she was back on her feet, she ran through the train car and across the gangway into the fourth car, diving into the seat where she had left her belongings.

She checked her bag for the handgun. It was still there—much easier to maneuver with than the R4.

"Jason? Drew?" the Cardinal's voice sounded sternly over the radio.

After discarding her bag on the seat, Emily poked her head around the armrest. The coast was clear … for now.

"We're on it, sir. Just give us a few seconds to finish up here."

Now what do I do?

There was still nowhere to hide.

Remembering that she had passed a ladder between the fourth and fifth cars, she dipped low from her seat and made her way back to stand in the gangway. Shoving the pistol into the front of her waistband, she shimmied onto the narrow ladder and started to climb.

The wind howled in her ears as she leaned around the side of the train. She could see Jason and Drew through one of the side windows, already starting their search through the third train car.

Leaning back between the cars, she stepped onto the next rung.

Emily's head popped above the train car like a meerkat, her choppy lob whipping her in the face from all directions. In the distance, she could see the man called Anthony coiling a data cable. He had already set up an antenna and was now kneeling while affixing it to the sheet metal roof of the train. Physically, he was much leaner than the other men—scrawny even.

Tech guy, no doubt.

She climbed onto the roof, stretching her arms out wide for balance. She looked ahead, willing Anthony not to turn around.

Emily approached the gap between the third and fourth cars and gauged the distance. Just as she was prepared to leap, the door below slid open, causing her to retract.

She peered into the gap from above, watching the two men make their way into the next car.

She took a deep breath, then ran hard toward the ledge and leapt over the gap.

The velocity of the train made it impossible to stick the landing, causing her to drop and roll. Being downwind, the loud thump of her hip against the roof seemed to escape Anthony's range of hearing. He didn't react.

Steadied on her feet once again, Emily pulled the gun from her shorts and held it firmly with both hands. Sidestepping, she snuck up on Anthony from behind until she was within range.

"Cardinal, we've got a lot of blood back here." Jason's voice sounded simultaneously from the radio on Emily's belt and the one on Anthony's chest.

Fuck! He definitely heard that.

Anthony's hand immediately sprang for the gun that lay beside him amongst the gear.

"Don't even think about it!" Emily demanded, pressing the steel of the Glock into the back of his head.

His hand stopped, slowly rising with the other into a stance of surrender.

She stepped forward, kicking his rifle over the side of the train and into the bushes below.

"The radio—toss it here!" Emily pushed the muzzle harder into the base of his skull.

Lowering his left hand, Anthony reached across his chest to grab the radio and tossed it aside as well.

Emily had no intention of adding to her body count, and yet, she couldn't shake the ominous feeling that she would have killed him already if it wasn't for the uncertainty of whether the shot would alert the others to her whereabouts. Still, at this point, she was bluffing, hoping the man on his knees wasn't as smart as he looked.

"Please don't shoot me!" he pleaded. "I'm just the computer guy! Please!"

Emily paused.

Maybe he's telling the truth. Maybe he isn't the real threat here.

He looked like he hadn't lifted a weight in his life, unlike his comrades.

In her hesitation, Emily hadn't noticed the train starting to turn a sharp bend, snaking along the cliffside of the Urubamba River. The terrain had become rugged, and in turn, was causing the train to rock. The car below them faltered and she lost her balance once again, drawing the barrel of the gun away from Anthony's head.

He hurried to exploit her imbalance, spinning around to grab her wrist that held the weapon and veer it farther away. A struggle to gain control of the pistol ensued, each tugging and pushing the other. With the train tipping up and down beneath their feet, neither could gain an opportunity to advance.

Anthony used his lanky arms to grab Emily and flip her over, sending the gun falling away from her hands to skitter across the roof of the train. With neither of them able to reach for it in time, the vibration of the train car caused the gun to rattle over its lip and into the rushing waters below.

Emily gathered herself to her feet, trying to stabilize herself with a strong footing as the train shook repeatedly with each angled turn.

"You've got yourself into some trouble now, you dumb bitch!" Anthony yelled.

He tried to kick her, but she blocked it with her forearm, causing him to stumble backward.

Anthony made a lunge for Emily, attempting to hold her arms at the shoulders. Using her body weight, Emily ducked and rolled backward, planting her foot into his sternum and lifting him up over her head and onto his back. Landing near the middle of the car, Anthony bounced along the roof, twisting as he started to slide over its edge.

He scrambled to grab the protruding lip of the train car, banging his body against the side of the train as he dangled. Looking from Emily to the jagged rocks waiting beneath him, he hoisted himself up by pushing his feet off the window ledge below.

Emily turned around and saw the cable Anthony had been using, still anchored to the antenna.

While he was busy getting to his feet, she reached down and grabbed the loose end of the cable, looping it around her torso. Pulling tightly, she knotted it around herself multiple times to ensure its security above her hips.

Stabilized, Anthony began walking toward her, clenching his fists as he moved across the roof of the train. Emily rushed to do the same, both hoping to get in the first attack.

This, however, was one of her least bright moments. She hadn't allotted for the amount of the cable she had consumed.

Just as they were about to collide, the cable around her waist tightened, wrenching her stomach as the sheer force shot her backward onto her behind, causing the crown of her head to snap against the sheet metal.

She looked up, stunned and bug-eyed from her miscalculation. As he stood over her with a cocky grin, he pulled back and split open her bottom lip with a right hook.

For a moment, her whole body went limp and dull. Her ears rang over the clack of the train tracks as the warm ooze of blood trickled along her chin.

Anthony stepped to one side. Lifting a slackened portion of the cable he had been using earlier, he draped it twice around Emily's neck, tightening it around her throat. He hauled on both ends, hoisting Emily's body from the roof of the train into an upright position so he could stand behind her, making the most of his leverage.

Her oxygen was immediately cut as the cable locked around her windpipe.

He was strangling her, grunting while squeezing tighter and tighter. Faint sounds were coming from Emily's mouth as she siphoned for air. She dug repeatedly at the cable with her fingernails, leaving claw marks along her neck.

But in her moment of panic, she remembered her knife that was still strapped to her thigh.

Reaching down, she plucked it from its holster and jabbed it into his leg. Feeling the cable loosen as he yelped, she leaned ahead and with a quick snap back, head-butted him away from her.

He fell backward, releasing a hushed groan.

Emily dropped to her knees, coughing, breathing heavily as she pulled the cable over her head. She hurried to stand again, readying for another attack.

But she quickly realized that there wasn't going to be one.

Whipping around, she found the sharp edge of the antenna protruding from Anthony's chest. His eyes were wide, his mouth gasping like a fish out of water.

She approached him with caution, retrieving her blade from where it was embedded deep within his thigh.

These people were just as dangerous as Dr. Alsafar had warned, and it was in that moment that Emily's remorse for killing Caleb suddenly disappeared. She looked down at Anthony as if relishing in her achievements.

Emily Owens is not to be fucked with.

Pulling him from the metal rod, she dumped his body off the roof of the train, sending it crashing against the wet rocks in the river below.

Emily wiped the blood from her mouth with her forearm before lying on her back, out of sight, staring at the clouds as they rushed by overhead. This was as good of a place to hide as any.

"Cardinal Valerius, we still haven't found Caleb. There's a lot of blood back here, boss, but there's no one on this train."

She lifted the radio to her chest, listening carefully for their next move.

"Return to the front car. We'll anchor down here until we reach Aguas Calientes," the Cardinal's voice commanded. "Anthony, get down here. We'll finish the rest when we arrive."

She knew that without a response from Anthony, they'd be looking for him next.

So much for being safe on the roof.

Emily shimmied her way to the edge of the train car and peeked over the rooftop to look through the side window. She could see Jason and Drew heading back through the cars toward the front of the train, just as they had been instructed.

Now was the time for her to make the trip back to the last car and stow away. If they had already looked there, there would be no reason for them to check again.

Leaping from one car to another until she was standing between the final two, Emily climbed her way back down the ladder. She slid the door of the fifth car open and stepped inside, turning steadily to close it right behind her. She pressed her forehead against its frame, pausing momentarily to take a few breaths of relief.

But the train car was eerily silent and filled with an aroma that hadn't been in the car prior. *Is that perfume? ...*

Her nostrils flared.

Without a chance to turn around, the blunt stock of a gun connected with the base of her skull, sending her body falling unconscious to the floor.

Emily's body swayed from side to side with the movement of the train as she drifted in and out of awareness. The back of her head pounded while the rough texture of rope gritted against her wrists. She lay on her side, tightly bound.

Struggling to stay conscious, she jolted at the nearby cock of a gun.

"Let me shoot her!" A woman's voice yelled from across the train car. "This bitch thinks she can kill our men and get away with it? Huh?"

THE MISTS OF MORNE

"Alex, settle down!" the Cardinal said, trying his best to calm her. "As I have said before, the Boar wants her alive. There will be no killing her … today."

Drew raised his rifle toward Emily now as well, sending a red beam trailing over her chest, showboating in front of the others.

"Who is this *Boar* anyway? Some guy hiding in the shadows telling us all what to do? He's probably not even fucking real. I say we kill her. Fuck what the Boar says!"

Instantly, the Cardinal withdrew a knife from his vest and slammed it into the eye socket of his own man. The rest of the Order members flinched, skulking away as he removed the knife just as quickly. Squirts of blood fanned the air as Drew's body slumped over.

"Would anyone else care to speak ill of our monarch? If so … now would be the time to speak up."

The others nervously looked around the room at one another in silence.

"Moving on then …"

Emily's eyelids flickered as Rico grabbed the dead man's body by the ankles and dragged it away, before she faded into a blackout once again.

CHAPTER EIGHT

It wasn't until some time later that Emily awoke, jarred by the sound of gravel churning beneath the weight of rubber tires. Her body rocked ever so slightly, bringing consciousness to the pain in her head. She opened her eyes to the sun bearing down through the tree branches that went zipping by overhead.

She sat up quickly, finding herself in the pan of a single-cab truck, surrounded by the remaining members of the Order. Alex and Rico were in the cab, while Jason and the Cardinal sat in the back with her.

"She's awake, boss," Jason said, motioning his head in Emily's direction.

She instinctively reached for her knife again. It was gone.

"Looking for this?" the Cardinal said, dangling her blade between his thumb and index finger, taunting her.

"Where the fuck are you taking me?" Emily seethed.

The brakes of the truck slammed abruptly as the vehicle slid along the mucky road.

The Cardinal raised his hand to point toward the mountainside, forcing her to look.

Parque Arqueológico Nacional de
Machupicchu
Un Patrimonio Cultural de la Humanidad
BIENVENIDO WELCOME BIENVENUE

They had reached the base of Machu Picchu.
There's still a twenty-minute drive to the top. Why are they stop-
ping now?
The Cardinal looked at his watch, then back toward the road.
"Right on schedule."

Emily could hear the sound of vehicles in the distance, followed by a cloud of dust barreling down the cliffside. From the
narrow pathway, seven or eight busses began to whip past the
truck, each seemingly filled to capacity with passengers who all
held a look of fear about them.

Jason and the Cardinal stood in the pan of the truck, holding
their weapons in plain sight. They stared at the tourists as the buses
sped along the suspension bridge that crossed the river to safety.
They must have made their arrival well known back at Aguas
Calientes when they got off the train.

When the commotion settled, Jason slapped the roof of the
truck, signaling to Alex to proceed up the mountain. They zigged
and zagged along the ascending path. Emily just sat there, never
taking her eyes off the Cardinal.

Alex shut off the vehicle's engine at the end of the roadway, in
front of the hotel near the entrance to Machu Picchu. The whole
place looked as if it had been deserted.

Jason leapt from the pan of the truck to unlock its tailgate,
allowing the Cardinal to join him on the ground. Alex and Rico
exited the vehicle as well, with the latter making his way around
to the rear.

It was only when Rico appeared behind the vehicle that Emily's eyes focused solely on him instead of their leader. At his full
height, he stood taller than the cab of the truck itself.

Bending forward, Rico grabbed Emily by the ankle, and in one
swift motion, dragged her to the edge of the tailgate. She started

to flail with kicks and screams, though he didn't seem bothered in the slightest by her combative behavior. He simply plucked her body out of the pan of the truck and slung her over his shoulder with ease. She continued to scissor-kick her legs while elbowing him repeatedly in the back where she had been draped.

Out of nowhere, the sharp sting of a slap rang across Emily's face.

Alex grabbed Emily by the jaw and squeezed her cheeks and lips together, crushing them between her fingers. Her smoky eyes shifted back and forth, looking deep into Emily's as if to bore into her soul.

"Listen, bitch. If you strike my man again, I'll cut these pretty little duck lips right off your fucking face. Do you understand?"

"Alex!" the Cardinal scolded.

She looked at him grudgingly, pushing Emily's face forcefully to the side.

Alex was strong. Not gym-strong like Emily considered herself to be, but more hardened, like a soldier. The vibe Emily got from her was that maybe she had been molded to be ruthless, as if maybe she hadn't had a choice.

Emily soon realized she would be dragged along with them no matter what, and decided it would be best to calm down and let her resistance subside, at least for now.

Rico carried her through a jungle-like walking trail, finally breaking into an open area filled with stone buildings, staircases, and walkways.

Emily knew from the pamphlet she had been given at the train station that they had arrived at Machu Picchu.

With a snapping thud, her body was thrown onto a grassy plateau as the four members of the Recreant Order spread out around her, looking curiously in all directions.

Her mouth formed into a crooked smile; it was then that she realized that they still didn't know the exact whereabouts of the relic they sought.

"Jason," the Cardinal commanded, "head to the Sacred Rock, and take the girl with you. I will go to the Temple of the Three Windows. Rico, you investigate the Royal Tomb, and Alex, you check out the Temple of the Condor."

Jason swooped over and grabbed Emily by the rope that had been knotted around her wrists to form a leash. Forcefully, he began to tug her along the way to his assigned post as the others disbanded to carry out their given objectives.

Hours passed without anyone discovering much of anything, while Emily sat on the ledge of the Sacred Rock being practically eaten alive by insects. Jason remained close by as he was instructed, while she watched the others weave in and out of the temple ruins in the distance. The boxes that the Order had brought with them on the train contained excavating tools, many of which she could hear being used to smash rocks and to knock away walls.

Without regard, they were destroying hundred-year-old architecture for something that may not even exist.

Pathetic.

Emily stood to stretch her legs. Slowly pacing in front of the large stone, she shook her head at all the damage Jason had done with a hammer and a chisel. He had now begun chipping away at its backside.

Every time he became occupied, she would make small attempts to free herself from the ropes, biting at the frayed knots around her wrists. But just as one knot finally began to loosen, she was interrupted by a loud crumbling noise, and a cloud of dust rising from behind the Sacred Rock.

She peeked around to see what had caused the commotion.

"Boss, on my location," Jason radioed. "I've found something."

Within minutes, the rest of the Order members had gathered around the back of the stone, which had completely shed a thin layer of crusted rock. Although each of them stood around with their hands on their hips scratching their heads at the rock's facet, little did they know that Emily knew what had been uncovered.

The image depicted a figure holding a bright yellow object in an outstretched hand. It was the mural she had kept stumbling upon in her research. Just like the others, this mural had the clouds of mist surrounding the figure, and the massive army rising from within it.

This mural, however, showed something more.

An additional panel showed the yellow object—which at this point, she could only assume to be the sunstone from Diego Gomes' story—placed on some sort of mantle, and from it, a large, arrow-shaped beam of yellow light shooting upward into the sky. As if telling a story, a third and final panel showed a figure sealing the yellow stone within the mantle, covering it with what appeared to be some kind of liquid.

Was this a clue left by Luis Gomes perhaps. After he brought the stone back from Switzerland?

"Everyone, follow me," the Cardinal suddenly demanded before storming off toward his initial post on the west side of the Machu Picchu site.

The other Order members formed a single file and kept pace with him, all the while dragging Emily along like a battered mule. They climbed several interwoven flights of stairs until they reached a small clearing atop a stone structure. There, rested another large ritual stone. Emily recognized it as the world-renowned Intihuatana of Machu Picchu—it was said to have been guarded by the Inca Empire for centuries.

Intihuatana, when translated, meant "a place to tie up the sun." It was a solid granite altar containing small, lopsided steps, leading to a slab-like fragment that jutted four feet from the top toward the sky.

The Order began to encircle the altar like vultures, while Emily helplessly wondered what exactly they were trying to determine.

Then, the Cardinal ran his hand along the altar, staring at it intently, almost as if he was studying it. Emily noticed that the part of the stone he was studying was a different material than the original granite of the Intihuatana.

The Cardinal hesitated for a moment and then shrugged his shoulders with disregard. "Rico, grab the sledgehammer. Smash it."

"No! You can't do this!" Emily screamed, pushing her way forward.

Jason flung his arm out across her chest, stopping her from advancing any farther.

On the one hand, she knew the integrity of her profession had to be upheld. This sacred site should not have been laid to waste, just to discover some ancient relic. But on the other hand, had she made it this far by herself, she wondered, what she would have done to ensure her own legacy if she had been the one to reach this location first.

She watched Rico grab a large sledgehammer from one of the boxes, tightly gripping its wooden handle. He ascended the stairs one by one, stopping on the highest platform, which contained the protruding, tablet-shaped portion of the structure. Tourists weren't even allowed to so much as place their hands on the Intihuatana, and now, he was defiling it with his mere presence.

He lifted the hammer onto his right shoulder, then swung it like a baseball bat against the rock. The first smack did little damage, but as the metal head resonated repeatedly off the rock, small cracks began to form. With his every swing, the fractures spread like a spider's web. He grunted as sweat poured down his bald head.

On Rico's last strike, the rock encasement shattered and crumbled away to reveal a smaller granite tablet underneath. It formed a sort of vertical shrine, a single circular hole bored into its center.

Emily used her shoulder to shove Jason's arm out of her way, inching forward to see better.

There, resting in the crevice of the Intihuatana, was an unsullied yellow stone.

Alex thumbed the button on her radio. "We've located the relic. Initiate extraction."

"On my way, sweetheart," a seemingly familiar voice responded from the other end.

Emily snapped from her awe and returned her focus back to the members of the Order.

A large grin of triumph had formed on the Cardinal's face, just as the setting sun hit the stone, causing light to refract against its faceted surface, creating the illusion of a glow. He took a hesitant step forward then stretched out his hand to lock his fingers around the relic. He removed the sunstone from its perch and slowly brought it back toward his body, looking down at it in the palm of his hand.

"For so long the Florentine Diamond has eluded us, but today, my brothers and sisters, we rejoice, for we have obtained what is rightfully ours! No longer will the Recreant Order be forced to move about in the shadows. Instead, we may now move within the light of God!"

Florentine Diamond? Emily furrowed her brow.

The Cardinal let out a triumphant yell, thrusting his hand that was holding the sunstone above his head.

Emily's head, like those of the rest of the Order members, swiveled around expectantly—looking for signs of the mist. Some mist was present, but no more than had already been there when they had arrived.

The army? Her head swiveled again. *Nothing.*

No war cries, and certainly no rush of warriors. Only silence.

"No! It can't be!" the Cardinal shouted, furiously bringing his arm back down to hold the diamond in front of his face. He raised it toward the sky once more, shaking his fist.

Still, nothing.

"Damnit!" His jowls trembled as his face flooded with rage. "It seems we have a fucking fake in our midst!"

He shoved the diamond into Jason's chest.

"Take it! We'll need to get it to that old fool for research. No doubt it still holds some value to the mission."

Emily could see that the Cardinal's failure was getting the best of him. She burst into laughter, with the sole purpose of pissing him off.

"Wow," she sneered. "That's embarrassing."

The Cardinal turned sharply toward her, pushing his way through his henchmen, drawing level with her face.

Emily stared at him, smiling without so much as a flinch as he puffed hot heavy breaths over her.

"You and your big bad team came all the way up here for absolutely nothing it seems." She giggled and snorted in an attempt to further irk him. "And here, I thought you had done all your research. Very poor execution, I must say."

He slapped her across the cheek with a firm backhand, sending her collapsing to the ground.

"So, you think this is funny, do you? Maybe I'll just tell the Boar you tried to escape, huh? Fell off the side of a mountain as it were?"

The Cardinal turned back to his attentive minions, then glared back at Emily with a dastardly grin.

"Alex … have your fun."

The female Recreant immediately became giddy at his words, slowly walking toward Emily as if to feast upon her vulnerability.

But before Alex could get her first lick in, she halted, her head snapping toward the sound of stomping and rustling coming from the Machu Picchu entranceway.

Tactical lights flickered over the clearing.

"SUAT," Rico said, stepping toward Alex to pull her back closer to him.

"Calm down," the Cardinal said as he stepped ahead of the group. "We knew it was only a matter of time before the authorities arrived. Stand fast."

Almost immediately, the chuff of a small helicopter approached from below the mountainside. Emily assumed it would be a tactical sub-unit arriving to rescue her, but that was until the helicopter appeared from behind the Intihuatana and cradled its way into an open area near their position.

She knew she had recognized the voice over the radio.
Dominik.

As he moved around the front of the helicopter, a smug look crept across Emily's face at the unsightly train track of stitches that ran across his forehead. His nose was covered with a nasal-strip bandage, and his eyes looked like those of a raccoon, swollen, black and purple with hints of yellow.

She smirked with pride at how badly she had messed up his face, but quickly turned back to the SUAT team members who were now within shooting range. She threw her bound hands above her head, surrendering to alert the SUAT team that she wasn't a threat.

It was too late.

A flutter of HK53 bullets ripped through the sod around her.

As the Order members hurried to find shelter behind the stone walls, Emily crawled on her knees and elbows away from the gunfire.

Alex was the first to lift her rifle to her chest, holding it against her shoulder as she leaned in and fired shots from her position amongst the ruins. Rico stepped around the corner of a wall as well, spraying shots in the direction of the SUAT team, laying down cover fire while Alex sprinted to join him.

The Cardinal had no choice but to wave for his team to retreat.

Darting from behind the walls, the Order members rushed through the gaps in the ruins, releasing a barrage of bullets in the process. As the back and forth of gunfire filtered through the stonework, clouds of grey dust filled the Recreants' escape route.

Emily watched the scene unfold from her fetal position, quietly praying to make it out alive, and glad that, for the moment, nobody's attention was on her.

She glanced toward the SUAT team to see the officers in formation among the ancient city, then back again to see the Order members helplessly cornered. She kicked off her shoe, then removed her sock and waved it above her head like a white flag.

"Let's go!" the Cardinal commanded, circling his index finger in the air. "Everyone in the chopper. We've run out of time. Forget the girl. We'll deal with her later."

The Recreants scrambled over the embankment, letting off multiple rounds as they ran to pack themselves one by one into the helicopter like sardines.

Dominik and Alex climbed into the front, while Rico grabbed a metal beam and hoisted himself into the body of the helicopter. Once inside, he turned to extend his hand to the Cardinal and then yanked him aboard as well.

The helicopter's rotors began to speed up, whistling in rotation by the time Jason had begun his approach. He only made it a few yards before another wave of gunfire from the SUAT team trailed him, clipping a ligament in his left calf. He dropped to a knee for a split-second before continuing to hobble toward the helicopter.

"Cardinal Valerius! Pull me in! Pull me in!" Jason's voice squawked as he limped toward his teammates, his face masked with terror as he stretched out his open hand.

"I'm sorry, Jason, but the Order thanks you for your service." With his hand on the helicopter's sliding door, the Cardinal raised his pistol and popped two rounds into Jason's temple, looking on as the body flopped forward and hit the ground. "Amen."

It was then that two SUAT officers crowded Emily and cut her loose from her restraints, while the rest of the squad aimed for the helicopter as it lifted from the ground. The ringing of their bullets against its iron frame echoed across the valley, subsiding only when the helicopter flew too far out of range.

The SUAT team proceeded to fan out and clear the rest of the structures, while an officer helped Emily to her feet and another radioed for medical assistance, assuring her that they would be arriving shortly.

The tactical unit left her seated next to the Intihuatana, looking on as the officers continued to comb the area, even though she had told them all the members of the Recreant Order had been accounted for and were all gone.

She stood back up and walked over to one of the smaller crates left behind by the Order. Her bag was tucked inside, nestled amongst the unused tools. She pulled it out and checked its contents: knife, phone, and passport. All still there.

She plopped herself back down next to one of the stone walls, just as two more SUAT officers dragged Jason's body over and laid it beside her. Once they had moved on, she leaned inconspicuously over Jason's body, optimistic as she hunted through his vest pockets to see if the diamond the Cardinal had handed him was still inside. Snickering at the irony, she held it in front of her face, twisting it under the light of the setting sun to admire its golden facets.

So they're searching for the Florentine Diamond?

Seeing the medics approaching her, Emily stuffed the diamond into her satchel and tucked the bag behind the small of her back against the wall. She brought her knees to her chest and crossed her arms, leaning on them to hang her head.

CHAPTER NINE

Emily sat propped up against a pillow, chewing on cold, lumpy hospital mashed potatoes. It was now morning, and she had spent the night in the hospital in Cusco after being transported there for precautionary measures. Her wrist was lightly sprained and she had a minor concussion; nothing that bed rest and painkillers couldn't fix. She sought sleep, but the constant wailing of ambulance sirens hadn't provided the greatest lullaby.

She spat the half-eaten mush from her mouth onto the dinner tray, pushing it to one side.

Wiggling her body, she tried to get a little more comfortable, having no such luck with the cuff clamped around her one good wrist, restraining her to the bed. Apparently, the Peruvian authorities weren't finished with her yet.

She stared at her bag that hung on the back of her room door, wanting to check inside it to make sure no one had rifled through her things during her transport.

Suddenly, a knock rattled the door.

"Hello, Miss Owens, may we come in?" a man's voice said. He was already pushing his way inside the room.

"Yeah, sure," Emily groaned.

A Peruvian detective approached her bed and leaned in to release the handcuff, while a second detective shut the door behind him as he entered the room.

A gesture of good faith for my co-operation, I presume.

Emily was trying not to think about what had happened the day before, let alone spell it out for the two authorities. On the other hand, she also knew that innocent people had suffered, so anything she could do to help was her priority.

"Miss Owens, we wish to ask you a few questions about yesterday evening's events," the detective who was approaching from the door said as he pulled a small notepad from his pocket, flipping it open. "Would that be all right with you?"

"Go ahead. I'll try my best."

"Who were those people on the mountain? Why were you the only person that they held hostage? Do you know why they were here?" He was badgering her, spit-firing questions without so much as a warm-up.

Thanks for asking if I was okay, asshole.

She thought for a moment, knowing that she should choose her answers very carefully.

Yes, she wanted to help, but she couldn't just spew facts about gifts from gods or a diamond that contained an army. They would throw her in a Peruvian nuthouse really quick if she did.

"They referred to themselves as the 'Recreant Order.' I don't know why they chose to only take me hostage—maybe it was because I was an easy target? I don't know why they were here exactly. I overheard them talking about wanting to search the ruins for something, but I don't know what it was they were searching for."

Her story was a mix of facts and lies, enough to blame the Order, but not quite enough to incriminate herself for having the same agenda.

The leading detective's pencil began to scribble across the page, while the other detective leaned over, whispering something too low for Emily to hear.

"So, Miss Owens, what about the bodies?" the lead detective continued.

"The bodies?" She sat up straight, arching her eyebrows to feign ignorance. "What bodies?"

"Well, for starters, the two bodies we found along the train route to Machu Picchu. One directly on the train tracks and the other washed miles downriver, found tangled in a thicket of branches. Both bodies had identical lacerations made by the same weapon, it seems. A weapon we have yet to locate."

"I'm sorry, but I have no idea what bodies you are referring to."

The officers squinted at each other before the less verbal of the two took a step forward to retrieve a phone from his jacket pocket.

The lead detective started in again.

"Caleb O'Brien. Wanted in Mexico for robbery and homicide." As he spoke, the officer holding the phone flashed a headshot of the first deceased man. "No?"

The officer swiped the screen again; another headshot.

"How about this man, Anthony Clarke? Wanted in the United States for extortion and cybernetic warfare."

She was absorbing everything they were saying, yet couldn't shake the realization that the Order had their hands on any resource they required.

"And what about these other two men, Miss Owens? Can you tell us what happened to them?"

The first picture was of Drew, dead on board the train.

"Andrew Docker. No criminal history retrieved yet, but we're sure it's out there."

She took a hard, deep swallow. Knowing the names of the men made the fact that she had killed some of them much more real.

"He was killed by the leader." She finally managed to muster a response. "They called him the Cardinal. Cardinal Valerius, I believe."

The officer nodded and made a note before continuing. "And what about this man?" Another dead body flashed on the screen. "Jason Simms. On the run from British authorities for armed robbery and grand theft auto. We were told by our men that they witnessed him being shot at by someone in the helicopter. Can you confirm this?"

"I can," she mumbled. Her mouth started to salivate, her throat irritated.

"And this man?" The officer raised yet another photo, this time of the train conductor, his head splattered across the platform of the train station. "What was his part in all this?"

With that, Emily leaned over the side of the bed and puked over the railing, her stomach heaving repeatedly.

"That's enough." The detective casually tucked away his notepad. "Thank you, Miss Owens, for your co-operation. We are also here to advise you that, due to the circumstances, we have arranged for your extrication from Peru later today. I suggest you try and get some rest. Your things are being transported here from your hotel as we speak.

"Please, allow me to go get a nurse."

As the men exited the room, Emily wiped away the residue from the corners of her mouth. Sliding onto her side, she became paralyzed as her eyes filled with tears.

Everything had hit her all at once.

She closed her eyelids for just a moment, in an attempt to ignore it all, but before the nurse had a chance to arrive, fatigue had won, and Emily had fallen asleep.

Emily was roused by a clamoring noise coming from outside the hospital. She shimmied herself off the bed and over to the window to pull back the curtain.

A swarm of news reporters, cameramen, and media vans were haphazardly placed throughout the parking lot, along with police, who had put up a small barricade to keep the media out of the building. She grabbed the television remote and turned on the local news station.

It was everywhere.

The photos of the Order's henchmen, the train, the deaths. Even flashes of the damage atop Machu Picchu panned across the television.

So much for working from the shadows, I guess.

The crowd, however, was there for her, the sole witness. The one who had made it out alive.

She wasn't ready to tell her story. Not yet. Not one that was so unfinished. She had to get out of there. Her business in Peru was over and it was time to go home.

Noticing her suitcase on a chair in the corner of the room, she removed her hospital gown and changed as fast as she could. She grabbed her satchel from the back of the door and checked inside: knife, phone, passport, and stone. Again, all were accounted for.

She slung the bag over her shoulder and softly opened the door to the room, surprised to find that someone from the local authorities had been standing guard the whole time.

"I'm ready to leave," Emily demanded.

The officer nodded, then walked her to an emergency exit at the end of the floor, one that led to a small staircase at the rear of the building. In turn, this led her to an empty alley where an unmarked vehicle waited to take her to the airport undetected.

As the vehicle began to weave its way through the streets of Cusco, all Emily could think of was her condo, her own bed, and her family. The short trip now felt like an eternity, and she was more than ready for her life to return to normal ... whatever that would be.

CHAPTER TEN

On the way back to her condo from the airport, the Sunday morning traffic rushed along the Grand Central Parkway, but things couldn't have been more serene. Something about New York City and its familiarity had put Emily at ease again.

She laid her head back on the headrest, simply listening to the sounds of the concrete jungle, taking long, deep breaths until the cab dropped her at the main entrance to her building. Running through the onset of heavy rain, she burst through the front door, rolling her suitcase along the tiled floor.

"Miss Owens! Glad to see you're back from your mini-vacation," Geoffrey bellowed from the front desk. "Oh, and a new hair cut as well, I see! Changing things up, are we?"

"Oh, how I missed you, G." She gave him a big hug. "So glad to see your face again."

It was the first time she had perked up in days, but as she drew away, it was Geoffrey's chipper attitude that had faded. She had totally forgotten that her face looked worse for wear.

"Oh, don't worry, G. Just a little rock-climbing accident, no biggie. And it won't be the last either! I'll be fine, I promise."

She could easily tell that he didn't quite believe her, but he chuckled as if he did, which was enough to save her the guilt for deceiving him.

Parting ways, Emily slid into the elevator and watched the numbers climb one after the other until she reached the 15th floor. Hurrying down the hallway, she stepped into her condo and dropped her bags just a few feet from the entranceway. She was exhausted from the events of the previous few days, and her body was still sore despite the brave face she had put on for Geoffrey. Leaving her bags at the door, she headed straight for the shower to wash away the dirt and grime that was still caked to her body after her escapade on Machu Picchu. Although she was anxious to continue her search, she knew that, for now, it could wait; she needed to rest.

The next morning, feeling fully rested, she wasted no time in rifling through one of the pockets inside her bag to retrieve the yellow gem. She moved into her living room and flopped down onto the sofa.

Holding the diamond above her face, a stream of sunlight glistened through the window and struck it like a prism, sending what seemed like a thousand sparkles dancing across every surface of the room. Just like the prayer had said, she truly felt like she was holding a piece of the sun.

The Florentine Diamond, hey?

Of course Emily had heard about the Florentine Diamond— but it was rumored to have been lost centuries ago, sometime in the early 1400s. Everyone who was anyone in the archaeological world knew that many explorers had gone in search of it to no avail, most even calling it a myth.

Emily was under the impression that the Recreants wanted the sunstone—the god's relic—not some heirloom diamond. But was it possible that they were one and the same? *Either way, this thing probably belongs in a museum. Fake or not, it has to be worth something to someone.*

At the risk of the diamond being completely fake, as the Cardinal had so aggressively announced, she figured it was best to see an appraiser first, before jumping to any conclusions. There was no way she was going to end up looking like an idiot in front of the museum acquisition boards, and as much as she needed to take a break after everything that had happened, the adventurer inside of her remained restless.

She remembered her mother had spoken highly of the Gemological Appraisal Laboratory of America—or GemLab—which had an office over in Midtown Manhattan.

This was certainly as good of a place as any to start looking for some answers.

Emily parked her car on W 47th Street, holding the collar of her jacket over her head as she got out and headed inside the building that GemLab was in. Up the elevator and down the hall, she came through a door to find a young woman with big, rounded glasses, sitting behind the front desk, grinning from ear to ear.

"Welcome to GemLab! How may we assist you today?"

Emily shook the trickling raindrops from her coat—the rain from the day before still hadn't let up—then hauled the yellow stone from her pocket and placed it informally onto the counter in front of her.

"I was wondering if you could perform an identification check and origin report on this piece, please. I need to know what it is, where it came from, and how old it is. Is that something you can do?"

"Absolutely!" the woman said, handing Emily a clipboard and pen. "I'll just need you to fill out these forms while I perform a brief initial inspection of the gem."

The woman stood, grabbing the stone from the counter with one hand and holding it under an LED light, while examining it with a hand-held magnifier held in the other.

Emily hovered curiously, watching as the woman twisted and turned the stone around to inspect it from all angles. The employee scrunched her brow, glancing periodically over the top of her glasses at Emily who would then glance away, rushing to complete the paperwork. As soon as she finished the last stroke of her signature, the young woman leaned over the desk and practically snatched the clipboard back to review the form.

"Where did you say you obtained this gem from, Miss … Owens?"

"Uhh, it was a family heirloom … from my grandmother."

Emily flashed a nervous smile. She was lying more these days than she cared for.

"I'm sorry, but a gemstone of this magnitude will take some time for us to properly examine, especially if you require the full spectrum of tests that you've requested. We will need to hold it for four to five days. Would this be all right with you?"

Emily looked around and noted the security cameras monitoring the area.

"Yes, I suppose that'll be fine. Can you please give me a call as soon as you find anything?"

"Of course. Please, give me a moment."

The lady placed the stone on a square piece of cloth, then laid both on a small stainless-steel tray before proceeding to carry it through a set of doors. As the door swung closed behind her, Emily could see other employees who were busied with computers and microscopes. She felt assured that she was leaving the diamond in good hands, hands that were hopefully not tainted by the far reaches of the Recreant Order. Otherwise, this would all be for naught.

"We will call you later in the week with the results," the receptionist said as she sat back down at her desk and wheeled in her chair. "Have a nice day, Miss Owens."

Emily stepped out onto the bustling sidewalk, standing beneath the building's awning as people ducked and weaved under the cover of umbrellas to escape the weather. Having no idea if the Recreant Order would show up out of the blue and finish her off, she was now in the habit of checking her surroundings and over her shoulder any time she was in a crowd. No doubt they would be looking for the stone, and more importantly, her as well.

Fortunately, she wasn't fond of waiting to be gunned down. She needed something to take her mind off of things while she waited for GemLab's results. Somewhere private. Somewhere out of the city.

She glanced down at the clock on her phone, lingering on her background screen. It showed a picture of her and her family that had been taken on a walk late last year in Central Park.

Her forty-nine-year-old mother had the complexion of a thirty-something-year-old, which was surprising considering that Peyton had been such a pain in the ass her whole life. Her mother had always said that because Emily's father always kept her laughing, it also kept her youthful, except for her hair, which had been brown with salt-and-pepper grey for as long as Emily could remember.

As for her father, his age showed a little more predominantly. At fifty-two, the folds around his aquiline nose were now creased more than ever, and every time Emily video called him, it seemed like the grey had slowly crept farther along the sides of his head above his ears. He always said that he was grateful to still have a full head of hair, and that the silver never really bothered him.

In the picture, he stood behind the three women of the family, who were all smiling because he had wrapped his strong, hairy arms around them, squeezing them so tightly together that it hurt.

Emily pressed the lock button on the side of her phone and tucked it back into her pocket, staring aimlessly into the street as the thunder pounded overhead.

Maybe now is the time to take my parents up on that visit. Spending a few days in the peace and quiet of Vermont would do me some good. The weather's probably better, too.

Her parents had moved out of New York to a beautiful property in the Vermont countryside near Chester. Birds chirped endlessly, and the colors of fall consumed the trees; it would be the perfect place to provide the relaxation that she so desperately needed right now.

There was nothing but clear skies and sunshine by the time Emily hit the I-91. Traffic had been clear and it was smooth sailing heading north.

She had never driven to Vermont before. All the other times she visited her parents, she had flown. It was nice just to have the radio on and admire the scenery, although driving one-handed most of the way due to her tender wrist sort of sucked some of the fun out of it.

She pulled up to her parents' house just before sunset, driving around the horseshoe-shaped driveway and parking in front of their large two-story home. It had yellow siding and blue shutters, with brick flower beds surrounding the whole perimeter. Its face was full of large, six-pane windows, which let in the natural light that her mother coveted so much, having never been much of a city girl.

Emily had decided not to call ahead to let anyone know she was coming, which caused her stomach to knot in anticipation of her parents' reaction to her surprise arrival. Stepping from her vehicle, she could see them just sitting down at the dinner table, right on schedule. Removing her suitcase from the trunk, she wheeled it over to stand in front of the house, waving ever so slightly to get their attention.

Her father noticed her first, pushing back his chair and waving to her through the window. Her mother jumped to her feet to join him as he ran through the foyer to the front door. With open arms, they scurried down the steps to embrace Emily from both sides.

"Come in! Come in!" her father beckoned, gesturing toward the house.

"Yes, let's get in out of this cold," her mother added, grabbing the suitcase from Emily's hand and dragging it along as she ushered her inside. "Did you do something new with your hair?"

Luckily, Emily had thought to wear a turtleneck, high enough to hide the ligature marks on her neck as if she were hiding a high school hickey. Her mother's profession had made her overly observant, to the point that Emily was actually surprised it had worked.

Once the greetings had subsided and they had settled everything away, her father threw another log onto the flickering embers in the dining room fireplace. For the first time in what felt like forever, Emily and her parents sat down to enjoy a meal together as a family—or at least three quarters of one.

"So, any new adventures to tell us about?" her mother asked, patting her mouth with a napkin.

"Yes, c'mon! Fill us in," her father added. "Your mother mentioned something about a trip to South America? Get up to anything exciting in your travels? Maybe something to do with that busted lip of yours?"

He was prodding. Emily felt as if he had seen right through her cover-up story of a rock-climbing incident. Nonetheless, she wasn't about to sit there and worry her parents with every detail of her trip. As much as she would love to open up to someone about it, her parents were not her first choice. They would've scolded her for being so careless.

"No, nothing exciting. I went to Peru chasing an artifact I thought may have been hidden there, but it turned out to be a bust."

"I've certainly been down that road," her mother said, reaching to rub Emily's back. "I'm sure you'll find the next one."

Emily hadn't really had time to think of her "next one." She had placed all of her focus onto this mysterious stone, and she had failed miserably.

Yet another disappointment to add to the list.

It wasn't her mother's fault by any means, but the wording she used suddenly made Emily lose her appetite.

"I'm sorry, guys, but I think I'm still a little jet-lagged from all the flights, and tired from the drive. May I be excused? I think I'll go lie down for the rest of the evening if that's okay. We can pick this back up in the morning, yeah?"

Her parents looked at each other, then back to Emily with reluctant smiles.

"No problem, Toots. I'll have breakfast ready for you when you wake up."

Emily entered the guest room with all of her things in tow and crawled onto the bed, her mind jumbled now with thoughts of how she would approach her career moving forward. Realistically, she knew no real decision could be made until the results came back from GemLab. And even then, with the Recreant Order now in play, she contemplated whether or not she should even continue down the path of chasing the sunstone, a path that was proving to be more dangerous with every twist and turn.

She plummeted her face into the nearest pillow and let out a muffled scream.

But almost as quickly, she sprang back up.

Her wallowing had somehow made her forget all about the info that she *did* have. Information that the Order had just let slip without even realizing it.

She jumped up from the bed and plucked her laptop from her suitcase, then flung it open and sat cross-legged in front of it. Sure, she knew *of* the Florentine Diamond, but she didn't know that much *about* the Florentine Diamond. It was time to try and figure out what had led the Order to think they were searching for the Florentine Diamond in the first place. Even a secret society would need to get its intel from somewhere, and the internet was as good a place to start as any.

She spent hours reading and researching, compiling a folder of information in her cloud storage, comprising any known facts about the lost diamond, along with the stolen files from the USB drive. Though concrete details from researchers and treasure hunters alike were scarce because so many different people had sought the Florentine Diamond, she was able to piece together two different origin stories—both of which were supported by consistent and reoccurring information.

The first known owner of the Florentine Diamond was Charles the Bold, Duke of Burgundy. It is said that he would often wear his prized jewelry into battle, adorning his battle armor, until his death in 1477 during the Battle of Nancy. It is suspected that the diamond was later found by a wanderer who took the gem and sold it without knowing its value.

In the late 1400s, the stone reappeared in Italy, where it was bought by a man named Ludovico Sforza. But from there it vanished, never to be seen again.

Unfortunately, this scenario didn't include many clues for Emily to go on.

She moved on to review the alternate record of the diamond's history.

The Florentine Diamond was acquired from an Indian king in the late 1400s by a man named Ludovico Castro, Count of Montesanto. In 1601, the diamond was presented to the Society of Jesuits in Rome, who, in turn, sold it to Ferdinando I de' Medici, the Grand Duke of Tuscany, some years later.

Once the last member of the Medici family died in the 1700s, the diamond became a part of the Habsburg Crown Jewels, which were kept in the Hofburg in Vienna.

With the fall of the Austro-Hungarian Empire in the early 1900s, the diamond was moved to Switzerland for safekeeping. At some point between 1917 and 1925, it was thought to have been stolen by someone close to the royal family and then taken to South America. The predominant theory is that the diamond was then cut up and sold.

Duke of Tuscany? Vienna … Switzerland … South America?

The story still had no mention of mist or an army, but all the small details explained why the Recreant Order had believed the Florentine Diamond to be in Peru.

She laughed at the fact that they must have been scouring the other locations for months, potentially chasing a false trail for years.

But something still wasn't adding up.

If the second storyline led to a replica diamond, at what point were the stones switched? And why?

She needed more information. Thankfully, she knew one piece of the puzzle was sitting in a lab in New York.

It was morning when Emily snapped awake with a jolt. Her laptop was still open beside her on the bed, her hand still resting on its touchpad. She shut its screen and tucked it to one side before heading downstairs, the smell of bacon greeting her halfway.

As she swung around the railing, her father was floating back and forth around the kitchen, whipping eggs and shaking a frying pan of sizzling pork. A quick peek through the front windows confirmed that her mother's car was missing from the driveway, presumably why he was so busy.

Emily pulled out a stool and sat at the bar-style countertop.

Immediately, she picked up a strange vibe in the air; something seemed odd. Her father hadn't yet made any eye contact with her and hadn't even said so much as a "good morning"—an obvious change in attitude from the night before. Instead, he just turned and slapped a plate full of food down in front of her without saying a word.

Unsure what to make of it, Emily slowly started eating, hoping that it was maybe just a woke-up-on-the-wrong-side-of-the-bed scenario.

She quickly realized it wasn't.

He eventually stopped moving around the room, coming to a stop with his back to her while leaning his palms on the edge of the sink. He stood still at first, staring off through the window into the backyard, before turning his face ever so slightly over his shoulder in her direction.

Still no eye contact?

"Toots, I want you to tell me the truth."

Her ears twitched at his stern tone.

She laid her fork down beside her plate and took a gentle swallow of juice. She knew he was referring to her trip and her injuries. *I guess he's not as gullible as I thought.*

"What truth, Daddy?" Emily said in her most innocent-daughter sort of way, hoping to play it off.

He hung his head and shook it, discreetly trying to control himself. His grip on the lip of the countertop tightened. His knuckles turned white as the veins in his forearms swelled.

"I'm not stupid, Emily. I'm very well-versed in world news. I travel for a living, remember?" He had called her by her first name. When she was growing up, he only did that when she was in big trouble. "You said you were in South America, in Peru. Did you think I wouldn't find out about that terrorist attack at Machu Picchu a few days ago? It's all over the internet! Now tell me. What happened out there? The young woman that survived, the one that got away—was it you?" His voice had grown deeper now, crackling.

She froze, unsure of how to respond to his accusations. Her father had never spoken to her in this tone before, with so much conviction.

"Oh, yeah, that," she said hesitantly. "I heard about that as well. I wasn't anywhere near there … Actually, I may have already left Peru when that happened …"

Emily's father spun around and pounded his fist on the countertop in front of her. Her juice sloshed out of the glass and the ceramic plate of food rattled against the laminate surface.

Their eyes locked, neither able to look away.

Emily just sat there with a widened stare, her bottom lip protruding as it started to quiver.

Her father was more intimidating than any member of the Recreant Order, and his outburst happened so fast that she hadn't even noticed how her hand had clenched around her fork in some sort of new defensive instinct.

Breaking the tension, the front door flung open with the sound of plastic bags rubbing against one another. Emily's mother had returned with a stock of groceries for the week, sending her father retreating to the sink to grab a bowl at random and start washing it.

Emily rolled up the sleeves of her sweater and wiped under her eyes, an attempt to evade any further questioning from her mother, who had started to put the groceries away. Emily kept her head down, quietly continuing with her breakfast, though every bite since the altercation made her want to vomit.

"Is everything okay?" her mother asked.

Neither Emily nor her father spoke.

"Emmet? Emily? What's going on? Is he on your case already about the rock-climbing mishap?" She was standing with one hand on her hip, eyeing the wasted juice.

"Willow, we're fine," Emily's father answered calmly.

"Yeah, Mom, everything's good."

"You two better be playing nice." Her mother lingered, her dagger stare unwavering. "I'm not dealing with this alpha-athlete nonsense anymore. Grow up, the two of you. I swear, you're more alike than either of you would ever care to admit."

"Mom! I said everything is fine. Trust me." Emily forced herself to smile.

She finished her food then stood from her stool, carrying her plate to the sink to join her father, who was still visibly shaking. She raised her heels and kissed him on the cheek, innocently enough that her mother simply rolled her eyes irritably before leaving the room.

Emily cupped her hand over her father's, and without saying so much as a word, the tension eased. She stole a quick glance over her shoulder to confirm that her mother wasn't lurking around, then turned back to him.

"Give me some time—then we can talk, okay? I'm here for a few days, just … give me a chance to open up. When I'm ready, I'll explain everything."

Her father flung his arm around her back, pulling her into a sideways hug.

"Okay, Toots," he said as he leaned down and kissed the top of her head.

Ultimately, she knew he was just looking out for his baby girl. She couldn't fault him for that.

Throughout the following days, Emily and her father would periodically find times to talk, whether it was while shooting glass bottles in the wooded area behind their house or simply sitting on the back deck with a glass of wine.

She told him everything about her search for the mysterious lost artifact—first the sunstone, now, potentially, the elusive Florentine Diamond. She told him everything she had found out about the Recreant Order; she even reluctantly told him about the men she had killed. Sitting in front of her father while she told him that she was now a murderer brought the sour taste of bile back to her throat and tongue, but she felt that sharing the details were necessary. Somehow, her father's approach was to take it all in stride, not once telling her she shouldn't have done what she did. If anything, he seemed to emanate pride.

He openly took comprehensive notes, which was both disconcerting and curious. Every name Emily mentioned, every location that she had visited or heard of, he recorded them all in a little black notebook. Even when she talked about the fighting and killing, he would stop to correct her, critiquing her methods and giving her what seemed to be pointers on what she should have done better in certain situations to be swifter, more efficient. Emily knew that regardless of the topic, he wouldn't have been himself if he hadn't acted this way.

But in these moments of critique, there were brief instances where her father seemed like someone she didn't even know, a stranger—but in an inexplicably good way. Their relationship was reaching a level that it never had before, a bonding that Peyton would be even more jealous of if she had only known.

By mid-week, everyone's mood had started to somber. Emily's father had been called for another last-minute contract. Another flight, another job, leaving Emily with a couple of days to spend solely with her mother. She considered telling her mother about everything that had happened to her as well, but instead opted for less-tense conversations so she could truly relax.

By Friday, the weather had turned mild. Emily and her mother were basking in the autumn sun, bundled up in the hammock that hung from two birch trees beside the house. The crisp air and a cup of hot chocolate made Emily's life seem much more pleasant than it actually was.

Taking her final sip, Emily's front pocket buzzed.

She pulled her phone from her jeans, lifting her sunglasses to see the screen before raising it to her ear.

"Hello? Emily speaking."

"Miss Owens, this is GemLab calling. We've just received the analysis results for your gemstone. We need you to come and see us as soon as possible."

CHAPTER ELEVEN

Emily wasn't sure if it was the whooshing noise of the water around the tires, the repetitive pricking of the rain hitting the window, or the mechanical sound of the wipers followed by their squeaky retractions, but it had all made the drive back to New York feel like it took forever.

It had begun to downpour in Massachusetts, and continued on through Connecticut. A drive that should have taken three hours, four at the most, had now taken her six because of the build-up of water on the roadways.

GemLab closed at 5:00 pm. It was now 4:35 pm. She was cutting it close.

She burst through the front door of the building at the corner of W 47th and 5th, and repeatedly pushed the call button for the elevator.

Come on, come on, come on!

Instead of waiting, Emily dashed to the stairs, making sure to skip over every second step on the way up. She flung open the door to the GemLab reception area, hitting the coffee desk behind it with a loud thud, startling the receptionist. It was the same woman from before with the rounded glasses, and she was now looking over her specs at the sudden commotion caused by Emily's graceless entrance.

Emily gently closed the door behind her, frequently apologizing as she stepped up to the counter.

"Hi, um, I'm … I'm Emily Owens. Not sure if you remember me, but I received a call this morning that my stone was ready for pick-up."

The receptionist began to thumb her way through a hefty stack of stapled papers before finally tugging out the one belonging to Emily. She quickly scanned the pages, then reached for the phone on the corner of her desk.

"I have Miss Owens here. There's a note on her file that says you would like to speak with her … Mhmm … Okay." The woman slapped the receiver back down then propped the file into a wire basket tray hanging on the wall. "The appraiser will be with you shortly. Please, take a seat."

Emily sat in the waiting area, unable to stop her heels from tapping the floor. Once five minutes had passed with no further acknowledgment from the receptionist, she was about to go ask what the holdup was, when a side door opened to reveal a man in a lab coat. He grabbed the file from the basket on the wall then glanced in Emily's direction. She was the only one waiting, so there was no guessing. With the flash of a smile, he waved for her to follow him through the doorway.

The man in the lab coat proceeded to lead her down a small winding corridor, eventually veering into a private office. Allowing Emily to go in first and take a seat at a large metal desk, he shut the door behind them and followed her in, sitting across from her. Along with the files, he placed a small wooden box on the table between them.

For a moment, she squirmed in her seat as the man pored over each of the individual documents. His eyes scanned over the pages like the escapement of a typewriter until he eventually closed her file shut once more and opened the box, turning it toward her.

Inside, nestled neatly on a piece of velvet cloth, was her stone, still faintly glistening.

"Okay, Miss Owens. First of all, my name is Professor Miller, and I am an expert gemologist here at GemLab. I want to let you know that we are in a private and confidential room right now, and nothing that is said will be disclosed to or heard by anyone else. This is strictly between us."

Wait … why am I in a private room? Am I being detained or stalled? Do they expect foul play? Maybe the police are on their way …

Her heels began to tap against the floor again.

"Why have you brought me back here?" Emily asked cautiously.

"Well, Miss Owens, it's policy that whenever we have a client with a significant appraisal, we like to disclose the information behind closed doors, so to speak."

"Significant?" she questioned him, now engrossed.

He flashed her another smile.

"Miss Owens, allow me to tell you that this gemstone you have brought to us is a diamond appraised at three million US dollars."

Her heart felt like it had been sling shotted into her throat.

Three million dollars! Breathe, Emily, breathe.

Flabbergasted, she reached for the box, practically petting the diamond with her fingertips.

Regardless, this journey had never been about the money. Her primary goal was still to achieve recognition as one of the greatest discoverers of her time. She *needed* to find the real diamond, and fast.

Remember why you're here. Remember your main reason for the appraisal in the first place: the diamond's origin.

She hurried to mask some of her excitement.

"Thank you, Professor Miller." Emily positioned herself upright, nonchalant. "And what of its other details?"

"Oh, yes, I have that right here for you." He reached into the folder beside him, once again fingering through the paperwork. "Ah, here. It says the diamond originated from India, and by its weight and color, we suspect that it has a royal origin. We've dated it back to the late 15th to early 16th century."

Emily instantly remembered her notes. One of the stories about the Florentine Diamond had mentioned that the diamond had been acquired from an Indian king around that time.

This can't be a coincidence ...

Professor Miller started to shake his head, chuckling aloud.

"You know, for a moment there, myself and my colleagues thought this was a very specific diamond. One that has been lost for centuries—"

"The Florentine Diamond?" Emily cut him off with excitement, leaning slightly over the edge of the desk.

"Yes, how did you know? But don't worry, it's not. I ran every test possible, and unfortunately it did not match exactly with the Florentine Diamond's known characteristics. Still, its color and even the nine-sided, 126-faceted double rose cut had us fooled. So close, yet so far. It was about twenty carats shy as well. If I didn't know any better, I'd say someone cut this diamond to replicate the Florentine Diamond. I'm not sure why anyone would go to such lengths to do so, but we've all seen stranger things, haven't we?"

He had just confirmed her initial thoughts. Someone must have cut this diamond to look like the real one on purpose. Now, the only question was who.

After signing off on the appraisal, Emily had taken the diamond and its documentation and headed straight back to her condo. She forced herself to remain house-bound for the next couple of days, her time consumed with scouring over the internet, trying to learn as much as possible about the lost artifact, but unfortunately, there wasn't much to find.

She was quickly starting to realize that to find the real Florentine Diamond, she would definitely need more sets of eyes on this than just her own; solo wasn't going to cut it any longer. She needed a team. Trustworthy people with a special set of skills. People who were just as headstrong as she was, but maybe only half as stubborn.

I have to start at the basics, back to where the story all began.

The Recreant Order had already cleared most of the possible locations of interest off the list. Tuscany, Austria, Switzerland, South America, all crossed off, one after another. Now, from the new info that she had, India was the only place left where the diamond was once known to have been.

Doing her due diligence, she checked the USB drive again. There was no mention of anything related to India or an Indian king in the stolen Duke of Tuscany files.

Maybe the Order just hasn't checked there yet. Or maybe, they felt that the history was too old to be relevant. Either way, I have to search there for myself. It's the only way I can be sure.

By Monday, Emily had begun to go a bit stir crazy from staring at nothing but her computer screen and notes for the entire weekend. Having felt that she had completed sufficient research, she looked at her calendar to see the bold black circle around the date that marked her routine gym session with Gabrielle.

She found comfort in being able to return to the ring, to finally get back into the swing of a regular lifestyle after being away for so long. Her body seemed to have healed up well, and she was excited but anxious to lace up her gloves and go a few rounds.

At the stroke of noon, Emily parked her car near the training center. With her gym bag in tow, she was whistling as she turned the last corner. She stopped in her tracks as she was faced by the rhythmic flashes of red and blue lights from two police cars that were staggered at the entrance to Gabrielle's gym.

Shards of thick-cut glass littered every inch of the adjacent sidewalk. The gym's windows had been smashed from someone inside the building, and at least five, forty-pound dumbbells littered the street.

Emily dropped the bag from her shoulder and ran over to the front of the building as fast as she could, oblivious to the fact that she was being halted by two police officers who were cordoning off the scene.

"Gabby! Oh my God, Gabby!" Emily screamed, stretching her neck to look around. "What's going on? My friend, she owns this place. Is she okay? Gabby!" she yelled louder.

"I'm okay!" Gabrielle's voice called out from behind one of the broken panes. "Let her through."

The officers parted enough that Emily could slip between them to console her friend.

Gabrielle stepped from the inner shadows of the gym, her arms crossed protectively across her chest. Her face still carried that unwavering brave façade, like she was a woman who perhaps wasn't allowed to show weakness. But her eyes revealed the lie that her body language was trained to portray. They were narrow and cold, with hollow glints of fear that Emily had never seen before.

"What happened?" Emily asked, meeting her halfway to hold her by the shoulders.

"I don't know, Em. Why don't you tell me? They were asking about you."

"Wait, what? 'They' who? Who was asking about me?"

"Three men—with guns—were asking if I knew where you were. Said they were going to kill me if I didn't tell them. Imagine, kill me, Emily. They were going to kill me just to get to you." A tear ran from the corner of her eye, just as she turned to take another look into her training facility. "They tore up the gym real bad inside, trying to prove their point. Apparently, it wasn't enough to threaten my life, they had to take away my life too."

Emily leaned to one side, eyeing the devastation.

The ropes to the rings had been severed. Busted punching bags dangled from chains, their stuffing protruding outward like that of a teddy bear chewed through by dogs. Weight racks, cardio equipment, training setups—all ravaged and tossed about with disregard.

"Hold on a minute, what did they look like?" Emily asked frantically. "Was there a woman? Was one of them big and tall and full of tattoos? Was one of them called 'the Cardinal?'" Emily asked urgently, pushing for a response.

"I don't know, Em! I was too busy being scared for my life. What do you mean 'big and full of tattoos'? What the hell have you got yourself into?

"All I know is they said they were going to go after everyone you knew until they found you. Said that they found you once, and they'll find you again. They kept saying you had something that belonged to them ..."

Emily backed away slowly, gripping the roots of her hair while her mind tried to process what was happening. *They found you. But how? You were careful. Weren't you?*

"So why didn't they kill you?" All at once, Emily's scattered brain refocused, causing her to blurt out the question.

"Officer Prescott over there was coming in for her yoga class, saw them with their weapons drawn and radioed in for back-up. Once they heard the sirens, they fled.

"Em, I don't know who else they would think of going after, who knows you like I do, but what if they aren't as lucky as I was?"

Oh no, Mom and Dad—and Peyton! What have I done?

Emily left Gabrielle standing on the side of the road as she sprinted back to her gym bag. She reached in, heaving furiously to remove her athletic gear until she scrapped the synthetic canvas at its bottom.

Empty.

She had left her cell phone back at her condo. Luckily it was only a few blocks away. She had to make it.

Emily weaved her car in and out of traffic so fast that slamming on the brakes only became an option once she reached the front of her building, leaving the car parked sideways in the middle of the road. She scrambled around the front bumper then burst through the door, almost falling into Geoffrey's arms as she entered the building.

"Whoa! Miss Owens, watch your step. Is everything okay?"

Without a response, she shoved him out of the way and blew past him to continue onto the elevator, then upward to her floor.

As the doors slid open once again, Emily immediately noticed that the door to her condo was ajar—certainly not the way she had left it.

Dashing away from the elevator, she squared her back to the nearest wall, creeping sideways until she reached her condo, hesitantly shoving the door all the way open.

She slowly peered around the doorframe to look inside.

Shattered ceramic from her dishes covered the kitchen floor. Soil from her upended plants had been tossed onto the accent rugs. Tables were snapped or overturned, and cotton was protruding from the otherwise plump cushions of her sofa.

She listened intently.

Silence, aside from the thumping of her heart.

Slithering her arm around the doorway, she pulled the drawer of her entrance cabinet open, grabbing the knife she had left there the night Peyton had woken her. Tensing her grip around the handle, she started drifting around her condo, surveying the destruction left in every room.

The place had been ransacked: her cupboards, her closets, her cabinets. It had all been picked through. Even her bedroom, where her phone had been charging on the dresser, looked like it had capsized from within.

She knelt at the wall, tracing her fingers along the white cord protruding from the socket to a dead end; her phone wasn't there.

Her heart started racing once again.

Emily started grabbing armfuls of the clothes that were strewn about the room and tossing them into a heap on the floor. Nothing. She moved furniture and curtains, her lamps and storage ottoman, all before bending to lift her mattress back onto the slats of the bed.

There it was.

She found her phone underneath one of the bedsheets swirled on the floor; it must have been thrown during the Order's search. Dropping to her knees, she plucked up the phone and thumbed Peyton's number. Her sister lived within the city and would be the next logical target.

No answer.

A wave of panic began to overtake her.

"Peyton, pick up your fucking phone!" she yelled.

Again, no answer.

Flicking through her contacts, she called both of her parents' cell phones. Straight to voicemail.

Emily sank to the floor, her eyes welling as they shifted around the room before stopping on the open set of bifold doors that led into her walk-in closet.

The small safe that she kept buried deep inside was wide open.

She sprang to her feet and rushed over to the steel lockbox, placing her hand on the lip of its gaping door.

It was empty.

The diamond, its documents from GemLab, the lipstick USB drive. Everything was gone.

The Recreant Order had promptly reclaimed all of the information they required to move forward with their objective, and then some.

All they needed now was to tie up the loose end—Emily.

Emily tried her best to focus on the road, continuing to call her family as the ringing echoed over the speakers of the car. Peyton and her husband lived on Staten Island, and if Emily couldn't reach her by phone, she was determined to make it there in person, hopefully before the Order did.

She sped halfway across the New Jersey Turnpike, running red lights and dangerously weaving in and out of traffic, all the while calling her parents and sister. Her mother finally answered her parents' home phone line.

"Mom! Listen to me. You have to get out of the house!" Emily yelled.

"Whoa, sweetie, what's going on? You're scaring me."

"Just trust me! Where's Dad? Get him and get out of the house. It isn't safe there."

"Emily, calm down. Breathe. He's right here next to me; I've got you on speaker. Can you tell us what's going on? Are you all right?"

"I'm on my way to find Peyton. I'm mixed up in something terrible. It's bad. It's really, really bad. Please, just get out of the house. I just really need you to go."

There was no reply, only a harsh, scratchy flutter on the other end of the phone's receiver.

"Mom? Mom? Are you there? Goddamnit, Mom!"

"Sorry, hold on a second, sweetie. Some strange men just pulled up in the driveway."

"No! Mom, it's them! Get out now!" Emily screamed, straining her vocal cords.

"Emmet, do you know those people?"

"Mom! Dad!"

Suddenly, the erratic pop of gunshots rang through the receiver, automatic weapons firing relentlessly. The sharp shattering of glass and lead bullets ricocheting off the wood made Emily cover her mouth. Suddenly the barrage of gunshots stopped.

"Mom?"

An eerie silence filled the car, broken only by the two single shots of a handgun that sent tears cascading down Emily's cheeks. She pounded the steering wheel over and over with her palm, while the dial tone of the phone buzzed over the stereo until it disconnected itself from the other end.

What have I done? …

She wanted so badly to pull the car onto the shoulder of the road, but she couldn't. Peyton was still in danger.

You should never have meddled in things you didn't understand. You should have known better. And what's worse—you were warned.

The tires of the car screeched along the driveway as Emily pulled up in front of her sister's house. She jumped from the driver's seat and ran along the stone retaining wall, up the concrete steps, and barged through the front door.

"Peyton!" Emily yelled repeatedly, circling from the kitchen, to the dining area, to the living room. "Peyton! Where are you?"

"What the fuck, Em?" Peyton finally responded as she approached the railing to look down from the second floor.

Her hair dangled to one side, crinkled and wet. She looked as if she had just gotten out of the shower—likely the reason why she hadn't answered Emily's calls.

"What are you doing here?" She started to walk down the winding staircase to where Emily was standing.

"Where's Graham? Where's Riley?" Emily grabbed her sister aggressively by the hand. "We have to get the three of you out of here."

"Graham is out golfing with his old military buddies, and Riley is with Graham's parents." She began rubbing the underside of her baby belly. "Em, you're worrying me. What's going on?"

"I can't explain right now. I just have to get you in the car and get you out of here. Some bad people are coming for you … because of me."

Just then, two car doors slammed in succession from outside the house.

Emily crept over to the curtains with her sister in tow and peeked outside.

Two men in black suits were eying Emily's vehicle while walking toward the front steps. A third man, the driver, sped off from the house without hesitation. Neither of the men were familiar to her, but they were armed with the same weapons as the Recreants from the train in Peru.

"They're here. We have to go. Now!" Emily once again tugged at her sister's hand.

But instead of panic or fright, Peyton's facial expression darkened, became stern. She immediately grabbed her wet hair and pulled it back into a small, tight ponytail.

She draped her arm in front of Emily, shoving her to stand behind her.

"Peyton, what are you doing? They're going to kill us! Come on!"

The two men entered the house.

Emily could see them through the adjoining archways search-ing room by room, moving in a loosely coordinated tactical for-mation. The thud of their boots knocked against the hardwood, with every creak in the floor drawing them closer and closer to the sisters' location.

Peyton parted her bathrobe and crouched down beside the sofa before casually extended her hand underneath. Emily, confused, remained standing and exposed.

Once the men finally entered the living room, they raised their weapons focusing on a woman each. The red dots of their rifles fluttered against the women's breasts above their hearts.

"Please! Don't shoot!" Emily begged.

She quickly threw her hands up in surrender.

"My water broke!" Peyton suddenly exclaimed, one hand still on her belly while the other remained beneath the sofa. "Please! I'm in labour!"

The men hesitated, looking to each other for some sort of approval.

So killing a pregnant woman is above the Order's standards?

Emily looked down at her sister, still having no idea what Peyton was trying to accomplish. She then looked back to the men, drawing nearer by the second, readying to pull their triggers.

Emily closed her eyes, accepting the inevitable.

This is it … The Owens legacy ends here …

CHAPTER TWELVE

First, there was nothing but darkness. Emily's eyes fluttered against their lids. She was curled into a ball behind the sofa, and her hands were cupped over the sides of her head. The ringing in her ears was a sharp, deafening pitch, like someone had let off a concussion grenade in the living room.

It took her a few seconds to realize that she was still alive. She lowered her hands from the sides of her head as she finally had the courage to pop open one eye. Discreetly looking across the room, she could see the two men lying motionless on the floor, staining the cotton rug with a deep red.

As her other eye unlocked from its squint, she turned to see her sister, who was standing tall instead of squatting.

Peyton's right arm hung at her side, a smoking M9 pistol clutched in her hand. She turned, noticing that Emily had stirred from her sheltered state, then reached down and pulled Emily by the elbow to her feet.

Emily's jaw dropped. She couldn't help but stare at the gun, then back to her sister, non-verbally asking what just happened.

Peyton walked boldly over to the bodies and raised her pistol to put one more shot in their chests for reassurance.

This woman moving so methodically around the room in front of her certainly wasn't the Peyton she knew.

"What ... what just happened?" Emily asked, finally able to speak.

It was as if Peyton hadn't even heard her. She was too busy reaching down over her belly, grabbing the bodies' limbs and tidying their position. It was apparent to Emily that this wasn't Peyton's first time in a situation like this, which was even more alarming.

Peyton disarmed the two men and moved their weapons to the kitchen table. She pulled a crumpled photo from one of their coat pockets and flashed it to Emily as she walked past her through the room. It was a picture of Emily, Peyton, and Gabrielle at a lakeside fire, pulled from one of Emily's social media accounts. The Recreant Order had known exactly who to target and precisely what each of them looked like.

Peyton laid her own gun on the kitchen counter, hauling the top drawer next to the sink open and pulling out a simple, dated flip phone.

Her thumb pushed the speed dial before she brought it to her ear.

"You were right." Her voice was firm, articulate. "They showed up just like you said they would ... It's taken care of ... Yes, she was." Peyton briefly glared over at her sister. "I'll sit her down and tell her ... Don't worry ... She can handle it ... Love you too, bye."

She removed the phone from her cheek and thrust it toward Emily, who didn't know whether to take it from her or be afraid she would kill her with it.

"Hell ... hello?" Emily answered the phone, completely unaware of what was happening.

"Hey, Toots."

Hearing her father's voice made her glossy-eyed as she held her palm over her mouth with both anguish and relief.

"I know you're probably scared and wondering what's going on. Peyton is going to explain everything to you shortly, I promise. Your mother and I are fine; there is no need to worry. Just remember that I love you, and that I have always done what I've had to do to protect you. Bye, Toots."

He ended the call before Emily had a chance to respond or ask a single question. She closed the phone and handed it back to Peyton, who tossed it back in the drawer. She then pulled her regular cell phone out from her purse and called her husband, Graham.

"Hey, sweetie, the baby came earlier than expected … Yup, that's right … Delivered right in the living room … Yes, I'm doing fine; Em was here with me … Oh no, just a little mess … By the way, we had twins—two boys … Can you send an ambulance? … I love you too."

Emily gave Peyton a quizzical look.

"Someone's always listening, Em. C'mon now, didn't you pay attention to *anything* Dad taught us?"

Once again, Peyton's demeanor returned to a neutral state as she laid her phone down, walking over to look through the curtains to the outside. She didn't seem to see anything, but she walked to the front door and locked the deadbolt for assurance.

Returning to the living room, she pointed to the sofa, motioning for her sister to take a seat.

Emily didn't move. She merely watched as Peyton eased her way onto her body pillow, patting the sofa cushion to indicate that she should join her. Emily was reluctant but eventually made her way over, seating herself on the opposite end of the sofa, away from this … stranger.

Suddenly, Peyton broke out into a huge grin.

"What?" Emily chimed, raising her brows.

"You know, Dad always knew you had your own path to follow. As much as he pushed you in his desired direction, you just wouldn't take." She laughed.

"What's that supposed to mean?" Emily asked, leaning a little closer.

"The gun range. The fighting lessons. He always wanted you to be like him … like us. But no, *you'd* rather play with all the artifacts Mom brought home from her expeditions. I mean, it's okay and all, but it's ironic how in the end it all comes back around."

Emily was still totally confused. She moved to sit at the edge of the coffee table, directly across from her sister.

"Peyton, tell me what's going on, right now!" she demanded.

"Em, you only know our dad as a father, but there is so much more to him that you don't know. Growing up, did you honestly think that all he did was shuttle people around? Did you think he just flew a plane, hung out somewhere for a few days, then flew home and made tens of thousands of dollars? Come on now, Em, I know you're smarter than that."

Emily started second-guessing everything she had ever known about her father. Her sister was making a valid point. She had never really let herself think of it that way.

"So, what are you saying?"

"You know what, Em, I'm just going to come out and say it. Dad is retired military, okay? A Night Stalker, or at least, that's what they call themselves. He was a part of a secret division of the U.S. Army Special Operations Aviation Command. He's likely killed more people than live in your condo building—and that's not even an exaggeration."

Her words were so blunt that Emily became hushed. Her mind couldn't process the information being presented to her. She felt as though her whole life was a lie, a fabrication.

"I don't understand. He's still working, isn't he? What do you mean by he's 'retired'?"

"He is. Has been since you graduated high school. Only works privately now, under contract. Gets paid a pretty penny, too. Now he *does* just fly people around, but if things go south, he helps out—acting sort of like a back-up plan. He has his own team now though—recruits—and a whole lot of resources. He called me a few days ago and told me you had gotten into some trouble with an organization called the Recreant Order. He said they're not a group you want to mess with."

"Wait a minute. So you're one of these … Night Stalkers as well? I suppose you're going to tell me that your job as a flight attendant is a lie too?"

Peyton stood from the sofa, rubbing her belly again and moving to stare out the window with a discomforting look.

"I'm not much of anything these days, except a shuttle for this little thing. But no, Em, I'm not a flight attendant. I'm also not a Night Stalker, although I was trained by Dad to be a part of his team … just like he started to do with you. The only difference was, I liked it. Every move he showed me, every shot he let me fire, I loved it all. It wasn't until I was eighteen that he started to show me things you don't learn at self-defense classes—that I can assure you. He practically taught me everything he knows, and I'm damn good at it. That much you should know."

She knew that Peyton was telling the truth. She could be an ass sometimes, but never a liar. Emily started replaying her adolescent years over in her head. She had always felt like her dad pushed her so hard as a teenager, but she just figured he was trying to compensate for never having a son; maybe he still was. But she never realized that he was just trying to teach her how to survive.

"And why now?" Emily stood as well, raising her voice, fueled with emotion. "Why wait all this time to show your true colors?"

"Because of Mom. She doesn't know any of this either, although after today, he doesn't have much choice but to come out with it all. I mean, she knew he had a military background, but she thought he gave it all up when they had us. When in reality, he continued to work for the military until he *did* officially retire.

"Do you think it was easy for him, keeping it from you guys? But now, Em, you've brought this on yourself. You've literally brought the bad guys to our doorsteps. Dad always said he could see Mom's curiosity inside of you, and look where it's gotten you.

"He isn't mad, trust me, but with me being pregnant, that's one less person to protect you."

"And who says I need protecting?" Emily puffed out her chest, broadening herself as she stepped closer. "If he told you everything, then you know I've killed people, too."

"You got lucky, Em. But I will give you credit—the story did sound pretty badass. Did you actually stab a guy in the neck? You ruthless bitch," Peyton chuckled.

A laugh started to build in Emily's stomach, breaking her frustration. Her sister always did have a way with words.

They stood, face to face.

"So, what now?" Emily asked.

"Well, for starters, Dad wants you to continue to find this thing you're looking for. He could hear in your voice how excited you were to be chasing down a lost relic. It would make him so happy and proud to see you accomplish what you've set your mind to. He believes you can do it. He also wants you to know that whatever you need, we are all here to help."

"What do you mean by 'all'?"

Suddenly, the rough sound of the deadbolt unlocking rattled from the front door.

Graham and two other men shuffled into the house. Working their way around the furniture, Graham approached Peyton first, looking her over to ensure that she and the baby were okay, while the other men began to roll the two bodies up in the blood-soaked rug, concealing them for disposal. Within minutes, they had picked up the rug and exited the house.

Must be one of those "resources" Peyton mentioned.

Emily still couldn't comprehend what she was witnessing. Everything was so organized and secretive.

She quickly turned back around to face Peyton and her husband.

"What's your part in all this?" Emily said, directing her question at Graham.

Peyton raised her hand, advocating to speak for him.

"Graham was trained by our father as well; works for him too. Remember how I told you that Graham and I met each other at a concert? That was also a lie. We met in training. You know, day after day, working out with each other. Then one night, I finally got up the nerve to tell him I wanted him to screw my brains out and we've been together ever since. Cute, right?"

Graham shook his head and looked at Emily.

"That's not *exactly* how it went," he chuckled.

Graham had always seemed like the strong, silent-type to Emily. She had just thought it was his personality but was now quick to realize that it may have been the pressure of keeping her family's secrets that had kept him so quiet around her and her mother.

She couldn't knock the authenticity of his love for her sister though. He was always a real gentleman toward Peyton, very much her sister's type as well. With a dirty blonde crew-cut, brown eyes, and a chiseled jaw, Graham had it all.

"Dad's having the same conversation with Mom as we speak. Trust me, I bet he wishes he *was* killed today than have to deal with her wrath," Peyton joked while going to the kitchen to get a glass of water. "Listen, Em, we'll be fine here. I suspect we've warded off the possibility of those Recreants returning for a second try.

"Go home and make your plans. Dad said he'll fly you wherever you want to go once you're ready. It'll be a lot easier to bring weapons along with you when he's flying the plane, so maybe this time you aren't stuck bringing a knife to a gunfight. By the way, what is it with you and those garter things anyway?"

Peyton had made yet another valid point. Now that the air was cleared, maybe Emily could avail herself of her father's resources— maybe get him involved in the next leg of the search. This may be exactly what he had been longing for all these years.

But secret soldier or not, Emily was determined to recruit her own hand-picked team to help her out. She wanted people she could trust, not just some randomly selected mercenaries recommended by her father. She had no idea what she would run into on her journey, but it was precisely that: *her* journey. This was *her* adventure. *She* was making the decisions now, and *she* was prepared to live or die by them.

Back at her condo, Emily stood amongst the mess, still trying to process the absurd amount of new information that had been dumped on her only an hour ago. It was like a conflicting new chapter had been cracked opened in her life, yet it had presented itself as a sort of odd, well-needed shake-up. She wasn't mad, just disappointed, mostly with herself. She understood why they had kept everything under wraps. She just wished she hadn't been so naïve for all those years.

To not to get stuck dwelling on the past, she instead began to assess the damage done in each room throughout her condo. Moving around as she tidied, her skin crawled knowing someone had been lurking through her living space when she wasn't there.

In the living room, hovering over her shattered trophy case, she bent down to extract her medals from the broken glass. It wasn't the material things she cared about—those could be replaced. It was the sentimental ones that had her holding her breath as she cleaned. For instance, her archaeology book collection that had started when her mother gave her *The World Encyclopedia of Archaeology* for Christmas at the age of twelve. Fortunately, her laptop was still intact, although it had been thrown into the bathroom.

As she placed her books back on their appropriate shelves, Emily happened across her Berkeley yearbook, which remained unopened since her graduation. Desiring even a brief return to normalcy, she cleared a spot on the floor and plopped the book down in front of her, lying on her stomach while casually flipping through its pages. She eventually arrived at the class pictures, scouring them for a few seconds until her eyes rested on a black and grey photo of herself.

Emily remembered her graduation day well. She could hardly wait to show her mother the diploma that she had worked so terribly hard to earn. She glanced over her shoulder at the expensive piece of paper that now sat in a cracked frame leaning against her heater, compliments of the Recreant Order.

Turning back to her yearbook, her attention shifted to the guy standing next to her in the group photo.

Seth Parish. The only person in the whole class that could show her up.

Seth graduated summa cum laude with a major in archaeology and a minor in geography, and had also been an avid treasure hunter since the ripe age of fourteen. Maybe life just got
busy, but seeing his photo made her miss his company. They used
to be close friends, engaging in a few make-out sessions while
late-night studying, but never anything more; she was a lot less
confident back then.

To her, he was the funniest man in the whole university at
the time, always making her feel secure in an environment full of
strangers. But, for no particular reason, they hadn't kept in touch
much since graduation.

I wonder what he's been up to.

She pushed herself up from the floor and into a seated position,
dragging her computer into her lap. She opened her social media
account and started to search, knowing they were still virtual
friends at least.

He wasn't hard to find. In his profile picture, he was lying on
a white beach in Greece, sporting his well-tanned, swimmer's
physique against the bright grains of sand.

Still swimming, I see. And a new sleeve piece as well? Interesting …

His soft brown eyes entrapped her, even through a photograph,
and his coal-black head of hair made her reminisce about all the
times he asked her to play with it as he lay innocently on her lap.
His beard was short and boxed—which was new—but no matter
how hard he may have tried, he still couldn't cover up that damn
smirk of his.

She caught herself twisting her hair, browsing through more
of his profile than necessary, when a recent status update caught
her attention.

*"All finished up here in Mykonos! Time to head home and look for
the next adventure I can rub in my friends' faces!"*

Sounds like he might have some free time on his hands.

There were albums full of photos from jobs he'd had on ship-
wreck expeditions all over the world. She recalled how he had

always been very self-willed, always looking for that next big challenge.

That's when the wheels in her head started turning.

Maybe I could reach out to him and see if he would be interested in joining my team. It's a long shot, but I could utilize someone like him in my search for the Florentine Diamond.

What do I have to lose?

Emily opened the message window and trailed her fingers along the keyboard, making sure to take the time she needed to write him a concise but enticing message. Once finished, she sat completely and utterly still, biting her thumbnail while staring at the screen.

What if he says no? What if he's busy? What if he thinks this is just a proposition for something ... more? Well, I mean, he is single ... No! Em, focus. This is serious.

She cleared her mind and pressed send.

And there it was. Her first real step toward pursuing the Florentine Diamond—if that's what it was she was truly after.

She flailed onto her back, smiling at the ceiling, scissor-kicking her heels against the floor.

It's happening! It's actually happening!

In her moment of triumph, she turned her head and realized that she still had a ton of cleaning to do. She sat upright and shoved the laptop to one side. She spent the next few hours placing everything back in order as best she could, until all that was left to clean was her bedroom.

Stepping inside to decide which tornado-swept corner she would tackle first, she rested her hands on her hips and passively studied the disordered contents of the room from the doorway.

It was then that a glossy piece of paper caught her attention, its ragged corner sticking out from under her bed.

She bent down to retrieve it, gently blowing on it to remove any dust. Her left brow arched as she surveyed the business card of the person who, without question, would be the perfect next addition to her team.

THE MISTS OF MORNE

Maggie Riggs
Explosive engineering & disposal
I build 'em, I Rigg 'em, I blow 'em
1-701-555-8745

CHAPTER THIRTEEN

It was a typical Saturday morning inside JFK airport as Emily bumped her way through the plethora of travelers, thankful that *she* wasn't the one doing the traveling this time. Between people getting ready to start vacations and the upper-class business moguls leaving for business trips, the entire building was crawling with people.

It wasn't until close to 9:00 am when she finally entered the Arrivals area, stopping next to a souvenir trolley.

Emily looked up at the large flashing monitor, standing cross-armed in front of it to ensure everything was running smoothly.

"Flight 180: Bismarck, North Dakota to New York, New York – Arrival – 9:05 am – On time"

Emily lowered herself into a small set of adjoining seats just outside the area with the conveyor belts, shifting from one butt cheek to the other in order to get comfortable. She barely knew Maggie, and the fact that Maggie had been so eager to come to New York, even though Emily had only provided half the details about the reason why, was eating at her. She would've disclosed all of the dangerous details over the phone, or with a text even, but she felt the information was too sensitive and preferred to provide it face to face.

Absolutely nothing about the upcoming trip was going to be safe. It would involve determination, hard work, and skill. She wasn't even fully prepared herself, so she knew she couldn't expect her teammates to be either.

Emily had begun to run scenarios of how the conversation might go, when the double doors opened, allowing a wave of bodies to enter the waiting area.

She sprang to her feet, standing on her tiptoes while erratically shifting her head from side to side to get a better view over the crowd.

Eventually, two orange, wispy updo buns came bobbing over a man's shoulder, their frizziness looking like a bad case of bedhead. Because of Maggie's short stature, it took a moment for her to come fully into view.

Emily raised her arm above her head, moving it in a wide waving motion. She could see Maggie's face light up with glee when she finally noticed Emily, running forward with a suitcase trailing from each hand, before letting them go to fling her arms around Emily's waist.

Emily had no choice but to hug back.

"Eek! You have no idea how excited I am that you called me!" Maggie shrieked.

For such a small woman, you're awfully loud.

"It's nothing," Emily said. "I'm just glad you could make it."

"Are you kidding me? I wouldn't miss this trip for anything!"

Emily grabbed one of the bags and helped wheel it to the airport parking lot, while Maggie peppered her with an endless barrage of questions about New York; apparently, she had never been.

"I'm sorry, Maggie, but we don't have much time for the touristy activities, at least not right now."

"Oh, that's okay!"

Arriving back at Emily's condo, Maggie dropped her bags just inside the entrance, awe-struck with admiration, her head swiveling from side to side.

"This is laid out a lot better than my one-bedroom back home!" Maggie gushed. "Sheesh."

Emily showed Maggie to the room she would be using for the next few days, directly across the hall from her own.

"Here," Emily said, extending her hand. "Take this spare key. That way, you can come and go as you please while you're here. Just, don't mess anything up—so to speak."

Emily turned and checked her cell phone yet again, the hundredth time that day.

Still no message from Seth.

She didn't even know if he checked his messages frequently, so at this point, her assumption was that he wasn't coming.

As she watched Maggie start to unpack, her stomach remained cramped and knotted, waiting for the right opportunity to explain everything.

It was then that a knock rattled the front door. Emily left the spare bedroom, leaving Maggie to empty her suitcase while she went to answer the door.

Graham had arrived holding two thick black cases. He carried them directly into the other spare room and flung them down onto the mattress.

As much as Emily wanted to do things on her own, she certainly wasn't stupid. With the Recreant Order lurking, she needed someone like Graham on her side for protection. After a lengthy talk with Peyton over the course of that week, they had decided it would be a good idea for him to tag along to provide just that. Meanwhile, Peyton had taken their son, Riley, and headed to Vermont, to provide a little extra protection for their mother in case the Order paid her another call.

Snapping the clasps on the cases, Graham opened them to reveal a copious amount of weapons and ammunition, all delicately laid among rigid foam padding.

"Whoa, whoa, whoa!" Emily did a quick double take over her shoulder, then moved into the room and quickly closed the door behind her. "You have to hide those!" she whispered.

"Why? What's the matter?" Graham said, furrowing his brow.

"I haven't *exactly* explained all the details to Maggie yet, and she's only in the next room."

Graham huffed irritably and shook his head, aggressively closing the cases again.

"Well, you'd better tell her soon before she catches me cleaning a rifle in the kitchen."

Emily playfully rolled her eyes and shuffled her way back down the hallway to Maggie, who had folded all of her clothing away. With her two laptops propped up on the dresser, she seemed busy enough that the tense conversation next door had gone unheard.

"All settled in, I see?" Emily asked, leaning against the doorway.

Maggie hauled herself to her feet and moved closer to Emily, staring up at her with innocent, sea-green eyes. "So then, what's the plan?"

There it was. The Question. The one that activated the nervous knot in Emily's stomach again. She was already visualizing her new friend storming off after all was revealed, but ultimately it had to be done. There was no point in delaying the inevitable.

Emily jerked her neck in a motion to lead Maggie out into the living room, introducing her to Graham, who was already sitting on the sofa in wait. She stood at the front of the living room, staring back and forth between her stern brother-in-law and the giddy redhead.

Her voice failed her.

As she searched for the right words to lead with, her lips produced nothing, saved only by a second firm knock on the door. The welcomed distraction drew her from Maggie and Graham's expectant stares. As she opened the door, she froze in disbelief in the entranceway.

"What's the matter?" Seth said as he eagerly brushed past Emily into the condo with his usual smug grin smeared across his face. "Didn't think I'd make it? I never get any credit, do I?"

He dropped his luggage in the middle of the room, then turned to lift Emily off the ground in a bear hug, spinning her in circles. She could tell he was showing off, but she couldn't help but notice the strength of his grip.

He placed her back on her feet, resting his hands above her hips for a fleeting moment before turning to shake Graham's hand in introduction.

Maggie stood abruptly, primping her hair and patting her clothes to adjust the wrinkles. She had just seen the man and was already ogling him; that was until she noticed Emily giving her a very unimpressed look, to which she retracted back into her chair with a shy smile.

"So, what's with all the secrecy?" Seth said as he slouched into the nearest chair, throwing his feet onto the coffee table. "You have piqued my interest, Emily Owens, now don't let me down."

Maggie remained secretly focused on Seth, turning repeatedly to Emily and raising her eyebrows to signal her approval. Emily, on the other hand, kept biting at her index fingernail trying to conceal her audacious smile.

"Okay. Okay," Emily whispered under her breath. "You can do this."

She took a short breath in through her nose, and let a deep exhale out through her mouth.

No more excuses.

She looked around the room at the three people before her, all of them staring back at her with vivid intent.

It's now or never, Em.

Over the course of the next several hours, Emily went into great detail on the events leading to this meeting. Peru, the Recreant Order, the Florentine Diamond. She withheld nothing. She even disclosed the background of her father's training, wanting to be as transparent as possible with her team from the get-go. She knew the key to any team's success was trust, and that if it was broken early on, then she would lose them all.

As her spiel came to a close, Graham was the only person not sitting stock-still. His attendance, at this point, was strictly observational. Seth looked a little shocked but intrigued all the same, while Maggie, on the other hand, looked fearful, just as Emily suspected she would.

Emily nervously brought her hand to her face while she waited for their retort.

Nothing?

There was utter and absolute stillness from all parties.

It wasn't until Maggie started to fumble through her jacket that the uncomfortable silence was broken. She hauled her inhaler from her pocket and jammed it to her lips. Two quick presses followed by a large breath in stopped her from hyperventilating. She then stood and paced along the edge of the sofa.

"I don't think I can do this. I don't think I can do this. What if we get killed? Or worse?!"

Emily didn't know what could be worse than getting killed, but she needed to somehow calm Maggie down.

"Yeah, Em. I dunno about this," Seth chimed in shortly after. "I'm all in for a good treasure hunt, but this sounds dangerous—even by my standards."

She was losing them faster than anticipated. She needed to rope them back in.

Emily turned to Graham with a pleading look on her face, but he just sat there, shrugging his shoulders with nothing to add.

"Nope, I'm out!" Maggie shouted, jittering. "I ... I ... I can't."

"Guys, I knew this would be a lot to take, but I honestly wouldn't have invited you here if I didn't think I *needed* you for this. This could be one of the greatest achievements of our lifetimes!

"Seth, you posted about it online yourself—you were looking for your next big adventure. Imagine unlocking the secrets of the past, untouched by anyone in recent times.

"And Maggie, the Florentine Diamond has been lost for centuries. It deserves to be discovered. Your career in explosive mining would literally blow up with your name attached to its discovery—no pun intended.

"The diamond needs to be found by the right people. It needs to be found by us.

"The Order has proven that they will stop at nothing to find the diamond. If they get their hands on it … if they harness the army—should the legends be true—they may as well be unstoppable. We have the opportunity to stop them before they go too far, and I believe the people in this room, working together, can do that."

Emily closed her eyes and hung her head, waiting for a brash response.

Again, stillness.

"Okay, I'm in," Maggie's voice squeaked from across the room.

Emily popped one eye open, seeing her friend seated once again.

"Well, I can't turn that kind of superhero speech down, I suppose now, can I?" Seth leaned back, sprawling his arms along the back of his chair.

Emily's other eye sprang open now too, as a look of disbelief came over her.

Have I really done it?

After a short frenzy of laughter followed by tears of joy, she thanked everyone in the room, making her way around to hug them all. She knew that total, brutal honesty up front had been the right choice.

Standing in the presence of these very talented individuals, all unique in their own ways, really gave her a sense of pride. But potentially putting them all in harm's way was selfish, which would constantly be in the back of her mind, making her feel uneasy.

"Well, everyone," Emily continued, "it's getting a little late. Might I suggest we get some rest? We have a lot to do over the coming days in preparation for the trip. It's wings up in four days."

In the days leading up to their departure, the goal was to try and get in as much training as possible, to have everyone be able to at least defend themselves if put in a less-than-desirable situation.

Every morning after breakfast, they headed to Gabrielle's gym for some hand-to-hand combat lessons with the owner herself, another person Emily had to disclose everything to in an attempt to right her wrongs. Once Gabrielle knew her friend's motivations for getting mixed up with the Recreant Order, she let the team train in her gym, even during the renovations.

Gabrielle would be waiting every day at dawn, ready to show the women her best techniques and takedowns: hammer strikes, groin kicks, elbow strikes—all moves anyone could use for self-defense, even against the largest of opponents.

Graham was tasked with teaching Seth some brute fighting moves that would prove useful if ever in close quarters: knee strike, throat punch, ax stomps—all ways to finish an opponent quickly and smoothly. Of course, three days was not enough time to *fully* prepare any of them to go hand to hand with trained combatants, but at this point, it was better than nothing.

In the afternoons, they headed for Emily's favorite gun range located near Greenwich Village. This fell under Graham's umbrella of training as well, who brought most of his weapons along so everyone could get a handle on them and see how they felt. He provided lessons on how to grip the guns, aim them, and how to contain their recoil.

Seth had done some hunting with his grandfather in his youth, but had never used artillery like these military-grade products before. And Maggie, well, she had never so much as seen a pistol in real life, let alone shot one. Her tiny wrists floundered with every bullet she fired, to the amusement of the others.

Emily watched from the sidelines, seeing each individual grow from rookie to teammate, helping one another to learn and progress. She was wholeheartedly happy with her selections, each person an adequate fit for the journey ahead.

As the sun set on the third and final training day, the group had collectively decided it was time to head back to the condo building and freshen up. Their bodies were tired from the fighting, and their hands sore from the grips of the guns. As an added reward for their tireless efforts, Emily had made reservations at a nearby restaurant for a night out before the mission, her treat.

After Emily was finished showering, she made her way toward the living room while wrapping her damp hair in a towel. She was going to let Seth know that the shower was free, but slowing at the corner, she found him prodding around her living room, making his way from wall to wall, seemingly admiring all of her achievements that were on display.

He picked up an old photo of Emily as a little girl smiling with her family.

"What are you doing?" Her voice broke the silence.

"I, um …" He started fumbling with the picture frame before placing it back down. "Just admiring your, um … work."

Emily was wearing a white satin bathrobe. She smiled as she tousled her hair with the towel, walking over to where he was standing to pick up the frame herself, staring at it intently.

"Those were simpler times, it seems," she said softly, more to herself than to him.

She returned the picture frame to the cabinet then walked over to the linen closet, fully aware that Seth hadn't stopped sizing her up since she entered the room.

Raking her hands over the towels, she pinched the lacey slit of her robe to hug the curves of her breasts, her chest still covered with beads of water from the shower's steam. Bending over to grab a facecloth from the lower shelf, she could see him watch her from the corner of his eyes as she projected the silhouette of her body through the gown. She was toying with him now, for her own enjoyment as much as his.

Shutting the bifold doors of the closet, the feeling of a re-kindled sexual tension between them was obvious until she approached him and shoved the towels hard into his abdomen.

"Go get cleaned up," Emily demanded, smirking devilishly as she headed into the next room.

Inside, Maggie was sitting in front of the mirror drying her hair. Emily flung her towel on the floor and began brushing the knots out from her own hair. It was nice to have another girl in the house for a change.

Just as Maggie shut the hairdryer off, Emily heard her cell phone ringing from her bedroom. She sprang from the bed and ran to grab it from her dresser.

"*Incoming Call – Dad*"

"Hey, what's up?" Emily asked excitedly.

"Just checking in to make sure we are all ready for tomorrow."

"We sure are. Everyone's very anxious to get started. You said to meet you at the airport at 3:00 pm right?"

"That's correct. When you get there, head to the east wing. Pull your vehicle through the gated area and I'll be waiting for you there. Once we load your equipment onto the plane, we should be able to take off shortly after."

"Did your friend's equipment arrive yet?"

He was referring to two large crates that had shown up on Emily's doorstep the day prior, delivered directly by courier and marked "Dangerous Goods." Maggie had explained what was in them, but she had lost Emily somewhere between lithium-ion and nitroglycerin.

"Yes, they did. They're here in my condo."

"Sounds perfect." There was a pause before he continued. "Toots, I only ask you this because I'm your father, but are you sure you're ready to do this? Once you go down this road, there may be no coming back. Are you prepared for the fallout?"

She paused for a moment, replaying his question in her mind.

"I'm ready," she replied confidently.

"I thought so. Goodnight, Toots. I love you. See you in the morning."

"I love you too. 'Night, Dad."

She walked back over to her nightstand and plugged her phone in to charge. After doing so, she turned around and found that Seth had left the ensuite door ajar, from which a faint cloud of steam was billowing.

She knew she shouldn't peek, but her curiosity got the best of her.

She crept toward the door to get a better view, gently grabbing the knob and pushing the door open just a little bit more.

The light from the bathroom was brighter than expected, forcing her to retreat into the shadows of her bedroom. Still, she could see him behind the glass shower panes as trickles of water dripped down his hard, naked body.

His core was solid and defined, dusted with a thin layer of hair that stretched upward to broaden across his chest. He was running the shampoo through his thick black locks, causing his biceps to flex unintentionally.

Emily was finding it both cruel and unfortunate that the condensation on the window had blocked her view from his waist down.

Her fingers slowly began to trace the inside edge of her robe, sliding ever so gently along her bust. The more he lathered his body, the more aroused she became, biting her bottom lip so hard that it was turning pale.

She stepped closer in hopes of getting a good judgment of his manhood, when the hardwood creaked beneath her feet.

Her eyes widened as Seth perked at the noise.

She took a soft step backward, slinking farther into the darkness of her room.

He turned, bobbing his head to peer out of the slit of the open bathroom door. Dismissing it a few seconds later, he turned back toward the showerhead and continued to rinse.

Closing her eyes, Emily let out a small sigh of relief that she hadn't been caught, when suddenly another creak of the floorboards echoed through the room.

She spun her head around, her wet hair smacking across her face.

"What are you doing?" A shrill voice came from a figure standing in the entrance to the bedroom.

Emily had no idea how long Maggie had been standing there, nor did she want to know.

She blushed, quickly tightening the crease of her robe to cover any cleavage that may be showing.

"I ... um ... was talking to my father about the dick ... I mean the *trip*! The trip tomorrow, that we are taking ... yes."

Emily's face had now turned as red as Maggie's hair.

Their eyes remained locked, each waiting for the other to say something, anything, before a loud blurt of laughter shot across the room, followed by Emily joining in. Both of them darted from the bedroom as Emily giddily grabbed Maggie's arm, diving back into the guest room and slamming the door behind them.

As suspected, a knock followed just minutes later.

Emily opened the door to find Seth standing shirtless and wearing nothing but his sweatpants, vigorously rubbing his head with a towel.

"Graham and I will be ready in ten if that works."

"Certainly." Still giddy, Emily turned to Maggie with a concealed smile, then back to Seth. "We'll meet you in the lobby."

At the restaurant, the team spent the evening catching up and getting to know one another a bit better. Even though Emily and Graham were family, Emily still felt somewhat estranged, especially since she had found out about her father's and his working relationship. She was looking forward to getting to know him a little bit better now that their relationship was no longer muddled by secrets.

Seth and Emily had a lot to catch up on as well. Their days in university together seemed like eons ago, and life had taken them both in quite opposite directions. And Maggie, being the newest to them all, seemed to have a never-ending well from which to draw stories, which was welcomed whenever an awkward silence kicked in.

As the night came to a reluctant close, Maggie turned out to be a little drunker than she had let on. Graham slung her arm around his neck, assisting her on the walk back to the condo. Emily was hoping the fresh air would help to bring her around.

Once they made it off the elevator, he chivalrously picked Maggie up in his arms and carried her the rest of the way into Emily's condo, escorting her into her bedroom. He returned seconds later, shaking his head, unsmiling, and headed straight to his own room without so much as a "goodnight."

Emily and Seth were left standing alone in the hallway, just outside her bedroom door. He grabbed her by the hand, lifting his other hand to her face, caressing her cheek with his thumb. Emily wasn't sure what *he* thought was going to happen, but *she* wanted to ensure he was prepared and focused for the days ahead.

Leaning his elbow against the doorframe, he seemed to be playing a flirtatious game of cat and mouse, as if he was waiting for something.

"Thank you for coming," Emily said. "This means a lot to me."

He stared at her, his eyes fixated on hers, as if he were trying to convey all the words he hadn't said that night, just by looking at her.

"Whenever you need me, just name the time and place. I'll be there." He broke into a pearly white smile, still searching her eyes. "All you have to do is ask. Goodnight, Em."

He leaned from the doorway and kissed her hard on the cheek.

She closed her eyes, frozen in the moment, only to open them again as his lips moved away from her face. Stepping backward into her room, she started to close the door, but at the last moment, she poked her head around the doorframe and with a devilish grin, said, "Oh, and by the way ... I hope you enjoyed the little tease earlier."

"Umm ... what?"

She winked at him as she shut the door, leaving him standing alone and slack-jawed in the hallway.

Seth Parish, speechless? There really is a first time for everything.

CHAPTER FOURTEEN

Thick, intertwining clouds of dust trailed behind the two vehicles as they pulled onto the tarmac of Teterboro Airport. Graham and Seth were in the first, driving toward the plane in an SUV that carried the large cases of equipment for the trip. Following closely behind in the second vehicle were Emily and Maggie, shuttling everyone's luggage. As they pulled around the side of the aircraft, Emily's father could be seen standing at its rear, next to the open ramp to the cargo hold.

Once parked, the men jumped out and began to unload their vehicle, grabbing a handle each as they brought box after box straight on board the plane. Emily, however, started off by giving her father a warm hug, who then offered to help her walk the smaller pieces of luggage through the side door of the plane and stow them safely overhead.

Maggie, on the other hand, was a little slower to join the others, rubbing her temples. Thankfully, her transition lenses were doing their job to keep the brash light from her eyes, as the liquor had done a number on her the night before; she was still paying for it though. Emily watched Maggie from inside the plane, hunched by the rear wheels of the SUV, puking up the remains of her amaretto sours.

Oh Mags, that must be one nasty hangover.

"I could use a co-pilot," Emily's father said as he stepped through the door of the cockpit, drawing Emily back with a wave.

She looked at him and brightened, knowing the fourteen-hour flight would give them more than adequate time to talk. Besides, she had gotten a little rusty behind the wheel; it had been years since she had co-piloted with her father. As a teenager, he had taught her everything he could about flying, even letting her take the controls a couple of times, but always as long as he was in the passenger's seat, never solo.

"So, how did Mom take the news of your double life?" Emily asked, smirking as she plopped into her seat. "C'mon, spill it."

He just stared at her with narrowed eyes and a grin, alluding to the fact that it was probably one hell of an unresolved argument. Emily looked back at the rest of the team readying to take their seats, then she turned back to her father.

"Your mother and I will be fine. And hey, bringing you on this trip means that I don't have to sleep on the downstairs sofa for another night, right?"

They laughed as the propellers began to churn, the metal sheeting vibrating beneath their feet. With a dash forward and a pull of the throttle, the plane began to lift, soaring onward through the sky above New York City and out over the ocean.

From her seat in the cockpit, Emily could see that Maggie remained in a supine position for the first few hours of the flight, clutching a bottle of water in one hand and a barf bag in the other. Seth and Graham, on the other hand, moved about the body of the plane, loading bullets into their appropriate clips and making sure their navigation tools were organized and updated.

It wasn't until about three quarters of the way through the flight that Emily noticed her friend finally starting to come around. It was weird for Maggie not to be her perky little self, but once she seemed to get a grip on her hangover, she managed to get up and move about the plane.

Without speaking to anyone, Maggie grabbed her laptops from the overheard compartment then opened them on a nearby table. Next, she wheeled over one of her crates and cracked it open. It contained multiple antennae and transmission wires, which she began hooking into her computers.

Maggie removed a foam pad from the crate and continued to rummage, her eyes focused and stern with concentration. It was a new side of her that the others hadn't experienced yet.

She began to haul what appeared to be vials of chemicals and various canisters out onto the table, spreading them out in front of her.

"Hey, Maggie! Are you sure that's safe to do on a moving aircraft?" Graham shouted from the rear, making sure to be heard over the hum of the engine.

She turned, slowly bringing her finger to her lips to hush him, then turned back to her work. She mixed and matched different chemicals, powders, and ingredients to create her explosives, categorizing them from smallest to largest along the table.

As time passed, Emily became more and more intrigued, eventually unbuckling herself from her seat in the cockpit to make her way back to Maggie's work station.

"So, what have we got here?" Emily asked curiously.

Maggie finally cracked a smile, working her way down the line while lifting each product to illustrate its use.

"This little guy right here is nothing more than your average grenade." She was holding a small device, approximately the same shape and size as a cigarette lighter. "I've modified it so we can adhere it to a surface if necessary, then detonate it from afar.

"This next one is a special type of pipe bomb, my own blend." She lifted a piece of galvanized conduit, secured with two caps on either end and a trailing wire fuse. "We would use this style of device if we had to place the explosive in a hole or a crack in a rock, to break it open from the inside out."

Emily was enthralled listening to her friend explain these foreign objects to her, taking each one in her own hands to admire it.

"And what about those ones down there?" Emily pointed to the far edge of the table. She was asking about the malleable composition encased in a dark green film.

"I call those our 'just-in-case bombs,'" Maggie said with a wide smile.

Emily gave her a quizzical look.

"Well, I figure if we get into some trouble with the Recreant Order, we'll need something to stop their vehicles before they get a chance to chase us, you know, like in the movies. I made sure these babies had enough power to do so. Hell, they could probably blow up a whole building! Wanna hold one?" She jutted the explosive in Emily's direction, causing her to take a few steps back.

"I don't think I'm quite comfortable doing that just yet."

"Oh, come on!" Maggie insisted. "It can't detonate without a shockwave, silly."

Suddenly, a hand snatched the explosive from Maggie's grasp, tossing it in the air like a juggler.

"Well, well. Not too shabby, Miss Riggs," Emily's father interjected. "Made a few of these myself back in the day, although not with this much workmanship, I must say. Good job!"

He tossed the explosive back in the air for Maggie to catch, then sat down with the other two men who were listening intently to the women's conversation.

"Okay. Now that everyone is vertical and mobile, Maggie, did you get those reports I asked you to find?" Emily said.

"One step ahead of the game," her father laughed. "I've taught you well, it seems."

Maggie had already scampered over to one of the laptops and begun vigorously striking the keyboard.

"Emily has advised me that we should always know our enemy before ever setting foot on the battlefield. A few days ago, I started to do some digging into the hierarchy of the Recreant Order."

Emily made her way over to Maggie. "And what did you find?"

Everyone else was standing now as well, crowding around the computer screen as Maggie began to go through a list of photographs and profiles she had collected, providing a commentary on each.

"So, I've determined that the Order members that you ran into in Peru are a part of the Recreant Order's core leadership team," Maggie said directed at Emily. "The older gentleman who you mentioned was bossing everyone around, his name is Jonah Valerius. The lower members of the Recreant Order refer to him as 'Cardinal Valerius' or just 'the Cardinal.' He was a good guy once, a trusted member of the Society of Jesuits, up until sometime in early 2001. He killed two members of the Society before disappearing, presumably joining the Recreant Order instead. It's still unknown what made him go off the deep end."

Emily cringed at the sight of his face appearing on the laptop screen. Flashbacks from her trip began racing through her mind, but somehow, she couldn't bring herself to look away.

"This man is Dominik Novak. He has a criminal record in multiple countries, including Russia, Brazil, and Saudi Arabia. His past goes cold somewhere around 2016, which I've predicted to be when he was most likely recruited by the Order."

Emily crossed her arms and hung her head to hide her disgust, staring at the screen over her brow. *I can't believe I almost slept with this guy.*

"This woman is Alexandria Hale; goes by 'Alex.' While serving as a U.S. Marine, she was caught in the head by shrapnel during a ship attack near Syria. She was sent back to the United States, deemed unable to serve due to the effects of the injury.

"Unfortunately, she didn't see it that way. Months later, after what *she* felt was a long enough recovery, she was found stowed away on a naval ship trying to return to Syria. She was immediately dishonorably discharged, unable to work even a government desk job. My guess is the Order caught wind of this series of events and took her under their wing."

It was apparent by the looks on everyone's faces that Emily's whole crew were finally realizing how tough the people on the Recreant's payroll were.

"And this bulking specimen right here is Rico Mauga, the Recreant Order's 6'7" powerhouse. He immigrated to the United States at an early age from Samoa after his parents' passing. He spent his life getting transferred from foster home to foster home, eventually ending up as a cage fighter in Slovenia. He and Alexandria met after she was recruited by the Recreant Order, with my records showing that they are currently engaged."

Emily rubbed the side of her face, recalling the hard slap she had received from Alexandria when she had elbowed Rico. *Ahh, now that makes a lot more sense.*

"Last, but certainly not least, we have 'the Boar.'" Maggie brought up a stock photo of a blank figure on the screen.

"Where's the photo?" Emily asked abruptly, squinting through her confusion.

"Well," Maggie continued, "from what I can gather, he's also referred to as 'The Monarch,' meaning he's likely the highest member on the Order's totem pole. He's a ghost: no images, no background, no existence. All I was able to retrieve were several pings from somewhere in Rome during conversations between him and the Cardinal. I imagine that's where the Recreant Order's headquarters are. I'll continue to run traces on the crew. Maybe they'll slip up eventually; the bad guys usually do.

"So ... any questions?"

Everyone was silent. They all stepped away from the computer for a moment to try and absorb all the information that they had just been given.

"That will be all, Miss Riggs," Mr. Owens said, shaking her hand before making his way back to the cockpit for the remainder of the flight. "All right, everyone, prepare for landing."

The team began to secure the freight and take their seats, buckling in as the buzz of the landing gear released with the plane's descent.

Emily's father had booked a private landing strip at the Hosur Aerodrome in Tamil Nadu, located in the southern region of India.

Two large, grey SUVs had been arranged and were waiting on the tarmac for the team as they deplaned. Working together, they unloaded all of their equipment and luggage from the aircraft and placed it into the back of the rentals.

As Emily slid into the driver's seat of one of the vehicles, she realized her father hadn't followed them, but had instead remained on the plane. Raising her index finger to Maggie, she exited the vehicle once again and ran on board to check on him.

"What are you doing?" Emily asked. "Aren't you coming with us?"

"Unfortunately not, Toots. This is your adventure, your story." He raised his hand and pointed toward the vehicles. "Those people right there … *they* are counting on *you*. It's time you show them the leader I know you can be."

Emily nodded, then hugged her father tightly before walking back off of the plane.

"So, where will you go?" she called from the tarmac.

"I have a job to take care of west of here. Don't worry, it should only take a day or two. I'll call you afterward to check in."

He pressed a button inside the plane and the rear hatch began to close. They waved to each other as he disappeared out of sight. Before Emily even had a chance to make it back to her vehicle, the plane's engine had begun to rumble and her father had taken off from the airstrip.

This is it.

Emily was officially on her own. Not in a literal sense, but it was her first undertaking as the official leader of the group.

Climbing aboard her rig, she waved her cell phone at the other SUV, signaling for the men to pay attention to their devices. As they pulled out of the airfield gateway, Maggie had already opened her laptop from the passenger's seat and had connected herself to the team's electronics. She began transferring all the files and documents that they would need for their trip—profiles, pictures, videos, anything that could possibly hold a clue. She even included the Peruvian news articles covering the attack on Machu Picchu.

Emily drove ahead of the men. She had arranged the rental for a two-story villa located about three hours north of the landing strip. Full of windows and archways, the villa resembled a small mansion—it even had a large decorative fountain in the front, and lush hedges and concrete statues around its sides and rear.

By the time the vehicles pulled through the front gate of the villa, darkness had fallen, and Emily could tell her teammates were weary after almost twenty-four hours of travel. It would be morning before the next move could be made, regardless of how anxious she was to start hunting for the diamond. The way her teammates' shoulders slumped as they once again carted their luggage inside, indicated that beds would be in their near futures.

Emily, on the other hand, remained bright-eyed and bushy-tailed. Once unpacked, her anxiety and its equally matched excitement kept her awake, so she decided to take a stroll through the villa, admiring every square inch.

Upon returning to the second level, she gently peeked inside one of the bedrooms to find Maggie snoring beneath the covers. Walking farther along, she listened at a second door as Graham was ending a video call with Peyton and Riley, saying goodnight before going to bed himself.

But it was after a few minutes of peeking in the rest of the rooms that she realized there was no sign of Seth. His bags were strewn about one of the bedrooms, but he was nowhere to be found. She continued through the winding hallways, stopping near a sheer curtain that was blowing inward from one of the windows.

Turning the corner, she found Seth leaning on the clay railing of a balcony, overlooking the rear garden while sipping from a bottle of beer. She couldn't see his face, but his posture and body language in the light of the full moon led her to believe that he was deep in thought about something.

She walked up behind him, bending down to retrieve a beer for herself from the ice bucket at his feet.

"Nervous for tomorrow, are we?" Emily asked playfully, hoping to get a rouse.

He didn't answer right away. Instead, he continued to stare off in the distance, tipping the bottle back for another swig.

Emily's stomach began to sink at his lack of response. He was always in a good mood, but his extended silence told her otherwise.

"Why this?" Seth said sharply, causing the beer to foam from Emily's mouth.

"Excuse me?" she said.

He turned his head toward her, his face cloaked with disappointment.

"Why did it take a trip halfway around the world—on some wild goose chase to find a diamond—for you to start talking to me again?"

Emily's heart buzzed inside her chest.

He had made a valid point, and regrettably, she had no idea how to answer him. There wasn't a particular reason for her distance over the past year; it just sort of happened that way.

"You never reached out to me either, Seth," she retorted defensively. "Don't try to make me out to be the only one responsible here."

They faced each other now, both clenching their bottles as their voices continued to rise.

"After graduation, when I saw you off at the airport before your flight back to New York, you kissed me on the cheek and said you would never lose touch with me! I waited for a call or message, Emily—you knew how I felt about you back then ... everyone did. Let's not act like we both didn't see what was going on. You flirted just as much as I did. But hey, maybe I was the only one who thought it was leading somewhere ..."

He turned back to look over the balcony, leaving Emily's mouth gaping at his outpouring of emotion. She huffed at his gall, putting the bottle back to her lips for another gulp, gazing off in the same direction he was.

He's not wrong.

"I knew how you felt about me, but I also knew you had big aspirations in life, and I didn't want to be known as the girl that held you back from them. I also have my own life to lead—not that I've done anything with it up until now."

She laid her bottle on the railing and looked at him from the corner of her eyes. To her surprise, she could see that he was smirking.

She turned toward him, slapping him across the arm with the back of her hand.

"What's so funny?" she barked, shifting into an unintentional smile.

He turned to face her as well, throwing his head back and finishing what remained of his beer, still smirking as he peered at her from around the bottleneck.

She went for another backhand on him, but he caught her by the wrist.

He laid his bottle on the rail beside hers, easing his grip while still ensuring that she couldn't pull away, holding her as if she had been snared.

Emily made no attempt to free herself from his grasp. Instead, she watched his eyes gaze upon her body in the pale blue moonlight. His pupils traced from her legs to her stomach, eventually landing in a locked position with her own as both of their expressions dropped from silly grins to more suggestive stares.

Seth pulled her wrist with a jerk, causing her to stumble forward into his arms. They stood nose to nose, his warm breath soothing against her skin. His jaw dropped ever so slightly, his bottom lip grazing along hers. His hands, tightening around her waist, edged below the waistband of her shorts.

Emily draped her arms around his neck, crossing them behind his head as she looked up through her lashes. His bottom lip rubbed against hers again, but this time, she met it with her tongue.

As if reading her mind, Seth's fingers dug into Emily's lower back and pulled her in, closing the final few inches between their bodies before locking his lips with hers.

Like two animals unable to control themselves, her hands became entangled in his hair, their mouths coming together like two opposite waves of an ocean. He spun her around, their bodies banging against the wooden shutters as their tongues forcefully swirled together.

He lifted her from her feet and pressed her hard against the cement wall, cupping his hands around her thighs for leverage. At the same moment, she wasted no time reaching down to viciously undo his shirt, ripping at the last three buttons holding it together and sending them pattering across the balcony. Her legs clenched around his hips as she pressed herself along his body.

Seth swiftly spun her from the wall and carried her a few short steps through the darkness, sitting her on the balcony's railing. The loud shatter of glass echoed from below, interrupting their kissing.

Both broke out into hysterical laughter, realizing that they had knocked their bottles down to the stone walkway below, hoping that they hadn't disturbed the others.

Dismissing the interruption just as quickly, they again stared at each other without saying a word.

Is this really going to happen?

She tugged at his shirt, pulling it halfway down over his shoulders as she kissed his chest.

He reached for the top button of her shorts, releasing it from its hold.

"Emily! Emily!" A voice shrieked from the hallway.

It was followed by a sharp, continuous beeping that was getting louder with every running footstep.

Seth lowered Emily to her feet from the railing. They were still putting their clothes back together as Maggie bounced around the corner. She was distraught and out of breath, holding one of her laptops open in her hands as Graham followed shortly behind, pulling a t-shirt over his head.

"What's wrong?" Emily asked.

"I've been running scans for any activity on the Recreant Order's leadership team—news reports, police scanners, basically anything that could give us the upper hand.

We must be on the right trail because I was notified that Rico just went through security at an airport in Italy. The flight itinerary shows that he's on his way here, and I don't think he's alone."

The teammates looked around at one another. They had no idea if Rico was coming for them, or if they were just chasing the same lead. Either way, this wasn't the news Emily wanted, leaving her to come up with a new plan, and fast.

"Okay ..." Emily's eyes shifted about the ground, searching for the right words to say to the others. "Well, at least we know he's coming, which is probably one step ahead of what he knows about us. But something tells me the others won't be far behind, if they haven't already found a way to get here without us knowing about it.

"Let's all just get some sleep, and in the morning, we can start hitting up the towns and temples as planned. If the diamond has been here, someone will have to know about it."

Everyone nodded in agreement. Maggie and Graham turned to make their way back in the direction of their rooms, leaving Emily and Seth alone on the balcony once again. She turned to see him staring at her with a caged, yet intimate aggression.

He made another advance, only this time, she politely stopped him by placing her hands on his chest.

"We *all* need to get some sleep," Emily said. "I'm sorry."

Seth smiled and nodded, then turned to saunter his way back to his room.

She listened for the thud of his door closing, followed by the clasp of the lock. She re-buttoned her shorts, turning once again to face the rear garden. She reached down to retrieve another beer from the bucket, pressing the cold glass firmly against her forehead.

Lowering the bottle to the balcony's railing, she twisted its cap with the bottom of her shirt and took a long, drawn-out sip.

"Seth Parish, what *are* you doing to me?"

CHAPTER FIFTEEN

The next morning, Emily left her bedroom and headed straight to the kitchen. From the upstairs hallway, she peered over the railing into the open-concept space below, finding that Seth had already beaten her to it. Coming down the winding staircase, she could see he had several maps and documents spread out on almost every inch of the available counter space.

Oh! Old school treasure hunting. I like it.

He was studying the documents intently, leaning over them with one hand placed on the counter while holding a peach with the other.

"Good morning," he said, taking another bite of his fruit, its juices foaming around his beard and mustache.

"Good morning, back," she replied.

The sexual tension still lingered from the night before, and yet, somehow, she knew that now was not the right time to discuss it. Today was a workday.

She grabbed the pot of coffee Seth had prepared beforehand and poured herself a mug. She approached where he was standing and bent over the maps as well, trying to figure out what exactly his game plan was.

"So, what are we thinking?" Emily asked, hoping all these papers had a purpose.

"Well, I was up most of the night going over the history of the Florentine Diamond you provided. As you noted last week, the history does indicate an Indian king who ruled the Vijayanagara Empire. Now, I've gone back centuries reviewing the old war histories of the Empire, hoping to find some sort of clue, and it seems that our best bet is to travel north toward Hampi, which is where the largest collection of temples from the Vijayanagara era is located. But first, we should check out the other temples along the way and see if they hold any clues."

He brushed away a few unnecessary documents before slapping a map of the Karnataka region in front of her, already filled with numerous jot notes in red ink marked along its margins.

"According to my research, there are about ten temples within a 30-minute radius of Hampi, each fitting the given criteria and time period of the diamond's known history."

Emily's eyes scanned back and forth across the pages.

Seth's smart. He wouldn't choose these locations if he didn't do his homework.

Upstairs, another door creaked open.

Graham emerged from his room, dressed in dark grey cargo pants with a black, three-quarter sleeve top, ready to greet the day. He had just finished clipping his handguns into his brown leather, double-shoulder holster as he joined them downstairs.

"Someone looks dressed to kill," Emily commented.

"The day is young," he replied, heading over to the coffee pot. "Do we have our coordinates?"

Seth slid the map across the countertop, double tapping the red dot of Hampi with his index finger.

Graham simply stared down at it, sipping his coffee and nodding. "So, is anyone going to wake the redhead?" he asked sternly. "We're losing daylight."

Emily rolled her eyes, removing herself from her stool.

"Maggie! You awake?" she yelled, trotting back up the staircase. "We have to get ready to go!"

Emily pushed open the door and peeked inside the room to find Maggie still asleep in her bed. She walked farther in to stand over her, watching as a faint trail of drool soaked a portion of her pillowcase. The blankets had been messed beneath her, and she had one leg flung outside the covers.

"Wake up, bitch!" Emily screamed, winding back and slapping Maggie's semi-revealed backside.

"Huh? Wha?" Maggie sprang up, disoriented, wiping away the fiery red hair that was stuck in the drool on her face.

"Get dressed. It's go time."

Graham had finished his coffee and was now rinsing his cup in the sink as the women finally emerged from their rooms, collected and dressed. Emily appeared first wearing beige khaki shorts, with a dark red, tight-fitting tank top, accompanied by a leather sheath strapped tightly around her right thigh, holstering her blade. Maggie followed promptly behind, sporting dark green capri pants and a loose, black crop top. Her tactical backpack was loosely slung over her shoulder, carrying her computers and any small explosives they may need on the fly.

As the three of them exited the front door, Seth had already packed up one of the SUVs for the day's journey. Sporting a dark blue t-shirt and off-white board shorts, he looked as though he had planned on going to the beach instead of searching for a long-lost artifact. The only useful article he was wearing was the holster strapped to his waist, concealing his handgun against his back.

Emily walked by him and glared, shaking her head with embarrassment before jumping into the back seat of the vehicle. Graham slid into the driver's seat, accompanied by Seth on the passenger's side, leaving Maggie to climb in the back to join Emily.

On their first day, one by one, the red circles Seth had circled on the route to Hampi were crossed off the map in sequence. All the temples they visited proved to be fruitless, showing nothing in relation to the diamond. Emily made sure not to let the failure of their first attempts get her down, understanding the fact that there were still many more temples to visit and explore.

By the middle of the second day, her patience was beginning to wear thin. Again, all the temples that they visited showed no sign of the Vijayanagara king, nor his army in the mist.

As they pulled away from yet another one of the temples surrounding the town of Hampi—again, a dead end—this time heading in the direction of the town of Hosapete.

Suddenly, Emily asked, "Has anyone noticed we haven't seen a single vehicle heading toward the temples? Wasn't it much more crowded this morning when we first set out?"

Graham shot Emily a concerned look in the rearview mirror, seemingly confirming that he had been in observation mode this whole time.

Graham reached for the vehicle's radio, turning the knob to adjust its volume.

The raucous sputter of an unknown dialect came over the speakers, repeating hysterically.

"What are they saying?" Maggie asked.

"Shhh, shhh," Graham motioned, raising his hand to cut her off. "It's Kannada. I learned some of it while I was here during a mission a few years back. I think … they're saying …"

Before he finished his sentence, he jerked the steering wheel furiously and whipped the vehicle around in the middle of the road.

"What's going on?" Emily screamed, digging her nails into the backrest for balance.

"The authorities have just declared a state of emergency. They've set up a roadblock outside of Hosapete. There have been reports of armed assailants, spotted around the Hampi temples. They're saying the local police force didn't have the firepower to stand up against them, so they've cut off city access until the military arrives. It just happened ten minutes ago, so by my calculations, the armed forces will be about an hour out. We've gotta move."

As the SUV sped through the domed gateway back into Hampi, a loud commotion could be heard coming from up ahead.

People were running and screaming. The streets had become crowded with both locals and tourists running in terror, so much so that Emily and her team were unable to get through.

Graham slammed the vehicle into park and everyone jumped out.

The four of them ran forward through the chaos, managing to break out into a small central portion of the town. Graham and Seth placed their hands on the grips of their pistols as dust clouds rolled across the roadways in front of them. People fled through the streets in all directions, while motorized bikes and scooters whizzed past them recklessly, beeping their horns to help move pedestrians from their paths.

Emily watched as a woman carrying a swaddled baby tripped and fell to the ground. With a stampede of people heading their way, Seth dropped to his knees and helped the woman up before she could be trampled.

Emily hurried to shove them both into a crevice between two buildings, motioning for Graham and Maggie to follow behind them. As everyone huddled in the small gap between the houses, the Indian woman continued to ramble and cry, oblivious to the fact that she had been hauled to safety.

"What's happening?" Emily yelled, placing her hands on the woman's shoulders trying to calm her. "Why is everyone running?"

The woman kept rambling; more Kannada.

"Men ... with guns. Heading for the temple," Graham repeated, trying to interpret.

Before they could get any more information out of her, the woman pushed Emily aside and rushed back into the street with her baby clutched tightly to her chest, leaving the team looking on as she joined the crowd and disappeared out of sight.

Seth crouched, urgently pulling his folded map from his back pocket and tracing his finger in the direction from which the crowd had been running. He then looked back up at the team.

"The Hazara Rama Temple. It's about 2 miles north-east of here," Seth said.

He folded the map again and stuffed it back into his shorts before unholstering his pistol. Graham removed both of his guns from their holsters as well, as the four of them hugged against the brick walls, looking for any sliver of clearance. They needed to get back to the vehicle, and luckily now that the crowd had subsided, a straight path back to the SUV had been left open.

Watching over one another's shoulders, they dashed through the open streets while the crackle of gunfire could be heard in the distance. Nearing the vehicle, Emily opened the back door to the SUV and shoved Maggie's head down, pushing her inside. The men slammed the front doors closed behind themselves, tossing their pistols onto the front dash right before Graham stepped on the gas, peeling off in the direction of the shots.

Shortly after passing the town's border, the winding road had transformed into an eerie desert, lifeless and desolate. The firing of bullets had stopped, and the flocks of pedestrians had made quick work of their getaway. As the SUV rolled onward, over hills and around bends, there were almost no signs of anything out of the ordinary.

Almost.

Graham stomped the brake pedal, sending the vehicle into a skid before stopping abruptly in the middle of the road. He nodded forward, motioning ahead so that the rest of the team could see what was lying in wait.

Two black SUVs were parked, crossed in front of one another to block the road while three armed men wearing black tactical gear dragged on cigarettes, preventing anyone from getting any closer to the temple.

"I say we plow through them in this baby," Seth said jokingly, slapping the dash. "We bought insurance … didn't we?"

"It'll never work," Graham said as he shook his head, confidently disregarding the comment. "Their weapons will rip through the vehicle before we even get close. This thing isn't bulletproof."

"Wait a minute!" Maggie shouted, unclipping her seat belt and leaning over the back seat into the rear hatch.

She started pushing over containers, rooting around half out of sight from the others. All they could see were two legs flailing about over the beige seats.

"Got it!" she yelled, falling back into her seat.

Maggie was holding a collapsed launching mechanism she had stowed away in one of her crates. Piecing it together, she slapped the latch to lock it, then fumbled around underneath her seat for the ammunition. Pulling out a small green canister, she clicked it into the chamber and snapped the trigger into place.

"This, to me, screams 'would you kindly move?'" She flashed a devilish grin. "Hopefully this will scare those baddies enough that they'll run away once their vehicles have been blown out of the way, and we can pass on through without a chase."

The rest of the teammates looked around at one another in uneasy agreement before Emily gave a slight nod to Graham, who grabbed the device from Maggie, insisting that he take the shot.

She doesn't need this burden on her conscience.

Seth got out of the SUV and moved around to climb into the driver's seat as Graham opened the sunroof and raised himself to stand on the middle console, shouldering the launcher.

He pounded the roof of the SUV, signaling for Seth to hit the gas.

The moment the vehicle began to pick up speed, the Recreant Order henchmen turned toward the approaching churn of gravel as the SUV barreled down the roadway. They pinched the cigarettes from their mouths and flicked the butts into the ditch, holding their hands to their brows to shield the sunlight. It took them all of three seconds to figure out that the SUV was heading straight for them, but before they had a chance to reach down and cock their weapons, Graham, who had them trained in his crosshairs, let Maggie's explosive device fly.

A loud bang followed by a large puff of smoke forced him to recoil while the rest of the team gasped, holding their breaths as the projectile coasted through the air with a light hiss. It struck the street just in front of the bumpers of the two overlapping vehicles, causing them to lift, flipping backward through the air before crashing onto their roofs. All three Order members attempted to dive into the adjacent ditch before the impact, but their actions were futile. The blast radius sent a cloud of flames outward that engulfed the men's bodies, propelling them across the dirt like discarded rags.

Seth hit the brakes once more, this time a few yards shy of the destruction the explosion had caused.

Everyone gawked at the bodies of the Recreants strewn across their path. Maggie, in particular, grabbed the backrests of the seats ahead of her and hauled herself forward. Emily knew she had never seen one of her devices used on another human being before, nor had she been prepared to.

Maggie's bottom lip began to quiver as her eyes welled with tears right before jutting her head into Emily's shoulder, sobbing heavily.

"Drive!" Emily commanded, her face fierce as she rubbed Maggie's back to comfort her. "I'm sorry, Mags. I should've said something …"

Graham hauled himself back down into the vehicle, throwing the steaming cylinder over his shoulder, onto the floor at the women's feet. He climbed into the front passenger's seat as Seth threw the vehicle into gear and headed farther along.

As they passed the wreckage, the crackling fire once again drew Maggie's face away from Emily's chest to gaze out the window at what remained of the Recreants and their vehicles. She cupped her hand over her mouth as tears streamed over her knuckles. One of the bodies lay motionless on the embankment, the man's face charred and peeling. The other two bodies had been reduced to mere parts, scattered along the road like a horrific human jigsaw puzzle.

Emily knew she should have been clearer about what her team could expect to happen on this trip. She had created a false impression for Maggie, one where her explosives would simply be used to scare the Recreants, not kill them. But now, the cards were on the table. Maggie had seen firsthand what her devices were capable of. She likely also realized that this was part of the reason that Emily had wanted her to be a part of the team—not just for her brain.

"Is she going to be okay?" Graham yelled as Maggie's body swayed with the bumps and turns of the road as they continued on. "It's only going to get worse from here. She knows that right?"

Maggie's bloodshot eyes winced as Emily grabbed her chin and turned her face back to meet her own. She looked into her eyes, trying to find the cheerful Maggie she knew inside.

"It's okay. Trust me ... it's okay."

Maggie seemed to absorb the words, but her reaction was minimal, weakly jerking her face away from Emily's hand.

"Listen to me!" Emily pulled her back again, trying to be a voice of reason. "When I was in Peru, I had to kill a man—several men—basically with my bare hands. I know what you're feeling. I know what it can do to a woman. It will pass, I promise."

Again, lies.

What had happened in Peru still ate at her to this day. She knew it would never pass. But she had to put on a brave front for her friend—if Maggie even still considered them to be friends after all of this was over.

"Just remember, if we don't kill them, they will not hesitate to kill us first. Do you understand me? Maggie—do you understand?"

"We're here," Seth shouted, snapping the women to attention before Maggie could muster an answer.

They all turned to look through the front windshield, their gazes met by a maze of walls surrounded by rubble lying about the ground. They had pulled up and parked underneath the branches of a low-lying tree, just outside the Hazara Rama Temple. It was a one-story structure surrounded by a brick wall, both of which were covered in carvings and man-made engravings. It was too difficult to examine the markings from afar, and by the looks of things, it would have to wait.

They were not alone.

Parked off to one side were two more vehicles like the ones they had just destroyed on the road. But these were empty.

Without a chance to contemplate their next move, a deep vibration shook the ground that sent huge dust clouds billowing up from the middle of the temple, venting through its arches and up into the air.

"C4," Maggie whispered, as if she knew just by the feel of it.

Seth and Graham grabbed their pistols from the dash and slunk out of the SUV, with Emily opening her door and sliding out as well, drawing her knife from its sheath. Maggie, however, remained inside, still paralyzed from the events prior, while the other three began to move in unison toward the temple's entrance.

But their advance was short-lived.

Getting no more than a few feet away from the SUV, five armed men rushed from the clouded entranceway. The men wildly fired their weapons in the team's direction, sending sand shooting up like tiny geysers as their bullets trailed behind Emily and her crew, forcing them to run for cover behind their vehicle.

Graham and Seth dove behind the front wheel well, as Emily ducked behind its rear. The ear-piercing clanks of metal followed them, as their enemies' ammo ripped into the body of the SUV.

Only when the gunshots subsided did Emily peer through the back window, looking at the movements and positioning of the shooters while they reloaded. It was then that she noticed that Maggie was still sitting upright in the back seat, carrying the same blank stare, completely unfazed by what was going on around her.

"Maggie, get out of there now!" Emily barked, attempting to stir her.

She didn't move.

The Order's henchmen snapped new clips into their guns and raised them again. This time, they were taking proper aim, squarely fixating their lines of sight on Maggie's head.

Before they pulled their triggers, Emily selflessly ripped open the door to reach up and roughly grab Maggie by her collar. With a large tug, she dropped the redhead to the dirt outside the vehicle, just as another streak of bullets pierced through the SUV.

The seats were shredded into wisps of cotton, as tiny shards of glass pelleted Emily's back.

Shit! It's only a matter of time before one of them hits the explosives in the back.

Graham leaned around the front of the vehicle, holding a pistol in each hand, while Seth stood above the hood and provided cover. Graham let out six fast shots, with one bullet hitting a Recreant squarely in the head, causing him to spiral to the ground.

In the background, Emily hauled Maggie from the dirt and leaned her against the back bumper of the SUV. Placing her fingers in her mouth, Emily whistled to the guys. Graham turned and under-hand tossed one of his guns in her direction. She snatched it out of the air, leaned around the rear tire of the vehicle, and fired two perfectly placed shots into the chest of another Recreant.

Two down, assholes.

Graham took another look over the bonnet. The Recreants were reloading for a third time while starting their advance. He flashed two fingers to the right, and a thumb to the left.

More shots began to fire from the Recreant's automatic weapons, popping the tires of the SUV, lowering it to the ground, hindering the team's cover.

"Maggie! Where are the grenades? What container are they in?" Emily screamed, trying to coax an answer from her friend.

More silence.

"Maggie!"

Seth stood and fired his pistol, catching one of the Recreants in the leg. This allowed Graham to fire more rounds and finish the job.

Three down, two to go.

Another clamor of shots circulated from the remaining Recreants.

The three active members of the team rose with their pistols all at once to retaliate. Firing relentlessly, their bullets connected with nothing, before the dull click of their guns indicated the chambers were empty. This left them no choice but to discard their weapons and cower behind the SUV once more.

"If my math is right, they're all out of ammunition too," Graham whispered.

"If you're *right*?" Seth repeated, unenthusiastic about his teammate's estimation.

Just as the words left his mouth, the Recreants' guns clattered against the ground, followed by heavy footsteps running toward the SUV. The first henchmen came around the back, grabbing Emily by the shoulders and tossing her to the ground. No sooner had her face bounced against the dirt, did Seth jump to her defense, tackling the Recreant into a scuffle on the ground.

Emily quickly recovered by tossing her knife to Seth, who caught it in his free hand and jammed it into the ribs of his assailant. He forced it deep inside as far as it would go, twisting it until the Order's henchmen became a slumped heap as he succumbed to the stab wound.

On the opposite end of the SUV, out of sight behind the front bumper, came repeated grunts and gargles, proceeded by the fading twitch of protruding legs.

Emily scrambled, thinking maybe it was her brother-in-law who was on the wrong end of the attack, but as she slid along the side of the vehicle's hood, she found herself pleasantly mistaken.

Instead, Graham was on his knees with the last Order member in a snug headlock. He looked up at Emily then jerked his arms, snapping the Recreant's neck before letting the body fall away. He wiped a small trail of blood from the corner of his mouth as he returned to his feet before instinctively walking back around to check on Maggie, like a lion protecting their cub.

"No bullet holes. She'll be fine," Graham mumbled. Much unlike their SUV, which now looked like a big hunk of swiss cheese.

As Emily and Seth brushed the dust from themselves, Graham walked on ahead toward the temple, clearing the area before he would approve of anyone moving further. He weaved in and around the temple's outer stone walls before disappearing into its hollow inner pathways.

Emily waited impatiently for his return, staring at her watch as the minutes ticked by. She paced back and forth, biting at her thumbnail until he finally emerged from under one of the archways, waving them onward.

"Emily, you're gonna want to come see this."

CHAPTER SIXTEEN

Emily grazed her hand along the walls of the Hazara Rama Temple, feeling the pictures depicted in the stones as she followed Graham. It was an old and magnificent structure, decorated with the portrayal of elephants, attendants, and horses, dating back to sometime in the 15th century.

Accompanying her close behind was Seth, who was trying to admire it just as much as she was. They had left Maggie in the parking lot, her body crouched into a ball at the base of a tree.

Emily came to a stop, eyeing the walls with deep concentration. They were filled with depictions of a horde of marching soldiers, all carrying spears and arrows, draped in what appeared to be primitive garb. She withdrew her phone from her back pocket, swiping to the photos of the Irisagrig tablets from Dr. Alsafar's exhibit. Opening one, she held it to the wall.

A perfect match. The shape and designs are unmistakable. There's even a clouded trail around the soldiers—could it be the mist?

"These pictures do not necessarily seem to depict the people of India," Seth said.

He neared her from behind, studying the display even more intently than she was.

"My thoughts exactly," Emily added.

He continued along the passageway, his brow protruding in his concentration. He wiped his forehead with his palm.

"If I apply what I've learned from my own research and the information you've collected, these images could certainly hold a very different perspective from what is currently known about the history of this region." He paused, taking a few steps back to get a better view of the images. "Here, for example," he said, pointing to a specific image. "This wall could very well tell of the great army of Vijayanagara. It appears to depict the arrival of a young peasant, who swept through the land with an army at his command. It appears that he overthrew the current king and then claimed the land for himself, thus assuming control of the Vijayanagara Empire."

I knew there was a reason I brought him along. He's good.

Seth continued around the corner of the wall, dipping and weaving along the artwork.

"And here could be the depiction of the new king and his army stealing from the people of the surrounding regions without mercy, quickly obtaining some of the greatest riches the world had ever seen. But over time, it seems as if he became paranoid, fearing that his people would turn on him to try and claim these great treasures for themselves.

"This next panel shows the king holding two stones. Perhaps this represents the duplication of the diamond; one with power, and one without. It appears that he then publicly sold one of the diamonds—presumably so that people would think that he no longer possessed so much power. Ironically, it appears as though this action also caused his downfall, as the true diamond was stolen shortly after the sale of the replica.

"With the neighboring regions knowing the king was now without the defense of his invincible army, it appears that they moved in and killed him in an act of revenge."

Seth turned around and looked Emily square in the face.

Both knew they were on the brink of unraveling the diamond's dark past.

"The legend has to be real!" Emily said. "It makes perfect sense now! The reason the Order hasn't found the Florentine Diamond yet is that, up until now, they've been following the trail of the replica diamond! The replica that the king created all those years ago. That must have been the diamond that was uncovered in Peru. The one that I had appraised and then was stolen!"

She threw her arms around Seth's neck, squeezing him for his efforts and assistance.

But their embrace was cut short.

A gunshot, followed by a loud moan, came from deep within the temple, as if someone was writhing in pain.

Emily and Seth fell away from each other and ran back to the entrance of the temple. Graham, who must have exited the temple from a different route, was already in the parking lot, forcefully hauling Maggie to her feet and over to join the others. Once regrouped, the team collectively made their way inside again, with Graham taking the lead, directing them toward what he had discovered earlier.

Another gunshot sounded from inside the temple, this time followed by a woman's grunt, faint and distant.

Reaching the innards of the temple, Graham pointed ahead to a large hole in the floor surrounded by fresh debris, which had been made directly in the center of four pillars within the monument.

This must have been the result of the blast we heard earlier.

Emily shook her head at the destruction of yet another historical site by the Recreant's incessant greed.

Crowded around the hole made by the blast, they could see a hidden staircase that led beneath the temple. A staircase that led to the source of the gunshots and echoing moans.

How did the Order even know that this was here?

Seth moved away from the hole to eye the pillars surrounding them. After studying their carved images, he said, "It appears that these four pillars represent four guardians ... who perhaps failed in their role?"

The teammates looked around at one another, then back at the hole.

"I'll go first," Graham instructed, letting go of Maggie to lower himself into the darkness of the pit.

One by one, the rest followed suit. First Maggie, then Emily, then Seth, slinking beneath the surface into the underground tunnelway.

Lit torches placed in sconces along the walls illuminated the tunnels as a light mist wafted itself along their feet. Emily was positive this had to be the mist from the stories, garnering hope that the diamond was drawing close.

Suddenly, Graham raised his arm to halt the team, pointing up ahead at what appeared to be two bodies lying face down on the ground, barely visible beneath the unnatural mist.

He waved only Emily ahead, and both of them crept in sync toward the dormant figures.

Standing idly over them, Emily examined the bodies to find that they were riddled with buckshot holes, likely corresponding to the emptied shotgun that had been discarded beside them. The blood was minimal, but the fatality was certain.

Graham stepped forward and used the toe of his boot to turn one of the bodies over.

It was a large man, draped in a royal-looking loincloth. His skin was pigmented a dark blue and he was barefoot. His long, coal-black hair had rough strands of silver. His physique was that of an ancient warrior, and he was still holding a bow in his stiffened hands.

Why is he here, underground?

Emily walked over to the other body, this one a woman, again, wearing nothing but a loincloth. The woman's skin, however, was instead laced with a yellow tone. Her ethnicity, although identical to the man's, was unrecognizable to Emily, who was unable to liken her features to a specific race.

Graham reached down to swat away the invading beetles that had begun to curiously approach the slain bodies and placed two fingers on the woman's neck to feel for a pulse. He looked up at Emily and shook his head. Both were dead.

"These people," Emily said, "they look like the people from the murals on the wall outside, wouldn't you say?"

She showed the photos to the team, holding the images above the bodies for reference.

"Impossible," Seth contended. "Those carvings are hundreds of years old."

"And what do you make of this?" Graham said, looking down at his fingers while rubbing them together. He had accumulated what appeared to be a sort of clay-like pigment from placing his hand on the dead woman's neck.

Seth walked over and inspected the substance on Graham's fingertips, smearing some on his own. He massaged it at first, then lifted it to his nose and smelled it.

"Is this …" Seth whispered. "Is this … paint?"

"War paint, perhaps?" Emily added, bending down to get a feel for herself.

Just then, another moan wailed from around the next corner, echoing through the tunnel.

The team perked up, with Graham once again taking the lead toward the source of the noise. Turning a corner, they could see a doorway up ahead that led into a well-lit chamber. A mist poured from its entrance like water flowing around the rapids of a river, filling the tunnelways.

More sounds of a struggle, followed by another hollow grunt.

Using a raised fist, Graham halted the team yet again.

Everyone fell quiet, listening. Nothing but the sound of heavy panting came from inside the chamber, and suddenly, the mist began to recede from around the team's feet, retreating back to its origin within mere seconds.

Something doesn't feel right.

The team proceeded, edging themselves along after the receding mist. Following it through the doorway, they discovered another female warrior, her skin painted a deep red, slumped against the wall with the shaft of an arrow protruding up through her jaw and piercing out the back of her skull. Farther inside, more torches were scattered about the room, revealing another four pillars, though there was still no sign of the diamond. The mist was all but gone, and Emily felt more exposed than ever.

A faint gurgling came from beside the team, drawing everyone's attention from the slain warrior on the left of the chamber to the ever-shifting shadows cast by the torches' flames. In those wavering shadows stood Rico Mauga, holding another blue-painted warrior by the throat, raising him from the ground.

Pulling a cell phone from his vest, Rico began taking photos of the markings on the inner walls of the chamber. He then shifted his thick head toward the huddled team, letting out an enraged growl before releasing the being in his grip to drop motionless to the dirt. As he turned the rest of his body to face them, a spear broken off at the handle, protruding through his right thigh was revealed.

Rico was once again adorned in black tactical gear, the same as he had worn in Peru, but luckily he showed no signs of having any weapons on him. That was until he reached down and gripped the wooden shaft of the spear with both hands and pulled it from his flesh without regard or hesitation. He flipped the spear around, holding it like a pointy club as he tucked the phone back into his vest.

"You're too late," Rico said convincingly. "We have what we need here."

Graham and Seth walked deeper inside the room, circling around Rico from behind in preparation for the all-but-certain fight to come.

Rico smirked as if their attempt was futile.

Emily grabbed a torch from the wall and held it as a double-handed weapon, approaching him from the front while Maggie stayed back, peeking from around the doorframe like a timid mouse.

Both men ran at the Samoan as Emily charged forward in an ill-prepared triangulated attack. She slid on her knees across the dusty floor as the sharp blade of the spearhead swooped above her head. Graham jumped onto Rico's back, flexing his bicep to tighten his arm into a headlock around the Recreant's windpipe. Seth grabbed for the arm holding the weapon, trying to grip and subdue the man's most lethal appendage.

Even with a three-on-one assault, it was hardly a level playing field.

Emily scrambled to her feet, swinging the flaming piece of wooden stave against Rico's abdomen. The disgruntled look on his face showed that he had felt the attack, but it was hardly enough to bring him down.

Oh boy.

Rico swung his arm to one side, sending Seth flying in one direction and the broken spear in the other. He then booted Emily in the stomach, causing her to tumble backward before reaching both hands above his head to grab Graham by the collar, flipping him over his head and onto his back.

"Maggie, you have to help us!" Emily yelled as she crawled to Graham, glancing back to see that her friend was still cowering. "This was what I told you about. He will kill us all. Please!"

Maggie didn't move. Instead, she remained staring at her teammates scattered about the room, who were getting completely manhandled.

Seth lifted the spear, holding it defensively in front of himself in an attempt to deter the Samoan.

Rico reached up and thumbed the clips of his weighted vest to release it from his body, gaining mobility as it landed with a thud against the ground.

"Fuck you, asshole!" Seth yelled, thrusting the spear toward the Samoan's head.

Rico dodged the attack, propelling a stiff elbow into Seth's ribcage, sending the spear spiraling across the room again.

Seth collapsed, coughing up a faint blob of blood. His breathing became stifled and short. To Emily, he sounded as if he had broken a rib.

Graham rushed Rico again, this time connecting with a followed-through hard-right punch to the Recreant's jawline. Trying to capitalize on Graham's hit, Emily, who was standing behind Rico, raised the torch above her head and brought it down with all her might, only to have Rico grab it by the burning wick, hastily rip it away from her grasp, and toss it across the room.

Graham squared himself up, ready to go hand to hand with the brute member of the Order. They traded multiple blows before Rico finally socked him in the gut. Then, holding Graham's head with both hands, he kneed him in the face, causing Graham to drop to the ground.

Emily took a long look around. Her brother-in-law's eyes were filled with fluid, and blood was pouring from both of his nostrils. Seth was attempting to stand but gasped with each contour of his torso. Her own head was pounding, and her knees looked like they'd been scraped by a cheese grater. Defeat was imminent, and Rico barely had a scratch on him.

But then, breaking the silence in the chamber, came a thumping noise over and over again like the beat of a low-sounding drum against Rico's back. The Samoan turned slowly. Maggie was standing below him while awkwardly beating her tiny, freckled fists against him.

At first, Emily looked on with a smile at her friend who was trying to come to their rescue, but it was a smile that faded into a tremble once she realized how much danger Maggie was truly in.

The Samoan shook his head with a light laugh, then wrapped his palm around Maggie's face like he was palming a basketball. He lifted her from the ground, all one hundred and twenty pounds of her, tightening his fingers around her fragile skull.

She screamed out as her glasses snapped against the bridge of her nose under the strength of his grip, her legs flailing beneath her. Using both hands, she struggled to pry his thumb away from the side of her face, but her attempts to free herself were useless. Just as Emily thought Maggie's life was over, Rico dropped her, taking a sudden inhale of breath.

Seth was now hunched behind the Recreant, with one hand cupping his ribcage and the other on the handle of the spear that was now jutting from Rico's lower-left side.

The Samoan leaned back, clocking Seth across the temple with another cocked elbow before once more pulling the spear from his body. All at once, he drove the spearhead forward, sending it through Graham's shoulder so hard that it forced him back against the wall.

In retaliation, Emily jumped up from behind and latched onto Rico's neck. In his moment of distraction, Maggie dove to wrap her legs and arms around his previously punctured leg. She dug her fingers deep inside his wound, causing him to howl in pain.

Rico stepped forward, dragging both of the women that were clinging to him, and with one swift movement, kicked the leg that Maggie was grasping to send her flying into one of the pillars. Her back smashed against the hard stone, knocking the wind from her lungs before sending her collapsing to the floor. He then reached behind himself, grabbing Emily by her hair and throwing her to land in a heap with the rest of her teammates.

As Rico advanced upon the group, Seth lunged from behind one of the pillars, and with a last-ditch effort, dropkicked Rico in his chest, causing the Samoan to stumble backward against the far wall. Seth tried to follow up with another tired charge, but Rico easily blocked him, lifting him above his head and tossing him to the ground in front of Emily and the others.

"You cannot win, you fools," Rico said smugly, laughing at them from across the room. "I was born for the fight. I breathe to cause pain. All you are is a collection of weak links!"

Emily was slumped motionless next to Graham, Seth was gasping for air on the floor, and Graham was severely bleeding from the spear wound in his shoulder. Yet, Maggie climbed to her feet, holding one arm against her injured back. She started laughing as well, causing Rico to halt mid-guffaw. She neatly held one half of her cracked lenses back to her face, then reached into her pocket to remove a small silver cylinder.

Rico glanced down at his thigh with unease to see a green light pulsing from inside his flesh, blinking faster with every second. His expression blanked as he turned his face back to the feisty redhead who was gritting her teeth, gripping the detonator in her outstretched hand.

"Now all *you* have … is a big fucking hole in your leg!"

With her words, Maggie pressed the button on the detonator. The blast cut through the bone of his leg, severing the limb from his body just above the knee. Blood and muscle coated the wall behind him.

Rico dropped onto his stump with a scream, clasping his hands down around the end of his missing limb. The acoustics in the chamber amplified his bellow as he flipped onto his back, holding his half-leg in the air with disbelief.

Seth hobbled over to the red-painted warrior's body, withdrawing the arrow from her jaw. As the rest of the team watched, he stood over Rico's head, and with a precise thrust, drove the arrow through the Recreant's left eye socket.

After that, the screaming stopped.

Emily hugged Maggie from behind, praising her for a job well done.

But the celebration was short-lived. Graham was in worse shape than anyone had realized.

"Maggie!" Emily exclaimed. "I need you to take Graham, get in one of the Order's vehicles, and get him to the hospital in Hosapete. Get yourself checked out as well; we're not taking any chances.

"Seth and I will do one last sweep here and meet you back there. Okay?"

Emily helped to drape Graham's good arm around Maggie's shoulders before helping him to his feet.

"You have about twenty minutes until the Armed Forces arrive," Graham said, slumped over Maggie as they shuffled toward the chamber's exit. "Whatever you have to do—I suggest you make it quick."

CHAPTER SEVENTEEN

The walls of the temple were filled with reoccurring words and drawings, seemingly painted with a person's finger: no brushes, nor tools. The colors of the paint matched those of the paint on the warriors' bodies. Everything looked primitive, yet so sophisticated all at once.

Emily and Seth took turns observing the unknown language, an ancient text repeated across the stone walls, words that neither of them were able to translate or understand.

But one thing was unmistakable: a yellow arrow smudged onto one of the walls, the wall that Rico had captured in his pictures. Emily realized that the arrow was almost an exact match to the drawing on the sacred stone at Machu Picchu; the only difference was the addition of four blue triangles drawn beneath the arrow, separated by what appeared to be rolling clouds of mist.

Perhaps these triangles depict water. And the mist, flowing freely over it.

Emily recorded everything she saw. She looked over her shoulder at the dead warrior, then back to the walls. *Did they do this?*

She started to bite her thumbnail again, looking down at Rico's motionless body. She knelt beside him, turning his hands so his palms faced upright. They were coated in the same substance as

Graham's fingers had been after he touched the warriors' bodies—some kind of blue and yellow pigment.

She stood again, walking around to examine the skin of the warriors, each one covered in the same substance, which resembled war paint.

As she tried to piece the puzzle together, she noticed the rhythmic puff of light breathing. By now, Seth was studying the walls of the tunnels farther out, so she knew it couldn't have come from him. The wheeze was dull and strained, like that of someone on their deathbed.

She spun around, half expecting Rico to be alive and standing behind her. However, his body remained as still as ever.

Emily looked back at the two dead warriors. Reluctantly, she held her finger under the nose of the woman first, the one who had once had an arrow thrust through her jaw.

Nothing.

She moved to the body of the other warrior, once more holding her index finger under his nose. It took a few seconds, but she began to feel a very faint puff of air striking her skin.

"Seth, he's alive! One of them is alive!" she yelled.

She grabbed the warrior's body and moved him into a sitting position against the wall, eyeing him intently for some sort of movement.

"Can you hear me?"

She leaned in with caution, listening, trying to gauge any sign of a response from the warrior.

Miraculously, his eyes shot open and immediately locked on hers as if he were staring into the depths of her soul. It was as if some force was holding her in place, immobilizing her. She could not speak, nor blink, nor even breathe. All five of her senses had frozen, and for those few brief moments, life was stilled.

Only once her body had surrendered in full did the man place his worn hands on her cheeks. A white mist began to billow from his body like smoke billowing from a smokestack. It circled the air around them, swirling, thickening like a dense fog. Then, without warning, it poured into every orifice of Emily's head.

She fell backward onto the ground, her body stiff like a board as the whites of her eyes rolled back into her head. Her body began convulsing, seizing at the mercy of the white clouds enveloping her.

The mist was taking over.

Emily opened her eyes. She was staring up into a star-filled sky as a light breeze blew across her skin. The mist had seemingly released its hold, like a weighted blanket being lifted from her chest.

She scrambled upright, disoriented, looking at her surroundings with an odd sense of familiarity. She was on a precipice above what looked to be a small village. The peaks of mountains rose in the darkness around her. Pit fires burned in the village below her. But there was no one around. There was barely even a sound aside from the crackling embers of dried logs.

Approaching the huts of the village, it now dawned on her exactly where she was. She was in Machu Picchu, though it was distinctly different from her visit just a few weeks prior. There was no destruction; the walls of the structures were in immaculate condition, and everything looked fresh and new, almost as if hundreds of years of deterioration had been erased.

Impossible. This can't be.

Emily jerked her head at the sound of a twig snapping beside her, catching a glimpse of a hooded figure running behind one of the huts.

"Hello?" she called out, hoping for a response.

She tried to catch up to them, but by the time she came around the corner, the person had vanished.

"Seth? Seth, are you there?"

Nobody answered.

As she stood outside the window of one of the huts, the firelight inside drew her attention. Peeking inside, she saw a Peruvian man dressed in a yellow poncho, wearing large golden jewelry, asleep on a bed formed from clay. He reminded her of the drawings depicting the Inca she had admired in the church in Cusco.

At the foot of his bed, two large, well-built, red-painted warriors stood watch like statues, holding their spears butted against the ground. Emily noticed that they looked nearly identical to the dead warriors from the Hazara Rama Temple.

Emily opted to move closer for a better look, but was halted when a ceramic pot shattered outside at the opposite side of the dwelling. Her head dipped low as the warriors stirred from their post and rushed outward to investigate the noise.

No sooner had the warriors taken their leave did the cloaked person appear again, this time creeping from a window adjacent to Emily's, moving with stealth toward the slumbering man in the poncho.

"Wake up!" Emily shouted, trying to raise the sleeping form. "Someone's inside!"

There was no use. It was as if she wasn't making any sound at all.

The figure dropped onto their belly, army-crawling their way across the floor to the edge of the bed. Reaching their arm up, the hooded figure ran their hand under the man's poncho, weaving like a pickpocket in and out of the folds of material.

A few seconds later, the hand of the cloaked figure emerged holding a vibrant yellow diamond.

The Florentine Diamond!

The figure paused and Emily could see that their cloak was clasped together with a decorative coat of arms adorned with what appeared to be three roaring lions and fleur-de-lis. The figure quickly stuffed the diamond out of sight and snaked their way back outside and over an embankment to make a running getaway.

Before Emily could comprehend what was happening, the white mist whirled around her again, engulfing her in a bright flurry that seemed to pull at every inch of her body.

As fast as it had appeared, the mist broke once more, this time leaving Emily standing in an open grassy field. The sun was beaming down instead of the previous starry sky, and there were no huts anymore, just the surrounding lush greens of hills and valleys. The sky was clear, unhindered by so much as a cloud, yet she could hear the distant sound of rolling thunder.

Something was approaching in the distance from the south, followed by a brown cloud of dust that was growing by the second. As the rumbling got louder, the earth began to shake even more vigorously beneath her.

With her hand to her brow, she squinted ahead to see a massive wave of men on horseback rushing toward her. Ten or twenty thousand soldiers easily, proudly carrying the flag of Switzerland above their stampede.

She immediately turned to run in the opposite direction as fast as her legs would allow, hightailing it through the yawning field. She kept her pace, running for the horizon until, yet again, the ground began to hum below her. But this time, it felt different, as if the movement was coming from in front of her rather than from behind. Breaching a small mound, she mustered enough strength to climb to its top. When she broke above the mossy bank, her eyes landed on the second source of approach.

A second army was rushing toward her, shrouded in a blanket of white mist. The army, which comprised knights in full regalia and the same warriors from the Hazara Rama Temple, approached Emily by the thousands, seemingly unbothered by her presence on the embankment.

First were the blue-painted warriors, the front offensive wave, sleek and agile. They lined the mound with their bows drawn, aiming their arrows toward the sky. With a quick release, they let their arrows fly in the direction of the approaching Swiss riders.

Next came the red-painted warriors, strong, tall, and burly, with hands gripped around the thick wooden shafts of their spears. Along with the armored knights, who were on horseback, they formed an impenetrable wall. Following the archers with another great battle cry, they ran full speed toward the opposing forces, seemingly determined and without fear.

The two armies collided with a reverberating crack, the soldiers and warriors slaying one another with their weapons of old.

Emily collapsed to her knees, placing her shaking hands over her face while working to control her breathing. Meanwhile, through the cacophony of battle, in her sheltered state, she could distinguish the sound of hooves trotting to her right, mixed with the sharp clanking of chains.

Removing her hands from her face, she saw a man dressed in full knight's armor sitting atop a regal-looking horse. On the man's breastplate was a crest in blue, red, and yellow, overlaid with three roaring lions and a pattern of fleur-de-lis—the same crest that Emily had seen on the thief's cloak in her vision of Peru. On his head, instead of a helmet, he wore a headdress adorned with multiple glistening jewels, and at its center was a large, yellow diamond.

The man's oblong face was unmistakable after all the research she had done on the diamond's history—*Charles the Bold.*

Charles gave a sharp tug on a chain that was draped in his clutches. Trailing behind the horse, restrained in a set of shackles, was an enslaved brown-skinned boy.

Charles had been accompanied by a third and final wave of warriors, their skin painted yellow. They were acting as a last line of defense against anyone who might try to attack him. Holding their stone daggers, they spread out to draw the attention of the Swiss invaders away from their keeper.

But it was upon their advance that the mist thickened yet again, blinding Emily to the unfolding battle.

The mist encircled Emily, cold air brushing against her arms and legs, contrasting with the mist that was already upon the battlefield. It lifted her, mere inches above where she had last stood, before placing her back into the middle of the same open field. Its landscape, however, was severely different.

The once shining sun had long disappeared behind a mass of grey clouds, ones that had opened the floodgates of rain onto the war-stricken grasslands.

Emily cupped her hand over her mouth, taken aback by the sheer extent of bodies that now littered the field like leaves on an autumn day. Swiss, Burgundian, and war-painted warriors alike were strewn amongst the forming mud puddles, covered in gashes and blood, impaled with spears and swords, some even missing entire limbs.

Unable to hold back, she leaned over her knees and vomited among the dead.

The mist had carried her to the aftermath of the Battle of Nancy, which concluded the Burgundian Wars in January of 1477. Reading about it was one thing; living it was another.

As the mist on the battlefield started to retreat, the slain bodies of the diamond's army began to dissipate with it, as if they had never existed. However, the bodies that had fallen outside of the trailing tendrils of mist remained, staggered among the lifeless Swiss and Burgundians covering the plains, evidently abandoned by the diamond.

But why?

The mist retracted farther still, all the way back into the Florentine Diamond, which was still affixed to Charles the Bold's headdress just a few yards away. As Emily's eyes followed the trail of the mist, the little brown-skinned boy emerged from beneath one of the horses, wading through the mud to approach Charles' lifeless body.

The slave's wrists were still bound, but his chain had somehow been severed in the events of the battle. He spat disrespectfully on the crest-adorned breastplate of the duke while bending down to rip the diamond from Charles' headdress, before turning on his heel and running as fast as he could toward the nearest wooded area.

As soon as the boy was out of sight, Emily's vision started to become a murky grey. Her body stiffened yet again, leaving her unable to move until once more the mist had rushed in and carried her away.

A finger twitched at first, then a toe, followed by a pair of agitated eyelids.

Emily lay on her back, returned to the secret chamber under the Hazara Rama Temple. For a moment, she was relieved, propping herself up onto her elbows.

Damnit, Seth, were you just going to leave me here?

Once back on her feet, she realized the chamber looked nothing like when she had last been in it.

There were no murals on the walls, no Rico lying on the ground, and there was certainly no Seth.

How long was I out?

"Seth?" she hissed. "Seth, where are you?"

Emily hugged the wall, slowly moving toward the chamber's entranceway. But as she neared the tunnels, the shadows dancing on the walls indicated a commotion at the end of the passageway. As the shadowy figures drew closer, she could hear heavy footsteps and incessant yelling.

As Emily peeked around the nearest corner, four painted warriors came into sight, holding their weapons at their sides and retreating backward into the tunnelway. Opposing the warriors was a gang of men, holding machetes, torches, and sickles, forcing them deeper inside against their will.

Emily scrambled behind one of the four inner pillars, hiding before they entered the chamber.

Once all of the warriors were sequestered within the chamber, one of the men stepped forward before ushering his companions to retreat, ensuring that the warriors did not follow. He turned to face them from the entranceway.

"Pathetic immortals. You were supposed to guard our king's diamond, not let it be stolen by some adolescent thief. There is no way for you to return now, you fools. As such, we leave you here to pay for your ignorance—for eternity!"

To Emily, the man looked to be Indian, but by some strange occurrence, Emily was able to understand his words perfectly.

Moments after the man took his leave into the tunnels, a harsh scraping noise, followed by a dense thump echoed throughout the chamber.

No, no, no!

Emily ran through the passage, realizing what the mob had done. Climbing the steps, she smacked her hands and fists against the stone barricade they had used to seal the only exit, trapping her, and the warriors, forever.

"Let me out!" she screamed. "Seth! I'm still down here! Get me out! Seth!"

Tears flowed down her cheeks, knowing her efforts were useless. Turning to sit on the steps, she closed her eyes and laid her forehead on her overlapped forearms, inhaling shallow breaths.

C'mon, Em, get a grip. This isn't real ... it's all in your head. There has to be a reason you're being shown this ... there has to be ... I know it.

Emily's thoughts soon became disrupted by the cackling of gulls cawing in the background. She creased her brow, lifting her head from her lap to yet another foreign, figment location. She was sitting on a bench in some sort of dockyard, and the weather was overcast with a light drizzle.

People walked back and forth in front of her, carrying on with their daily conversations without the slightest indication that she existed. She rose to walk aimlessly among them on the cobblestone streets, dragging her feet with exhaustion from the visions into which she'd been haphazardly thrust.

Stopping along the water's edge, she observed a crew of men throwing barrels of rum and sacks of food over wooden planks to other workers who were loading them aboard large ships.

From the far end of the dock, another man wearing a long mantle and a puffy beret-style hat walked toward her in the middle of the street. His beard, white as snow, was long and forked. Behind him, a court of other men pranced, following his every move. He veered right, climbing the rickety wooden ramp onto the biggest vessel that was stationed at the dock, his followers piling on board behind him as well.

But one of the men in his posse trailed behind, seemingly less enthralled than the others. He was much younger than them too, likely closer to Emily's age by the looks of him. He stopped at the bottom of the ramp and began rifling through the inner pockets of his regal cloak.

She stepped closer, hovering to get a better look at what the man was fidgeting with, when, from his cupped hands, she saw a yellow glint of light. A trickle of mist began to seep through his fingers and gather in a pool around his feet.

This time, however, Emily looked around, furiously searching for a landmark, a clue, anything that could help her identify her surroundings. She needed to know exactly where she was, or at least what time period she was in. This was the missing piece of the timeline she required—the events that took place after the diamond left India.

But it was too late—she couldn't see anything aside from the ships and the enshrouding mist.

As the ships' anchors began to draw out of the water, the bearded man appeared again from the top deck of the boat, raising one leg onto the rail and leering down at the young keeper.

"Ludovico! Stop fooling around. Make haste. It is time we embark."

"Yes, father!" the young man shouted back.

Once the man named Ludovico had boarded the main vessel, he returned to the bow of the ship, looking back at the port with pride.

"Farewell, Bristol, my love. I shall miss you dearly."

At once, the ships began to push away in unison, heading for the open ocean as the mist retreated with them, vanishing into the rolling seas.

Bristol? As in Bristol, England?

Emily tried her best to memorize her surroundings before the mist inevitably consumed her all over again. It wasn't long before she felt the all-to-familiar stiffening, and everything around her faded to white.

When Emily opened her eyes again, the ships and dock had disappeared. In their place was only a hellish heat, caused by a roaring fire that lit the night sky with a pulsing orange hue. She stood, watching as a city was engulfed, burning in an unforgiving blaze. People were running and screaming in all directions, while others used buckets to haul water from the ocean with composure, trying to contain what they could of the flames.

The mist was visibly present, but it had been tainted with the coal-black clouds of smoke from roasting brick and wood. Many painted warriors ran through the burning city streets, fighting with different clusters of white men. However, it appeared as if the diamond's forces were protecting the city, not destroying it.

I need to get higher.

Finding a suitable crag to ascend, she climbed until the screams below the clouds of smoke and mist began to dwindle. The wind blew fiercely, blowing sparks and embers through the air, catching more of the city on fire as they swirled around.

Now atop a rocky hill, a few hundred meters above sea level, she could make out the body of water below, leading back into the sea between two gigantic outcroppings of rock.

From the opening to the sea, three large ships were penetrating their way into the depths of the defenseless harbour. The city was under siege.

From one ship's stern, two spheres of fire shot outward from the vessel, trailing across the skyline and plummeting into the shore. The bang of cannons followed close behind, creating huge explosions below the haze. The weapons of the white man had evolved and were now much too powerful for the diamond's army of warriors, who were unable to contain cannon fire with wooden bows and arrows carved from rock.

Heavy footsteps came from behind Emily, drawing her attention from the battle. A man came running through the white blanket of cloud, wheezing and coughing, resting his hands on his knees to catch his breath. He could barely make the steep traverse.

Still gasping for air, he reached across his chest into his breast pocket to pull out a glowing yellow diamond, ensuring it was safe before snuffing the light again so as not to draw any attention to himself.

Emily followed him as he continued along the beaten path, to the top of one of the rocky cliffs. She watched as he suddenly dropped out of sight, as if he had disappeared straight into the ground itself. The mist quickly disappeared behind him.

Again, Emily tried to look around for some sort of bearing, something to indicate where she was, but there was no use. The city was being practically reduced to ash. Smoldering structures and flames were all that she could see.

Eventually, the vision passed, as they all did, the smell of singed flesh replaced with the more elegant sound of the breaking of waves washing against breaching rocks. A breeze tousled Emily's hair, and she could hear the light brush of leaves rustling in the wake of the low-lying wind.

Emily was left standing alone, waist-deep in water, staring into the widened end of a ravine. And yet, her skin crawled with an unsettling feeling that someone was watching her.

Her eyes wandered over the trees, squinting as tiny figures moved in the distance, scattering themselves along the cliffs and shoreline. The water's edge soon became lined with red-painted warriors, and for the first time since the visions had begun, she felt like they could actually feel her presence. Each warrior clanked their spear against the rocks, pairing in time with some sort of rhythmic chant, calling to her as if they somehow needed her to be their witness.

A bright yellow light shot from the center of the ravine and lifted high into the clouds, towering from her field of view. The chanting stopped, and the red-painted warriors dispersed into the forest behind them.

From the base of the mountains, the mist returned, seeping over the water like fingers reaching out for her body. It swirled around her one final time, tugging at her limbs while forcing itself back inside of her.

Her eyes rolled into her head, sending her body crashing backward into the water.

"Emily!" A man's voice echoed from above.

She opened her mouth to respond, but the mist was still restricting her from speaking.

"Emily!" The voice came again, this time from beside her. She could feel someone shaking her.

Her eyes sprang open, glossy at first, staring at a decrepit stone ceiling while Seth's face hovered above her, looking down upon her with concern.

Lifting her, he wrapped his arms around her shoulders, kissing her cheek while he held her tightly, smoothing the base of her neck.

"Thank God! You're awake. What happened to you?"

CHAPTER EIGHTEEN

Emily sat with her back against the wall of the temple, her arms crossed over her knees with her forehead pressed against her arms. Seth stood across from her, leaning against the closest of the four pillars, rubbing at his ribs while tapping his heel repeatedly against the floor. And Rico, well, he had already settled into pallor mortis, which was an unsightly view for the duo who weren't accustomed to the sight of death.

"So? Are you going to tell me what happened?" Seth asked, breaking the uncomfortable silence that had consumed the room since she had awoken.

Emily raised her head, her eyes holding an empty stare. Her face was covered in dust, stuck to the sweat and tears that had accumulated while she was unconscious.

"It was so real," she whispered. "Like … I was there, you know?"

Emily felt as if she had been locked inside her visions for hours, when in actuality, it had only been mere minutes. Seth had found her spasming on the ground and hadn't been able to wake her. From the oblivious look on his face, she soon realized there was no way he could know what she was referring to.

"Where are Graham and Maggie?" she asked.

Seth paused for a moment, using his shoulder to leverage his body from the pillar.

"You sent them to the hospital in Hosapete, remember?"

She remembered as soon as he said it, but everything was still a blur.

He reached out his hand to help her to her feet. He gently parted the tangled hair away from her face, then cupped her cheeks in his hands, focusing on her pupils. She embraced the warm touch of his hands on her, eventually giving him a weak smile before walking a few feet around the chamber, twisting her back and neck to relieve the tension built up from the spasms.

Nearing the muralled walls, she turned a shy eye toward Seth.

"What?" Seth questioned, breaking into a smile of his own.

"If I told you something—anything—would you believe me?"

"Em, you've asked me to chase you around the world to look for a diamond that *supposedly* houses an army of warriors. I think belief was thrown out the window a long time ago." He started laughing, until he noticed that she was not. He became serious. "Yes, of course I'd believe you. Always."

She looked down at her feet, searching for the right way to explain to him what she had witnessed. She then pointed across the chamber to the red-painted warrior slumped on his side.

"Him. He showed me ... everything."

Seth side-eyed the warrior who was clearly no longer among the living.

"He showed you what, exactly?" He said with reservation.

"He revealed it to me through the mist, like scrying in the smoke of a crystal ball. I know where the Florentine Diamond is, and has been."

"Wait, what? That's great news! Isn't it?"

Before Emily could even begin to explain, Seth's phone began to beep.

"Oh, shit! Em, we have to go."

Seth picked up Rico's vest, retrieving a set of keys. He then grabbed Emily by the wrist and led her to the tunnels so they could weave their way back to the parking lot outside.

"That was the ten-minute mark, which gives us about ten more to get out of here before the authorities arrive, and that's *if* Graham is as good as you say he is."

He helped Emily into one of the Recreant's SUVs, then slid into the driver's seat. They sped from the temple as quickly as they could.

After passing through several small towns, with the silhouette of the Hazara Rama Temple behind them, Emily still hadn't lifted her head from the window of the vehicle.

"Do you want to tell me what you 'saw' now?" Seth asked. He had given her a twenty-minute window of opportunity to speak, but she had remained mute.

She knew he was poking fun; he wouldn't have been Seth Parish if he didn't.

"I sort of know where the Florentine Diamond is, okay? I've seen its location—or at least, all of the locations it's been—but geographically I have no idea where it ended up."

"Good thing you brought an expert then, huh?" He laughed again, turning toward her, waiting for a response. "Well? Spit it out. What did you see? C'mon, walk me through it."

"I saw *them*," she replied, once again referring to the warriors. "They were gathered among some sort of cliff formation, watching me—no, waiting for me."

"Cliffs. Got it. Creepy, stalker, warrior dudes. Got it. What else?"

"I saw a city burn to the ground next to the same cliffs, or at least, I think they were the same. Someone had the diamond there; of that I'm certain. And before that, ships. The diamond traveled on large, wooden ships."

"Ah-ha! Now we're on to something—my specialty. How many ships were there? Did any of them have emblemed sails? Who was the captain? Did you see any of the crew members' faces?"

"I did, but I didn't recognize them. All I know is that one young man was named Ludovico. Their accents were … Italian maybe, with a hint of British." Emily closed her eyes and rubbed

THE MISTS OF MORNE

her temples, trying to remember all the details when suddenly she sprang forward. "The docks! I was at the docks! In Bristol. Yes! I remember that part for sure."

"Bristol, hey? Interesting. Now, are we talking modern-day Bristol or ... ?"

"No, no, no. It wasn't recent at all. The people in my vision were wearing houppelandes, for Christ's sake."

Emily's tone had become frustrated as she tried to remember every minute detail of her visions. Seth, on the other hand, was patient as he pieced together the trail of breadcrumbs she kept feeding him.

"Okay, hear me out. What if you were shown ships that were leaving on a voyage? Maybe someone took the diamond and departed from Bristol, hoping to use its army to conquer a new world? Although, now that I think about it, Bristol was a gateway for so many explorers back then, that locating the person you saw in your vision would be like finding a needle in a haystack."

Emily removed her phone from her pocket and started swiping through the photographs of the temple walls, tracing her fingertips over the blue triangles and yellow arrow, which she now realized must be a beam of light surrounded by water.

"This is where the diamond is. I've seen this water, and I have seen this light. The warriors want me to find it. I can feel it."

She swiped left once more, staring at the previously unknown language written on the chamber's walls.

Wait a minute. Something's different ...

Somehow the text had become understandable. She began reading it aloud, fluently in the foreign tongue.

"Emily? What the fuck did you just say?" Seth said, somewhat disturbed. "You're freaking me out a little."

She took a moment to gather herself before translating it for his benefit.

"Men and women watch. One yellow sun, guarded by the protectors. Two red homes, we occupy the cliffs of the morne.

Four divine waters, divided by the archers." She turned to Seth, pale and quivering. "It's ... their language."

"How ... how do you know what it says?"

"I'm not sure. I just do."

Maggie had texted Emily to let her know that they had secured a room on the second floor of the Sushruta Hospital in Hosapete. Once Emily and Seth had arrived, they parked the vehicle and wasted no time rejoining the others.

Upon reaching the room, they found Maggie cheerfully dealing out cards onto Graham's dinner tray, his left arm well wrapped and placed in a sling. Maggie had only a few small bandages and was sitting with an ice pack pressed against her back. When Emily asked about her new pair of glasses, she had happily explained that she was so clumsy that she always brought a back-up pair.

Emily swooped in and hugged them both, thoroughly checking to make sure they were doing okay. The fight had taken a heavy toll on everyone, and knowing her friends were in good hands meant it was due time for her and Seth to get checked out themselves.

Forty minutes later, they returned to the room, already feeling better than when they had left. Emily, much like Maggie, only had a few scrapes and bruises, while Seth, on the other hand, couldn't stop lifting his shirt to show everyone his bandaged torso covering his two cracked ribs.

But the happy reunion was quickly cut short when a familiar beeping noise came from underneath Graham's hospital bed. Maggie reached down, pulled her laptop from beneath the bed, and opened it on her lap, pushing her glasses up the bridge of her nose. She furiously clicked across its keyboard.

Looking up from the screen, Maggie spun the laptop around to show the others.

"Alexandria and Dominik have landed at the Hosur Aerodrome."

No doubt they were here to join Rico—but they'd be in for a nasty surprise once they found him.

Emily fell right back into panic mode, pacing the room while Seth tried to calm her. Graham still had to be admitted for another twelve hours for precautionary observation. They couldn't all just up and leave. It would raise too much suspicion and unwanted attention.

"Go," Maggie said politely, stopping Emily in her tracks. "It's okay. I'll stay here with Graham until they discharge him. You and Seth get back to the villa and get our things together. We're going to have to move fast once we meet back up."

Emily didn't like the idea of leaving her teammates behind, but it was looking like the only option. Someone had to stay, and someone had to get everything ready so they could head to Bristol while they were still one step ahead of the Recreant Order. She turned toward Graham, who, with nothing more than a nod, gave his approval.

"Besides," Maggie piped up again. "No one from the Recreant Order even knows what Graham or I look like ... I hope. We'll be safe. It's *you* I'm worried about."

Graham let out a restrained groan, shimmying his way upright to elbow his pillow behind his back as a prop.

"Take the Recreants' SUV, but make sure you ditch it before you get back to the villa so the local authorities can't trace it back to our rental," he instructed. "Once you're there, load what you can into our remaining SUV and get some rest. Meet us back at the airstrip tomorrow morning at 10:00 am. No matter what happens, no one goes looking for the others. We *only* meet at the airstrip. Your father has arranged for a plane to be available for us. That's the play. Do you understand?"

Emily could hear the strict tone in his voice, but she had no problem letting him call the shots on this one. This was his element, not hers.

"Understood." She leaned in and kissed his forehead then turned back to Maggie. "Are you okay? I mean ... with everything that happened back there?"

"I think I'll be fine. I get it now. I've seen it. The Recreant Order is full of bad people, and they deserve what they get. You won't see me hesitate again, that I can promise."

"Take care of him." Emily nodded toward her brother-in-law. "My sister will kill me if anything happens to him. As soon as he's discharged, you head straight to the airport, do you understand?"

"Understood!"

"Call or text me if anything changes."

Night had fallen by the time they reached the villa. Seth dropped Emily off before leaving to drive a few extra miles down the road to ditch the vehicle. While he was gone, Emily was left with the task of loading everyone's belongings back into their remaining SUV before returning inside for the night.

Once she was finished, she scurried upstairs to get undressed. Her body yearned for the warmth of an overdue shower. As she slipped beneath the scalding hot water, a certain comfort spread through every bone of her body. Closing her eyes, she moved her face under the showerhead to let the water continuously wash over her skin. The puddle at her feet quickly became a murky copper tone as the dirt from her body mixed with the dried blood from her wounds, more euphoric than painful.

By the time she had finished and shut off the water, the bathroom had filled with a ghost-like steam, floating through the air and making it difficult to locate even her towel. For a second, she hesitated to come out from behind the glass door, as the vapor caused her to flash back to the mist from her visions.

She clenched her eyelids shut, drawing a breath through her nose before opening them again.

C'mon, Em. You can do this.

Finding the courage to step out of the shower, she snatched up her towel and ruffled it over her hair before wrapping it around herself with a firm tug, folding its crease into the crease of her breasts. She pulled at the door, opening it just a few inches to let the chilly air casually mix with the steam from the shower and eliminate the damp haze.

That's better.

Much to Emily's surprise, Seth had returned earlier than she'd expected, slamming dresser drawers open and closed at the far end of the villa. Continuing out into the hallway, she repeatedly ran her fingers through her hair to loosen the knots, leaving a trail of wet footprints that ended at his bedroom door.

She rapped with her knuckles, nudging it open without invitation.

There he stood, barefoot and shirtless, wearing nothing but an undone pair of jeans, dangling a gangly pair of white socks from his palm. His physique resembled that of a downward arrow, the ripple of his abs and their V-cut contour pointing Emily's eyes to whatever was concealed behind his open zipper.

"Is this all you left for me to wear?" Seth chastised her, causing her to snap from her visible admiration. "A pair of jeans and some tube socks? Really?"

She shot him a raised eyebrow accompanied by a provocative smirk, suggesting that he wasn't as funny as he thought he was.

He laughed, tossing the socks onto the foot of the bed, but stopped to cough while grabbing his bandaged ribs in the process.

Emily tensed, moving closer to place her hand over the bandaged area as if it would help, holding it there noticeably longer than she was required to.

"Are you ... okay?" she asked softly, gazing up to stare into his eyes.

"I am now." He placed his own hand over hers, both cradling his torso.

"Thank you for everything today, Seth. I'm sorry if I scared you back there."

"Honestly, I just didn't want to lose you." He lifted his other hand, brushing a few loose strands of wet hair from her cheeks and tucking them behind her ear. "I felt so powerless when I wasn't able to wake you. If you could try not to do that again, it would be great."

He was the epitome of a wordsmith, always making her smile. *Sarcastic and charming rolled into one. He hasn't changed a bit.*

Before he had a chance to jest any further, Emily raised her finger and pressed it against his lips to hush him. Maybe it was the aura of danger, or maybe it was the fact that both of them were half-naked, but she most certainly hadn't forgotten their hot mess from a few nights before. Only this time, there would be no interruptions.

His lips pressed back, kissing her finger. His eyes captivated her, lowering her hand from his mouth to trail it intimately down his side.

It seems he hasn't forgotten either.

She slid her index and middle fingers into the belt loops of his jeans and tugged, bringing him closer. His skin smelled just as she had remembered, mineral and sage, only now it had the undertone scent of soil from the temple. It didn't matter. The wait was over.

Emily rose to stand on her tiptoes, propelling herself higher to reach his lips with hers. His hands were laid gently at the base of her neck, resting on her collarbones. For a moment, she felt like he was too shy to indulge her, until their tongues met furiously.

She dropped her heels to the floor and fell away from his face, looking up at him with a genuinely smitten grin. He had been left hanging, his eyes still shut, as she placed her hand against his chest and playfully shoved him away. When he opened them again, Emily had taken a few steps backward and had her thumb driven into the knot of the towel between her breasts.

His brow was raised, almost daring her to do what she was insinuating. So she did.

Digging her nails into the slit of the towel, she released it from her body, unwrapping herself like a present as the cotton towel hit the floor with a waft around her ankles. Her hair, still wet, draped over her shoulders, sending small beads of water trailing down her bare body.

He didn't break eye contact for so much as a second. Even as she stood naked before him, he focused solely on her face. Taking initiative, he stepped toward her and placed one arm around her waist, sliding his other forearm down her back, curving under her, and hoisting her effortlessly—a move that sent goosebumps descending down Emily's spine.

She instinctively clenched her legs around his hips, giggling as they collapsed upon the bed. The kissing grew vigorous, gaining in passion. She reached between their bodies to finish undoing his jeans before sliding them down over his stiffened bulge with impatience.

Got him.

CHAPTER NINETEEN

Maggie & Graham

"Full house!" Maggie yelled, spreading the cards across the dinner tray in front of Graham.

He folded his cards while refraining from a grin, nodding to congratulate her on the win. He had beaten her in the twenty-six games prior; it was long overdue.

She gathered the deck again and started to reshuffle the cards. Maggie could see that Graham's arm was starting to aggravate him. He was wincing ever so slightly while rolling his shoulder. In fact, being confined to a hospital room was making them both a little antsy.

She had just started to deal the cards again when her stomach expelled a gurgling rumble, apparently as contagious as a yawn, as Graham's growled right behind. They looked over at the spread of hospital food that a nurse had brought them several hours prior. It looked like someone had thrown up, ate it, and thrown back up again—Maggie was positive she had seen a filth fly land on the tray just a few moments ago. Scarfing that down wasn't an option.

"I got this," Maggie said, recalling the small shop they had passed earlier on the first floor while they were being admitted.

She stood from the side of the bed and dug into her pockets, withdrawing a scanty number of rupees and counting them in her palm.

Graham laughed, nestling himself back into his pillows.

"So ... just a snack then?" she said, blushing with embarrassment.

Riding the elevator to the first floor, Maggie noticed there wasn't much activity going on, just a handful of nurses tending to the emergency room and an on-call doctor or two visiting their patients. Luckily, the shop was open twenty-four hours.

She walked inside, pawing her way through the small selection of snacks they had to offer. But she was unnerved by the fact that she didn't recognize any of the products before her.

Grabbing some bags of the closest things to chips as she could find, she placed them on the counter, looking up at the clock behind the cashier; 3:45 am. They still had another hour or so before Graham would be discharged.

She passed the rupees to the clerk and began trotting back to the elevator.

Suddenly, bright red lights started to flash along the ceiling, followed by all the nurses dropping their clipboards and running toward the front door of the hospital.

Maggie lingered curiously to see what all the commotion was about, as the ear-splitting wail of an ambulance approached from the distance.

Oh no. It must be a serious emergency.

She tucked one bag of chips into the back of her waistband, then scrunched open the other to snack on while she watched the unfolding chaos. Peeking from around the corner, she could see the ambulance roll up to the front door as paramedics scurried to pull a stretcher from the back. With all the people crowded around the door, it was hard for her to see much else, especially for someone of her height, or lack thereof.

Startling at the harsh bang of the double doors, she halted her chewing as two more paramedics crashed a gurney feet first into the medical center. Through the scrambling of the staff, she caught what she thought was a glimpse of Rico's body lying motionless on the trolley. Climbing atop a stool placed by the wall, she could now see the arrow still sticking from his eye, reassuring her that he was most definitely deceased.

Phew.

As the paramedics veered through a second set of doors, a doctor rushed behind, accompanied by a Black man dressed in a well-tailored suit. Maggie had seen this happen many times before—albeit mostly on television—so she wasn't particularly alarmed. She knew a doctor had to officially pronounce the death, so it was only logical they brought Rico's body to the morgue if he was DOA.

Why so long after, though?

Retrieving her phone from her back pocket, she called Emily to report.

All of the action had made her hungrier than she had anticipated, looking down to find only crumbs left in the bag. Pacing the center of the hallway awaiting an answer, she lifted the bag to her face, tipping her head back to tumble the crumbled remains into her mouth while crinkling the foil bag to make sure she got every last morsel.

The entrance doors banged open a second time.

Maggie casually lowered the bag from her mouth and turned her head to discover that standing a mere seventy-feet in front of her was Alexandria of the Recreant Order. She was grabbing at her neck, clutching it in a panic of stifled sobs, pacing in her distress over not being allowed to follow Rico's body. She began tossing patient charts and paperwork, littering them along the nurses' station through her emission of inconsolable anger.

She soon became swarmed by nurses who tidied up the paperwork and offered their condolences, but in a befitting manner of unacceptance, she rudely began shoving them away one at a time.

Maggie couldn't afford to be spotted. To her knowledge, the Recreants didn't know what she looked like or that she was even accompanying Emily to India, but the Order had many resources. There was always a chance they had profiles on all of Emily's teammates, just like Maggie had profiles on theirs.

She turned on her heel, ejecting herself around the corner of the wall to hide. Hanging up the unanswered call, she realized the first floor had become deathly quiet since the commotion had settled. She peeked one eye around the corner again, confirming that Alexandria hadn't seen her. The female Recreant remained leaning over the nurses' station, her head buried into her folded arms.

Maggie Riggs is in the clear! All right.

She leaned back against the wall in relief, when upon connecting, a loud pop echoed from behind her like a shot from a gun. She squeezed her eyes tightly shut with regret, then opened them just as quickly.

The chips!

"Fuck!" Maggie hissed under her breath as crumbs began to patter down her backside and fall around her legs.

Reluctantly, she peeked around the corner once more, staring nervously down the hallway.

Alexandria was now standing upright, alert, and pointing her pistol in Maggie's general direction, the red light still strobing. The nurses and ward clerks shrieked at the sight of the gun, scattering like ants from the common area. But as far as Maggie could tell, she was still undetected as she watched the Recreant aim from side to side trying to find the origin of the noise.

Maggie looked across the hallway at the elevator doors from where she had come, knowing it was her best chance of reaching the second floor. On the other hand, the likelihood of her being shot if she made a run for it right now was all but certain.

"Think, Maggie! Think!" she scolded, foolishly slapping her palm against her forehead in self-punishment.

Just then, a bell sounded from the lift across the hall, as the doors of the elevator slid open, allowing two custodians to leave its confines, unaware of the events unfolding at the other end of the hall.

Here's my chance!

Overhead, the wailing of an alarm cut her advance off at the knees. The siren was nearly deafening and was accompanied by bright flashing white lights that replaced the red ones.

One of the fleeing employees must have hit the security buzzer.

The two custodians moved into the corridor to see what was happening, giving Maggie the opportunity she needed to dart from behind the corner. Running behind them, she slid into the elevator across its grated floor.

Alexandria glimpsed her getaway, firing a barrage of shots toward the elevator and subsequently striking the custodians, lacing them with bullet holes. Maggie witnessed their bodies slam hard against the tiled floor outside the lift. She covered her cringing eyes with one hand while thumbing the button for the second floor with her other.

Maggie could see Alexandria running steadily down the corridor toward her. More bullets rang against the metal door of the elevator as she closed the distance, causing sparks to fly around Maggie's lowered head.

Alexandria arrived just as the elevator doors were shutting. It was long enough for the two women to make eye contact but not enough time for her to pry the doors ajar. As more shots clanked outside the metal box, Maggie felt a sense of relief as it finally began to rise.

She took out her phone again to call Emily, ripping the mangled chip bag from the back of her capris. Rings kept going through, but yet again, no answer.

Unfortunately, there was no time to keep trying. She had to get Graham and get the hell out of there.

When the doors opened on the second floor, mass hysteria had hit. The sirens and lights were just as predominant, with nurses and patients alike trying to gather their belongings and get out.

Maggie pushed and shoved people from her path as best as she could, taking a few bumps herself as she forced her way back to Graham's room. By the time she scurried into his unit, his bed was empty, and there was no sign of him anywhere.

This can't be good ...

Her bottom lip began to tremble as her heartbeat quickened. In desperation, she grabbed her backpack and hastily headed back out of the room in search of Graham.

Standing in the hall, she did a double take in both directions. Alexandria had managed to climb the emergency stairway and was once again locking eyes with Maggie from down the hall.

Well, that's a death stare if I've ever seen one.

Alexandria raised her gun, seemingly with no regard for the people who were crisscrossing through her line of sight. Luckily for Maggie, there were too many obstructions to get a clean shot.

Seething with frustration, the Recreant started her advance, keeping the gun raised toward Maggie as she bluntly bulldozed bodies from her path.

Maggie had nowhere to run. All the entrances were blocked by people trying to flee. She simply stood still, awaiting the hot sting of the bullet that was sure to rip through her at any given moment.

Suddenly, Graham sprang from an adjacent room, using his uninjured shoulder to body check Alexandria. She was sent flailing into a stationary surgical cart, upending it and falling onto the floor.

"Run!" he shouted, waving for Maggie to follow him.

Maggie was certain he would have stayed and fought the Recreant, but with his arm in a sling, he was the embodiment of one hand tied behind his back. Instead, he reached around the doorframe to grab his bag, then placed his hand on Maggie's back and guided her to the stairway. As fast as they could, they navigated their way out of the building and out into the parking lot.

They made their way to the Recreant's SUV that they had taken from the temple earlier that day. Maggie climbed into the passenger's seat, throwing their bags into the back as Graham turned the key in the ignition, shoving the gear shift into reverse. As they peeled out of the parking lot, shots fired from the second-story window snapped against the hood of the SUV before they sped out of range.

Maggie stared at the clock in the dash; 4:31 am. She pulled out her phone to try and reach Emily yet again.

No service.

"What do we do now?" she asked, slamming the cell phone onto the seat beside her in a huff, hoping that Graham had some sort of plan.

"Well, first of all, stop using that damn thing in your hand, it's practically a homing beacon. Shut it off—now. Next, we head straight for the airstrip. We meet up with the others there, just as planned. We need to get out of India as soon as possible."

Maggie pressed her head hard against the headrest.

Neither of them had slept since the night before, and aside from the adrenaline rush, it was starting to take its toll.

"Go to sleep," Graham instructed. "You'll need your rest. This day isn't over yet."

His eyes remained focused on the road while Maggie scowled. His tone was so harsh toward her, but she sensed a protectiveness about it just the same. She laid her head back against the headrest and closed her eyes.

"Thank you," she whispered.

An hour and a half later, Maggie awoke to the hiss of a transport truck engaging its air brakes. The vehicle was stopped. By this point, her head had shifted to the ledge of the passenger window, leaving line patterns dented into her face.

She quickly spun her head to the driver's seat. No sign of Graham.

Panic began to build at the base of her stomach until she realized that they were at a gas station and that she could see him through the back window pumping gas. She let out a sigh of relief before opening the door to join him.

"Feel any better?" he chuckled, clinking the nozzle against the tank and returning it to its holster.

"Much better. You seem better too, by the looks of it."

He had removed the sling from his arm while she slept.

"I'll be all right."

"So ... where are we?"

"I'm not sure of the town, but I estimate we should be about three hours from the airstrip. We should probably get some *actual* food here if possible."

Maybe he has a sense of humor after all.

Maggie ran inside to grab them something to eat, while he approached the attendant and paid for the gas. Graham pulled the SUV away from the pumps to park beside the building, out of view of the road so they could eat peacefully, just in case.

"You don't suppose the Order has gotten to them, do you?" Maggie asked, her mouth full of sandwich.

Graham turned, wiping his mouth with the back of his hand.

"In my line of work, you always prepare for the possibility, but I'm sure they're okay. They're probably still sleeping, which is what I'd like to do if you don't mind taking the wheel for a while. Think you can handle that?"

The two swapped seats, and Graham propped one of his shirts into a makeshift pillow against the passenger window. He was asleep before they hit the highway. Even though he fronted toughness, in his sleep, he couldn't hide the fact that his shoulder was still bothering him, flinching periodically from discomfort.

After an hour and a half had passed of desolate roadways and no conversation, Maggie's eyelids began to flicker with a weighted nod. Graham was still sleeping, so she wasn't about to bother him again to drive just yet.

Although the sun was starting to rise, which helped a little, she needed something more to stay awake, determined to push through. Pressing her finger hard against the button on her armrest, the driver's side window opened to allow a breeze of air in to strike her face.

That ought to keep me focused!

She looked down at her phone resting in the center console, then over to Graham. She hadn't turned it off as he had instructed, only because Emily had told her to keep in contact, and to be honest, she was more afraid of her wrath than his. She dialed Emily's number and lifted the phone to her ear, listening to the tones, hoping someone would pick up the receiving end before she got caught.

Suddenly, the tail-end of the SUV dramatically rocked and swerved about the road.

Graham shot up into a seated position as Maggie yelped while trying to get the vehicle back under her control.

"What are you doing?" He spun around to face the rear windshield, investigating the cause; another SUV was trailing behind them at a dangerously close proximity. "Goddamnit, Maggie!"

He ripped the phone from her ear, powering it off before throwing it onto the dash.

The pursuer sped up and rammed them from behind again, sending another jolt shuddering through the vehicle.

Maggie eyed the rearview mirror, trying to get a glimpse of the assailant. It was Dominik.

"They've tracked us," Graham muttered. "I knew it. Fuck!"

"I'm sorry, I'm sorry!" Maggie pressed the pedal to the floor and sped away, but the Recreant stayed tightly behind them in pursuit.

As she swerved over the center lane, Graham struggled to reach back and grab his bag, which housed his firearm—a modified assault rifle—and was able to eventually pull it into the front seat.

Maggie, on the other hand, was confused at first. She knew he wasn't able to use the weapon—not with only one good arm at least. Then she realized what he was up to.

"No, no, no, no, no! I am not using that thing. I can't. I won't."

Graham just stared at her intensely as if she had a choice in the matter.

"Fine! Damnit," Maggie huffed.

Graham flung the gun onto the dash and grabbed the wheel, allowing Maggie to crawl over him so they could switch places.

Another jolt.

Dominik had clipped them again, this time sending Graham forward into the steering wheel, causing him to grunt, and toppling Maggie down into the passenger's seat.

Reaching forward, she grabbed the gun and dragged it into her lap. She could barely hoist its weight, let alone fire it.

"Put the strap over your head and grip it like this," Graham instructed, motioning what to do. "Rest the butt of it against the roof of the SUV and aim with the green laser. Whatever the dot is on when you pull the trigger is where the bullets will go. Understood?"

She nodded nervously.

Graham pressed the button above his head to retract the sunroof. The wind wafted through the vehicle, sending Maggie's orange hair into a tizzy. Mustering all of her strength, she lifted the gun up into her arms while stretching the thick leather strap around her neck and shoulder.

Another bump from behind, this one flinging their vehicle forward so that Graham had to stomp on the break, screeching the tires against the asphalt.

"What are you waiting for?" Graham yelled.

She planted her feet on the passenger's seat, inching her head through the hole to stare back at the dark vehicle, with Dominik smirking devilishly from the driver's seat. He reached across his chest, pulling a handgun from his breast holster, then lowered his window and leaned out with one arm, pointing the barrel in her direction.

She ducked, scrambling back into the hole just as fast, as three bullets ricocheted off the roof of the vehicle, and a fourth that caused the back window of their SUV to shatter.

Graham began to swerve, hoping to create a moving target that would be harder for Dominik to strike.

"Get back up there! C'mon!"

Maggie took a hard swallow, then popped up through the sunroof once again. This time, she dragged the gun up with her, planting the body of the rifle on the roof to aim the laser sight just as she had been instructed to do. Through the scope, she could see the prism as it reflected through Dominik's front windshield. She rested her jittering index finger against the trigger, steadied the gun as best as she could, then pulled.

The recoil shot her back at first, sending the rifle to fumble against the roof.

Dominik dodged just as the bullet tore through the front windshield of his vehicle, creating a circular hole in the headrest of the driver's seat. Returning upright, he placed his hand on the window, and with a push, sent it tumbling away against the road.

"Fuck you, sweetheart!" He spewed with what seemed to be a shout of enjoyment.

Maggie picked up the weapon again and steadied herself for another attempt, but Dominik had gained momentum, pulling broadside now with the SUV. He rammed them from the left, causing Maggie to flail backward against the roof. She hurried to grip the gun with one hand while grabbing the edge of the sunroof with the other to keep her balance.

Bastard!

Dominik fired more shots, blowing off their side-view mirror in an attempt to hit Graham.

Maggie turned the gun and squeezed the trigger again to unleash a flurry of bullets that created a pattern of holes along the side of the Recreant's vehicle, forcing him to hit the brakes and retreat. He had become a cockroach that just wouldn't go away.

Another acceleration launched him back into their bumper, only this time dislodging it, leaving it barely hanging on by one side.

Maggie began to eye his tires. It was the best way she knew how to throw him off their trail, but there was no clear shot.

That's when something resonated in her explosive-oriented mind.

She raised the rifle once more and fired it from her hip, summoning an unrelenting crackle of shots at the hood of Dominik's SUV. He ducked again as each bullet penetrated the protective cover of his engine. Within seconds, smoke began to billow from the holes before finally catching afire.

She watched the blaze spread across the hood like it was tinder, forcing Dominik to slam on the brakes. Through the cloud of smoke, she could see him flipping his middle finger before launching himself from the driver's seat and onto the tarmac as the whole vehicle burst into flames.

"I did it! I did it!" Maggie exclaimed, dropping back into the cab of their SUV.

"And you didn't even have to kill anyone," Graham added.

She leaned over for a high five that woefully was not reciprocated. Graham just faced back toward the road and continued to speed along.

She was aware that it wasn't time for celebration just yet, but *some* recognition would've been nice.

In the final hour, Maggie and Graham had arrived back in Tamil Nadu, rushing for the Hosur Aerodrome in hopes of meeting the others. After seeing a plane departing in the distance, they knew the airstrip had to be getting close.

Maggie looked at her watch; 10:12 am.

A few minutes off target—but hopefully not too late.

Whipping into the lot, their rental SUV lay up ahead, confirming that Emily and Seth were already there. The plane that Mr. Owens had prepared was still sitting in a hangar up ahead.

Pulling up alongside the rental, Maggie noticed half of the team's weapons and equipment were not in the vehicle, but there was no sign of their teammates anywhere. The keys were still in the ignition, and their phones were resting in the cup holders. It appeared that all that was missing was their backpacks.

They can't be too far ... can they?

Graham and Maggie both walked over to the hangar that housed the hired plane. Although there was no sign of Emily or Seth there either, they did find the other half of their equipment nestled into the cargo bay of the plane.

Graham turned back to Maggie, scratching the back of his head and shrugging his shoulders.

"I'm sure they're around here somewhere," he said. "Maybe they're speaking to the pilot? Do you mind grabbing those bags and helping me finish loading the equipment onto the plane?"

As they moved the equipment on board, Maggie continued to scout the airstrip until her eyes settled on another large hangar a few hundred feet away with its doors wide open.

"Do you think they went over to that one by mistake?" she asked, jerking her head toward the other hangar.

"Not likely. If so, why would half the gear be moved? Still, they should be here by now." He tossed the last bag in, then waved to Maggie to approach. "I'm starting to think something isn't right. We should check it out. Follow me, but stay tight."

Midway across the tarmac, they came across several employee uniforms lying discarded on the pavement. Entering cautiously through the main door of the hangar, they found two white planes inside, and an empty space that would accommodate a third.

Taking a single step inside, Graham bluntly shoved his forearm into Maggie's chest, halting her from going any farther. There was a man tied to the metal shaft of the wheels of one of the remaining planes, the distinguished tattoo of the Recreant Order visible on his wrist.

Graham withdrew his weapon and scanned the room for others, while Maggie stayed cautiously behind him. Once cleared, he lowered his weapon, leaving them both to gaze upon the man's humility.

"Here to rescue your friends, I see," the Recreant spat at them. Maggie and Graham exchanged a suspicious look. "You're too late. Your friends are as good as dead," he cackled.

Graham lifted his gun and shot the Recreant in the forehead without so much as a warning, sending Maggie shrieking as the blood splattered across the belly of the aircraft like a bug meeting a windshield.

"Don't you think we should have found out where they were taking them first?" Maggie yelled, stomping her foot. "You know ... before you put his brains back by the rudder!"

Graham holstered his gun and turned to face her.

"We *do* know where they are taking them—to 'The Boar,' remember? Emily told us that they kept saying they wanted her alive. As for Seth, I'm afraid it's probably too late for him."

Just then, a cluster of footsteps approached from the direction of the runway.

"Maggie!" Graham yelled, grabbing her forcefully by the bicep.

They rushed through the main door, as rounds of ammunition pattered along the interior of the sheet metal walls; more Recreants were coming through the bay doors.

Graham was practically dragging her as they sprinted back across the tarmac toward their hired plane, as more shots clacked around them with nearing accuracy. Rushing into the hangar, they slammed the door shut, Maggie darting to one side while Graham boarded the plane without hesitation.

"What are you doing?" he shouted from the door of the cockpit. "We have to go! Now!"

Disregarding his command, she stopped to rummage through one of her crates that had yet to be loaded onto the plane.

As Graham started the plane's engine, she ran back to the door and clamped a charge on its left side, then zipped a wire across the footer to another charge on the right, pressing its dormant green button.

She scrambled back to the plane as it wheeled forward, her feet slipping against the concrete as she hurried to scramble inside. Graham wasn't about to leave her behind, but he damn well sure made her work for it.

When the members of the Order finally ran through the doorway, the tripwire snapped, releasing an explosion that sent them flying backward in disarray underneath the steel slab of the door. Grinning at her success, Maggie shut the plug door just as

Graham throttled forward and shuttled the aircraft from the metal dome onto the runway, raising them into the air.

They sat in the cockpit, both staring out the window in total silence, broken only by a resounding beep from Maggie's laptop back in the cabin.

After she returned to the cockpit with her computer, she propped it open on her lap. A notification flashed across the screen showing that the Cardinal—Jonah Valerius—had left an airport in Italy and was headed for Iraq.

"Why would he be going to Iraq?" Maggie asked, turning the laptop to Graham while pointing at the screen.

"I don't know, but my concern right now is finding Emily and Seth. We know they've been taken by the Order. Put away the computers and the phones. We don't want to give them any inclination we're coming."

"What do you mean 'coming'? Where does this leave us? Where are we going?" Maggie said, gauging him for his assessment of their next move.

"We're going to go find them. We're going to Rome."

CHAPTER TWENTY

Emily & Seth

The warm touch of sunlight shining through the slats of the window shades awoke Emily from her sleep. Already stirring, she reluctantly opened one of her eyes while letting the other remain shut for a few extra seconds.

She reached beyond the ruffled blankets, patting for Seth's body, but he wasn't there. Rolling over to grab her cell phone from the nightstand, she realized that it wasn't there either, remembering that she had most likely left it in her own room the night before. Still completely naked, she swung her legs out from underneath the covers.

Slipping from the room, she floated her way down the hallway and headed for her bedroom to see the charging cord dangling at her bedside.

Where the hell did I leave my phone?

Throwing on some clothing, she gathered her things and progressed to the kitchen, enticed by the aroma of cinnamon and steeped arabica beans. Dropping her bag at the front door, she walked around the corner to find Seth smirking at the kitchen counter before she even spoke a word. She swung along the edge of the countertop into his arms for a long, smooth kiss, an emphatic reminder of the night before.

"Good morning, Emily Owens," he said nonchalantly, whilst handing her a cup of coffee.

"Good morning, Seth Parish," she jested back, lifting the cup to sip the hot beverage.

"So, any word from Maggie or Graham?"

"Good question, but I can't seem to find my phone. Regrettably, *I* didn't sleep in *my* room last night."

"Regrettably?" he asked, playfully raising his eyebrows.

"You know what I meant."

He reached into his back pocket and removed her cell phone, dangling it in front of her face.

"Found it this morning in the bathroom upstairs. Figured you'd need it."

"Give me that." She snatched it away from him, thumbing the screen to unlock it.

Her remnant glee was fleeting, her stomach quickly sinking into a knot when the notifications for three missed calls from Maggie appeared on the screen. The first two had come through close together at 4:00 am and 4:11 am; the third had been more recently at 6:40 am.

"Jesus, that was only twenty minutes ago."

Why didn't she text me?

"Em, what's wrong?"

Her worry prompted her to immediately call back—a call that went straight to voicemail. She motioned to check her own voicemail, and there was a single message: a mix of silence and scuffling for ten straight seconds, then finishing with what sounded like Graham yelling, "*Goddamnit, Maggie!*"

"Em, are you going to tell me what's going on? You're scaring me."

Without saying a word, she lowered the phone and dashed to the common area. Turning on the television, she changed the channel to the local news, entranced by the screen as every news outlet in the Ballari District reported of a second attack in the Sushruta Hospital, sometime in the early hours of the morning. The authorities believed it to be linked to the gunmen at the Hazara Rama Temple earlier the previous day.

"Hey, isn't that the hospital where we left Maggie and Graham?" Seth asked, joining her.

"We have to get to Hosur Aerodrome. Now!"

Emily spun away and tugged him by the shirt, hauling him toward the front door to grab their bags. Without so much as locking the villa, they set the navigation in the SUV and headed for the airstrip.

Pulling onto the open airfield, Emily and Seth parked outside a domed metal hangar that housed a sleek black plane, just as her father had informed them there would be.

They began loading the bags and equipment onto the aircraft, when a voice called from the tarmac.

"Excuse me, are you Emily Owens?"

She turned to see two light-skinned men walking toward her, wearing coveralls and safety vests; they looked nothing like the men that had been working at the airstrip just days prior when they had arrived.

"Yes, that's me. Is something wrong?"

"Not at all, Miss Owens. Your father has told us to escort you to your next destination upon your arrival."

"Really? Well, we were just about to finish loading all of our equipment on board."

"Oh, I'm sorry for your efforts, but that's no longer the plane we will be using. A malfunction was discovered this morning during the inspection. I must ask that you come with us, as we have prepared a new plane for your takeoff. I do apologize for the inconvenience."

Emily shot Seth a look of suspicion before staring back down at the two men.

"Have Maggie and Graham arrived yet?" she prodded.

At Emily's words the man's ears seemingly perked. He shot his companion an aggressive glance, one that transformed back into a forced grin as he returned to face her.

"How stupid of me, I forgot to mention. They're already waiting on board the plane. Come, let's get you seated and relaxed."

Where's their vehicle then?

Emily and Seth climbed down and began to follow the men toward the other hangar. The man who hadn't spoken left them to join a group of others who wore the same coveralls, all glancing over their shoulders, watching every move she and Seth made as they headed inside.

To her surprise, three planes were parked neatly beside one another in the center of the hangar. She let out a short sigh of relief at the fact that they were actually being led to another aircraft, until she overheard one of the workers speaking Italian as she passed by.

Italians? Working here, in India? That seems strange …

As a matter of fact, now that she thought about it, all of the workers were white, none of them looking to be locals. She recalled that when they had landed just days before, all of the airstrip employees had been Indian.

She quickly switched back into defensive mode.

"Seth, something's going on here," she hissed beneath her breath.

"You're telling me! Looks like we've been upgraded to first class."

"Seth, I'm serious! It doesn't feel right."

"Okay, okay. Yeah, I felt that too. Let's just stay calm. Where's your weapon?"

"In my backpack. Yours?"

"Same. We might want to keep them close, just in case."

Both casually slid their backpacks to their fronts, fumbling around as they walked side by side.

"Hey!" The worker who was directing them shouted from behind. "What are you two doing there?"

They turned, one hand each in their bags while the other held their bags by the straps. The worker, too, had one hand driven into the oversized pocket of his coveralls.

Emily studied the left side of his chest and the predominant name tag that was sewn onto it.

"Mohammad"? Strange name for an Italian.

The man followed her line of sight to the name tag before sharply pulling a handgun from his uniform.

Too late.

Emily and Seth had already dropped their bags during his withdrawing motion and now stood with both hands clutched on their own pistols, aiming squarely at the man's forehead.

"Drop it!" Emily commanded, gesturing her barrel downward.

The man dropped his gun without contest, gradually raising his hands to surrender. In doing so, his sleeves shortened, revealing the Recreant symbol tattooed on his wrist.

"Don't even think of yelling for help," Seth threatened, "or I'll drop you where you stand."

"And you think a gunshot won't attract the others?" the man retorted. "You dumb piece of shit."

He chuckled, then spat at Seth's feet.

Emily looked to Seth, then back to the Recreant.

He has a point.

"Keep him there," she said as she lowered her aim and moved to retrieve the man's gun and tossed it toward the back of the hangar.

She then jogged to the nearest plane, a white private jet that had *Quinntech* plastered across its side like some high-handed banner. Emily climbed its dropped steps to scout inside but returned just seconds later.

"No sign of Maggie or Graham."

Grabbing a coil of nylon rope that had been laid on a nearby container, she wrapped it tightly around the Recreant's wrists before leading him to the next plane and tying him to the landing gear.

"What time is it?" she asked, creeping past Seth on her way to the main door to peek outside.

"A little after 10 o'clock. Why?"

They're late …

On the tarmac, the workers had started shedding their coveralls, revealing tactical clothing and automatic weapons underneath. Farther past them, the billowing dust clouds from another of the Recreant's black SUVs that was approaching at top speed—no doubt loaded with more reinforcements.

"We can't wait for them any longer," Emily ordered, drawing from the door. "The plan has changed. We have to go."

"But Graham said …"

"We have to move—now!"

Seth holstered his gun and grabbed their backpacks from the concrete floor, following Emily on board the plane as she took one last look from the stairway at the bound Recreant.

"*Aiutami! Aiutami!*" he shouted profusely, flashing Emily another smug grin.

Emily didn't speak Italian, but she knew they had to move fast. She entered the plane's cockpit and slid into the pilot's seat.

The Recreant's henchmen poured into the hangar with their weapons at the ready, ringing several shots around the plug door as Seth was hauling up the stairs.

"How much longer, Emily?" he shouted anxiously, pulling the plug door shut and securely locking its latch.

As bullets rang against the body of the plane, Emily lined herself up on the runway and steadily pulled forward, pressing her feet against the rudder pedals to accelerate the plane to take off.

With the Recreants becoming tiny black dots on the runway as the plane gained altitude, Emily's legs started to relax just a little, and her vice-grip hesitantly began to release the controls.

"What the fuck was that?" Seth asked, standing in the doorway to the cockpit, wiping the beads of sweat from his face.

She peered around him into the body of the plane, its interior riddled with bullet holes from the Order's ambush; luckily, none had penetrated its outer shell.

"I don't know, but I'm sure that whoever owns this thing won't miss it. Looks like they can afford to have it replaced."

"How the hell did the Order even know where to find us?"

"Who knows. More of their resources, I imagine."

"What about Maggie and Graham? Do you think they survived the hospital or … ?"

"Graham's smart, and you saw how protective he is over Maggie. I'm sure they're fine … wherever they are."

"So, where does that leave us?" Seth slouched into the seat beside her.

Emily's eyes shifted to the fuel gauge, something she hadn't thought of checking before their impromptu takeoff. It only had three quarters of a tank, which was the equivalent of about three thousand miles.

"This plane isn't big enough to make it all the way to Bristol. And unfortunately," she said as she began tapping on the glass window of the gauge, "we wouldn't be making it that far even if it was."

"Assuming the others are safe, aren't they going to wonder where we are? We left half of our shit back in the vehicle, remember?"

Her eyes moved back and forth across the dashboard as she gathered her thoughts.

Assuming they're safe? Maybe it's too late for them. Who knows what Maggie was trying to call and tell me …

"It'll be okay. We'll figure it out. A brilliant man instilled in me at an early age that worrying gets you nowhere."

Suddenly, she perked from her chair, looking frantically about the cockpit.

"There! Pass me that!" she instructed, pointing at a piece of paper sticking out from the side of Seth's chair. He hauled it out to reveal a folded navigation map.

She snatched it from his hands and spread the paper out in front of her with a heartening smile, tracing her finger over the paper to a single black dot. She looked back up at Seth, who was leaning forward to see what she was pointing to.

"Iraq?" he asked skeptically. "Why would we go to Iraq?"

"Not just Iraq, Seth. My mentor, Dr. Alsafar—his laboratory is there. He can help us! I'm sure he can."

They had enough fuel to make the trip, and it was the only haven she could think of, though her giddiness was overshadowed by Seth's wary stare, as if he wasn't sure that it was the sanest suggestion.

The diminishing six-hour flight had felt like an eternity. Even with the autopilot allowing them to rotate sleep, Emily found it difficult to stop thinking of her friends she had so selfishly left behind. Graham would be tough, she knew that, but Maggie would be so scared.

Once the aircraft crossed the Iran-Iraq border, a mix of hisses and crackles rattled over the headset that rested near the dash. She leaned forward and snatched it from the console, wrapping it around her head and pressing it against her ears.

A person on the other end was relaying something in Arabic.

She had trouble gathering what they were saying at first, trying her hardest to ensure she understood the message correctly.

"Flight … 86 … do you … we will …"

The relay kept cutting out, making it impossible to piece together the whole transmission.

She kicked Seth's shin to wake him.

Once he realized something was happening, he lifted himself from his seat and bent over her shoulder to listen—not that he could understand any of it.

"Flight … 31986 … you respond … we … fire."

Emily reached toward the knobs and began to fiddle with the radio frequency to try and get a better signal, the needles swaying back and forth on the prompter as she twisted the knobs.

"Flight 331-1986 … do you respond? … We will fire … if necessary."

Her eyes widened as she grasped what was happening. It was stupid of her not to consider the consequences of flying an aircraft through potentially volatile airspace unannounced. She cleared her throat, hoping that her Arabic was pronounced correctly.

"Yes! Please, yes! Mayday! Mayday! Who am I speaking with?"

"This is the air traffic controller located at the Mandaean Research Center. You are flying into restricted airspace. Please divert your aircraft immediately."

"We are not a threat! Please!" With each pause, her heart began to knock against the inner hollows of her ribcage. "My name is Emily Owens! I've traveled very far to speak with Dr. Alsafar! We are not a threat! I repeat, we are not a threat! Do you copy?"

Seth flung himself back into his chair with both hands cupping his forehead as a brief moment of white noise filled the headset.

Emily started to scramble with the knobs again, fearing she had lost connection.

"If you do not turn your plane around, we will take it down. This is your final warning."

"No!" she screamed. "Listen to me! I need to speak with Dr. Alsafar! I have to land this plane! Please!"

Another moment of white noise ensued.

Neither of them moved a muscle, expecting at any moment to be blown out of the sky by a missile.

"Hello!" Emily shouted. "Hello! Anyone?"

"This is Alpha 1989-231. You have been cleared for temporary landing. Prepare for your aircraft to be boarded upon arrival."

Emily flung her head against the backrest, struggling to control her erratic breathing. Ripping the headset away from her skull, she shakily grabbed the controls and pushed forward, watching the gauges spin counter-clockwise as she started their descent.

Without so much as a chance to remove their seat belts after landing, the door was ripped open by two officers carrying AK-47s, who proceeded to force their way into the plane. Emily and Seth already had their hands held high in the air, only to be aggressively cuffed as the security personnel lifted them from their seats, ushering them through the gangway and into the adjoining building.

They were made to walk at a fast pace, onward through a labyrinth of double doors and white corridors, all of which contained workers in hazmat suits and lab coats, littering the aisles.

The small group stopped at a bright red set of doors. The escorts pushed them open and nodded for Emily and Seth to enter. They had arrived in some sort of living quarters complete with plush sofas, a sizable television, and a glass-top bar in one of the corners. On the opposite wall was another set of red doors. Panning cameras hung from the ceiling, focused on them both like watchful eyes, as they waited like criminals about to go on trial.

The room filled with a long, uneasy silence until the other set of red doors finally clicked open. Emily was surprised at first before her legs unwillingly thrust her forward.

"Dr. Alsafar!"

He had emerged from the doorway with a light jog, meeting her in the middle of the room with his arms spread wide to clasp her into a hug.

"It's okay, Emily, you're safe now," Dr. Alsafar rubbed his hand in soothing circles against her back.

Ending the embrace, he reached down to unlock their handcuffs one at a time.

"Sorry for the informality; precautionary measures, I'm afraid. And who might you be, young man?"

"Seth Parish." He rubbed his wrists as he took a step forward to grip the doctor's hand in a firm handshake.

"I see, I see. Well, yes, come along then!" The doctor waved, leading them into yet another corridor.

Their trek ended at Dr. Alsafar's office, which to Emily, seemed very much like a personal apartment within the complex; it had a bed, a kitchen, sofas, and even a small, discrete lab station. Dr. Alsafar lifted the tail of his lab coat and plopped himself into a puffy leather chair, laying the handcuffs to one side before interlocking his fingers and placing his elbows on the desk in front of him.

"Take a seat, Emily. Tell me, why are you here? What has happened?"

She sat impishly in the chair across from him, fully knowing that he would be angry if she revealed all the facts that had led her there. He had warned her weeks ago to stay away from the Recreant Order, but she had ignored him outright, making it her own fault that things were in the state that they were.

"Do you remember when you called me, warning me about the symbol I sent you and how it related to the Recreant Order?" She took a deep swallow, trying to play it off as innocently as possible.

"Yes, I do." His face sank, changing from optimistic to a sullen, predetermined disappointment. "Please, tell me you heeded my warnings."

She looked to Seth, who seemed to be trying to remain as neutral as possible.

"No, we didn't ... *I* didn't."

Emily spent the next hour retracing their steps, informing Dr. Alsafar that she was already in Peru at the time of his call, and how she felt she had to continue her search for the sake of capturing the legacy she so badly desired. She explained that it was only after those events unfolded that she understood how important it was to find the diamond before the Recreant Order did, hoping he would understand her reasoning.

Just as she had hoped, he never retorted in anger once. There were a lot of huffs and headshakes, but never a moment of displeasure. He listened, which was all she wanted him to do.

Once her explanation was finished, the doctor rose from his chair in thought, scuffing the soles of his shoes along the floor as he paced back and forth across the room.

"Did anyone know you were coming here to see me?" he said, jittering. "Were you followed?"

"No! This was a snap decision. This was the only safe place I knew I could come to. Please, Dr. Alsafar. Can you help us or not?"

"Emily, I care for you, I do. I love your family, and our history together runs deep. But for your safety, I cannot allow you to stay here. I'm sorry."

"Wait, what ... what do you mean we can't stay?" She was harshly taken aback by his lack of hospitality. "What safety?" She scowled, raising her voice at him and ejecting herself from her chair.

The doctor hung his head in despair, rubbing at his eyes.

"Your plane is being refueled as we speak. I will provide you with food and lodgings for the night, but in the morning, you must go. That is final." His voice had also raised a level in retort.

Emily stood slack-jawed at his cowardly lack of eye contact and said nothing, letting her displeasure be known when she turned to storm out of the room, slamming the door behind her in the process.

"Wait up!" Seth yelled as he ran to catch up with her.

He grabbed her by the arm midway down the hall to ease her back.

"Can you believe this?" Emily was fuming, her face a crimson red. Her jaws were puffed, and her eyes had long surrendered their usual pleasant aura. "He's just going to dismiss us? Really?"

Just then, another set of doors hissed open next to them, releasing more security guards. They were carrying linens and two key cards that were attached to lanyards.

"Dr. Alsafar has arranged these for you. They will grant you access to the common areas within the facility, including your rooms. Your belongings are waiting for you there."

As the hours ticked by into the night, Emily had opted not to leave their room, especially not to reconcile. Instead, she lay on her bed with one arm tucked behind her pillow, staring daggers at the ceiling.

She looked over at the clock; 12:05 am.

There was too much on her mind to sleep. She still had no idea where Maggie and Graham were, and even less of an idea of how close the Recreants were to finding the Florentine Diamond.

Growing more and more restless by the minute, she decided now would be a good time for a late-night stroll, one that might clear her head instead of encasing her in gloom between the four walls.

Hauling her bag across the floor, she withdrew her handgun. She had tucked it into the waistband of her pants just before the security personnel had boarded the plane—one of the perks of her new paranoia.

She popped the clip of the gun open to confirm that it was loaded, then snapped it back into place, shoving it into the rear of her waistband while standing to grab her key card from the nightstand.

Out in the corridor, she found that the aisles were now deserted. No workers, no security—almost peaceful in a way. One by one, she weaved through the different rooms of the research facility. The canteen, the lobby, the scattered archaeological laboratories: all containing fascinating high-tech equipment, but nothing else that was particularly intriguing.

Near the end of her self-given tour, she scanned her key card against the pad of a unique steel door, one that was noticeably more fortified than the rest.

"*Access Denied*"

She scanned it again.

"*Access Denied*"

Emily huffed, shaking her head at the fact that the automated systems mocked her with their denied entry.

Well Em, now might be a good time for that reconciliation after all. If I remember correctly, the doctor never did go to bed early.

She was soon face to face with his office door, knocking softly with the hope that he was still awake. She wanted to talk to him—privately.

No answer.

She reached for the doorknob, turning it to find that it was unlocked. She poked her head inside and called out to see if he was there.

Again, no answer.

Moving inside, she had all intentions to wait while perusing around the office to admire all of the accolades that hung on the wall. When, from the corner of her eye, she saw another key card laid atop a filing cabinet—one that looked slightly different than her own, more sophisticated somehow.

She snatched it from the cabinet and headed back out into the corridor.

Step by step, she slid along the corridor with her shoulder tight against the wall, peeking around each corner as she navigated her way back to the steel door. She scanned the new key card against the pad, this time initiating its automatic open.

As she slipped inside, the motion-activated lights above powered on by her movement, revealing what looked to be some of the doctor's most recent works in progress. Fossils, parchments, diagrams: all things one would expect from a busy world-renowned archaeologist.

Browsing through what she presumed to be his private lab, Emily came to a control console placed in front of a tinted set of windows. The console had a slit that looked as if a key card would fit perfectly into it. She placed the card into the slot and pressed down with her palm, activating the console's power source.

All at once, the console began to illuminate, energizing the previously dormant work station.

At first, she was amazed, reveling in the technologically advanced laboratory that she could only dream of one day owning for her own research. Dr. Alsafar had everything an archaeologist could ever want, right at his fingertips.

But her awe was temporary.

As the screens that lined the walls of the rooms began to operate, each one flickered in sequence, revealing each one of her documents from GemLab. The history, the origin, the appraisal of the Florentine Diamond replica; all of it was there.

She turned from the screens to the windows, her eyes welling as she began to comprehend what was happening while staring into the black nothingness behind the glass panes. In slow succession, bright lights and mechanical humming began to activate behind the panes, allowing her to make out what was concealed behind them.

She covered her mouth with her hand, leaning over the console in shock to witness a human incubator that housed one of the red-painted male warriors. He had tubes and monitors hooked up to his body like some sort of ill-considered test subject. More surprising was the fact that this wasn't one of the warriors from the Hazara Rama Temple, which could only mean one of two things: either Dr. Alsafar had found this individual elsewhere on his own, or the warrior had been otherwise provided by the Order. Either way, the Recreants reaches ran deeper than she had ever thought possible.

Her legs became weak and tingly, barely holding her up as she hyperventilated against the work station. Someone who she thought had loved and supported her throughout her entire life had betrayed her, leaving her feeling equal parts hopeless and foolish.

How could I have not seen this before?

As her down-turned face wavered above one of the monitors in front of her, she noticed a button with the words *"Initiate Tuscany Protocol"* on its touch screen.

What else are you hiding?

She thumbed the button, causing a cylindrical canister to slowly eject from the side of the console. Her glossed eyes widened as they were met by a brilliant yellow hue.

The replica diamond! That son of a bitch.

Stepping closer to the encasement, she removed the replica from its housing, fumbling it as she looked at it with a rekindled admiration before slipping it into her front pocket.

I'll be taking back what's mine, thank you.

Pressing the touch screen once more caused the empty canister to retract back into the console. Emily paced around the room, trying to figure out how best to get Seth and get out of there without getting caught. There was no doubt that the cameras had captured her every move, but in the off chance they hadn't, her new knowledge of Dr. Alsafar's dark secret was on her side.

She pulled the key card from the slot in the console, sending the room back into its unpowered state.

Scampering back to Dr. Alsafar's office, Emily hoped to return the key card before he ever noticed it had gone missing. The less of a footprint she left in her wake, the better. But upon her return, she found the doctor's door ajar. She could see silhouetted shapes moving about on the other side of the door through the light of its crack.

Shit!

Standing with her back against the doorframe, she listened to the brash voices of two people arguing about something. One voice belonged to Dr. Alsafar; she could tell that much with ease. But the other proved to be more elusive, yet she felt that its heavy rasp was familiar just the same.

Soon the arguing got louder, more hostile, and was followed by a harrowing grunt from Dr. Alsafar and the sound of metal utensils striking the floor.

That's when Emily pushed open the door and rushed inside, pulling the gun from her waistband and pointing it directly ahead. But her aim wasn't trained on the doctor like she thought it would be. Instead it fell on another man—one whose voice had given her the urge to vomit since the first time she had heard it.

Cardinal Valerius had the doctor clutched by the collar, tightening it around his throat while holding him pinned against the metal trolley that had previously been covered in lab tools.

Dr. Alsafar stared vacantly in her direction. Emily could see that his pupils were dilated and that he appeared to be bracing himself as blood ran from his nose down over his white smock.

The Cardinal eased his grip, tilting his head to look past the barrel of Emily's gun and straight into her eyes.

"You'd love nothing more than to blow my face off right now, wouldn't you?"

His words seeped through the corner of his cocky grin.

"You're goddamn right I would," she replied, thumbing back the hammer of the gun. "Let him go."

"No! Emily, don't!" Dr. Alsafar begged, holding his hand out to emphasize his urgency.

"Why not? Is it because you're one of *them*? I've seen what's in your 'laboratory,' you sick fuck. I trusted you. *My family* trusted you."

"I'm not one of them! You have to believe me, Emily! I swear it!"

Sweat began to trickle down the doctor's forehead, beading at his hairline and temples.

The Cardinal, on the other hand, remained overtly calm given the situation, tugging the doctor to his feet before shoving him away. He proceeded to spread his arms from his body, as if he was taunting Emily to end him, and she could see no reason not to.

"What's the matter, Miss Owens? Can't shoot an old, unarmed man? I thought by now you were a stone-cold killer, no? How many of my men have you killed? Five? Six? You're racking up quite the body count, I do believe."

He continued to smile as he taunted her. She gritted her teeth at his every word.

"Dr. Alsafar, what's going on?" she shouted. "Tell me!"

He nervously looked at the Cardinal, then back to Emily.

"He … He …" The doctor's lip quivered beneath the weight of his stutter.

"Spit it out, you old bastard," the Cardinal snapped as he reached into his pocket.

Emily took two steps forward, reminding him she still had the gun pointed at him.

Regardless, he pulled out a phone and began thumbing through its contents, stopping on a video recording and pressing play as he turned the phone in her direction.

Within seconds, tears lined her cheeks as she watched Dominik mercilessly beating her father who was strapped to a chair.

Her stomach buckled and her calves tightened. She braced herself with one hand on her thigh to stop herself from collapsing.

The hand holding the gun began to shake, though unwavering from the Cardinal's head.

"You see ..." the Cardinal continued, placing the video on repeat while laying the phone down. "Your father thought he could save his little girl by coming to find us first. Let you look for the diamond while he came to Rome to try and slay the beast, or should I say, 'the Boar.'

"But we were waiting. We're always waiting."

"Where is he?" Emily screamed, firing one round off beside him, the bullet lodging in the drywall.

Without so much as a flinch, he raised his index finger and wagged it back and forth.

"Now, now. As the doctor here so kindly asked, I wouldn't shoot me just yet. You see, I have a contingency plan in place that you just might be interested in hearing. If I don't return within twenty-four hours to headquarters, then your father dies. Now, you don't want that, do you?"

Emily's knees grew weaker as she periodically glanced from the video to Dr. Alsafar and then back to the Cardinal.

"What do you want from me? And what does Dr. Alsafar have to do with any of this?"

"You know what, Miss Owens, you're right. He doesn't have anything to do with this ... not anymore."

With that, the Cardinal grabbed one of the trowels from the trolley and slammed it into the doctor's ear socket. As the pointed blade severed the cartilage of his ear canal, it sent blood spattering across the Cardinal's beard and face. A waterfall of deep red gushed down the doctor's neck and arm. His limp body swung in a circle with the impact, making soulless eye contact with Emily before careening to the floor.

Muting her own squeal, she covered her mouth with her hand, sending more tears cascading over her fingers.

"Again, you can't shoot me," the Cardinal said with a shrug. "Oh, and don't worry, no one will be coming to help. Let's just say, I've sent security on a little ... break.

"Oh, how it must be eating you alive not to fuck my day up right now, huh? Such a shame. And speaking of a shame…" The Cardinal trailed off as he sat in the doctor's puffy leather chair, leaning forward over the doctor's twitching body. "The Order thanks you for your services rendered, Dr. Alsafar."

He leaned the chair back and placed his feet crossed onto the table, resting the back of his head against his interlocked hands.

"Apparently, there are a lot of people who will do just about anything to keep *you* alive, Miss Owens—you know, like study a diamond or examine an ancient warrior, for example. Did you really think the Order would allow the likes of Dr. Alsafar to join our ranks? Please. One little threat against the Owens family and he was broken, ours to exploit. Hell, even the Boar seems to have taken a liking to you, wanting to keep you alive and all.

"What do you say? Care to join us in the hunt for the Florentine Diamond?"

On his final word, the Cardinal's eyes shifted to the doorway. Seth had arrived.

"Em, what's going on?" he asked.

The gunshot must have woken him.

He approached her from behind, bringing into sight Dr. Alsafar lying in a pool of blood on the floor. He wrapped his hand around Emily's fist that was firmly clenched around the pistol, allowing him to take over her aim as she crawled across the floor to her mentor, whose life was long gone by now.

Seth spotted the video playing in a loop on the desk, then furrowed his brow empathetically down at Emily.

"Ah, the *boyfriend*," the Cardinal laughed, still unbothered by the gun pointed at him. "Here to save the day, are you?"

Emily pulled Dr. Alsafar's lifeless head and torso from the floor, rocking back and forth as she cradled him.

"Seth, don't. We can't kill him."

Her lips narrowed, gently lowering the doctor's body back onto the tiles. She climbed to her feet and walked over to the desk, reaching for the handcuffs. Swiftly turning to the Cardinal, she jerked his arms back, strapping him to the chair he was so confidently lounging in.

"This probably won't hold him for long. I'm sure there are more Recreants on their way here right now." She latched the restraints so tight that it broke his skin. "But it buys us enough time to get out of here."

She grabbed the Cardinal by his thinning white hair and yanked his head back, leaning in so they were nose to nose. "And the answer to your question is *no*. Because there won't be a Recreant Order left when I'm through with you."

"Emily? Emily!" Seth shouted, jarring her from her threatening posture. "Leave him. Come on, we have to–"

"*We* have to save my father." She turned toward him, dead-eyed. "No more running, no more hiding, no more bullshit.

"Let's get back to the plane. We're going to Rome."

CHAPTER TWENTY-ONE

Maggie & Graham

Maggie laid her head back, resting it against the ceramic lip of the jacuzzi. Its bubbles popped against her fair skin, brightened by the sunlight. She could hear the bustle of the city below, a relaxing white noise as she intermittently reached for the decreasing glass of champagne.

The October air was brisk, and the warmth from the tub was welcomed. The honeymoon suite of the Hotel Artemide was the only suite available upon check-in. Graham wasn't a fan, but they didn't have much of a choice. She, on the other hand, loved every minute of it. A free bottle of bubbly, a basket of chocolate, and a private hot tub on the rooftop balcony.

"When in Rome!" she snorted while taking another sip from the flute, giggling at her own joke.

She reached over and grabbed the clock radio to see the time; 2:00 pm. Graham had left hours ago, following a lead on the Recreant Order. Rome was a big city, and the two of them had very little to go on, assuming that Emily and Seth were here at all.

Just then, a beep sounded from inside the room, the lock releasing as Graham shoved his way through the door. He walked straight to the balcony.

"Let's go," he commanded, picking up a towel and flinging it at Maggie to catch.

She could tell that he must have found something, given the new cuts and bruises on both sets of his knuckles. Hopping from the jacuzzi, she scurried across the room, dripping and slipping as she ran barefoot past him into the bedroom to change.

"I'll be downstairs," he scowled. "Meet me outside the main entrance."

The door slammed as he exited the room.

It was the first time he had asked her to leave the hotel since they'd arrived. Maggie knew she wasn't the best of help when it came to this sort of thing, but she thought he could have at least been a little nicer after all they had been through.

Maybe I just need to prove myself a little more.

By the time she flung herself through the glass door onto the sidewalk, Graham had already unfolded a tourist map and was tracing his thumb along the page. As Maggie joined him, he tucked it into his back pocket without a word, nodding his head for her to follow his lead.

They started weaving through the cobbled streets. He remained silent during the whole twenty-minute venture. Maggie couldn't determine if he was too focused on the task at hand or still holding a grudge about not listening to him when he had told her to turn off her phone when they were in India.

Continuing up a slight grade, they came to a stop in front of the obelisk located in Piazza del Popolo. Maggie noted that they were at the base of the famous Pincian Hill.

"What are we doing here?" Maggie asked, hoping to discern the reason for his urgency.

Graham reached into his other back pocket and hauled out a pamphlet, discretely handing it to her.

"Let's just say that when all of your members sport a matching tattoo, they aren't that hard to spot.

"And don't worry, the man that I pried that pamphlet from won't be needing it anymore. Trust me."

She unfolded the handout to reveal that it was actually an invitation with the symbol of the Recreant Order blazoned across the top. The invitation read:

Masquerade ball on Pincian Hill
Your presentation of the sun is requested
Join us in celebration of our people
October 31st, 2019
Doors open at 20:00

She looked up from the paper at Graham's expression. It was the first time in a while that he didn't seem defeated and frustrated.

This was their in.

She gawked around the open plaza at the many buildings branching in all directions.

"So ... which one is it?" she asked.

"Well, that's the next step. We have two days until the party to find out where it'll be held—and if we're lucky, the party will lead us straight to their headquarters. Now that our search area has been narrowed, it should make things a little easier. I say we spread out and look for anything embellished with a Recreant symbol.

"I'll check the south side. You head north."

Graham handed her an earpiece and a communications receiver with synced frequencies. Maggie clipped it onto her belt. She knew it was the only technology he felt safe enough using without the fear of being tracked again.

"If you see anything, report it back. You got it?"

"Got it!"

Maggie crumpled the pamphlet and tossed it like a basketball in an attempt to land it in the nearest trashcan. It hit the rim and bounced to the street. Graham just shook his head while he walked away, leaving Maggie to blush with embarrassment.

They spent the next two days surveying every inch of Pincian Hill. Alleyways, side streets, parks, even the sewer systems—just in case. But, nothing.

It wasn't until the afternoon on the day of the ball that they caught a lucky break.

Wandering through a back street, two white courier vans passed Maggie. Normally, she wouldn't have given them any heed, but both vehicles were plastered with large catering decals across their sides. She hadn't eaten all morning, which was probably why they had caught her attention in the first place.

That's when it registered.

Two vans mean two loads of food. Two loads of food likely mean a large gathering of people. That must mean the masquerade ball!

She ran as fast as she could in their direction, trying to keep up, too focused and flustered to report back to Graham. The streets, crowded with tourists and locals, hindered the progress of the vans, but this allowed her to easily keep them within her range of sight.

Half a block behind them, she turned the corner around a gated building to find the vans had parked at a side entrance to a large stonework mansion. She hid beyond the iron bars, watching as the caterers opened the back doors of the vans and began to unload tray after tray of food. A well-built man guarded the same door, and as he turned to let the caterers enter, sure enough, Maggie could see the Recreant insignia positioned above his right elbow.

Jackpot!

"Graham, come in," she whispered. "Do you copy? Over."

"Yes, I'm here. Did you find something? Is everything okay?"

"I've found it. Meet me just west of the Fountain of Aesculapius, by the black gate on the corner. I'm in a shrub."

Maggie hunkered down for twenty minutes until he arrived, pointing through the slats of the fence for him to get a good look as he approached. He patted her firmly on the shoulder, the first sign of recognition that made her feel like a real part of the team—assuming that there still *was* a team to be a part of.

They eyeballed the large three-story building, with its many upscale windows and unique architecture. From there, their eyes shifted to the precast steps of the main entrance, as men and women trickled through the armed security detail waiting at the ready. As each guest neared the colossal set of wood-paneled doors, they presented their Recreant tattoo and the guards waved a UV light over the ink to ensure its authenticity.

Maggie's attention veered to the caterers once again, over-hearing two of the workers venting their frustrations in Italian about some ill-regarded co-worker.

"I'll try and translate," Maggie said, cupping her hand around her ear in their direction.

"You speak Italian now?" Graham questioned, his face riddled with confusion.

"I spent a year abroad in San Marino with my parents. You're not the only one with skills, mister. It's not my fault you kept me cooped up in the hotel these past few days. Now shush and let me listen."

She turned back to the conversation.

"I can't believe that bitch quit," Maggie repeated. "On today of all days, leaving us shorthanded like this. What a joke."

She gasped, looking up at Graham with wide eyes.

"Not a chance." He dismissed her insinuation without the slightest hesitation.

"Graham, you have to let me. I know I can use this opportunity to get inside."

"Maggie, you can't. You have little to no training, we haven't had nearly enough time to scout the premises, and on top of everything else, we've no doubt been marked by the Order for termination on sight. If they mark you, they *will* kill you, and then they'll probably stuff your body in that dumpster over there without batting an eyelash."

Hearing him lay it all out at once like that made her take large gulps of air to release the sticky lump in her throat. But just the same, this was the bold chance she had been waiting for to prove her worth.

"Listen! You just heard me say they're down a server. I bussed tables for three years in university, so don't tell me what I can and cannot do. I'd be perceived more innocently than you would if you were to go traipsing in there, and I'll stick out a lot less too. Besides, I'll have you in my ear the whole time to guide me, remember?"

Graham wiped his palm down his face, confirming that she had made a valid point.

"Okay, now *you* listen. We do this my way. You get in, you serve people their cocktails, and you stay invisible. When you get the chance, you sneak away to look for Emily and Seth. But Maggie, you must prepare yourself. You may very well find them dead—or close enough to it."

She hadn't really thought of that, and to be truthful, she had no idea if she *was* prepared.

"I understand."

She placed her hand on his shoulder and leveled her eyes with his before backing away into a light jog toward the vans.

After a few minutes of mingling with the caterers, she left them to casually skip back to Graham, who was standing with his arms held awkwardly out from his sides as if awaiting a response.

"I start at 8 o'clock!" Maggie bounced up and down on her heels, clapping her hands. "I have to come pick up my uniform at 5 o'clock.

"Funny that the Order is throwing a Halloween party while their higher-ups are searching for a long-lost diamond, huh? I guess cult morale must have its worth."

At 7:50 pm, they returned to the fence, slinking beneath the dimmed hue of the nearest streetlight. Hiding behind the hedges, they took cover with each passing headlight as the valets pulled around the front of the building.

"Here we go," Graham said, pulling a black ski mask down over his face. His body was draped in a form-fitting graphite tactical suit,

Maggie thought it was probably military grade. "Report everything you see to me. I want to know any and all characters you run into. If someone sneezes, you tell me from what direction. You got it?"

"I got it," she said mockingly. "Graham, look, if this is going to work, we need to be a team. I need you to trust me, okay?"

Maggie pulled her hair into a high-top ponytail, snapping the band of her masquerade mask around her head. It was one of the requirements of her catering uniform along with her black pants, black apron, white dress shirt, and a forest green bowtie to cap it all off.

"I'll be up there." Graham pointed to a rooftop opposite the mansion. "If you can, stay close to the windows. That way, I can not only hear you, but also keep an eye on you through the scope of my rifle.

"Oh, and Maggie ... I do trust you."

He ran off down the street and disappeared into one of the side alleys.

Maggie took a much-needed puff of her inhaler, tucking it into her apron as she walked over to the side entrance of the building to knock on the door. It was opened by a member of the catering staff.

The woman grabbed her by the wrist and proceeded to drag her onward through the kitchen.

"Okay, Maisie, was it? I'm putting you on drink duty. Just walk around looking pretty like you young ones normally do. You'll be paid cash in full after the event, and tips are split equally among the servers. Got that? Good. Get out there."

Before Maggie even had a chance to correct her name, she had a silver platter forced into her hands and was shoved toward the bar.

Wading through the dense crowd of guests, she couldn't help but feel like a fish surrounded by sharks. The majority of people in the room were killers, criminals, or an affiliate of either.

There were people of many different races and cultures, bringing together an assembly from all corners of the world. The fact that everyone was wearing a mask kept Maggie constantly at unease. She felt as if it were symbolic of them hiding their ugly truths.

Moving throughout the Recreant-infested halls, her head bobbed and weaved with every venture from the bar to the ball-room as she examined as much of the mansion's infrastructure as she could to relay back to Graham. Making a mental blueprint was harder than she had expected, between having to avoid the groping hands of entitled rich men and the incessant nag of tipsy women trying to summon her for another drink.

"Excuse me, miss, over here!" One such woman snapped her fingers as if that somehow made her more important than the rest.

Maggie turned to find an athletic brunette, wearing a beautiful bright red dress with a high leg slit, waving her over.

"If you don't mind, I'll take two of those." The woman rudely snatched two glasses of wine from the tray without even so much as a thank you, ignoring Maggie outright.

"Dumb bitch," Maggie muttered, carrying onward back into the crowd.

She had yet to find anything of importance, and her patience was running thin.

The more hours that passed, the more prominent the buzz of the crowd became. The music had gotten louder too, meaning now was the time for Maggie to make her move; she may not get another chance.

There doesn't seem to be much going on down here. Best I start checking the floors above.

Sneaking away from the party, Maggie climbed up a set of winding stairs from the foyer to the second floor, pressing her shoulder to the corner as she looked down the length of the stretched hallway. She slowly started making her way along, trying doorknobs as she moved. Midway down the hall, she finally encountered one that wasn't locked.

"Graham, I'm in."

Turning the knob, she slid into the darkness of the room and cautiously closed the door behind her. She flicked on the light switch, finding herself in an open room filled wall-to-wall with shelves full of books. Maggie was startled to find a masked woman slouched in a leather chair sipping scotch.

"What are you doing?" the woman slurred, shifting upright in the chair, her eyes bloodshot and swollen like she had been crying. "You aren't allowed in here. The party is on the main floor. Get out before I snap that twig-like neck of yours."

She took the last swallow of her drink, laying the empty glass on the table beside her.

Maggie stood completely still, stunned. She had never been spoken to like that before.

"Maggie, what are you doing? She's clearly just a woman drowning her sorrows." Graham's voice hissed over her earpiece. "It's clear that nothing's out of the ordinary here. Get back out and start looking. We haven't got much time."

"I am so sorry!" Maggie said to the woman, slinking her way back to the door. "Would you like the light off again, ma'am?"

The woman just flopped her hand, motioning for Maggie to leave, so she simply flicked the switch and backed out of the room.

Out in the corridor, she closed the door gently and quickly looked both ways to confirm that she hadn't been detected before creeping to the other end of the hall. Once there, she found another flight of twisted stairs, this one leading up to the third and final floor.

The third floor was quiet, unaffected by the rumblings of the gathering below. If anyone were to find her snooping this far away from the ball, she knew she'd be in serious trouble.

If Emily or Seth were being kept anywhere, it'd be here. I can feel it.

She crept from wall to wall, trying the handles of multiple doors, but all were locked.

"Maggie, they could be in any one of those. You'll have to bust the doors in."

"Graham, have you seen me? All I'm gonna do if I try to muscle one of these open is get a bruise."

A mumbling noise suddenly caught Maggie's attention. She launched herself around a corner for cover, just as a door swung open at the other end of the hallway.

"Fine! Starve for all I care, you stupid bastard!" Dominik appeared from the threshold, slamming the door on his way across the corridor and onward through a set of double doors.

"Maggie?" Graham's voice crackled in her ear again.

"Yeah, go ahead."

"That's the room. If they're feeding someone, it's to keep them alive. It has to be them. I can see your route through the window. If you run, you're clear. Get inside, get them out of there, and get back to me. I've dropped the fire escape for you.

"On my mark …"

Maggie exhaled against the dated wallpaper, peeking around the corner while focusing on the brass doorknob as her target. She reached down and removed her shoes, hoping that her bare feet would be less likely to cause a disturbance.

"Go! Now!" Graham ordered.

At his command, she sprinted as fast as she could down the hallway, her eyes shifting to the room that Dominik had entered, praying that the double doors didn't crack open as she passed.

Reaching the knob, she took one look back at the doors, then injected herself into the room.

The eerie silence was immediate, broken only by the sound of the latch clicking as she pressed the door shut behind her. Another dark room. She traced her hand along the wallpaper, feeling for a light switch, to no avail. She tried the other side of the doorway as well, but again, nothing.

"Graham, there's no light in this room. What do I do?"

"There has to be one somewhere. It's probably an interrogation tactic. Try searching farther inside."

She wandered into the black abyss—there didn't seem to be so much as a window in the room—unless it had been covered. Taking hesitant baby steps, Maggie stretched her arms out in front of her, waving them crisscross, hoping not to face-plant into anything. Beneath the bare soles of her feet, she felt a cold, slippery surface that crackled with her every step: a plastic tarp, which meant someone was trying to keep the place from getting messy.

That's not a good sign.

With a wide swipe of her arm, her hand finally brushed against a dangling pull chain. At its tug, the sudden burst of light from a makeshift lamp-stand accosted her eyes, forcing her to cover her face with her hands for a moment so her eyes could adjust.

Through the protective crease of her fingers, she examined the room to see that it was under much-needed renovation, indicated by the paint cans and plywood that had been left strewn about.

That's when she noticed the spattered crescents of red forming a dotted path along the outer edge of one of the tarps on the floor. Fear had stopped her from turning any farther, predicting that she would find at least one of her friends' bodies lying dead at the end of the gore-ladened trail.

Trying to save her dinner from making a reappearance on the floor, she mustered the courage to gaze farther to her left, only to find something neither she nor Graham had expected.

"Graham." Maggie pressed her finger to her ear. "We have a situation here …"

"What situation? Did you find them? Are they alive? Maggie, talk to me!"

"Technically, I didn't find *them*. And the alive part I, well … it's to be determined. Graham, it's Mr. Owens."

Emily's father was slumped in a chair, with nothing but ropes keeping his limp body in place. His face was swollen and mangled, like a boxer after losing twelve consecutive rounds.

"What do you mean 'Mr. Owens'?" Graham harped. "What the fuck is Emmet doing there?"

Maggie felt her mouth moisten, her stomach churning at the grotesque scene. She took a rough swallow then dropped to her knees to start untying him. On the final knot's release, his body fell forward, causing her to collapse beneath his inert weight.

He was breathing, but barely.

"He's ... alive," Maggie puffed, squirming to get out from underneath him.

"Maggie, listen. You have to get out of there. That bastard from the airport must have been baiting us. Serves him right that I blew his head off. Emily and Seth must have never been captured by the Order. Goddamnit! You have to hurry."

It was easy for him to say that. He wasn't the one responsible for transporting a two-hundred-pound, unconscious man down two flights of stairs and undetected through a crowd of five hundred people.

She squeezed Emily's father's face, hoping that it would help to jar him from his unconscious state.

Suddenly, his eyelids popped open and his eyes rolled back into his head like the reel of a slot machine before eventually falling back to focus on her.

"Mr. Owens, it's me, Maggie. I need your help right now, okay? I'm going to get you out of here, but I'm going to need you to stand up. Can you do that?"

"I ... I can ..." he gargled as a lump of blood poured forth from his jowls, "... do that ..."

Maggie placed his arm around her neck and began to hoist him as he helped push himself up with his other hand using the seat of the chair.

"Graham, where do we go from here?" Maggie asked, moving to shuffle their way back across the plastic toward the door.

"Give me a second!" he snapped. "I'm scanning the building. I can't see any plausible escape route for you. There are too many fucking people on the second floor now, blocking all the windows. We're gonna have to make a blind move."

"What exactly is a 'blind move'?"

"Maggie, in a few seconds, I'm going to shoot one of the Recreants through an open window on the second floor. When you hear the ensuing chaos, you open the door and you run. Get deep into the crowd and make your way to the nearest exit. Do not stop. Do you understand?"

"Okay ..." She clenched her hand around the doorknob, staring at Emily's father, who nodded weakly in confirmation. "We're ready."

Maggie heard Graham take four short breaths over the communications receiver, which was then followed by two gunshots and the high-pitched scream of a woman below.

At the signal, Maggie opened the door and started to hobble down the hallway as quickly as possible.

"We're on the move!"

"Maggie, wait! That wasn't me!" Graham shouted, oblivious to whatever had just happened. "Don't move yet!"

"What! It's too late for that now. We're halfway down the first flight of stairs."

Emily's father grunted with every drop in step, gripping the railing as tightly as possible until they reached the second floor. Continuing with their heads held low, they joined a crowd of people and veered with them through the winding hallways down to the first floor.

From the corner of her eye, Maggie could see multiple Order members with their hands on their weapons, attempting to perform crowd control as a swarm of people flooded through every exit and poured into the streets.

She and Mr. Owens followed right along with them, and somehow managed to make it out undetected. Once in the clear, they met Graham at ground level, who had climbed down the fire escape of his building to assist them.

"Let's get him onto the roof." Graham transferred Mr. Owen's weight from Maggie to himself. "Once they realize he's missing, they'll sweep this area to look for him. We have to hide."

Back atop the roof, Graham slumped Mr. Owens against the brick lip of the rooftop and picked up his rifle once again to peer into its scope.

"Looks like about fifty members of the Order are still inside, maybe more."

Maggie had her hands in the deep pockets of her apron, drawing Graham's attention as her inhaler clanked against something else she had been concealing.

"What are you doing?" His brow shriveled with curiosity.

"You remember," she began, "when I went to pick up my uniform earlier today?"

"Of course. Why?"

She smirked, pulling a familiar silver object from her pocket, thumbing its lid to reveal a blinking green light.

Graham's expression dropped in an instant, turning back to his scope to examine the base of the structure. Blinking green lights were strategically scattered along the base of the building, one placed on each load-bearing point.

"You crazy, freckled mite," Graham whispered, releasing a hushed laugh and flashing Maggie one of the biggest grins she had ever received.

She puffed out her chest proudly, walking to the edge of the roof, readying herself to bring down the Recreant Order once and for all.

"How's this for proving myself?" She raised her hand, never taking her eyes off the building, knowing this was the only way to end the Order's reign.

She placed her thumb on the detonator, and with a gentle squeeze, she began to press.

"Wait!" Graham shouted, causing her thumb to quickly withdraw from the button.

He stood up from his post and ran with the rifle to the far end of the rooftop, squatting to prop the bipods onto the ledge and stare into the telescopic lens.

"What's wrong?" Maggie asked, chasing after him.

"They have her! They have Emily! She's inside."

Maggie rapidly closed the lid of the trigger, squinting to look into the building. There were moving bodies, sure, but identifying them was impossible with her naked eye.

Graham waved her over, allowing her to use his scope.

Through a large window at the center of the third floor, Dominik could be seen encircling Emily, with some sort of automatic weapon flung over his shoulder. She seemed to have been badly beaten, and her hands looked to be tied behind her back.

Graham dropped to one knee and rolled his neck with a distinct crack, exhaling softly as he leaned forward and aligned the scope.

Maggie placed her hand gently on his shoulder, a subtle sign of her faith. She watched him slide his finger into the guard, resting it firmly against the trigger, awaiting her command.

"Do it."

CHAPTER TWENTY-TWO

Emily & Seth

Emily held her head in her hands while she sat on the steps of the obelisk at the center of the Piazza del Popolo. Emotionally, she was a wreck. Every time she closed her eyes, Dr. Alsafar's lifeless stare haunted her. Physically, she was drained. She and Seth had found nothing after a full day of looking for clues to her father's location. They had searched all over Rome and hadn't seen so much as a sign of the Recreant Order.

Time was running out.

Just when she felt as though all hope was lost, a crumpled piece of paper blowing along the plaza like a tumbleweed caught her attention as it came to rest at her feet. She looked down between her palms and noticed what seemed suspiciously like the symbol of the Recreant Order amongst its folds.

She leaned forward and snatched it up, surveying the plaza as she unfolded it in her lap. It was an invitation that read:

Masquerade ball on Pincian Hill
Your presentation of the sun is requested
Join us in celebration of our people
October 31st, 2019
Doors open at 20:00

Two days from now?

She stood, again looking around for a sign of where the crumpled paper might have come from.

"Emily, do you copy?"

She stirred, placing her finger on her earpiece and pressing it tightly.

"Yes, Seth. Go ahead."

"I'm sorry, but I've got nothing over here."

She stared back down at the invitation, then once more at the people milling about the plaza.

"Forget it. Meet me back at the hotel. I think I've found something."

The following days consisted of Emily and Seth meticulously combing over every inch of Pincian Hill, trying to find even the slightest indication of where the party would take place. While searching on the day of the ball, Emily suddenly slung her arm across Seth's chest, practically forcing him into a row of bushes.

She pressed her index finger against her lips and turned back toward the street, pointing to the main entrance of a large three-story building, one filled with upscale windows and stone archways. Two armed security guards holding UV lights stood like statues at a set of wide wooden doors. They scanned the Recreant tattoos of the people approaching the door with the light before granting them entry.

Emily could hear grumbling in Italian coming from the side of the building, and she shifted her attention to two white vans parked at the side entrance. Behind the vehicles were people dressed in black and white uniforms—the caterers, no doubt—though neither Emily nor Seth could understand anything they were saying.

"Emily, that's your way in! Go over there and somehow explain to them that you're looking for work. Your entry will be undetected *and* you'll have a mask on. No one will be able to recognize you!"

She thought about it for a moment, but then quickly dismissed the idea.

"Seth, it'll never work. No one in their right mind would assume that's a good idea. Instead, how about I try going straight in through the front door."

Standing from her crouch, she started walking away from their hiding spot, leaving Seth to jog and catch up.

"Uh-oh. You've got that look in your eye, Em. I don't like it." He grabbed her shoulder, spinning her around. "What's your big plan then, huh?"

She dragged him a little farther, pointing at a tattoo parlor just across the river.

"Are you serious?" He took a large step between her and the road ahead.

"Move." She rested her hand on her hip, staring at him with a look of unwavering determination.

With a reluctant expression, Seth finally gave up and stepped aside to let her walk over the Ponte Regina Margherita, right to the front door of the shop.

Entering the tattoo parlor, Emily rushed toward the counter and slapped a large pile of euros on the glass display. Taken aback, the artist wasn't even able to open her mouth before Emily had thrown the invitation down in front of her, pointing aggressively at the Recreant symbol without saying a word.

The artist seemed agitated, having obviously seen the symbol before. She started profusely shaking her head as she repeated something in Italian. Pressing the money against the countertop, she shoved it back in Emily's direction.

At first, Emily thought the woman was refusing the work, until she stood from her chair and moved to the door, flipping the sign over to read "*Chiuso*": Closed. The woman avoided eye contact at all costs, only waving, indicating for Emily and Seth to follow her to the back of the shop.

Sitting upright, Emily undid the top four buttons of her blouse to reveal the midsection of her sternum tattoo. She smirked, rolling her eyes at Seth, who was apparently now more concerned with her cleavage than what they were actually trying to accomplish.

Emily lay back, allowing the artist to wheel over her stool and begin working. But every time she would bring the buzzing needle close to Emily's chest, her hands would begin to shake uncontrollably.

"Relax!" she demanded, reaching up to grab the woman's wrist holding the tattoo gun. "Just do it."

She wasn't sure if the woman had understood, but her hand stopped shaking.

Emily never flinched, as the needle carved the symbol into her skin, hiding it within the already intricate design beneath her breasts. The illuminating dye was almost unrecognizable to the naked eye.

In thirty minutes, the tattoo was complete, and Emily was already storming back out of the shop without so much as a thank you; imperative that she keep up the façade as a true member of the Order.

Later that evening, Seth lounged around the hotel room, preparing their gear, while Emily readied herself for the ball. Occasionally, she would catch him eyeing her with adoration as she softly flicked a wand against her dark lashes or slid creamy gloss across her lips.

Each time, he became self-aware, and she would see him flush before shying away.

At the final hour, she emerged from the bedroom wearing a scarlet red dress, tight-fitting on her torso but flowing loosely from the hip down. Her right leg graciously protruded from the lengthy slit in the gown's right side. She had purchased the dress from the hotel's boutique earlier that day, making sure that it would compliment her new tattoo.

She made sure to wear her garter knife on her left leg, well-concealed and so far up her thigh that if security did reach that close, they would be getting a knee to the face regardless.

"You look beautiful," Seth said as he raised his head from loading his handgun.

She walked over and turned his body to face her, planting a vigorous kiss on him that left a glossy residue on his lips. Smiling, she retrieved a red mask that completed her outfit. She slid it gently over her head and flicked her hair out from underneath the band before looking down at her wrist.

7:50 pm.

"Showtime."

By the time they reached their hiding spot from earlier that day, it was half-past eight.

Fashionably late always was a good look for me.

Emily popped the communications piece into her ear then adjusted her mask, inhaling anxiously through her nose.

"You sure you want to do this?" Seth asked while shoving in his own earpiece.

"I have to. I know he's in there. I have to save my father. Whatever it takes. With his help, I know we can track down Maggie and Graham."

Her radiant confidence meant that there would be no talking her out of it.

"I'll be outside the whole time," Seth added. "If you run into trouble, I'm coming in to get you, no matter what. Okay?"

Without saying a word, she kissed him once more before turning away and commencing her trot toward the belly of the beast.

Guests were still funneling into the party as Emily started her ascent of the building's precast steps, blending in with the crowd so as not to draw any unnecessary attention. The Cardinal would have already warned the Order that she was coming to her father's rescue, and no doubt the whole staff had been put on high alert.

As expected, she was no exception to being halted at the door. As the male security guard waved her forward, she seductively pried open the front crease of her dress, showing him the tattoo between her ample breasts. He helped himself to a long, vulgar look, just as she had predicted he would, ogling her chest as he waved the UV light.

"Bit of a looky-loo, isn't he?" Seth chimed from her ear. "Perverted bastard."

"Yeah, like you wouldn't." Her voice came through the clenched teeth of her steadfast smile. "Now shush, before you get me caught."

"*Entri*," the guard said finally, winking at her as she slipped by.

She wasn't aware of how massive the building actually was until she made it past the entrance. There were easily four hundred people doing their rounds, with more still outside waiting to get in. Fortunately, there was still plenty of room to mix and mingle.

"I'm in."

Emily hadn't planned to drink, but after seeing everyone else with a glass in hand, she needed to keep up appearances. There were a number of servers floating around, but none were headed in her direction. That was until she spotted a red-haired server quickly passing by her—moving almost too quickly, as if it was her first day on the job. She was carrying a tray full of white wine yet offering it to no one.

Must be new.

"Excuse me, miss, over here!" Emily barked, rudely snapping her fingers to grab the server's attention. "If you don't mind, I'll take two of those."

She snatched two glasses of wine, hoping to avoid the trouble of finding another server later. Disregarding the server's muttering as she walked away, Emily took a long sip to conceal her wandering eyes. Her gaze panned back and forth over the crowd as she planned her next move.

With a glass of wine now in hand, she floated through several rooms of the house, sparking conversation with anyone who would indulge her, trying to garner any inkling of how the Recreant Order operated. She trod lightly, making sure not to tip anyone off to the fact that she wasn't actually a member of the Order.

An hour passed faster than expected, with Emily covering most of the ground-floor rooms without any luck. Once it was apparent that downstairs had nothing left to offer, Emily realized that if anyone was being held there against their will, it would be on the upper levels and away from the party.

Laying her empty glass on the bar, she headed to the foyer toward an ill-patrolled set of winding steps, ones upon which she had kept a watchful eye since arriving.

Breaching the top of the stairs, she leaned discreetly around the corner of the wall.

The same red-haired server she had grabbed the drinks from earlier just so happened to be emerging from a door in the middle of the hall. The server looked both ways before closing it behind her and creeping hastily to the stairwell at the end of the corridor.

What could she be up to?

"Seth, I might have a lead. Stand by."

"You got it."

Walking leisurely down the hallway, Emily pretended to admire the outdated decor, when she suddenly swooped inside the room the server had just exited, shutting the door behind her with a firm press. She traced her hand through the darkness along the edge of the door until she found the latch of the deadbolt and turned it. Reaching up to flick the light switch, she placed her thumb under her mask and lifted it from her head.

"Can't I just sit here in fucking peace?" a woman's voice slurred from across the room, surprising Emily as she spun to press her back firm against the wooden slab of the door.

A lone woman sat in an armchair. Her gaze was piercing as it landed on Emily's face, which she had momentarily forgotten was exposed.

"Oh, I'm sorry! I thought this was the bathroom," Emily slurred as well, hoping she could pass off her snooping as a drunken mistake.

The woman remained fixated, barely acknowledging that Emily had spoken. She raised herself from the chair, reached up to her own mask, and snapped its elastic as she ripped it away.

"Emily, who was that?" Seth asked.

"Alexandria." Emily's face hardened, her gaze unwavering from the woman in front of her.

The Recreant grabbed the empty glass beside her and flung it at Emily's head.

She ducked, as shattered crystal rained down on her after its impact against the door.

All right, Em … here we go.

Lunging forward, she tackled Alexandria by the waist, charging her backward until her tailbone slammed against a wooden desk. But as though it had gone unfelt, Alexandria proceeded to bring her elbows down relentlessly upon Emily's back.

She grabbed Emily's hair and wrenched it back so that her face was revealed, pounding her knuckles into Emily's jaw three times before Emily was able to retreat, wiping a trail of blood from her already swollen lip.

She hits like a damn marine, that's for sure.

They made a run at each other again.

Emily ducked under a vicious swing, raising her heel to connect her stiletto with Alexandria's chin. She hooked her arms around the Recreant's waist and raised her from the ground, tossing her over the desk and into a pile of worn books stacked on the floor.

Emily walked around the table while sliding her right hand through the slit of her dress, grabbing the handle of her garter knife and withdrawing it from its sheath. She thrust the blade downward, just as Alexandria spun around to block it with a hardcover book.

Jerking sideways, Alexandria flung the knife-pierced book across the room. She climbed to her feet, swatting Emily across the cheek with a different hardcover book, forcing her backward across the library. Emily's face was becoming red and puffy, her cheeks throbbing with every smack.

Emily had nowhere to go.

Alexandria knelt, thrusting her elbow deep into Emily's gut, leaving her weak and nauseated, vomiting the small amount of wine she had consumed earlier.

Alexandria simply laughed, watching as Emily made a mess of herself.

"Disgraceful," Alexandria said as she reached to tuck loose strands of hair away from Emily's face, who began to cough uncontrollably as trails of spit spilled from her mouth. "It's a shame that I have to fuck up this pretty face."

She grabbed the shoulder straps of Emily's dress, pinning her hard against the bookshelves while reaching forward to remove a thick bible from above her head. Staring at it with great intensity, Alexandria bobbed the book around so that the fore-edge was clenched in her hand. She raised it above Emily's face, holding it horizontally while digging her nails into the cover for a steadier grip.

"Matthew 7:7 – Ask, and it shall be given you … and *this* bitch will finally get her wish."

Upon uttering the words, Alexandria thrust the rock-hard spine of the book into the bridge of Emily's nose, fracturing the cartilage and causing blood to pour from both of her nostrils.

"That was for Rico."

Clenching her jaw, she hit Emily again with more aggression than the last.

"And that was for me."

Through Emily's watering eyes, she could see that Alexandria was relishing in her punishment, licking the blood from the bible's spine like a true psychopath—one who had become completely unhinged by life.

Alexandria released her grip on Emily's dress, sending her slumping to the floor. She could feel the Recreant standing over her, casting her in shadow before the cold circle of the barrel of a gun pressed against her forehead, followed by the click back of the hammer.

"You know, maybe I should cut your leg off first, huh?" Alexandria spat through gritted teeth, lowering the gun and pressing it into Emily's already swollen eye socket. "Or maybe put a bullet through your eye, perhaps. Would that suit you better?"

As the chamber pressed against her orbital bone, Emily let out a scream for help that fell on nothing but the ears of her assailant.

"I don't know why the Boar wants to keep a pathetic piece of shit like you alive anyway. What is it he sees in you, I wonder? You're weak. Look at you! But unfortunately for him, you've taken away everything that gave me meaning in this world. Because of you, I have nothing left to lose. I welcome death now, and so should you."

Alexandria brought the gun back to Emily's forehead, readying for a kill-shot. But just as she was about to pull the trigger, Emily grabbed Alexandria's wrists, forcing her aim upward, to which she reactively sent two shots into the ceiling above.

Emily twisted the Recreant's arm, slinging her over yet another sturdy desk.

The guests, who by now seemed to be littered throughout the second floor as well as the downstairs, reacted to the shots by running and screaming, trying to make their way back toward the stairs that lead to the ground floor.

"Emily! What just happened?" Seth's voice hissed in her ear. "Your comms keeps cutting in and out. I think I heard shots."

The knob of the door began to jiggle vigorously, followed by the thud of someone's shoulder pounding against it, trying to break it open.

With her one good eye, Emily looked around the room and located another door on the back wall. She staggered toward it, but just as she placed her hand on its handle, it flung open from the opposite side, causing her to stumble backward onto the floor.

"Valerius …"

He entered the room swiftly, closing the door behind him.

As she slid herself back along the carpet, he walked toward her with a devilish stare, eyeing her as if she was his prey.

"No!" he shouted, lifting his open hand into the air while his attention shifted sharply across the room.

Alexandria had gotten back to her feet and raised her pistol to point directly at Emily. Her face and eyes twitched like she was trapped in some sort of dilemma.

"Give me the gun, Alex." The Cardinal began making his way diagonally across the room toward her.

She didn't move, but instead kept the gun trained on Emily, who by now had raised her hands into the air with a look of uncertainty about what was happening between the two.

On his approach, the Cardinal clasped his hands around Alexandria's, gently taking the gun away without contest.

With pistol in hand, he made his way back over to Emily.

"Well now, isn't this convenient. All this time, *we* were looking for *you*, and now here *you* are. You know, payback is a funny thing."

He removed a set of handcuffs from his back pocket, dangling them from his index finger. "Alex, be a doll and restrain Miss Owens, would you."

He stretched out his hand holding the cuffs until Alexandria walked by and snatched them, kneeling behind Emily to tighten the metal around her wrists.

"Someone would very much like to speak to you, Miss Owens," the Cardinal continued while moving toward the door. "In fact, he's been waiting quite some time for this."

The Cardinal led the way to the third and final floor, following a faint trail of fresh blood droplets that led up the stairs and to a room at the far end of the hallway. Expecting this to be her destination, Emily was surprised when they stopped short, with the Cardinal reaching out to rap at a large set of double doors located midway down the hall. Seconds later, Dominik opened the doors, smirking as they dragged Emily past him into the shadows of the room behind him.

A man was standing with his back to the room, staring out the large windows that overlooked the city. Alexandria pushed Emily down onto her knees before joining the Cardinal and Dominik, who were already standing at attention by the man's side.

"Monarch, we have brought you Emily Owens," the Cardinal announced. "As you have so often requested."

This must be the Boar.

The man's back remained facing her. His white dress shirt and suspenders were tightly fitted against his broad, athletic shoulders. His beard was dark and full, yet sprinkled with a casual grey, and his neck-length hair was loosely thrown into a disheveled bun. On the upper part of his neck, about two inches behind his right ear, rested the symbol of the Recreant Order etched into his skin.

As she processed his physical features, Emily was struck by a moment of recognition, and her heart began to race.

No ... it ... it can't be.

Without having the chance to even speak his name, the man turned to face her, his piercing blue eyes harshly reminding her of her journey's cruel beginning.

"Everett ... fucking ... Taylor."

She spat the words from her mouth as if they were sour on her tongue.

"Now, now, Miss Owens. I thought you only saved words like that for the bedroom, if I recall." Everett chuckled, taking a few small steps to where she was detained. "You are a hard woman to get a hold of, I must say."

He walked past her to pour a glass of scotch from the bar, taking a sip as he came back to stand over her.

"Tell me, do you still fantasize about me?" He was now gloating to the others.

She looked up at him as seductively as she could with a fractured nose, then she pulled back and spat into his face. He paused at first, removing a handkerchief from his pocket to wipe away her blood and saliva, laughing as he looked back at his inferiors.

Using the same handkerchief, he intimately wiped the blood from Emily's face, taking his time to ensure he removed every last streak. Then, he elegantly covered her face with the cloth to grip her nose, and with a loud crunch, twisted it to snap it back into place.

She released a muffled scream into his hand, almost fainting with the pain. He caught her before she hit the floor, propping her back onto her knees.

"Shhh," he whispered, wiping the remnant trickle of tears from her cheeks. "Shhh, it's okay. I've got you now."

"What is it you want from me?" Emily was practically blubbering from the shock of the pain.

"Oh Emily, it's not what I want *from* you. I simply want, well, *you*. Ever since our night in New York, I was convinced that you were unique. You do remember what happened that night, yes?" He grinned again.

"I don't understand. Why me? Why come after me and my family?" She was diverting him from the path of his sick little mind game.

"You see, I knew I wouldn't get a good girl like you to join the Order without a little ... persuasion." Emily shook her head, disgusted that he thought she would ever join the likes of the Recreant Order. "You laugh, but your destiny is to be with us ... with me. You're a smart young woman, Em."

"Don't you dare call me that!" she spat, quickly cutting him off. "You don't have the right."

"Fair enough, *Emily*." He started to pace back and forth in front of her. "I want you with me when I find the Florentine Diamond. I could use someone like you by my side.

"Once I am the Vicar of Christ—the keeper of the holy Florentine Diamond—I will have the power to spread the ways of the Recreant Order across this world, no matter how brief of a time it may be. I will exercise my right, unhindered, to unify the people and rid the world of the unholy and impure. It will be *I* who takes care of all souls. The Society of Jesuits—the Pope included—will bow before me."

She watched as his demeanor slipped from slightly crazed to purely psychopathic.

"Doesn't it sound glorious?" he added. "Don't you want to be a part of this magnificent movement?"

"Where does the Florentine Diamond play into all of this, exactly?" Emily queried. She was wracking her brain for the most opportune questions to ask, hoping Seth was still listening at the other end.

"Oh, come now, Emily, we both know you're cleverer than that. Think about it."

He gave her a moment to consider what she knew about the diamond and its power, recalling every hint buried within Everett's riddled words.

"The Pope ... Are you going to target the Vatican City?"

"The Vatican City!" Everett repeated with joyful cheer.

"The mist ... You want to send the army in to attack the Vatican from the inside out. You sadistic son of a bitch. Don't you realize that if you take control of the Vatican City, that Interpol, the Italian military, Christ, even the FBI will immediately try to put a stop to your plan? Guns versus spears and arrows are no contest, you fool. Your little plan is flawed at best."

"I think you mean sadistic genius," Everett corrected her. "You may be right, but the world will thank me by the time I am done. Neither my intention nor my expectation is to make it out of this alive; why, that would merely be a bonus! The Vatican is but a stage, one I can use to garner all the media attention I will need.

"Once the world's religious populations see the powers of the diamond, see that a higher being *does* exist, my mission will be fulfilled. The perspective of the world will forever be changed, and you, Emily Owens, will have played such a pivotal part in all of it. I am offering you a front-row seat to free this world of the ungodly chains it has been bound by for centuries. Please, allow me to reward you for your assistance."

"My assistance?" She scrunched up her face at him.

"Oh yes. Why, without you, I'd never be mere steps away from finally knowing the location of the Florentine Diamond."

Her confusion lingered; she was oblivious to exactly what he was alluding to.

He laughed again, walking amongst the other Recreant Order members.

"That night, in New York, do you think I was there by coincidence? Do you think *you* were? Did you actually think that *you* would get an invite just because of your family name?

"Think for a second. What better way to heat a trail gone cold than to have a fresh, young, beautiful set of eyes take a look at it. My followers are great researchers and treasure hunters, but sometimes the bigger picture eludes us, you see? And the way I'd heard Dr. Alsafar ramble on about you in our past encounters, well, he unknowingly made you an easy target."

Emily's mouth gaped with her inability to decide if she believed his allegations.

"I will admit, however, the sex was not at all in my intentions, but once you threw yourself at me for more information, well, I am still a man after all."

Emily squirmed to her feet and lunged at him, only to be halted by Alexandria's gun in her face once again, allowing him to continue rambling on.

"Dr. Alsafar really should have invested in a better firewall as well. His emails were easier to hack than I anticipated. We do appreciate the lead in Peru, by the way: Machu Picchu, of course. I mean, that was the turning point to our success, no doubt. By the way, you really shouldn't buy a train ticket with your credit card when you're trying to be discrete, you know."

Everett stopped in front of Dominik with a grim expression. "If I'm not mistaken, you almost did away with this one that night; am I right? Not that you didn't do a good enough job on your own of keeping this scum away from you, but trust me, he paid for what he did when he was back in my presence."

As Emily began to relax, Alexandria finally lowered her gun, standing back in position beside the Cardinal as Everett continued to speak.

"I did make one mistake, though, and that was sending some of my less-educated followers to New York to retrieve the replica diamond. I should have been clearer when I told them *not* to take your USB drive. But no matter; two out of the three paid for their indiscretions. Tell your sister I said thank you, by the way."

"So why tell me this now?" Emily snapped, wishing he would just get whatever he was going to do over with.

"Well, it seems as if we've come to another roadblock. As a matter of fact, if it wasn't for your father coming to save his precious little girl, we wouldn't have even known you were in India. I'm very surprised, by the way, that you let Rico and the others get to the temple before you—God rest his soul. Dragging your heels, were you?

"Oh, and about your old friend, Dr. Alsafar. He was useful for a while, I suppose. You know, he couldn't shut up about you and your family, praising you at every opportunity. He was right too, as it seems your father is craftier than we anticipated, slipping out during the commotion you caused earlier. An Owens for an Owens, I suppose."

Emily hung her head so she could conceal her smile.

"Seth, did you hear that?" she whispered. "My father's safe!"

She lifted her head again at the sound of crinkling paper as Everett pulled something from his pocket and unfolded it in front of her.

"Have you seen this on your path to foil me? Any chance you know what it means? My people found this in an abandoned cathedral near Venice."

She looked over the picture hanging in her face. The yellow beam of light shooting into the sky was once again unmistakable, but there were no blue triangles this time. Instead, there were two larger red ones, and they weren't beneath the light like the others, but instead were placed on either side of the arrow-shaped beam.

"Two red triangles with a yellow arrow between them?"

"Emily, if you help me on this quest, I'll let you live, I promise. Or, you can remain the stubborn girl that I know you can be, and we say our goodbyes. It really is your call."

"Nope. I'm sorry, I have no idea what it means." She felt no regret in saying that she couldn't help him. She just wanted Seth to be able to hear her over the transmitter. She could have easily agreed in order to buy more time, but she knew they would just use her and then dispose of her like the others before her.

"All right, then," Everett said, motioning for Alexandria and the Cardinal to open the double doors. "Have it your way. You know, I had much higher hopes for you ... for *us*. You really could have been something special."

"I think I'll live," Emily muttered, turning her gaze from him.

"Funny you should say that ... because I don't think you will. Dominik?"

"Yes, sir?" Dominik took a step forward with his hand already gripping his gun.

"I've run out of patience with Miss Owens. She's been given enough chances. Would you kindly dispose of her, please? And try not to make a complete mess. One bullet will do."

Before exiting the room, Everett approached Emily one more time. Lifting his hand, he grazed the curves of her chest.

"Don't *touch* me!" Emily pulled away from the contact. "You disgust me!"

"Oh ... that's too bad. Because I truly admire you. We could've done great things together, you and I. It's sad, really. Now, if you don't mind, I think I'd like to take something to remember you by."

He neatly pushed open the slit of her dress to expose her left breast and grasped the barbell piercing her nipple with his middle and index finger. Before she could react, he ripped it from her skin, causing her to scream in anguish before readjusting her dress to cover her chest. Stuffing the jewelry into his pocket, he left the room, leaving Dominik to finish the job, as Alexandria and the Cardinal followed, closing the doors behind them.

Now alone, Dominik moved closer, grinning as his eyes feasted upon her for the last time.

"Oh, how the mighty have fallen, wouldn't you say, sweetheart?"

She closed her eyes in an attempt to block out what was happening.

Good luck, Seth.

"We never did finish what we started in Urubamba." Dominik went to check the door before returning to stand in front of her. "Maybe I'll just take what I'm owed, you know, *before* I put a bullet in your head."

CHAPTER TWENTY-THREE

There was an unexpected thud against the hardwood floor, and Emily's face was sprayed with a warm, wet liquid before she was overwhelmed by the sharp metallic smell of blood. She tilted her head to try and drain the liquid from around her closed eyelids, managing to clear one of them so she could see what was happening.

Dominik lay slumped in a heap in front of her with a gaping hole in the back of his skull.

She twisted around to see the cracked circle in the window, then back to his body, scrambling to bring her arms down around her body and underneath her legs so that they were now cuffed in front of her. She immediately dragged her hands down along her face, staring at her palms now drenched in a garnet red.

Motioning to stand, she hovered over Dominik's corpse and kicked him repeatedly, a post mortem reminder that you don't fuck with an Owens.

She shifted back to the window frame, peering out below to find the street filled with party guests and onlookers, not to mention nearly a dozen police cars. The building was crawling with members of the Recreant Order, all of whom were unable to leave without a fight. It wasn't looking like she would be able to walk out the front door either. Her face held the evidence of Alexandria's wrath, and her chest tattoo clearly brandished the Order's mark.

Well, Em, how are you going to get out of this one?

"Emily, can you hear me?" Seth's voice buzzed over her earpiece through the static.

"Yes! Seth, you have to get away from the building. The Boar is Everett, Everett Taylor. The guy I stole the info about the diamond from. He's been one goddamn step ahead of us this whole time."

"Oh, really? Is he that douchebag-looking guy I just passed walking with Alexandria and the Cardinal? If so, he looks pissed."

Emily froze, processing what he had just said.

"Seth, please tell me you're not inside."

Just then, the double doors swung open, causing her to stumble backward and take on a defensive stance.

"I'm not inside," Seth said sarcastically, standing in the doorway, sweating and short of breath. "My God, are you okay?" Grabbing her by the back of the neck, he moved in to kiss her before drawing away to examine her lacerations. "What did they do to you?"

"What are you doing here?" she asked, ignoring his questions outright.

He draped her wrist over the edge of the bar, smashing the chain of her cuffs with the stock of his gun.

"When I heard the gunshots, people started rushing out of the building. And when you wouldn't answer, I slipped past the chaos and came in through the side door. Once I made it to the second floor, I started to search the rooms, but it wasn't until I saw the three of them coming down the stairs that I knew you had to be up here somewhere. I told you I would come for you."

Just then, another bullet whistled through the window and into the back of Dominik's carcass.

Seth grabbed Emily by the torso and swung her behind him protectively, but her instinct was telling her that they weren't under attack. If someone wanted her dead, they wouldn't have missed.

She leaned forward, peeking across the road at the buildings in the distance. Unable to get a clear sight, she reached down and removed Dominik's gun from around his body, using its scope to get a better view.

"Is that … Maggie?" she muttered. "Oh my God. Please tell me it's her!"

Spotted across the courtyard, the tiny redhead was practically doing jumping jacks on the rooftop. At the same time, Emily panned right and found Graham crouched beside her, sequentially flashing a light to get her attention. The flashes were accompanied by him holding his fingers up to relay a signal.

"5 … 1 … 3." Emily called it aloud, trying to understand what her brother-in-law was trying to tell them. "5 … 1 … 3."

She looked over her shoulder at Seth, but they were both perplexed.

"Wait! 5-1-3," Seth repeated, reaching to his waist for the communications receiver. He twisted the dial, switching through its frequencies before handing the radio to Emily, who pressed its button with her thumb.

"Maggie? Graham?" she shouted. "Do you copy?"

"We copy," her father's voice crackled back.

She looked to Seth, her eyes sparkling through their swollen state.

"There's no time to waste, Toots. We've got to get you out of there."

"Everett Taylor is the Boar," Emily added. "He's out there somewhere with the Cardinal and Alexandria. Be careful. They could be anywhere."

"All right, everyone, this isn't going to be a walk in the park," Graham said. "I need you to listen to everything I say. You got it?"

Emily and Seth flashed Graham a thumbs up, then turned back toward the doorway. But as they tried to move from the room, Emily stumbled to her knees. Her mouth was still bleeding heavily, and her nose hadn't even started to clot yet. She kept her hand pressed against her breast, hoping to use the dress as gauze, but

THE MISTS OF MORNE

it was getting more and more soaked with blood by the second. Her injuries had left her in a weakened state.

"C'mon, Em, we're almost out. You got this." Keeping one hand on the trigger of his gun, Seth helped her to her feet, using his other arm to support her from the side.

Slipping back in to the hallway, they saw no immediate signs of any of the Order members. They hobbled toward the staircase that led down to the second floor, hurrying as fast as they could, until a pair of voices resonating from below stopped them in their tracks.

"Two men in tuxes are coming up the stairs," Graham advised. "Hide."

Emily and Seth hugged the corner, readying themselves to pounce, when two light sounds of punctured glass resonated beside them. The two men dropped to the floor and tumbled head over heels into a heap at the bottom of the steps.

"There, I've made a path for you," Graham said. "Use it."

They hurried down the flight of stairs, stepping over the mound of henchmen.

"I remember seeing an emergency exit a few hallways over while I was searching for you." Seth veered them left, then took another sharp right. "If we can find it, it will be the quickest way out of here."

They maneuvered through every corridor unnoticed, making it to the red *uscita* sign above the door, which appeared like a beacon of freedom.

Seth pushed his back against the panic bar of the emergency door so they could slip out into the night.

Red and blue lights strobed against the surrounding buildings as Emily and Seth scurried into a nearby alley, pausing within the shadows so Emily could have a moment of rest. After every couple of minutes, they would make another dash, distancing themselves as far from the crime scene as possible.

The chuff of two police helicopters and a news crew hovered over the Recreant Order's mansion as circles of harsh light crossed against the building's façade, combing for any sign of movement from within the structure.

"Where are you now?" Graham's voice hissed again into their earpieces.

"We are about two or three blocks away from the party," Seth answered. "Heading south."

"Then plug your ears," Maggie instructed, masking a faint repetitive beep in the background.

Seth crouched with Emily behind a parked car on the side of the street while they both cupped their hands over their ears. Seconds later, explosions began going off in succession around the base of the Order's headquarters. Towers of orange flames, followed by large black billows of smoke, rose high into the sky and encircled the perimeter of the building.

Scattering into the streets for cover, civilians and officers screamed in unison as the helicopters above rolled sideways with a quick ascent to evade the blast overpressure.

Windows shattered and pillars began to fracture. Shards of rock and marble rained down from above on their way back to the ground after their initial skyward toss. But only when the building's segments started to collapse did the last of the Order members come running out, despite the police presence, dropping their weapons and surrendering to the officers who were returning to their posts outside the building.

Soon, the roof of the building caved in on itself, with the rest of the structure following suit, and with a thunderous crackle, it imploded into a pile of stone and ash. The remaining flames licked the night sky from within the rubble.

"What the fuck was that?" Emily asked with panic.

"Let's just say the Order has had a few dozen resignations," Maggie quipped, giggling at her own joke once again. "I told you I wouldn't hesitate next time."

"And Everett?"

"I haven't seen him. Only a few members of the Order were lucky enough to escape the blast, Em. He must have been inside,

THE MISTS OF MORNE

and no one's walking away from that. Except Alexandria. She made it out before the crash. But don't worry. The last we saw of her, she was being shoved into a police cruiser—very unwillingly, I might add. She won't be bothering us anytime soon."

For a moment, Emily was saddened but then was immediately relieved. This was an end. No longer would she, her friends, or her family be plagued by such a vile group of people.

She regretted nothing.

Their business in Rome was complete.

A short distance from the hotel, the groups rejoined each other with smiles and tears, but most of all, relief. Maggie and Graham were able to turn their electronics back on for the first time in days, while Emily wrapped her arms around her father and squeezed him so tightly that both their wounds pained from the embrace.

"Sorry, give me a second, guys," Graham said as he wandered a few steps away from the reunion. "I'd better call Peyton. She'll have my head for not checking in these past four days."

As he stepped to the other side of the street for privacy, the others dispersed as well, taking a moment to rest and recount the evening's events while Graham made a call. From where Emily sat, she could see his face oozing with concern, an expression that was immediately replaced with excitement.

Shortly after ending the call, he rejoined the group, smiling from ear to ear.

"Divorced?" Seth joked.

"No, but it looks like we finished up just in time. Peyton's on the way to the hospital. Her water broke ten minutes ago!"

Maggie started jumping up and down and clapping, while Mr. Owens grabbed him by the shoulder and congratulated him. Before saying anything, Graham looked to Emily with a sheepish expression, eyeing her as if to ask for some sort of permission.

"Go," she said. "You are not missing the birth of your child because of me. Besides, now that we've saved my father *and* taken down the Order, I think we can take care of ourselves from here on out, wouldn't you say?"

"Thank you," Graham said, hugging her tightly. It was the most affection he had shown her since joining the family.

"But please," Emily continued, "take my father with you. He needs medical attention, but not here. It's too risky—there will be too many questions. Where's the plane now? Can you get him back to the U.S.?"

"Emily, I'm not leaving you!" her father retorted boldly. "You're in bad shape yourself."

"Dad, I'll be fine. *We* will be fine. Trust me."

She shot him her puppy dog eyes combined with an innocent grin.

"Yes, I suppose you're right." He began to cough repeatedly before shaking it off.

"Go on, get out of here. I love you both."

Graham assisted Emily's father down the stretch of road before hailing a taxi to take them to the airport.

"So, where does that leave us?" Maggie asked. "I have your phones and belongings back at our hotel. I grabbed them at the Hosur Aerodrome before we took off. I thought you might need them."

"First, we rest." Emily looked around at the sprawling view of the city, then back at her teammates with a swollen smile. "Tomorrow, well, we'll see where it takes us."

Seth and Maggie looked at each other and burst into laughter, wrapping their arms around Emily.

"So," Maggie asked curiously, "what happened to you guys back in India anyway?"

CHAPTER
TWENTY-FOUR

From across the aisle of the airplane, Emily watched over Seth and Maggie with an almost parental expression as they lay slumped over in their seats getting some well-deserved rest. The night of the ball had been long and draining, and they had only had one full day to rest before hurrying to pack up and catch an early morning flight to Bristol.

She turned back to her lap, staring at the open tabs on Maggie's computer screen, detailing any hits on either Ludovico Sforza or Ludovico Castro, both of whom were mentioned in the diamond's recorded history. The man from her vision had to be one of them; she just knew it.

Ludovico Sforza once ruled as the Duke of Milan. Born July 27, 1452. He was acquaintances with Leonardo da Vinci.

Emily was able to find page after page of information about Sforza—his love life, his ruling, and his eventual demise. But when it came to Ludovico Castro, aside from a single reference to him being the Count of Montesanto, there was very little information to go on.

She did, however, find an arrest record from 1495 of someone who had gone by the alias Ludovico Castro, caught performing acts of thievery in Venice. It seemed that his father had had some pull with the bureaucracy there. They had let him off with nothing more than a slap on the wrist before he voluntarily joined the crew of a Portuguese explorer who was searching for a sea route to India.

The words on the screen were beginning to blend together. Digging her elbow into the armrest, she leaned her cheek onto a fist as she pondered. She held the replica diamond in her hand, slowly twisting it back and forth to catch the light.

C'mon, Em. What are you not seeing?

"Can't sleep?" Seth's voice came softly from across the aisle.

He hadn't even opened his eyes yet. He probably could've sensed her obvious restlessness. Either that or the constant click of the keyboard had woken him.

"Something like that," she replied.

He finally lifted his eyelids and studied the collection of information she was compiling.

"What do you expect to find when we get there? This may not be the final stop, you know. I don't want you to get crushed if we come up a little short again."

"I know, I know. As much as I want this to be it, I know the probability isn't there. Remember how I told you about my visions and how I saw those men boarding ships? The diamond went with them on one of their voyages, and it's up to me to discover which.

"I know we're going to find the next clue in Bristol. I can feel it."

Emily was the first one off the plane when it landed, swerving around people in the gangway as if the Bristol airport was going to leave without her.

As the team exited the building to catch a taxi, each of them drew their jackets a little tighter as they stepped onto the sidewalk, rubbing their hands together as they waited their turn in line. They had received a minor cold shock, as the temperatures were much cooler than what they had become accustomed to on the journey thus far. It reminded them that November had approached hard and fast.

Pulling one of his hands out from under his armpit, Seth raised it high into the air. The gesture was promptly followed by the arrival of a short blue taxi.

"Station road, please. Henbury," Emily instructed the driver, scooting in a few extra inches so Seth could squeeze in beside her. "If you don't mind waiting, it'll only be a short stop."

They were straight back to business, and Emily would have to be the embodiment of their map. She was the only one who had seen the visions, and the only one capable of guiding them to wherever it was that the diamond rested.

She made sure to pay the driver enough money to have him wait twenty minutes while they checked into their hotel, after which, Emily wasted no time in directing him to the one place she knew she had to see first and foremost: the dockyard.

Large pebbled beaches surrounded by lush greenery rested in the distance as the Bristol Channel came into view. Emily's skin crawled with goosebumps as she stared out over the waters of the oddly familiar port from the back seat of the taxi.

With the taxi pulling to a stop, she threw another wad of money over the driver's shoulder.

"Wait here," she instructed.

The idling taxi sat at the roadside, a trail of thin, white fumes emanating from its exhaust. Emily removed herself from the vehicle and began her recollective walk along the channel as Seth and Maggie followed some ten feet behind.

Time had changed the scenery of the port, but to her, it was as if she had just been standing there, all those centuries ago. Bending down near the shoreline, she placed her palm flat against the ground, closing her eyes and inhaling deeply as she lifted her face to the sky. With a heavy exhale, she opened her eyes again, gazing out over the never-ending view of the water.

"It was here. I stood right here," her voice carried calmly, barely loud enough for the others to overhear.

With a hand each draped across her back, her friends stood at her sides, trying to see whatever it was she was referring to in the distance.

"Are you okay, Em?" Maggie piped up. "All I see is boats and seagulls."

Seth reached up and gave Maggie a gentle slap on the back of her head, then shushed her with his finger.

"Over there." Emily pointed to the tattered point of the dock. "That's where the men boarded the ships. And right here! This is where Ludovico stood holding the diamond. And there! This is where the bearded older man shouted at Ludovico to come aboard so they could depart. This is the place. I know it!"

"Em, I believe you. I really do." Seth walked around in front of her, holding her by the hands. "But there must have been hundreds of ships that left these docks, traveling to only God knows where."

"And who's to say the diamond never came back here?" Maggie chimed in as well. "Sure, you might have seen it leave the docks, but what if they brought it back? We have no idea … do we?"

Emily remained entranced, just nodding her head along with the words they were saying.

Maybe they have a point …

Just as fast, she snapped to attention.

"No! We just need to find the most logical next step. Let me just close my eyes for a moment and see if I can recall any papers or documents … Maybe I'm forgetting something that could help us, you know?"

She was starting to realize that this would be harder than she had expected it to be, no matter how long she stayed in denial.

"Wait a minute! That's it! Documents," Seth said with a jolt. "Em, remember when we were in university and had that guest lecture about Christopher Columbus? The lecturer spoke of his discoveries, sure, but they also spoke of the ports Columbus frequently visited, one being right here—in Bristol!"

Seth had piqued her interest. She focused her eyes on him with intent as she waited for him to continue.

"The lecturer mentioned a building, one that housed all the comings and goings of the port, known as the Bristol Record Office. I believe now it's called the Bristol Archives. Surely, if these men in your vision left from here, someone would have documented it, right?"

"Seth, you're a genius!" Emily hugged him, leaving Maggie to awkwardly wrap her arms around them both from the outside. "C'mon, let's go!"

They all ran as fast as they could over the embankment and back to the waiting taxi, slamming its doors as they climbed inside.

"Bristol Archives, please!" Maggie shouted, pointing her index finger through the front windshield. "And step on it!"

The driver raced along the Portway, which bordered the River Avon for twenty minutes, swerving around every car in their path until they reached their destination. The taxi slowed to let them out near the Cumberland Basin.

The three of them started to jog across the streets, dodging waves of oncoming traffic before approaching a tall, brick building, nine or ten stories high, nestled on the outskirts of the roadway. Once inside, they directed themselves to the community lockers located in the foyer, temporarily storing their possessions in an attempt to hasten their search.

Maggie led the way farther inside with her laptop tucked under her arm, as Emily and Seth trailed a few steps back, readying their phones in preparation to photograph any pertinent information they might come across. However, their rush was put on hold when they were stopped by an older woman at the entrance to the facility's searchroom, instructing them to show their I.D.s and sign in.

The teammates looked at one another with slight hesitation, knowing full well it was best that nobody knew that they had been there. However, they knew that they had no choice but to oblige if they wanted to gain entry to the archives.

Emily reluctantly signed first, then stepped around the counter to survey the room, only to be stirred from her observation by the woman's voice from behind the counter.

"Ah! Margaret Riggs, you've arrived sooner than we expected," she said gracefully. "My apologies, it will be just a few more moments before one of our staff members brings down the documents you requested from the strong room."

Emily and Seth side-eyed each other in confusion, then turned back to Maggie with wide grins.

"Margaret?" they said in unison.

"What?" Maggie looked back at them and shrugged her shoulders. "Someone had to be proactive. I booked an appointment on the ride over here. Told them I needed everything related to the port of Bristol concerning anyone named 'Ludovico' from the 15th and 16th centuries. You're welcome."

Emily nodded at Maggie in approval, and they all turned to follow the woman in single file to the center of the searchroom. They sat at a large table that was used to spread out and study original documents.

Just as they were pulling in their chairs, a young man appeared from around a corner, wheeling a trolley that carried a multitude of large boxes and books. He promptly came to a stop next to their table and placed three large pillows onto the table, then carefully propped the many books onto them. This was a method the Archive used to preserve the integrity of its documents. He then walked to the other side of the trolley and carefully opened the boxes, spreading individual papers across the table.

"Here's everything we have," he said, moving the trolley away. "Good luck!"

For two hours, Emily and her crew scoured through thousands of pages of records and what must have been a dozen books. Everything from financial transactions to government contracts to sailing requirements to labour laws. They continued their search until the woman from the sign-in desk came to check in on them.

"So, how is everything going thus far?"

"Good," Seth replied. "Although, it sure seems like Ludovico was a popular name back then. There are so many records."

"Does this 'Ludovico' you're searching for have a last name, perhaps? Maybe I can help you along. I find that many people who come here end up leaving more confused than when they arrived—without some guidance, that is."

"Castro," Emily chimed in. "How about 'Ludovico Castro.'" She was hoping her hunch wouldn't let her down.

"Hmm," the woman sounded, resting her index finger on her chin. "I've been working here for forty years, but I've never heard that name before. I'm not saying he doesn't exist, but you just might not find what you're looking for inside this registrar. I'm sorry."

Emily slumped back into her chair, blatantly reeking of defeat. *We're getting nowhere, fast.*

"Though," the woman continued, "are you sure you don't mean Ludovico *Caboto*? One of the more popular Ludovico's from this city's rich history. I mean Castro … Caboto … similar, are they not? Perhaps you were misinformed on the spelling?"

The woman leaned over Seth's shoulder and pulled one of the larger books closer to the trio. Flipping through its pages aggressively until she reached a centerfold, she tapped her finger on a photograph that showed a cluster of men gathered on the steps of an old courthouse.

"There you go. One Ludovico Caboto."

Emily leaned farther over the table, disregarding the integrity of the other documents in the spread.

"Guys, that's him!" she exclaimed, pulling the book toward her and spinning it around. "This picture matches the man from my vision perfectly! It even says that he was of Italian descent. I knew I heard a hint of an accent in his voice."

"Excuse me, did you say 'vision'?" The woman's face shriveled into a look of misunderstanding.

Emily let the woman's comment go unacknowledged. Instead, her eyes trailed across the picture to the faces of the other men, soon coming to focus on the man standing beside Ludovico, the one with a familiar forked beard. It was the same older man that had boarded the ship and called to Ludovico from the railing.

She looked to the woman, pointing to the man with the forked beard.

"Do you know who this man is?" Emily asked, furrowing her brow.

"Ah! Now you sound more like one of our usual visitors. That man right there is Ludovico's father, one of the most recognized explorers of his time. His name was Giovanni Caboto, an Italian navigator and explorer. His most famous voyages departed from this very city."

Emily's chin dropped slightly as her eyes shifted to Seth, then over to Maggie, then back to the woman.

"… Although, because he was employed by the king of England, his English name is often used in the history books. You may know him, instead, as John Cabot."

CHAPTER
TWENTY-FIVE

"Guys, listen to this!" Maggie said, hovering over a publication. "John Cabot was a voyager who received full authority from King Henry VII to leave England to discover new lands. He intended to find alternative routes to China, although he never achieved that goal.

"His wife was Mattea Caboto, with whom he had three sons: Ludovico, Santo, and Sebastiano. It says here that he and his sons received public approval to investigate, claim, and possess any new lands they found, but only those which were not yet known to all Christians. It also says that Ludovico Caboto was known for his thieving tendencies, and after a brush with Venetian authorities, joined Vasco da Gama's exploration of the Indian Ocean."

"Wait a second—wasn't Vasco da Gama the explorer who found the first sea route to India?" Emily added, swinging to Maggie's side. "What if the mysterious thief Ludovico Castro *is* Ludovico Caboto after all!"

"Here, it talks of John Cabot undertaking three significant voyages in his lifetime, all leaving from Bristol," Seth interjected, plopping a thick book onto the table. "Details of the first voyage are scanty. It seems Cabot left Bristol in the summer of 1496, but due to a number of unforeseen and ill-fated circumstances, he returned without having found much of anything.

"His second voyage took place in 1497. It appears that a general chronicle of this journey has been pieced together with letters sent during the trip. He is the earliest known European explorer to have reached the land that is today known as North America on his ship, *The Matthew*. However, upon his return to England, it was noted that he had garnered a sense of urgency to set sail again as soon as possible.

"It wasn't long after that he was granted permission to set out on his third and final voyage, returning to this new land, for which he procured five ships and headed to sea once more with his son, Ludovico. Neither were ever to be heard from again—no ships returned, and no bodies were ever found."

"Great, so he disappeared, and nobody knows where," Emily huffed. "If that's the case, then we're no further ahead than when we started." She began to bite at her thumbnail, looking over the documents once more. "Wait a minute! You said that Cabot returned from his second voyage with a sense of urgency, right? That would have been around the same time that Ludovico returned from India. It makes perfect sense that Cabot would be eager to return to the new world once he was reunited with Ludovico! With the diamond's army at their disposal, Cabot and his son could share its power, practically conquering any land or peoples they encountered. It doesn't seem like he wanted to be an explorer for the money, nor did he want to be a public figure—if he did, he would've just overthrown the king, don't you think? Why rule England when you can rule a whole newly discovered land?"

"You know," a hoarse voice interrupted from behind them, "you could also go visit the tower if you want the full John Cabot experience."

The team lifted their eyes to see the young man, who had delivered their documents earlier, standing awkwardly off to the side, sporting his lanyard and name tag.

"Tower?" Emily questioned.

"Yes, ma'am, just over on Brandon Hill. If you want, I can point it out to you. There's a pretty clear view of the tower from the storage room on the 10th floor."

Without hesitation, they pushed their chairs back and waited for the young man to lead the way. He ushered them to the nearest elevator and thumbed the button to start their ascent. At the sound of the ping, they poured from the metal box, moving collectively to the north-facing side of the building.

"You see that peak in the distance? That's her. That's Cabot Tower." The employee spoke as if he were an automated recording, monotone and to the point. "Built to commemorate the 400th anniversary of John Cabot landing in what would later be known as North America."

Emily stared out the window as her hot, saturated breath spread across the pane, obscuring her view.

If there was ever a clue to be found, it would be there.

"Let's go!" she commanded. The three of them turned and bolted back to the elevator, leaving the young man unappreciated and alone in the depths of the musky storage room.

The tapping of Emily's heels only ceased once they had reached the ground level of the Archives, and the doors of the elevator slid open to release them back into the searchroom. They hurried past the sign-in desk to grab their things from the lockers, without so much as signing out before heading back out into the city streets.

"Taxi!" Seth called, followed by a whistle that proved fruitful to secure them a ride. "Get us to Cabot Tower, and promptly!"

"Maybe Ludovico hid the diamond inside the tower!" Maggie exclaimed, bouncing with excitement as everyone piled into the taxi. "Who knows what we'll find!"

"Maggie, the tower was built four hundred years after the fact," Seth said, inadvertently shutting her down.

"Yeah, Mags, sorry. I have to agree with Seth on this one. I explicitly saw two large cliffs in my vision, and there's nothing of the sort around here anywhere."

As the taxi pulled to a halt at the base of Brandon Hill, the team began to rush through the winding stretch of open fields surrounded by retaining walls. Fall had already left the trees barren, littering the ground with crisp orange leaves that crunched beneath their feet as they pushed ahead, butting through multiple tour groups to cut a path.

Eventually, they found themselves on a paved walkway, one that led farther up the hill and directly to the tower. Over the treetops, the tower's pointed, gothic-inspired peak could be seen in the distance, leading them to a small wooded area where the structure came into full sight.

According to the interpretative display outside, the massive stone pillar stood over one hundred feet tall, accented at the top by a slender octagonal spire. The entire body of the structure was comprised of red sandstone, underlined by cream-colored ornamentation. Inside, it housed a unique spiral staircase that led to the condensed viewing area at its top.

All of them arched their necks so they could see the tower's peak.

"Well," Seth moaned, "we might as well check out the top of this thing, right?"

Emily went first, placing her hand against the cold inner wall while climbing the winding staircase as the others followed in succession. When reaching the top, she stepped through a doorway that led them into the discrete observation area, one that could fit no more than twenty people at most.

Wasting no time, they each began pushing on bricks or pulling on ornamentation that hung from the walls, searching for anything that may come loose or give way to a hiding place within the tower. But still, they found nothing, only the suspicious looks tourists were giving them as they moved by.

After an hour of searching, they gave it a rest, lining up against one of the iron railings of the viewing area. Leaning forward, they could see the whole city of Bristol, stretching out in every direction, as they casually scanned the crowds of people below.

"Well, this seems like a bit of a dead end, doesn't it?" Emily said, pouting with a short sigh of irritation.

But no sooner had the words left her mouth did her attention shift to the ominous chop of flags blowing in the wind. Their furious clap came from around the edge of the tower's platform, pulling her to turn from the others and walk in the direction of the noise.

Seth and Maggie watched as Emily moved away from them with an overly focused look in her eye, one that they had become accustomed to since she had experienced the visions.

Listening intently, Emily leaned back to get a clear view of the top of the tower. She could see a short steel mast, securely affixed to one of the smaller spires. There was a flag she had never seen before, although it seemed eerily familiar in design as it flapped between the Union Jack and St. George's Cross.

She pulled her cell phone from her coat pocket and zoomed in to take a photo, bringing the picture on the screen closer to her face for a clearer look. Her jaw lowered like that of a drawbridge as she stared at the image, her breath uneven as the device trembled in her hands.

"What is it, Em?" Seth and Maggie said in unison, joining her to peer at the photo.

As they looked at the image of the flag, they were all struck with the same realization at once. The white flag contained four small, solid blue triangles. To their right was a large yellow arrow—like a beam of light—and on either side of the arrow were two larger, hollow red triangles.

Without so much as a moment of hesitation, each of them retrieved their cell phones from their pockets and began swiping vigorously through all the information they had collected.

Seth pulled up a photo first. It was of a sketch Emily had made, from memory, of the picture Everett had shown her the night of the masquerade ball. Maggie stopped at a photo that had been taken of the murals below the Hazara Rama Temple.

Emily brought up hers last: the yellow arrow smeared onto the giant rock atop Machu Picchu. As the three of them placed their screens together, it formed a perfect resemblance to the flag that was flying above their heads.

Nobody moved a muscle, each unsure of what to do next.

Suddenly, the tower door banged open, jarring them from their moment, as a group of tourists packed the viewing area with a guide at their lead. Emily was the first to snap from her reverie. Clutching her phone, she took a few steps away from the others, swiping back to the photo of the flag from earlier.

Without saying a word, she shoved through the strangers and grabbed the tour guide by the elbow, holding the picture of the flag up to the woman's face.

"This flag—what is it?" Emily asked unmanneredly.

"Oh, hello, young lady!" the guide replied, overly cheerful given the abruptness of Emily's approach. "Are you enjoying the great Cabot Tower? You know, it's funny, this flag has been a very popular topic of conversation today! Although the other gentleman was much more civil about it, I must say. If you wouldn't mind unhanding me ..."

Emily momentarily lessened her grip.

Who else would have such an interest?

"I'm sorry, I just need to know about its meaning. Please!"

The woman stared at Emily with a forced, on-the-job smile, then turned back to her tour group.

"This young lady has asked a marvelous question, ladies and gentlemen. She would like to know the history of the flags adorned above our tower, here."

Seth and Maggie emerged from behind the onlookers, gently placing their hands on Emily's shoulders to draw her back a little.

"You're not listening to me!" Emily scolded the guide. "This flag, what does it mean? I need you to answer me!"

"Ma'am, you're going to have to calm down. I will get to that part of the tour in due time!"

Emily's eyes flared with an impatient rage. She gripped the tour guide by the collar around her scrawny neck and pushed her back a few steps until she was pressed up against the railing.

The crowd of people shuffled backward, letting out a collective gasp.

"Listen, lady, I've had a long fucking week." Emily gritted her teeth, holding the phone an inch from the woman's nose.

The guide was shaking as she looked back and forth between the ground below, the flag on the screen, and Emily's dark, glaring eyes.

Seth tugged at Emily's shoulder a little harder, trying to ensure she wouldn't take it too far.

"What does this flag mean?" Emily spat out. "Tell me, goddamnit!"

"Newfoundland!" the woman gasped, her knees knocking together in distress. "It's the flag of Newfoundland."

CHAPTER TWENTY-SIX

"Ladies and gentlemen, we are now boarding flight 479 departing from Heathrow," the electronic voice repeatedly hummed over the airport speakers. "If you are traveling with children under the age of five, or traveling with someone who may need extra assistance boarding the aircraft, please, come see an attendant at the podium."

Seth was staring across the lounge absentmindedly while Emily and Maggie huddled together under a throw blanket as they all waited on standby. A promising direct flight was all that stood between them and their next location on the easternmost province of Canada, the island of Newfoundland.

"Excuse me, Emily Owens?" An attendant's voice stirred the women from their chairs. "We would like to inform you that we finally have room available on this flight. It will be boarding in just a few minutes."

Emily flung the blanket to one side. She and Maggie stood to stretch as Seth scrambled to gather everyone's bags.

"Oh, I'm very sorry," the attendant continued, "I should have been clearer—we have only one seat available at this time. If you wish to travel together, I'd be more than happy to inform you when we can better accommodate your entire party."

"Argh! We are never going to get out of here, are we?" Maggie huffed, flopping back down into her chair.

Resting her elbows on her legs, she dug both knuckles into her cheeks, staring impatiently up at her friends under the skewed rims of her glasses.

"Something will come along," Emily said. "We just have to wait, that's all."

Seth's gaze lingered on the attendant as she walked back to her station, before looking back to Emily and Maggie.

"You should go, Em. Maggie and I can wait for the next one. They're completely sold out. Besides, I've read somewhere that due to the weather in Newfoundland, it can be a nightmare to land flights. You might want to take this one while you can."

"Maggie?" Emily turned, gauging her for a second opinion.

"He has a point. I hate airports, but you're our best shot at finding this thing."

Emily bent over and pecked her friend on the cheek before standing to hold Seth in a more passionate embrace.

"Thank you," she whispered, moving from his lips to lay her head on his shoulder. They hugged one last time before she took her leave.

She reached down and grabbed her jacket from the chair, then wheeled her suitcase over to the attendants' station.

"I'll go." She laid her passport on the counter and slid it toward the attendant. As her documents were being checked, she casually glanced back to watch Seth walk over and slouch down next to Maggie. Moments later, she was ushered past the station and down the gangway. She turned to wave to Seth and Maggie through the glass doors before disappearing out of sight.

Once on the plane, she placed her backpack overhead and wiggled into her seat before smiling down at the freshly printed, one-way ticket she had pinched between her fingers.

"Destination: St. John's, Newfoundland – YYT"

It was afternoon when Emily stepped from the airport terminal, greeted by an unwarranted mix of fog and drizzle that
whooshed across her already reddened face. As cars and taxicabs
splashed past her at the Arrivals gate, she slipped into her wind-
breaker before attempting to flag down a ride.

Eventually, she managed to hail a cab, proceeding to throw
her bag aboard before sliding into the warmth of the back seat.

"Where to, darlin'?" the driver asked, observing her from his
rearview mirror.

"I need a hotel, sir, one next to the harbour preferably. I would
like something with a view of it all, please. Any recommendations?"

"Hmm, a view, huh? How 'bout the Alt Hotel? It's right on
the harbour front. A beautiful place to watch the ships come and
go. If you're lucky enough to get a suite, you'll have a great view
of Signal Hill from there." He began to laugh. "Not hard to tell
you're a mainlander."

He spoke so fast she had a hard time understanding him, and
she wasn't sure what a "mainlander" was, but his proposal was as
good as any.

"The Alt Hotel it is!" she instructed as the driver pulled steadily
from the airport and headed in the direction of the city's downtown.

The driver parked at the front of a black, modular-looking
hotel. Emily paid the man with an added hearty tip, then watched
from the front steps of the hotel as he sped off along Water Street.

Entering through the sliding glass doors of the hotel, she
moved swiftly toward the front desk, where she was quickly greeted
by one of the guest service agents.

"I am told you may have a room with a view of the harbour?"
Emily asked, already pushing her passport and credit card across
the desk. "If so, may I have it, please?"

"Sure, Miss Owens, let me see what I can do." The lady behind
the desk reviewed the travel documents while Emily anxiously
awaited her response. "Looks like you're in luck! Please, follow me."

The agent led her through the lobby and into the elevators, escorting her up to the fifth floor of the hotel. Two hard-angled lefts, followed by a stretch down a narrow hallway, led them to a solid black door at the rear of the building, where the woman slid a key card into the slot in the door. Walking into the room ahead of Emily, she placed the same card into a slot in the wall to activate the power to the room.

Emily dropped her bag from her shoulder, watching as the blinds automatically raised, allowing daylight to fill the previously dark room with a dejected and dreary grey. Nonetheless, it was the perspective she had come for, not the poor weather.

"Quite a view isn't it, Miss Owens?" the attendant claimed, fixing the curtains that dangled slightly crumpled on either side.

"Breathtaking, certainly." Emily took a step forward, captivated as she touched her nose against the glass.

"Obviously, here to your right, you have a view of the St. John's harbour, but if you look just over there to your left …" The lady pointed at two large cliffs just off in the distance. "You will see what is referred to as the Narrows."

As instructed, Emily looked to her left and gazed upon the mouth of the harbour, when suddenly, her visions came flooding back. Her lashes thrashed against the chill of the window while she braced her palms against the pane to keep herself upright.

You have definitely seen those cliffs before. Water leading to the open ocean … This was it.

"Is everything okay, Miss Owens?"

Emily was momentarily speechless as she stared at the aptly named Narrows.

"Was there ever a fire here at one point?" Emily asked, squinting as if she was taking an educated guess. "One that burned parts of the city, perhaps? Maybe within the last couple hundred years or so?"

She turned from the glass, hoping the attendant would have a knowledgeable answer.

"St. John's has had a few fires in its history. However, I suspect you're referring to the Great Fire. On the 8th of July in 1892, the center of the city and its downtown core were more or less reduced to ash, sending the townspeople into widespread panic. Sound like the one?"

"What caused the fire exactly?" Emily continued.

"Records show that the fire was started by a simple accident—a horses' stable caught aflame and quickly burned out of control."

That doesn't make any sense.

Emily had seen the attack vividly in her vision, but clearly, this lady wasn't aware of any of it.

Emily turned her attention to the left and pointed to a square-shaped structure atop the cliff on the left side of the Narrows. "What's that?"

"That's Signal Hill, and resting on top is our famous Cabot Tower—named after the explorer John Cabot. Its construction began in 1898, just a few short years after the Great Fire, in fact. It was designed by William Howe Greene, although it wasn't completed until the year 1900. They call it Signal Hill because it was where Guglielmo Marconi received the first trans-Atlantic wireless message. Cool, huh?"

Emily tried to hide her surprise as she moved around the edge of the bed, staring intently across the water at the structure.

Another Cabot Tower.

"So, this John Cabot fellow, everyone here knows of this man, yes? He's honored around these parts and in England as well?" Emily enquired.

"Oh yes! We wouldn't be the province we are today without him."

Emily simply nodded, mildly impressed that this woman was able to spew so many facts about the city.

"I won't take up any more of your time, Miss Owens. I'll let you settle in. If you need anything further, please just dial '0' on the phone, and someone will be able to help you. Enjoy your stay!"

The woman exited the room and shut the door behind her, leaving Emily with her gaze still trained upon Cabot Tower.

There's no point in waiting. If the diamond is in that building, I need to find it sooner rather than later. My vision brought me here for a reason, and now, it's time to find out why ...

The cab driver swerved back and forth through the winding roads of the city's downtown, climbing the grade through the askew rows of crooked townhouses. Emily had instructed the driver to take her directly to the top of Signal Hill, where the houses eventually faded away and the road became surrounded by lichened rock and barren alder beds. Passing a small information center located halfway up the hill, she had another flashback; her head swiveled from side to side in the back seat as she surveyed the rocky peaks and surrounding cliffs. She was certain this was the same area from her vision, the place where she had seen the man with the diamond emerge from the mixed blanket of smoke and mist.

"Stop!" she yelled, causing the driver to slam on his brakes in the middle of the road.

"Jesus, maid, what's your problem?" he hissed.

"This is far enough."

She felt that it was in her best interests to try and recall the path she had seen the man in her vision take before he disappeared out of sight between the rocks. Driving to the top of the hill in the back seat of a cab wasn't going to be much help.

But the hill was much steeper than it looked, and her legs quickly grew weary with the long trek to its top. It had been a while since she had to traverse anything more than a few flights of stairs, and the unforgiving crag caused a blister to form on her heel in no time.

As suspected, the trail had led her right to the foot of Cabot Tower. She looked at the giant metal mast on its roof, similar to that of its sister tower in Bristol, with its flags flapping continuously in the wind.

At that same moment, from around the corner of the octagonal tower, she saw tourists opening a wooden door and entering the building.

Might as well check it out.

Emily hurried to blend in with a small group of women who were just about to enter the tower.

The porched entrance had barely enough room for two people to get by each other, its woodgrain floor scuffed so badly that the color had been stripped. From the look of the stonework outside, she expected the interior of the tower to have retained some of its original features; however, it was apparent that the building had been recently renovated—or at least renovated since its completion in 1900. The walls had been drywalled and painted, and at some point, the main level had been converted into a gift shop.

She pretended to look around at the items in the gift shop, all the while looking for any sign or detail alluding to the diamond or to a place it may be hidden. It was too hard to get a read on the building with so much reconstruction. However, she did notice a small stair case she had missed on the way in, which led to the next floor.

Shuffling back to the porch, she climbed the winding stairs to reach an uninspiring second level. It was filled with historical interpretation boards, aimed at tourists, and a display of items from centuries gone by. Still, nothing related to the diamond, and the information that was provided gave no further leads.

Another set of stairs presented itself, this one leading to a third floor which consisted of a small windowed lookout for tourists, to sightsee more so than anything. It also contained a slender door that led onto the tower's rooftop, which provided a more predominant—albeit windy—viewing area.

Emily fought against the wind to open the door, struggling to make her way onto the roof with the other visitors. Once outside, she walked to the edge of the rooftop and rested her elbows on its thick stone barrier, admiring the harbour below before shifting her eyes across the sprawl of the city. From her lookout, she could see where the cab had dropped her off, halfway up the hill. She traced her eyes along her route to where she was now.

This has to be where that man disappeared in my vision. What am I missing?

As she was about to turn away from the ledge and head back inside, a little boy below caught her attention. He was crouched with a yellow plastic shovel, digging at the rock beneath him while his parents took photos of the landscape.

"Of course!" Emily exclaimed, running back through the door and scurrying her way back down the two flights of spiraled stairs.

I completely forgot that the man in my vision went beneath the rocks!

She burst into the gift shop, circling the room to find a door hidden behind some concession racking with signage that read, *"Employees Only"*.

By now, most of the tourists had dispersed, leaving just her and the timid young employee working behind the counter. Emily approached her slowly with an innocent smile, itching to coax her into providing a little off-the-record information. She grabbed a pocket-sized flashlight from a nearby basket, hoping to gain some trust by making a purchase.

"Um, excuse me." Emily laid the item down on the counter. "I was wondering if you could tell me what's behind that door over there."

The young girl looked to the door, then back to Emily.

"Oh, that door only leads to the basement. It isn't open to visitors. It's just where we keep all of our supplies and things."

"Oh, the basement, hey?" Emily raised an eyebrow. "Has it been renovated like the rest of the building or … ?"

"No, it's mostly original, very dark and dingy. Kind of spooky, actually. The foundation is definitely original, though, aside from a coat of paint maybe."

Emily sized up the door again, her mind already made up. Gaining access to the basement would be her best bet at finding anything.

"Any chance you could take me down there?" She nodded in the direction of the door. "I've traveled a long way to get here and would love to get the full, immersive experience of the long-standing Cabot Tower!"

The girl pondered for a few seconds, shifting her eyes about to avoid contact with Emily's.

"I … I'm sorry, I can't. I'm very new here, and I don't want to jeopardize my job. But, please, here, take this number and call the Parks Canada office." The girl grabbed a pen and paper. "We open to the public again at 10:00 am tomorrow, but I'm sure someone would be willing to come by earlier and help you out with your request."

Emily snatched the tiny piece of card-stock from the employee's fingers, knowing full well that she wasn't going to call them.

"Thank you," she mumbled as she left the gift shop, glancing back one more time at the integrity of the door before heading outside.

She immediately crumpled the paper and flung it over the crest of the hill, watching as it tumbled away with the breeze. She already knew that she would be paying the tower another visit—but that she would be doing it alone.

She trotted down over a rocky embankment, standing alone to stare out over the ocean as the waves crashed against the base of the cliffs below. The scent of saltwater singed her nose as she took hard, deep breaths of frustration.

She and her team had taken down the Recreant Order, shutting their entire plan down once and for all. She had come too far to stop now. Now was the time for her to prove to the world that she was capable of being one of the best treasure hunters and archaeologists the world had ever seen.

She wasn't just going to just follow in her parents' footsteps—she was going to create her own.

The Florentine Diamond will be my *legacy!*

CHAPTER TWENTY-SEVEN

Emily had traveled to the center of the city just to find a rock-climbing facility. It was late, and there were no other patrons in the business. A young man greeted Emily as she walked toward the front counter.

"Hi … Joel, is it?" Emily asked, leaning forward over the counter, indicating toward the man's name-tag. "I was wondering if I could rent some climbing gear. I know it's late, but I need it for tomorrow morning. I hope that won't be a problem," she said, batting her eyelashes.

"No … no problem at all. What exactly do you need?" the man replied, seemingly regaining his composure.

She took a moment to look over the selection of equipment, then expertly started pointing at items from the display.

"Give me one of those sixty-meter dynamic ropes, a harness, adequate belay tubes, a belay device, some webbing, and throw in a couple of carabiners."

The man looked at her, flabbergasted, admiring the way her request had just rolled right off the tongue.

"A woman that knows what she wants. I like it," he said, eyeing Emily. She didn't even acknowledge his attempt at flirtation, so he instead turned to grab each of her requested items from the display.

Emily was preparing to make the payment when she caught a glimpse of something glinting from high up on the wall. It was an ice axe hanging by a roped handle.

"On second thought, how about you grab me one of those too," she said, motioning toward the axe with a nod. "Just in case."

He stepped up and grabbed the axe by the handle, then laid it on the countertop.

"That one's been here for quite a while, but she's definitely a beauty; I'll give you that."

Emily picked up the axe and hefted its weight in her hand. Its curved orange shaft wound upward to its steel head, which contained a toothed pick and adze. It was lightweight, likely made of fiberglass or titanium. Turning it toward herself, she ran her thumb along its jagged teeth.

Perfect.

She tossed it into the bag with the rest of her purchases, threw her cash on the counter, then headed out the door before Joel got up the nerve to ask her out on a date.

Back at her hotel room, Emily set her alarm for an early rise, ensuring she had adequate time to search Cabot Tower before any of the employees showed up for the day. From her window, she stared across the harbour, once more at Signal Hill, and the iconic building positioned at its top that was illuminated by strategically placed floodlights.

She pulled out her phone, drafting a text to Seth and Maggie.

"Hey guys! Guess what. There's also a Cabot Tower here in St. John's. Clues from my vision are leading me to search beneath the tower. I'm hopeful that I'll find the diamond there tomorrow morning. Safe travels. I'll see you guys soon, xoxo."

Emily sent the message then hit the lock button on the side of her phone, sending the hotel room back into darkness. She thumbed the button on the wall before crawling underneath the bedsheets, staring at the ceiling as the automatic blinds closed beside her.

Emily's alarm sounded at 5:20 am. She shut it off just as quickly as it had started. She had been wide awake long before it ever went off. She was dressed now, sitting at the foot of the bed and pulling on her boots. Her attempt to get some rest before the excursion was unsuccessful.

She stood and walked to the bathroom, meeting her reflection in the mirror. Her eyes and the bridge of her nose had finally turned to a purple hue from the beating that Alexandria had given her just days before. She pulled at her shirt to check her bandaged breast. The tenderness had almost passed, but the sight of the bandage still left a very emotional scar of the Recreant's power, one that she knew may never fully heal.

She turned the faucet, letting the water pool in her hands so she could splash her face—a symbolic cleanse of her past encounters. She stepped from the sink and lifted her duffle bag, swung the door open, and headed for the stairs, avoiding all employees along the way so she could slip outside undetected.

Hitting the street under cover of the still-dark dawn, she hurried on foot in the direction of Cabot Tower.

As she reached the top of Signal Hill, Emily looked down at her watch; 6:01 am. She had less than four hours to find a way beneath the tower, potentially retrieve the diamond, and exit the tower—maybe less if one of the staff members decided to come in early.

There's no turning back now, Em.

She climbed the wooden steps to the tower's entrance, knowing that she needed to work fast. She removed the ice axe from her bag first, swinging it at the crease of the doorway to wedge it in between the facing and the latch. With a firm jerk, she popped open the door and tumbled inside as it swung inward.

Gathering herself, she reached outside and grabbed the duffle bag, quietly closing the door behind her. From there, she scrambled into the gift shop, feeling her way through the blackness until her hand found its way to the knob of the basement door. Already unlocked, it released without a struggle, allowing her to creep farther inside, closing this door just as gently.

Before taking another step, she rifled through her bag until she felt the handle of her flashlight, pulling it out and clicking its rubber button to turn it on.

The young girl from the shop was right. The basement was dull and dingy, and gave off an old musty scent that made Emily cover her nose with her arm on the way down. The stairs formed a narrow, stone spiral. At the bottom, an already opened steel door led into a storage room, again as the employee had advised.

The place was a bit of a mess. There were disorganized boxes of products and tangled wiring, not to mention all the pipes and ductwork running along the ceilings that forced her to duck in order to move around. And although she had been told otherwise, some of the basement walls had, in fact, been renovated.

She moved around the room, looking for any signs of original stonework. Eventually, she turned a corner, and the beam of her flashlight fell on a large, black, steel door. It was tightly shut, and there was a large padlock dangling from its latch. A sign that read "*Electrical Room*" was positioned in the middle of the door. She had checked everywhere else. This was her only remaining option.

Plopping her duffle bag down onto the floor, she placed the flashlight between her teeth and directed the light to shine on the door. Once again, she grabbed the ice axe, this time sliding the pick between the lock's body and its looped shackle. She applied an upward force on the handle with all her strength, trying to snap it off, but to no avail.

After taking a few short breaths, she made a decision. She couldn't continue with the quiet approach any longer. She had to take a risk.

Emily grabbed the axe by the base of the handle, and with a swift motion, she swung it so that the flat side of its head came down and hit the lock. The lock let go and fell to the dusty floor, bouncing away to one side.

Flipping the latch of the door, she pushed the metal slab open to enter the electrical room, a tight area full of data cables and small blinking lights. She swept the room with the flashlight, trying to make out the walls behind the equipment.

Her light stilled upon a small section of wall that appeared to match the original stonework of the building's exterior. Even though it had been painted over with a slate grey, the authenticity was unmistakable.

She kicked the obstructing electrical supplies out of her way, clearing a path to give her room to work. With the adze portion of her axe, she started to hack away at the mortar between the stones, chipping it to loosen the rock. She hammered relentlessly, breaking only for short intervals, which proved fruitful once the end of the tool finally broke through.

A howling gust of wind came from the hole, brushing her hair along her cheeks and neck. She flipped the axe back around to the pick, sliding it into the hole she had made. Then, she repeatedly used it as a fulcrum to break away the rocks, creating a pile of rubble around her feet.

Once she had created a sizable hole, she leaned inside with the flashlight and panned the light in all directions. The inside was too deep and dark to see very far ahead, revealing that the tunnel ran farther under the cliffs as she had expected.

Turning back from the hole, Emily ripped open her bag and began preparing her climbing gear. Starting with the harness, she clipped everything on, piece by piece, until each accessory was affixed, then slid the flashlight into her shoulder strap, pointing it forward into the cavern.

Carefully, she climbed through the hole, feeling with her right foot until it planted onto an uneven shale path. Once she had her balance, she carefully pulled the rest of her body through the opening, surrendering herself to the mouth of the passageway.

Ten minutes into a winding descent, Emily eventually came to a hollowed-out, cylindrical cavern that dropped deep down within the cave. Tracing her light along its sides brought into view a carved-out staircase, one that had severely deteriorated over time, as complete sections of its rocky steps had completely crumbled away.

Looks like all this climbing gear will come in handy after all.

She took a leaning step forward to try and estimate the distance to the bottom of the cavern, when in doing so, she saw an amber light glowing from below.

The diamond!

Her heart began to race at the sight of the golden aura revealing a flattened surface on which she could safely land. It was hard to judge for sure, but the cavern looked to be at least a hundred-and-thirty-foot drop, maybe more.

Pulling back from the edge, she released her bag from her shoulder, sifting through the gear to begin rigging herself an anchor using the pick of the axe, some carabiners, and the webbing. The head of the axe had become damaged and loose after the prior bludgeoning but still looked capable of supporting her weight for the descent.

Once everything was secured, she threaded a rope and tossed it into the shaft, watching as it uncoiled into the pit and finished with a snap. Turning her back to the hole, she affixed her belay tube to the harness and rope, and slowly inched her way over the rocky edge.

Closing her eyes, she took a leap of faith backward and began to rappel.

As Emily descended farther and farther into the hole, the brighter the yellow light seemed to glow, almost as if it knew she was coming for it. When her feet struck against the ground, she unclipped herself from the rope and quickly surveyed her surroundings.

The area was large, perhaps big enough to house at least a hundred people. Wooden crates, oil lanterns, and tattered cloth littered the area around her. Human and animal skeletons alike lay dormant, some together as if they had been embracing one another before an untimely death.

Just then, the light brightened again, catching Emily's attention.

She moved toward the source, hoping maybe she would find the Florentine Diamond lying in wait, perhaps tucked away in a nook.

Instead, she found that the cave wall had been punctured with four-inch holes, each leading to the outside of the cliff face. The light was coming from the amber sunrise breaking over the Atlantic. She knew the holes must have been strategically placed to light the cave during the day to save on fuel. Dismissing her immediate disappointment, she looked again at the lanterns, undoubtedly only used after sunset, once the cold night had set in.

She began to scavenge through the items in the room, searching for anything that may have been left by the man who retreated to this place in her vision. She checked every crate and every skeleton, even checking the pockets of the dead in search of the gem. All attempts were unsuccessful.

Emily looked at her watch. She was wasting time. With the sun coming up, it meant her window of opportunity was closing. She began to pace back and forth across the cavern, frantically grabbing at her hair and muttering aloud. In her rage, she drew back and kicked a pile of ashes from an old fire pit at the center of the room, sending its contents fluttering across the cavern floor.

She caught a glimpse of something solid lying amongst the disturbed soot. She bent over and picked up what appeared to be some sort of pocketbook or journal. Brushing away the coating of black residue, she discovered its pages to be made of a thick parchment, while its cover and backing were a leathery material, both lightly singed.

She removed the flashlight from her harness and stuck its barrel in her mouth, clenching it between her front teeth while aiming it down at the pages. Only the edges of the book had been burned by the fire, which meant whoever had the intention to get rid of it had failed.

Commencing her hastened investigation, she vigorously flipped through its pages and started to read at random.

We have finally returned to the new land we discovered. Our flag still flies on the shores of the harbour. My father has instructed me to take the diamond and the army of warriors to clear the surrounding area of inhabitants. We will rule this new land … together.

L. C. – July 1st, 1498

"L.C.? Ludovico Caboto maybe?" she garbled aloud, flipping a few more pages ahead.

I have come upon this journal in our family's estate. It appears to have belonged to my great grandmother and her father before her. Along with it, I found a gorgeous yellow diamond, one that—in accordance with the text on these pages—holds a mysterious power. And here I thought the stories we were told as children were simple folklore …

Howard Greene – January 13th, 1635

Emily flipped to the next page.

The army has proved to be of great assistance with our workload. The building of houses and structures has progressed rapidly, not to mention our farming. We are slowly teaching the warriors to hunt and fish from the boats, a useful skill in the coming winter.

Howard Greene – September 6th, 1635

Emily flipped to the last few pages, anxious to find the latest whereabouts of the diamond. As much as she wanted to, she couldn't waste her time reading all of the entries.

As I had feared, the Europeans have come for my family's diamond. I watched as they attacked our beloved St. John's, burning it to the ground. I have retreated to the sanctuary beneath the cliffs with our heirloom, along with my closest family and friends.

The community laughed when I created this place, but now, all I hear are their unbearable screams in the distance.

I have released the army from the mist. Some have remained in the burning city to try and fend off our assailants, while others I have summoned to guard the entrance of the cavern. They will be our last line of defense if we are discovered.

I have not yet told the others, but the food and water will not last much longer: weeks maybe, a month at the most. I hope we will not need to hide here that long.

Joseph Greene – July 8th, 1892

Emily paused for a moment, realizing it was plausible that Joseph Greene was the man from her vision, the one she had followed. The timing seemed to correlate, and his knowledge of the fire being an attack instead of an accident also made sense.

She turned to the last page of the journal.

I have lost everything. My wife and children perished several days ago, along with the rest of our people. Only William and I have survived long enough to live through this hell. Rations have been depleted, and we cannot stay here any longer.

It has been quiet outside for some days now. Using my scouting holes in the rock, I've witnessed the European ships retreat back to the Atlantic.

Still, this location is no longer safe for me or the diamond. People will continue to come for it. I know they will.

I covered this entire island in mist and sent the warriors out in search of a new place to settle. They have returned to tell me of something they refer to as a 'morne'. It seems to be some sort of mountain located to the west of here. I have decided to travel there on foot, in hopes of living the rest of my days in solitude. No one should suffer as I have. The diamond will forever rest with me.

I have instructed William to help rebuild the city with the remaining inhabitants once I have left. I have made him promise to build a structure atop this cavern so that no one shall ever know of its existence ... or of what happened here. This sanctuary will serve as a forgotten grave, allowing the souls of my family to rest here in peace.

Joseph Greene – July 29th, 1892

Emily closed the journal and stared down at her watch; 9:05 am. Her time was up. The tower's employees would be showing up within the hour, and she still had to climb her way out.

She stuffed the book into her waistband and started the grueling ascension back out of the cavern.

CHAPTER TWENTY-EIGHT

Emily untied the rope from the handle of the axe, letting it drop to the floor of the grotto. She placed the remaining climbing gear into the duffle bag and tossed it down as well, retaining only the ice axe, which she secured to her side. With fewer things weighing her down, she made a hasty retreat back to the hole in the wall.

Crawling back into the electrical room, she quietly shut the steel door behind her before creeping out through the basement and back up to the top of the stairs. With one hand on the door-knob, she turned off the flashlight with the other, cautiously opening the door that led into the gift shop. She peeked through the opening. The daylight pouring through the windows now made everything visible, an unwanted hinderance to her stealthy escape.

She stood still and listened. Neither morning gossip, nor the smell of bad coffee. There was only stillness, meaning she could still beat the clock.

She shoved the door open wider, but without warning, some-one kicked it from behind, crushing her hand into its crease. She let out a terrifying wail as she dropped to her knees, staring down at the throbbing numbness of her fingers as the door was ripped open from the other side.

An outstretched palm grabbed a handful of her hair, pulling her through the doorway and slinging her across the floor. The journal was sent spiraling, sliding to a rest against the boots of the man standing across from her.

"No ... it can't be ..." she whimpered.

"Well, well, well. I would say it's a surprise to see you here, but we both know that isn't true, now is it?" Everett Taylor said mockingly as he towered over her.

He bent down, casually picking up the journal and skimming furiously through its pages. Reading the last few paragraphs, he glanced at her then back to the journal, reaching into his back pocket to withdraw his cell phone and snap photos of its pages.

"Cardinal Valerius will love to see these," Everett said. "Within the hour, he will have landed on the west coast of this godforsaken, foggy island in Deer Lake—right where I need him, it seems. This journal appears to contain exactly what we've been missing. I knew that if I left you alone long enough, you'd find the next clue for us."

Just as Everett sent the text, Emily mustered to her feet, unclipping the ice axe and taking a swing at him. His head managed to avoid the attack, but his cell phone wasn't as lucky, flying from his hand and crashing against the wall before smashing on the tiled floor. He retaliated by withdrawing a pistol from his waistband and taking aim at Emily, but the gun was also knocked away by Emily's backswing.

With each swing of the axe, Everett was backed farther toward the wall. In an offensive maneuver, the next time she raised the axe, he lunged forward and placed one hand around the shaft of the axe, while gripping her arm with the other. He lifted his knee into her abdomen, sending her careening into a glass display casing that shattered under her weight upon impact.

"I really don't want to do this, Emily," he said, walking steadily toward her. "I gave you a chance to avoid all of this, remember?"

Picking her up from the shards by the collar of her jacket, he tossed her like a rag doll into the tower's entranceway.

"You truly are exceptional, you know that?" He stepped forward, pushing her up against the main door. "Yet, you're a woman who is very much wasting her talents. *We* are the future. God is smiling down on *us*. Don't you see?"

During his speech, she managed to wiggle one arm free, uppercutting him in the chin and causing him to stumble backward. She turned, opening the door in an attempt to escape, but once again, his fingers grabbed a fistful of her hair, slowly wrenching her head back toward his. She grabbed at the wooden doorframe, ensuring he couldn't drag her back inside, as he pressed his mouth intimately against her ear, filling it with his immodest breathing.

"I *chose* you!" he whispered, staring past her cheek to the southern hills flanking the Narrows. "Don't you understand? All of this could be *ours*. All you have to do is submit yourself to me."

Emily allowed her body to release its tension, giving him a false sense of security that maybe she was, in fact, considering his offer. But as soon as she felt his grip loosen, she dove forward and thrust the heel of her boot upward between his legs, connecting hard against his testicles.

Like any mortal man, his grip instinctively let her go as he reached down to cradle his throbbing scrotum. With that, she bolted through the door and slammed it behind her, hobbling down the wooden steps in search of the nearest getaway. But the top of the hill was almost barren. There were only a few wooden benches and a low-lying stone wall that surrounded the tower. Hiding was out of the question.

Seconds later, the bang of the tower's door swinging open sounded from behind her. Everett re-emerged, now enraged, gripping the handle of Emily's ice axe. His eyes were fixated on her as he took his time to waddle down the stairs, one by one.

She shuffled farther away, bracing herself with one hand against the low stone wall as she rounded a bend atop the steep embankment. But Everett had hastened to pursue her. The shrill noise of the pick scraped tauntingly against the stone wall as he followed.

She veered from the asphalt trail, cresting a mossy ridge to see the jutting rocks below, as the distinct scramble of loose gravel churned beneath Everett's footsteps. He had narrowed the gap between them, and with a resounding clatter, the head of the axe crashed against the rock wall as he made a swing at her skull.

Moving farther along the wall, Emily periodically glanced over her shoulder, trying to analyze the integrity of the weapon's head. The bolt that held the pick to the handle looked as if it had snapped, meaning that Everett couldn't afford any more missed attempts. But she had nowhere left to run.

"Emily, stop!" Everett dangled the axe at his side, lowering his threat level as he inched closer to her. "This is ridiculous. I know I can make you see the light."

She had little choice but to allow him to approach her, keeping her eyes focused on his, strategizing her only play.

"I can see that you want great things for this world, as do I," he continued. "I have vowed to remove the stigma that there is no higher power. It is my destiny—can't you see that?" He placed his hand on the side of Emily's face, brushing the grime and hair from her cheek.

She drew away at first before opting to indulge him just a little longer. She looked up, drawing him in with a seductive gaze, then too placed her hand on his face, softly running her thumb back and forth along his lower lip and beard.

"Everett," her voice crackled, "Everett, I … I …"

"Yes? Say it!"

"I … I think you're a delusional piece of shit!" Emily yelled, hardening her grip on the side of his face pushing with all of her might to topple him over, smacking his head against the rocky partition.

His temple split open, and a rush of blood poured from the wound.

She did it again, this time with the added leverage of him being on the ground, enabling her to really put some force behind the strike.

He crumpled, but adrenaline allowed him to lunge forward and tackle Emily by the waist, sending them both tumbling down over the rocky hillside. Their bodies rolled against the sharp crags, taking their breaths away. The axe bounced along with them, landing nearby as they came to an abrupt halt on a lower bend of the trail that encircled the hill.

Emily was the first to move. Her arms and legs had been reduced to patches of raw skin, each ingrained with soil and dirt. She dove for the axe, but Everett was still much closer to it and was able to snatch it from his prone position.

Stumbling back to his feet, he came toward her once again, lifting the handle of the axe firmly in his hand. One side of his face was masked with a dark red, rendering his right eye unusable.

To Emily's right, she could see a large outcrop, a naturally formed lookout over the Narrows. It was a decisive dead end, but ultimately, she had nowhere else to go.

Carefully, she lowered herself over the rock, coming to a rest just shy of its furthest edge. Leaning forward, she peered over the cliff at the barbed rocks in the ocean below as a rough influx of water crashed around them. There was only a slim chance she would survive the five-hundred-foot fall if she jumped, but at this point, she was considering it.

"Emily!"

The sound of Everett's voice calling her name had become insufferable.

She whipped around, glaring at him with venom. She had reached a boiling point, and his presence was something she was ready to be rid of.

I'm done running, Everett.

He squeezed the handle of the axe, looking down on her from above. He passed a hand through his hair and flung his head back in laughter, reaffirming his unstable mental state.

"Ironic, isn't it?" he gloated. "My first cleanse of this world ... is you. After all this time keeping you alive, it is *you* who I am required to dispose of in order to move forward. *You* are my test

... my deliverance!" He started to climb down toward her, carefully maneuvering around the curvature of the rocks so as not to slip. "Sometimes, our emotional tasks outweigh the physical ones, but today ... today it is time for me to begin my purge. And you, Emily Owens, you've already had your chance to repent."

By now, she had tuned out his words, focusing only on distancing herself from the cliff's edge. Once Everett had stepped into her range, she swung at him with a right hook, only to have him block it with ease and then grab her by the forearm. She tried to jerk away, but his grip was too strong.

Holding her steady, he raised the ice axe high over his shoulder, bringing it down like a strike of lightning into the upper right side of her chest, lodging the pick just beneath her collarbone.

The pain was so immense that Emily wasn't even able to form a scream. Her mouth just gaped, trails of spit stringing like a web between her lips. Her eyes clamped shut as flashes of red and black pulsated beneath their lids. Numbness filled her elbow, shooting down her arm into her pinky and ring fingers.

Standing there, she could feel his breathing, warm and heavy against her face as he leaned in, relishing in her suffering. Sweeping her legs out from under her, he knocked her onto her back with a thud. Her body arched from the rocks upon impact, causing her eyes to snap open wide to the sky above.

He placed his palm around the handle of the axe and knelt over her, his sight trailing from her flushed face to the edge of the cliff as if he was contemplating his next move. He grinned sadistically, but only for a moment before standing to wrench the handle of the axe.

Emily was finally able to let out a piercing howl as the teeth of the pick grated against her skin and muscle, knocking against her clavicle inside of her chest. Her breathing became rapid and short, and she soon realized that his intention was to drag her.

Grabbing at the head of the axe, she struggled wildly to remove it from her chest. It budged, but not before he began to pull her across the outcrop toward the cliff's drop-off, the teeth of the axe grinding against her bone with every yank.

Her heartbeat fluttered, and her pupils enlarged into two black holes. The pain from her wound had become so immense that it had seemingly subsided; she became acutely aware of her surroundings. The distance between where she lay and the edge of the cliff was closing. She needed to act fast.

Her left arm protruded from her body feeling around at the ground within her reach, searching for a loosened piece of rock. Only once Everett had managed to drag her but within a few feet from the edge did she manage to grab a sizable stone, hefty and spherical. With a broad stroke, she swung the stone at the weakened joint of the axe, cracking the handle away from its head.

Everett whipped around to look at the useless handle in his hand. And like a stick that one would throw for a dog, he tossed it off the cliff to fall into the saltwater below.

Emily rolled onto all fours, pressing the rock she was still holding against the ground for leverage. As he took a step toward her, she lifted the rock into a wide, horizontal swing, smashing it against his ankle.

The crunch of bone and ligaments was overshadowed by his cry of agony. As he fell to one knee, she managed to push herself up from hers, staggering to stand above him. With the rock still in hand, she struck him in the forehead, opening yet another gash.

Stunned, he grabbed her by the pant legs, pawing at them to steady himself from falling. He looked up, one eye still shut from the blood, while the other watered from the recent blow he had received.

Emily found it oddly satisfying to see his fear, to feel it even when raising the rock again, fully prepared to finish him with it. But instead, she wanted this to be personal. She dropped the stone, listening to the crackle as it bounced along the outcrop and out over the cliff.

"Everett, *you* are the one who needs cleansing, not this world. People like you hold no authority to cast judgment over the acts of humanity. Yours is but a short-term solution to a long-term problem."

She balled her left fist, leveraging him by the collar as best as she could with her other hand, landing a flurry of blows on him as the clench of her jaw drew tighter with each strike. Using the lingering anger of every event that had led her up to this moment, she wanted him to feel the pain she had felt, channeling it through her every strike.

Once his body became limp, she stopped.

Grabbing his chin, she raised his mangled face, forcing him to look at her from his one good eye.

"I am *not* one of you. I will never *be* one of you. The Recreant Order ends here, do you understand? May the mercy I show you now lead you to see that we can change to be better versions of ourselves.

"We cannot stop the sin. We are *not* perfect. We are *not* gods. You have no right to try and play one."

Emily released him, slowly stepping away to climb back up the hill.

"You're wrong, Emily," Everett muttered, standing on the favor of his good ankle. "When I find the diamond, it *will* recognize me as deserving. It *will* allow me to show the world the way. I'm sorry, but I cannot allow you to stop me when I am this close to achieving divinity!"

She turned, dumbfounded that he would not accept defeat.

Rather, he lunged toward Emily with a wide-swinging fist, only to have her duck it, which caused his ankle to give way. Following with a delivered kick to the back of his legs, she brought him to his knees once more.

His head slumped forward and he let out a gasp as his eyes stared blankly down into the water below.

Emily looked down at the piece of metal still protruding from her chest. She smiled, wrapping both of her hands around the center of the axe head, and with every ounce of strength she had left, she pulled.

Even though the pain was almost unbearable, she never once flinched. She did not shout nor cry, nor did she scream in agony. The gritting of her teeth was the only indication of discomfort that she revealed as she pulled the object from her body.

She approached Everett from behind, sliding her fingers into his long, knotted locks. Jerking his head back, she pressed her lips to his ear, just as he had done to her back at the top of the hill.

"I believe your words were, 'you've had your chance to repent.' But like *I* always say, Everett, this really is a cut-throat industry."

With that, Emily curled her arm around his neck, leisurely sliding the jagged teeth of the pick against his throat, retracting it like a bow across the strings of a cello. The blood oozed forth over her knuckles, flowing a blackened red as it ran down his chest and onto the ground, creating rivulets as it trailed through the crevices of the rock.

She stepped back, and with a swift kick, drove the toe of her boot into the center of his back. She watched as his body tumbled forward without resistance and disappeared over the cliffside. Taking one last look at the blood-soaked pick, she threw that over the cliff as well.

Instantly, a sense of relief consumed her, and she found herself smiling widely even though she had just killed a man. There was no regret, no remorse. Just relief.

But the fight wasn't over.

Emily snapped back to reality once she remembered that the Cardinal was still out there, somewhere, with all the info he needed to finish the Order's mission. Just because Everett was out of the picture didn't mean the organization would collapse in his absence.

She turned and hobbled steadily up the hillside, coming to a stop once she reached the bend in the trail where she and Everett had landed after their tumble. In the entanglement, his pockets seemed to have spilled, and sitting in the middle of the trail were his keys and her USB drive. Her barbell was also there, sitting amongst the blades of grass, a final reassurance that she had just done the world a favor.

While collecting the USB drive and keys from the ground, her attention moved to the sound of rustling and whispers. Her head shot up to discover that runners, hikers, and tourists alike had begun to gather all around. Some were taking pictures, while others had presumably recorded the whole interaction with their phones.

Uh-oh ...

Without them knowing the true history of her struggle, she would surely be labeled as a murderer by witnesses and media alike. Her face would be everywhere, or maybe it already was. She turned her face toward the city, listening over the intermittent gusts of winds.

The faint sound of police sirens echoed in the distance, drawing nearer to Signal Hill.

CHAPTER TWENTY-NINE

Emily dragged herself back up to the tower, sifting through the parting cluster of onlookers. Limping onward to the parking lot, she raised the fob on Everett's keys. She thumbed its buttons frantically until the yellow signal lights flashed on a black SUV, parked near the entrance to the main parking lot facing down the hill. Bracing herself against the driver-side door, she opened it just enough to grip the steering wheel and haul herself aboard.

But her attempt to flee the scene was quickly interrupted when she noticed a small unfolded map of the island of Newfoundland on the passenger's seat. A red, hand-drawn circle marked Cabot Tower. She could see that St. John's was located on what was labeled as the Avalon Peninsula. From there, she trailed her index finger westward, hoping to pinpoint the location the journal had referenced.

She lifted her face from the page as the sirens got closer, peering through the windshield to find that the police cruisers had reached the base of Signal Hill, speeding their way toward the information center. Behind her, the chuff of a helicopter was approaching from over the ocean.

It was too late to run. She was trapped.

She urgently dropped her face back to the map, tracing the highway westward until she discovered the place Everett had mentioned in his spiel: Deer Lake, a town on the west coast of the island.

Damnit. He must have been telling the truth about the Cardinal.

The helicopter had moved closer, growing louder as it flew in to hover over the tower. Hurrying, she focused her eyes north-west on the map, glossing over a widened stretch of protected reserve. She leaned in, unable to believe the words that were printed across the large, green portion of the island: *Gros Morne National Park.*

Morne? …

She pulled her phone from her jacket, and quickly searched for information on the park. Almost immediately, her device was flooded with images showing her the exact gorge from her visions. The water, the cliffs, the trees—all of it was sitting there in plain sight for anyone in the world to see. Labeled as a world heritage site, Gros Morne National Park was full of eroded valleys and glacial mountain ranges, much like Peru.

She looked up from her phone. The police cars were no more than half a mile away at best. With the looming rumble of the helicopter from above, brush and grass were sent swirling around the vehicle.

Emily prepared another text to her friends, attaching the pictures of Gros Morne and a geotag of its exact location.

"I hope this reaches you guys in time. I don't have time to explain, but the Cardinal is still alive, and he's close to the location I have just sent you. The gorge is located at the mouth of Western Brook Pond. Find it. Search it. You have to before he does, or the Order's reign will never stop. It's up to you two to find the diamond now. I know you can do it. Take care. I love you both."

After sending the message, she threw her head back against the seat, fading fast as she awaited her impending arrest.

Oddly, her phone pinged with a message notification. It was from Maggie and contained a blurry photo of what looked suspiciously like a birds-eye view of the vehicle Emily was sitting in. She propped open the door of the SUV. Sheltering her eyes enough to see the helicopter floating to land in the open parking lot, she spotted the goofy grin of the man hanging from the body of the aircraft.

"Care for a lift?" Seth shouted, shooting her a wink.

Slumping from the vehicle, she took a few weary steps forward. Teetering, she happily reached for his outstretched hand, one that very well could have been a lightheaded illusion brought on by the morning's exertion.

She stopped short, her eyes heavy as her eyelids fluttered. Everything around her faded into a blur as her knees caved under her own weight. The last thing she saw was Seth jumping down from the helicopter to catch her before she collapsed onto the pavement.

Hours later, Emily awoke from the prominent vibration of the helicopter against her back. Using her elbows, she lifted herself from her seat in a panic, her head swiveling from side to side.

"Where ... where are we?" she asked, reaching down to rip an IV from her forearm.

"Whoa! Take it easy," Graham yelled, steadying her. "You passed out from the blood loss. What the hell happened to you?"

He proceeded to hand her an earpiece so she could communicate properly over the loud hum of the helicopter's blades. Shoving it into her ear, she looked between Seth and Graham with a confused expression.

"The Cardinal! Where's the Cardinal?"

"We're coming up on the gorge now, Toots," her father said from the pilot's seat, still looking a little worse for the wear, but carrying a smile of relief. "If he's here, we'll find him."

From his right, a lovable face popped around the cushion of the co-pilot's headrest.

"Co-pilot, Margaret Riggs, reporting for duty, Miss Owens!"

"I really wish people would stop calling me that," Emily laughed and cried all at once with elation.

The flight through the gorge felt both majestic and unnatural. The cliffs were lined with the bright reds and yellows of fall foliage, intermingled with dark evergreens, creating a contrast against the pale grey rock. Aside from the blades of the helicopter, everything was still and peaceful. The whoosh of four separate waterfalls created an uncanny white noise as their waters fell from above, into the wind created by the rotors.

While taking it all in, Emily's eyes trailed to the floor of the helicopter. An open medical kit, a threading needle, and blood-soaked gauze were discarded at her feet. She pulled her shirt and jacket across her chest, seeing that her wound from Everett's attack had been sutured shut.

"Emily?" Seth asked. "What happened back there?"

"Everett, he … he was one step ahead of us this whole time. I'll save you the details for now, but let's just say, he's no longer in the picture." She shook her head profusely. "But what are you all doing here! How did you even find me?"

Maggie poked her head around her chair once again with an eager answer.

"We got your first text just as we were taking off from Heath-row. I forwarded it to Graham, but before I could reply to you, I lost service. You said you were headed to Cabot Tower, so of course, as soon as we got off the plane and saw that the local social media was blowing up with reports of a fight atop Signal Hill …"

"It wasn't hard to know where *you* were," Seth chimed in. "As always, smack dab in the middle of trouble," he laughed.

"And the helicopter?" Emily questioned.

"Apparently," Maggie continued, "your father has had con-nections in the town of Gander ever since 9/11. He and Graham flew to the military base there right after receiving my text. They loaned him the chopper, he picked us up at the St. John's airport, then we headed straight for you."

"Military base, huh? I guess that explains this thing?" Emily nudged her head in the direction of the M134 Minigun mounted near the door of the helicopter.

"There!" her father shouted, breaking up the reunion. "On the shore."

Emily lifted her gaze to the front window. Crashed onto the pebbled beach of the inlet was a red and white boat, which looked to have been taken from the local tour company that they had flown over a moment ago.

He must be here.

"Take us down," she commanded.

Emily's father approached her while shaking his head. Seth and Graham hauled three bodies from the boat. Each one had a bullet hole in their back, and unfortunately, none of them was the Cardinal.

"They're still warm," her father said. "He can't be too far. Ten, maybe twenty minutes ahead of us."

Emily looked toward the woods, then back to him.

"I'm going to stay on the ground. We won't be able to see everything from above with all of these trees. Someone needs to stay on foot."

"But you're injured," Seth said, stepping forward to voice his concern. "You should be in the chopper, resting. Let us handle this."

"I'll manage. I'm the only one with any idea about where to start looking for the diamond, and my visions were from ground level, not from the sky. It'll be best if I stay low."

Her father tossed her a gun, grinning as she snatched it out of the air.

"Still remember how to use one of these?" he asked.

"Better than you, old man," Emily smirked, pulling and releasing the slide. She lifted the pistol to scan the tree line with its sight, then lowered it again and tucked it away. "Good to go."

She hauled out her phone and brought up a map of the park using the internet.

"Gros Morne is a huge area, but I saw this specific gorge in my vision. Because of that, I'm thinking the diamond will be somewhere within a three-mile radius of here. We have to start somewhere, right?

"Dad, Graham, Maggie. I want you back up in the air. Seth, you stay with me. If we find the diamond before the Cardinal, we're going to need a speedy extraction. Got it?"

No one disagreed.

Seth turned to grab an assault rifle from the helicopter's hatch as Emily's father and Graham departed from the group and climbed aboard the cockpit.

"Here, take this," Maggie said, thrusting something into Emily's sternum. "It's a flare gun. If you get into trouble, use it, so we know where you are.

"And Emily, thank you for being my friend. Please, be careful, all right?"

They hugged before Graham arrived to impatiently usher Maggie on board. The helicopter lifted high above the gorge and out of sight over its ridgeline.

Under the dissipating thrum of the helicopter, Emily and Seth had moved no more than a few steps from the shoreline when Emily heard a branch snap to her right. She spun to remove her pistol from her waistband and pointed it in the direction of the noise.

"Em, is everything okay?" Seth asked. "Did you see something? Is it him?"

She didn't see anything, or at least, she didn't think she did. She couldn't have.

Suddenly, another branch crackled up ahead, this time, to her left.

She turned again, almost instinctively pulling the trigger, stopping herself only once her aim focused on the non-hostile origin of the sound. A warrior with yellow-painted skin was standing just beyond the tree line, his eyes fixed on Emily as he lifted his hand and waved her forward. It was obvious that he wanted them to follow him.

"Do you see that?" Emily asked, nudging her gun toward the trees.

Seth bobbed his head over her shoulder, then turned to face her. "See what?"

She took one last uneasy look around for the Cardinal. Seeing that the coast was clear, she began to jog recklessly into the woods without so much as a word, leaving Seth behind. She soon reached a grove within the dense forest, but the warrior had vanished, leaving her standing alone and confused, turning in circles in an attempt to find the man that had summoned her. She began to bang gently at the side of her temple, trying to shake any possibility of a delusion.

Maybe I'm concussed from the altercation with Everett?

"Emily!" Seth hollered, finally catching up with her through the brush. "What are you doing? We're supposed to stick together. That was your call, remember?"

At his words, another crunch sounded in the distance.

Emily looked through the trees and saw yet another yellow warrior, a woman this time, standing atop a small mound and waving her onward with what seemed like a heightened sense of urgency.

They're leading me to the diamond. I can feel it. Perhaps they can sense the impurity of the Cardinal's intentions? He must be getting close.

"Follow me!" she shouted, tugging at Seth's wrist to indicate that they had to move quickly.

Jumping over logs, splashing through streams, and almost losing her shoes in the deep mud holes of the forest, Emily fought to keep up with the warriors. Every few minutes, another one would appear to show her the way, leading her deeper and deeper into the gorge.

After some time, Emily and Seth broke through a large thicket into a clearing, its ground laden with moss-covered stones and unsettled dirt. A faint trail of mist drifted through the air amongst the trees, but here, the warriors were no longer present. Emily became uneasy with their sudden absence, like the feeling one gets when something bad has happened, but they have yet to uncover all of the details.

"Em?" Seth called, crouching near what appeared to be human remains embedded in the ground.

She looked down at the remains, decayed from years of environmental exposure. Beside them was a rucksack that looked similar to the items she had found under the tower at Signal Hill. Both the body and the ground around it looked to be undisturbed, yet the bag had clearly been recently moved, like someone had ravaged it and then tossed it aside.

"We're too late, Seth."

As if their discovery had been anticipated, a maniacal laugh trickled through the underbrush from just up ahead. They sprang to their feet, weapons readied, snaking their way in tandem between the trees to get a closer look.

"Miss Owens." The rasp of the Cardinal's voice floated from a distance. "Why am I not surprised to see you here so soon?"

She continued to try and hone in on his location, but the density of the interwoven branches made it impossible. She motioned for Seth to head to the right while she veered left in an attempt to surround the Cardinal.

"If you made it all this way, then I assume poor Everett wasn't so lucky. I always knew he was a proper fool."

Emily cringed, addled by his every word.

"He always was an idealist, thinking he could change the ways of the world. I knew it would never work. I do commend you for taking him out, however. In the end, it would've been hard on me to do so, but in reality, his death was unavoidable."

Emily tucked her gun into her waistband, using both arms now to push the branches aside, inching her way closer to the origin of his gravelly voice.

"He was so naïve, so unaware of what I had *actually* discovered in that lab of your Iraqi comrade.

"As soon as I dangled the image of those red triangles we found in Venice in front of him, he became oblivious to everything else that had been discovered—like a soldier of the mist, for example.

"All it took was the technology from that Iraqi doctor's lab attached to the head of one of the warriors! He showed me everything—from his abandonment by the young European, right down to this very spot in the woods. I didn't even need the location from that stupid journal. I knew exactly where to look all along. But what I did require was the opportunity to slip away. Once I was made aware that you were headed to St. John's, I also knew that Everett would want to follow you. Do you think it was really *his* idea for us to split up? Oh, no, no, no. Fortunately for me, the fog provided a convenient excuse ..."

"You're insane!" Emily screamed into the wilderness, still trying to locate the Cardinal's position.

"Maybe, but not as crazy as you for thinking that you could find the diamond before the almighty Recreant Order. Although, I do applaud you and your team for chasing me here so swiftly. I take it that's your helicopter I've heard hovering overhead? Did those warriors show you the way through the forest of their own free will? How futile."

Finally, Emily pushed through the conifers, coming to an area that was littered with fallen tree trunks and stumps. The overhanging sprawl of pine needles lay low over her head, as she pushed her way through their weight.

And there, standing plainly in the middle of the forest, was the Cardinal, still spouting his rambling speech.

"With the Florentine Diamond, I will lead the Recreant Order with the power it deserves! No longer will we fall under the command of idiocy, victims of our shortcomings." He reached into his waistband and removed his gun, dropping it at his feet. "I do not desire the use of man-made weapons, for with this army, I will bring the world to its knees. And it all starts with this province ... this pathetic ... little island."

The Cardinal turned so that his eyes locked with Emily's, who by now had drawn her own gun. His fist began to glow a bright yellow as he stretched out his hand to an open palm, exposing the diamond in front of him.

"No!" Emily shouted, stumbling as she tried to jump and weave over the terrain to stop him.

"Now, Miss Owens, shall we see what this army can really do?"

With his words, a solid beam of light shot forth into the sky in a pillar of brilliance. The white mist poured like water from the diamond's surface and out over his hand, filling the ground around him before ultimately consuming his body. The mist drifted high above the treetops, enshrouding the woods like a thick wool blanket.

Emily stopped about a hundred feet shy of the mist, watching as the Cardinal was consumed by it, nothing visible but the dim glow of the stone through the shroud. The mist began creeping its way forward, slowly at first, but exponentially increasing in speed as if it had a mind of its own and yearned to reach her.

She turned, running as fast as possible along any pathway she could find through the forest while the mist reached for her with translucent fingers amongst the vegetation. Every time she looked over her shoulder, the mist was gaining momentum, and before she knew it, her field of vision was consumed by an unwholesome grey.

"Emily? Emily!" Seth's voice came in over her earpiece. "Where are you?"

She stopped, her heart racing as her eyes shifted within the cover, unable to see more than fifty feet in front of her. She applied pressure to her throbbing shoulder, as the commotion of her escape had torn at a few of her stitches, pulling the sutures through her skin.

But an untended wound was the least of her worries. The rumbling that followed was the real threat, as the ground began to tremble beneath her feet, and the thump of heavy footsteps resonated all around her.

She timidly gripped her pistol, resting her back against the nearest tree trunk to hide, as if that was even possible.

Under the Cardinal's control, the blue warriors were the first to appear, carrying their bows and arrows, running toward her through the thickening mist with the intent to kill.

Emily raised her gun, shooting the first three dead into a heap on the ground, though it mattered little, as from the mist, more immediately replaced them in a relentless assault.

I need to keep moving. They won't stop.

Rolling from the tree she was hiding behind, she started running without direction, taking meaningless lefts and rights that would keep the warriors at her back. Arrows pierced the bushes beside her, every shot getting closer, leaving her no chance to radio for help.

A deafening war cry forewarned of the warriors' hunt as they gave chase. But over her stifled breaths of distress, Emily could hear more than just their collective approach in the background.

The helicopter!

Her trajectory had led her to a steepening hillside. With the chuff of the helicopter now coming from directly above, if she could climb high enough to break through the mist, she might have a chance to radio for help or even flag the chopper down.

Breaching the clouds, Emily found herself at the top of a barren cliff, a sight she had become accustomed to as of late. The tower of light was to the north, piercing the mist and traveling high into the clouds. To the east, the helicopter was heading dangerously fast toward the same yellow emission.

"Dad, turn around! I'm behind you!" she screamed, pressing her finger to her ear. "Don't approach the light!" She waved her arms frantically, trying to make herself more visible.

Her screams were swallowed by the depths of the gorge while also giving away her position to the hustling army below who were already making their ascent. The Cardinal had unleashed the red warriors now, and they were coming forth through the mist like a pack of wolves, readying their spears to heave in her direction.

Emily ducked the thrust of one spear and then side-stepped another, firing bullets into the chest of any being that emerged from the mist. For each warrior she shot, it seemed as if two more took its place. The forgiving high ground was her only advantage.

Breaking the army's advance, she waved her arms furiously once more while keeping a steady eye to the mist-line, noticing the helicopter sharply turn, heading in her direction. She smiled, jumping higher now, widening the stroke of her wave as her father approached from afar.

But her relief was short-lived.

The mist had begun to climb, funneling farther up the cliffside to pull her beneath its cloak once again. Once it had encased her, she was unable to hide. Her inevitable death could come from any direction.

Emily's hands were clammy, shaking against the grip of the pistol. She could hear that the helicopter was close—it seemed as if it was right above her—but with the density of the mist, signaling her location was out of the question.

Just then, a whipping snap behind her caused her to turn, prematurely shooting stray bullets into the mist before realizing that a black rope was now dangling from above her. It was out of her reach, indicating that it wasn't meant for her to grab on to. Then, through the mist, a body descended the rope, dropping at her side.

"I forgot to tell you. You're an aunt to another healthy baby boy." Graham stood tall, carrying his assault rifle slung across his shoulder, chuckling lightly. "Figured I'd drop in to let you know in person."

She looked at him with adoration before wrapping her arms around his torso and releasing a short sigh of comfort, one that was broken by a startling gunshot from behind.

Releasing each other to draw their weapons, they saw an approaching warrior suddenly sent falling out over the cliff.

"You didn't think I would let you guys do this alone, did you?" Seth asked, taking the last few strides to reach the hilltop, flashing his charming grin.

Emily motioned to kiss him but then shoved his shoulder out of the way to take out more approaching warriors with her handgun.

"We have to stop the Cardinal!" Emily instructed, still firing bullets into the army's ranks. "We can only hold off these warriors for so long. We're going to run out of bullets if we stay up here. We have no choice but to make a push!"

"I can still see the light!" Maggie's voice interrupted over Emily's headset. "If you head north from your location, it's a straight shot to the Cardinal. I'll provide cover fire from above with the Minigun. I got a twenty-minute crash course on how to fire this thing on the way here while you were unconscious. Point and shoot! Point and shoot!"

Her voice didn't sound as confident as her words let on.

"You just need to worry about firing those flares," Maggie continued. "When the warriors are behind you, launch a shot into the sky above them, and I'll make it rain bullets." She giggled. "Now *that* sounded kinda cool."

"Toots, we don't have much time. The Cardinal has already started spreading the mist farther throughout the park. There are hundreds, if not thousands, of visitors and hikers in this area that the warriors could kill with his mere command. Rocky Harbour, Deer Lake, Corner Brook … If he spreads the army into the towns outside of the park … it'll be a massacre, never mind if he targets the whole province. You have to stop him, Toots. I know you can do it."

Her father's voice once again gave her the boost to persevere. He was right. *She* had to be the one to stop the Cardinal. It was the only way.

"Boys," Emily said, stern and focused. "Tear me a path."

With that, she led her teammates to slide down the mud of the embankment, running in a straight line through the woods.

Graham and Seth littered the trees with bullet casings as waves of warriors tried to swarm them from every opening.

The army was only attacking in small groups, small enough that the assault rifles were able to keep them at bay, giving the team a clean break for the first few minutes. However, the momentum of the diamond's power suddenly seemed to shift.

"Hey, guys?" Maggie's voice trembled into Emily's earpiece. "That yellow light just got a lot wider and a hell of a lot brighter."

Coinciding with her observation, the pursuing army seemed to have ceased, giving Emily and the others a chance to catch a much-needed breath. Almost simultaneously, the mist started to spread, thicker and wider over the vast range of the surrounding mountains, eventually consuming all six hundred and ninety-seven square miles of Gros Morne National Park.

"Wait, do you guys hear that?" Seth said, gawking in multiple directions through the forest.

From deep within the mist, more war cries could be heard, followed by the sound of splashing water and cracking tree limbs. Hundreds of red warriors now emerged from the mist, unopposed and slinging their spears in the team's direction.

"Jesus Christ, Emily!" Graham grabbed her by the jacket, hauling her forward into a run with him. "Fire the goddamn flares. Now!"

She hurried to load a cartridge into the gun as they moved, sprinting through puddles and piles of wet leaves, trying their hardest to create distance between themselves and the closing army. Once readied, she stretched her arm straight above her head, sending a red shot hissing from the chamber that broke through the haze and hung in the sky, high above them.

"There!" Maggie shouted. "All right, guys, here it comes!"

The six-barrel chamber of the Minigun began to rotate, buzzing furiously as Maggie pressed the triggers, littering sparks into the mist from above. Trees were ripped in half by the ammunition as sprays of mud flicked into the air. Row after row, the warriors began to crash against the ground as the assault of bullets pierced through their bodies.

"It's working!" Emily yelled. "It's slowing them down, but it's going to be impossible to stop the army completely. The Cardinal's will is proving to be a powerful one."

With the helicopter following close above, she loaded the flare gun again and fired another round. This brought a second shower of bullets to fall behind her, carving another hole into the horde of pursuers.

"Guys, you're getting close," Emily's father said, providing guidance from his point of view above the clouds. "That last flare puts you about half a mile away from the Cardinal's location."

Arrows whistled past the head of each grounded teammate, digging into the back of the trees beside them. The blue warriors had rejoined the hunt, providing ranged attacks to make up for lost ground.

Seth and Graham swerved to flank opposite sides of the path they were taking, leaving Emily to rush up the middle, providing a moving target for the warriors. But the Cardinal was wisening to their tactic, now bringing the army in from all sides to surround them, trapping them.

Emily snapped the chamber of the flare gun, ditching the empty cartridge so she could reload another. When she raised her arm to fire the next flare, her forearm was punctured with an arrow, causing her to pull the trigger instinctively.

Right away, she dropped the gun, mustering a gritted scream while wasting no time to use her other hand to pull the arrow from her arm, creating a tattered hole in her flesh.

"Emily, are you okay?" Seth called out.

"I'll be fine, but I wasted a good flare. Bastards got me in the arm."

"Emily, what do you mean you 'wasted a flare'?" Graham shouted. "Where the fuck did it go?"

She looked back at the approaching warriors and then around for the flare, hoping that it had become lodged into the trunk of a tree somewhere. Seeing no sign of it, she listened for the hiss, arching her neck to stare straight above her at the red light dangling high in the sky.

Oblivious to what Emily had done, the helicopter had already started swooping in.

"Maggie, don't!" Emily yelled, a little too late.

It was impossible for Maggie to have known that Emily hadn't moved since firing the flare, leaving her, Seth, and Graham on the ground, like sitting ducks.

"Run!" Emily shouted, scurrying behind a large nearby boulder as the rattle of metal was accompanied by the spit of bullets, popping all around her.

While she sat tight under cover, Seth and Graham hopped over logs and climbed over underbrush, doing whatever they could to get as far from the radius of the flare as possible. Bullets crashed against the boulder, and Emily had to wait until the gunfire let up before she could move any farther.

As soon as it did, she sprang from behind the rock and continued running forward, disregarding her mistake.

"I've been hit!" Seth's voice stuttered into her ear. "A stray bullet ... ahh ... my leg!"

"I had to break away, Em. The warriors were on me everywhere," Graham added. "You have to get to the Cardinal. If you don't, none of us are going to survive this."

"You've almost reached him, Em," Maggie advised, "Just a few hundred feet!"

Emily looked ahead, now able to see the yellow glow pulsing through the mist.

She took another glance back over her shoulder. There was no sign of the army anywhere.

Something's not right.

"Toots, Graham is right. You need to hurry." Her father's voice was stiff and laced with worry. "We've got a situation up here."

Emily couldn't see that her father's helicopter hung between two clifftops, surrounded by hundreds of warriors, all lining the peaks of the cliffs. The red warriors had their elbows cocked back, holding their long, slender spears, and the blue warriors had their bowstrings drawn tight; each one's aim focused on the spinning blades of the helicopter, certain to take it down.

Emily had no idea what her father meant, but she knew there was no time to hesitate. She reached down and popped the clip from her pistol. *Empty.*

Just as quickly, she let the gun fall from her grasp.

Jogging in the direction of the Cardinal under the cover of the mist, she used any thick tree trunks that she could find to shelter her advance, creeping her way closer. Once in range, she peeked to find him standing in the same clearing with a grin plastered across his face, still firmly gripping the diamond. His eyes were a murky white, as if the power had made him all-seeing.

"Warriors of Inti," the Cardinal cried, "let loose your weapons on those who dare to defy me. Take down their airborne vehicle and send it crashing into the mountains be—"

Emily tackled him, sending the diamond flying from his hands and over the hillside as she and the Cardinal tumbled down over the embankment. Their bodies crashed against stumps and broken branches, coming to an abrupt stop in a shallow body of water that had formed across a moss-filled bog.

Both stumbled to their feet, staring at the Florentine Diamond that had landed directly between them. The mist had begun receding back into the diamond almost instantly, shedding the light of day on the park once more.

Emily smiled, triumphant.

No keeper ... no power.

At the same time, they each dove for the diamond.

Emily reached it first, cupping her hands around the yellow diamond, curling herself into a ball to protect it from the Cardinal's reach. While she acted as a human shield, his boot pounded repeatedly against her ribcage, forcing her to roll away, dropping the diamond behind her in the process.

He bent over and picked it back up, but without enough time to call forth the mist, she tackled him once again, causing the diamond to launch across the mire. They clawed over each other for the diamond, neither coming up successful.

She grabbed the Cardinal by the ear, pounding her fist into the bridge of his nose in an attempt to stun him. Instead, it merely enraged him, fueling him to stand up and grab the back of her head, hauling her face down to meet his knee.

Emily flopped backward into the water, blood spewing from her nostrils and down over her mouth. She crawled backward on her elbows, creating some distance between them and the Florentine Diamond, hoping he would follow. Her plan was to use his anger to her advantage, to distract him from his desire to possess the diamond.

It worked.

The Cardinal waded over to her, grabbing her by the back of the neck, raising her so he could strike the side of her face with a series of blows. But with each strike, she simply laughed, her normally bright white smile now tarnished with a reddened hue.

The Cardinal stopped for a second, confused, then followed up with another hardened punch.

She laughed more, doing so just to piss him off.

Shaking his head, he dropped her body into the water, turning back to collect the diamond. Plucking it from the ground, he squeezed it tightly in his hand.

"I'm not sure what you find so funny, Miss Owens, but I assure you, you won't find this next part so amusing." He raised the Florentine Diamond, his hand protruding out in front of him in preparation to call forth the mist.

Nothing happened.

He shook his arm and closed his eyes, yelling to summon the army.

Again, nothing.

Emily continued to cackle, struggling to raise herself out of the water. Her eye was half swollen shut, and her bottom lip had been split wide open. Her hair was wet, full of twigs and leaves, and blood dripped from her forearm. Her body was badly cut and bruised from the scrapes of her multiple falls. Still, she laughed.

"See, that's where you're wrong," she gloated, reaching into her pocket to pull out a yellow stone, identical to the diamond the Cardinal held in his hand. "I think that I *will* find this next part quite amusing."

His expression paled. He stared down at his own hand clutched around the diamond, then across at hers, gritting his teeth and shaking his head with incredulity.

"Emily? Come in," Seth's voice hummed into her earpiece. "Where are you? Are you okay?"

"I'm sorry guys, this next part's on me," she whispered, unconcerned, reaching for her earpiece and tossing it aside into the bog. She lifted her hand, confidently holding the newly revealed diamond outstretched in front of her. "You see, *Cardinal*, while you were busy trying to hide your agenda from Everett … killing Dr. Alsafar in front of my face … manipulating these beings for your own gain … you were missing the real threat …" Emily's face brightened with a smug grin, her eyes consumed with an opaque grey. "*Me.*"

Suddenly, the mist poured forth from the diamond in Emily's hand, seeping through her fingers and spreading across the surface of the bog. Her face tensed, staring at the Cardinal with a distinct hatred while his lips trembled with fear. The mist crept all around him, encircling him.

"I guess you were too busy … trying to report back to the Order … that you hadn't even realized … that I stole back what was rightfully mine." Emily's voice hovered in the air, near, then far. "The thing you took from me … while trying to find your own way here … the replica diamond."

"You stupid bitch!" the Cardinal barked. "What have you done?"

"I believe *you're* the stupid one … Was I too quick for you? Switching the diamonds while we fought … Didn't even notice … did you? Now the army is mine … and you? You can't escape."

He started running, climbing his way back to the top flat of the hill from where they had fallen. He rushed through the trees and across the ground, picking his pistol back up even though he had so casually discarded it earlier. Shakily, he pointed the gun in all directions at the mist.

"What happened to ... not being in the need of ... 'man-made weapons'?" Again, Emily's voice trickled from different places within the mist.

"Come on! Come and get me, then!" the Cardinal shouted. "I'll kill you where you stand!"

As the warriors approached the Cardinal, he fired his pistol aimlessly over and over again into the mist.

Then there was absolute silence.

Emily could sense him spinning around, the clicking sound of his empty chamber the only noise that could be heard through the mist.

It was in that very moment that Emily knew his fate had been realized.

"Goodbye, Jonah."

On her command, eight red warriors leaped forward from the mist, each one impaling the Cardinal through his torso with an upward thrust of their spears. Briefly, he was hoisted from the ground, falling back down onto his knees only once their spears had been removed. Each warrior then backed away, butting their spears hard into the dirt as they stood tall around him. The gun fell from his hands, and with both arms, he cradled the intestines that had begun to spill from his gut.

Emily appeared from the mist, coming to a stop between the warriors. She was now adorned in garments that matched those of the warriors. Her skin was laced with their yellow war paint, and she radiated a golden aura—a true recognition of the diamond's keeper.

The Cardinal tried to form words but produced nothing, only blood and spit as the mist dissipated back into the diamond, returning Emily to her normal state.

Crouching to his eye level, she traced her hand delicately along one side of his face before softly placing her forehead against his.

"Tell Everett I said hello."

Standing to walk away, she savored the moment, leaving the Cardinal's body to tip over and fatally convulse.

Emily only made it a couple of hundred feet before flopping against the rough bark of the nearest tree, sliding down into a seated position amongst the moss. Using her hand, she swiped away the blood that had tainted her mouth with the taste of iron.

"Emily!" A voice called to her, unrecognizable.

For the second time that day, her loss of blood had made her far too weak to even acknowledge the sound.

"Emily! Where are you?"

The source of the voice was Graham, who had just broken through the woods with Seth's arm draped around his neck. Emily was slumped on the ground ahead of them, barely able to make eye contact past her wilting lids. The men looked at each other and shook their heads in astonishment.

"Guys, we've got her," Seth said, pressing his finger to his earpiece. "She's in rough shape, though. We need to get her airlifted out of here ASAP."

"What's your location?" Maggie responded.

Seth came to a rest next to Emily, while Graham looked around for some sort of landmark, but the canopy of the forest made it impossible to see above the treetops. The thrum of the helicopter was nowhere to be heard, and making the steep traverse was out of the question.

"Graham? ..."

With her last drop of energy, Emily lifted her arm, pointing her index finger toward the bright orange handle of the discarded flare gun poking through the leaves.

Graham retrieved it, then returned to remove the last cartridge from her pocket and slide it inside the chamber. As Emily began to fade, she looked up at him, peacefully revealing the Florentine Diamond clutched tightly in her hand.

Relaxing her body into his, he raised his arm and shot the remaining flare high into the sky.

"Got you loud and clear," her father's voice said proudly. "Hang tight. We're on our way."

EPILOGUE

Waves of saltwater lopped against the hull of the Canadian Coast Guard's MOB boat, slowly drifting its way through the Narrows. Early morning reports were coming in about a disturbance that had ended with what witnesses claimed was a female individual, tossing a man over the cliffs of Signal Hill.

Divers had been in the ocean for an hour looking for any signs of human movement, or lack thereof. They knew the rescue would quickly turn into a recovery.

"Hey!" one of the divers shouted, waving his arms from the surface near the North Head shore.

The mates held their respective breaths as everyone's attention focused on the coastline when the FRC sped in.

"Jesus Christ!" the diver said, coughing and urging as the mates used a gaff to haul the body aboard the boat. "His god-damn throat is slit wide open. Must have hit a rock on the way down or something."

"Coastguard, here," the bosun radioed. "We've recovered the body."

Suddenly, the man spasmed, spitting out a mix of water and blood from the gaping gash in his throat. Crew members flung themselves at him to provide aid, comforting him as he regained consciousness.

"We need a fucking ambulance right now!" the bosun barked into the radio. "This guy's still alive! We're pulling in."

Once the man's body had been transferred onto the dock, the bosun knelt at the man's side, trying to get the man to focus on him to stay awake.

The bosun reached into the man's pocket, retrieving his wallet to study his identification.

"Sir, do you know where you are? Do you know what happened to you?" The bosun gripped the man's face, now making firm eye contact with him. "Mr. Taylor, can you hear me?"

ACKNOWLEDGEMENTS

To my wife, Alyssa. Thank you for supporting me during this crazy endeavor, where at the age of 30, I woke up one day and decided to write a novel. Thank you for your patience and your understanding that this was something I had to do, for me. I love you.

To my friends, family, and co-workers. From seeing me scribbling ideas for my cover design on a paper placemat with crayons at a restaurant, to watching me literally act out scenes from the book like a one-man casting call. Thank you. What may have looked crazy from the outside kept me sane on the inside.

To anyone and everyone who helped me in my writing journey: Mom and Dad, Brennon, Clay, Diyar, Andrew, Julia, Shane, Stephanie, Chris, Jeremy, my editor, my beta readers, and the helpful employees of Parks Canada. Without you all, the Florentine Diamond would remain lost forever. Thank you.

Manufactured by Amazon.ca
Bolton, ON

28342886R00219